The Trouble with Flying Solo

A Chemistry Matters Novel

H. Adrian Sexton

Published 1/5/2023

To Team Sexe:

Sabrina
Andrea, Brianna, India, and Chrystiaan
Kyra and Makai

I love you all!!!

Quote

No one ever made it to the end based solely on
what they knew when they started. Getting to the end
requires faith, growth and learning along the way.
Start, explore, learn, grow, and find YOUR ending.

Adrian Sexton

Previous works by this Dude

Altared Ego

The Chemistry Matters Series

Chemistry Matters
Curves, Edges and Perfect Imperfections

The Trouble with Flying Solo

PROLOGUE

SOLOMON SHIVERED INSIDE THE DANK, sixty-five-degree holding cell. His breathing labored by a heaviness in his chest. He rubbed his hands across his legs for warmth, then wiped away tears and surveilled his overnight dungeon. He leaned back against the cold concrete, closed his eyes and wished for the pleasure of sleep. A pleasure interrupted moments later by a dead bolt exploding through a hazy fog of semi-consciousness. The cell door clattered open and a scrawny guard shouted in a big voice, "Wake up, Alexandré! You have a visitor."

Solomon sensed a large presence enter. When he heard *Are you alright, Son?* he sat board straight and mumbled, "Mister Trey?"

Josiah Thomas the third, or Trey as his friends called him, entered the cell wearing an exquisitely tailored, navy-blue pinstripe suit. At Solomon's recognition, he conceded, "Lawrence called me. Told me about yesterday's episode at the house," in a calming tone.

Lawrence and Kenny Didier's father was Trey Thomas' college roommate. They are his godsons. Right out of law school he was hired onto the Governor's general counsel for racial justice. At thirty-five, he was the State's Assistant Attorney General. At forty, he resigned and opened a private practice. Now, twenty years, three books and nineteen million dollars later, he has represented high profile clients and is one of the most sought after criminal defense attorneys in the state of Washington.

Moments later a bulky guard in a green uniform entered the cell and ordered "On your feet Alexandré." Solomon cleared his throat, averted his gaze from Trey to the guard then back to the floor.

Trey shifted himself between Solomon and the guard. "I'm Doctor Alexandré's attorney and we're not finished talking."

"According to my watch you are." The guard sized Trey up and sneered, "It's interview time."

Trey checked his watch, then stepped aside and the guard escorted Solomon out of the cell.

Two minutes later they entered a small, windowless room with a square metal-topped table, four chairs, a two-way mirror and an erratically spinning ceiling fan that stirred hot, stale air.

"Sit down," barked the guard as he shoved Solomon into one of the chairs facing the mirror.

Solomon was tired. He had been up since the previous morning. And now a thousand thoughts of what happened to Jordyn were wearying his mind.

The guard shackled Solomon to the table.

"That's not necessary," Trey objected.

"Just protocol, Sir," the guard said as he mean-mugged Solomon. He didn't know Solomon, but he was aware of the nature of the accusation against him and everyone inside the jailhouse walls frowned upon violence against females. Before leaving, he growled in Solomon's ear, "Good thing for you that pitbull in a suit is here."

Solomon didn't acknowledge the guard, but stared at his shackled hands remembering the officer in his yard stating the word *murder*.

Trey cleaned his glasses then reached into his attaché and pulled out a leather-bound pad-folio. "Relax son, we'll get you through this." He clapped Solomon on the shoulder and placed a copy of the arrest report on the table. "But first, we need to address this."

Solomon found comfort in Trey's words. He took three deep breaths then blew air and feigned a smile for his father figure of an attorney.

Twenty minutes later, a bead of perspiration trickled down

Solomon's spine. His heart pounded after reading the arrest report for the third time. He knew he could never hurt Jordyn so what he read totally confused him. He was exhausted and yearned to lay his head down and go to sleep. It was approaching noon in the little, muggy room, but he'd been awake for so long that it felt more like evening. If he could only go home to his king-sized mattress and lay down, he knew he'd sleep the sleep of the dead.

Handcuffed to the table, he blinked away sweat, shifted in seat and laid his forearms on the table to comfort his heavy head. He shut his eyes and, not a minute later, sent soft snores vibrating across the table.

Then, the door opened suddenly and in rushed a pock-faced man in a wrinkled suit and nondescript black leather shoes. Solomon woke with a start when the door banged shut. He was stiff. He tried to focus on the newcomer in the room, but his eyes and temples throbbed. He jumped when he noticed the man in the chair next to him. Trey smiled an easy, comforting smile that reassured Solomon.

"Mister Alexandré, I'm Detective Leland Chrystopher." The pock-faced man paused when he saw the fatigued look on Solomon's tired face. "I need to ask you some questions when you're umm…ready."

Solomon made a monumental effort to focus. He put his palms to his eyes and rubbed his closed eyelids. He cleared his throat, had trouble recalling why he was there as he tried to comprehend the detective's words.

"Would you like some water?" Detective Chrystopher asked.

Solomon whispered. "Yes. Please."

As if teleported from the Starship Enterprise, a police officer entered the room with a paper cup. Solomon checked that it was water, not coffee, then wrapped his hands around the outside to cool them.

"Drink up." Trey's voice broke through the fog in Solo's mind.

After a few drafts of the cool water, the reason for the detective's appearance in the muggy room became clear.

Solomon and Jordyn were never in what most couples would consider a committed relationship. He lived in Seattle, and she lived almost 300 miles away in Spokane. They spent time when one visited the other's hometown and tremendously enjoyed each other's company. Once while cuddling after making love, Solomon asked her *What am I to you? You know, do we have labels?*

He remembered Jordyn hesitating, then exhaling deeply before she replied, *You, Mister Alexandré, are my friend, my caretaker at times, my lover, and my brunch and New Girl partner.* A somewhat briefer pause preceded, *For someone who is not my actual boyfriend, you are my everything!*

Despite being ten years his junior, she had made quite an impression on him, and it was impossible for him to sit handcuffed to that chair and understand how anyone who'd ever seen them together could think that he'd done what they were accusing. Other than that one incident which they'd promised each other to never speak of again, Solomon couldn't understand how the word *murder* could have been related to him when it pertained to Jordyn.

"Spokane police found this at her house." The detective laid the envelope on the table. All of the pictures inside are of you."

Solomon looked at the pile of mutilated photos. He and Jordyn hadn't been at odds the last time he had visited her in Spokane, so it was hard for him to fathom why she'd cut his face out of their pictures.

"Help me understand, Detective. If my face is missing, how did you get my name?"

Detective Chrystopher opened his folder. "Police report from Spokane says that they interviewed a couple of her friends, and they told them who they thought was in the pictures."

"Mel and Savannah?" Solomon begged.

When the detective started to speak, Trey cut him off with, "We have no further comment at this time, Detective. If you'd excuse us,

I need to speak to my client in private."

The detective glared at Trey for a beat. In the silence, Solomon pushed the pictures away and lowered his head to the table. Detective Chrystopher regarded Solomon, then slid out his chair to exit. The detective waved his hand over the items on the table and said, "I'll just leave these here to see if they jog your memory."

Before the door closed behind the detective, Trey ordered, "And you can tell whoever's behind the mirror that they can leave too." He rose from his seat, locked the door, gathered the pictures, stuffed them in the envelope and shoved the envelope in his briefcase.

Trey folded his arms and after a long contemplative silence, tried to explain to Solomon what would happen next. "Weekend arrests are the most challenging because the police can legally hold you without charging you for 48 hours. So, despite any threats or arguments I make when I leave here, I'll probably have to call in a favor with a judge in order to get around the D.A. and get you released before Monday. If I can't convince a judge, then your arraignment probably won't be until Monday."

"Probably?" The terror in Solomon's voice was unmistakable.

"Yes, Son, and even then, the judge may possibly deny bail."

"But I didn't do anything."

"That said, the DA may blowhard about *Murder charges being a serious accusation*, and argue that your ample income can support a means of flight, but with you being a lifetime Seattle citizen, your mother living here, and you owning your own business, there's no solid reason to deny your release. If the judge does grant bail, it'll most likely be under the condition that you surrender your passport." Trey scrunched his nose then pushed his glasses up with his index finger, giving the conversation a moment to breathe. When Solomon appeared somewhat receptive, he said, "The biggest thing going for us is that they haven't charged you yet. Those pictures are merely circumstantial evidence that you and this woman know each other. Nothing I saw was any proof or evidence that you committed a crime. The detective I spoke to in Spokane said they do not have a body." Trey's chair was uncomfortable so he stood. "Like I said, they don't have a solid motive. I'll get Detective Chrystopher to provide a timeline of this lady's disappearance, so I can work on establishing your alibi. But, the only *fact* the D.A. can provide a judge right now is that they consider this woman missing."

Trey took a beat, looked for a sign of hope in Solomon. When the silence lasted longer than suited him, Trey commanded, "Pick your head up and look at me boy!" When their eyes met, he said with conviction, "I've known you and my godsons most of my adult life, and if you say you didn't do what they're accusing you of, then I will do everything within my power to get you released as soon as possible. But until then I need you to buck up and be a man about this. The same way you were being a man when you were with that girl."

That last statement surprised Solomon. He'd always seen Trey as a father figure solely because of his age and for being his friends' godfather, but with Trey standing before him barking orders, the father figure loomed larger than ever.

"Do you understand me, Solomon?"

"Yes, *Your Honor*," Solomon said weakly.

"Cut that shit out," Trey barked. "You know who I am."

"I'm sorry Mister Trey." Solomon yanked against the handcuffs. "I…I just. I just…" His words never came. But his tears did.

"Look son, if you didn't do this, then hold your head up and tough out the weekend. I know you're strong enough for that." Trey checked his watch. "Now, before I go, I have a couple questions."

Solomon looked at Trey intensely before breaking his silence. "Let me guess, bottom line, you want to know *how I got here*?"

Trey sat down across from Solomon. In a comforting tone he said, "Yeah, Son; more or less."

Solomon slouched, laid his head back and focused on a crack in the ceiling. He closed his eyes and thought back three years to before all of this mess started. Before Jordyn. Before his wife Mareschelle's death. Back to before his life ended. Eyes still closed, his voice cracked when he said, "I guess that's the million dollar question we both want answered."

CHAPTER 1

THREE YEARS AND TEN DAYS before Solomon Alexandré was arrested, Reverend Draymond Carroll officiated the homegoing service of Solomon's wife, Mareschelle Renáe Betancourt Alexandré. Her parents, Mr. Darnell and Mrs. Rachel Mae Betancourt, loved their fellow congregants of Eternity in the Light Church of God in Christ, but were exhausted from the social accompaniments of laying their daughter to rest. The last week had tired them out and they were ready to leave the repast, so Mr. Be— as only Solomon called him—told Solomon to have the pastor offer the benediction.

Reverend Carroll kept the prayer short, and when he finished, Solomon escorted his in-laws from the church auxiliary hall to their car and said, "Call me if you need anything."

Mrs. Be slunk wordlessly into the front passenger seat.

"She'll come around, Son," Mr. Be said. "Give her some time."

"Time," Solomon countered, "the one thing we all want more of."

They walked around the car, then hugged before Mr. Be got in and lowered the window.

"Make sure you ring me when you get home." The Betancourts lived less than ten minutes away, but Solomon's request was an adoption of a ritual Mareschelle shared with her parents to ring the phone twice to inform the other that they'd arrived home safely. Mr. Be nodded and Solomon tapped the trunk as they drove off.

When he turned around, his mother summoned him. She had corralled Reverend Carroll—an attractive, six-year-widowed sexagenarian. The silver fox of a pastor was definitely Vivienne Alexandré's type, and Solo knew he was the only person in the building capable of saving The Rev from Viv's clutches. Vivienne said, "The reverend was telling me about some of the community outreach programs at his church."

"That's great, Ma."

Viv weaved her right arm inside Solomon's left while batting her lashes at Reverend Carroll. The church's auxiliary porch lights illuminated the baby smooth complexion of her dark, glowing skin—and Reverend Carroll noticed. No wrinkles, no crow's feet, no prominent signs of aging, only worn, tired eyes. She looked to be more in her late forties than her late sixties. Her spirit bordering on nobility. Her demeanor and pronounced posture suggested dignity. She radiated femininity, bangled hoop earrings and a satin head wrap like the rural women of Africa. "And I was telling him that I'd be available to help him serve the church in any way he saw fit."

"I bet you did." Solo extended his hand to shake the pastor's. "Sorry it's been so long, but good seeing you, Reverend."

"Can't wait to see you again, son." Reverend Carroll gripped Solomon's proffered hand. "Just maybe under better circumstances."

"And thank you for your kind words today."

"Think nothing of it, my boy. Mareschelle has been a part of our flock since before she could walk. It pains me when a young life is lost, but I know our Angel is in a better place now." He checked his watch then said, "I hate to eat and run, but I better be going." Reverend Carroll tipped his hat toward Vivienne. "I have sick and shut-in visits to make before I head home."

"If you need, Pastor," Viv offered zealously, "We can bring you a plate of food on our way home."

Solo shot a glance from his mother to the pastor. The joint look of embarrassment on both men's faces precluded the need for words.

"What?" Viv feigned innocence. After Reverend Carroll got into his car, she kissed her teeth. "Let me tell you something, Boy. That man is single, and fine as frog hair. If I don't offer him the pleasure of my company, some less deserving heifer will."

"But do you have to be so obvious about it?"

"I'm seventy, Boy. I have to be obvious about everything I want."

After Reverend Carroll departed, Viv supervised the cleanup by the Ladies' Auxiliary while Solomon farewelled departing guests. When the hall was empty, Solomon drove his mother home, then went to Lawrence's house to grab his suitcase before going to his own house for the first time since Mareschelle's passing a week prior.

CHAPTER 2

IT WAS ALMOST EIGHT O'CLOCK when Desmond Woodson checked the screen on his cell and answered after the first ring. "What's up, KD?"

"What's up, Big Wood?" Kenny Didier asked emphatically.

"Nothing," Desmond answered with a listless laugh.

"Yeah, you sound like it."

Out of his own restlessness and desire to find a temporary escape from his humdrum widowed life, Desmond asked, "So, what are you…or should I say…*who are you* getting into tonight?"

"I'm not making too much noise tonight. To be honest, I've been thinking about slowing things down with these broads." Kenny was the Don Juan of the Four Horsemen—the moniker he had bestowed upon his quartet of himself, Desmond, Lawrence and Solomon during their college years. In addition to being the lightest of the group, he had the smoothest complexion, two big dimples, a cleft chin and wavy dark hair. He was handsome, eloquently spoken and naturally debonair. He partied hard and dated more women than a gigolo, but had no interest in a relationship. "Actually," Kenny continued as he flipped through the channels, "I'm looking for the game. Gotta watch our Knights bust the Monarchs' asses."

"Me too," Desmond replied.

"Check it out Wood; I just talked to LD, and he told me that Solo stopped by his place, scooped up his bags and was headed home."

"For real?" Desmond asked. "The way he was snotting and boohooing at the funeral, I figured he'd be staying with Lawrence and Annette for at least another week."

"That's why I called. I'm not talking about tonight, but now that the funeral is over, we need a plan to get our boy back out there."

"Damn Kenny, you know how crazy Solo was about Mareschelle. What makes you think he wants to start looking for some *new*?"

"Nahh, Wood, you got me all twisted. Even I ain't that insensitive."

Solomon's friend for life had never been as consistently negative about any other woman his friends had dated, but from the day they met, Kenny and Mareschelle maintained a hate-hate relationship. *You in over your head with that bougie chick,* he had professed when Solo announced that they were officially dating.

A beat later, Desmond said, "Then what kind of *out there* you talking about?"

"I'm thinking maybe two or three weeks from now we take my man out and let him find some bougie chicks," Kenny replied. "You know Solo likes 'em bougie, and that new club *Destination* is always full of uppity tricks." Kenny popped the top off a beer.

"Man, Destination is crowded as hell every night except Thursday. And I'm not really up to waiting in anybody's line."

"Dawg, stop tripping," Kenny reassured. "We just theorizing on how to get the Homie Solo out of his head and back into someone's bed. I'm talking about one night, not a lifetime."

"I'm telling you KD, he ain't ready for that."

"I'll tell you what Wood, since my half of the Hang Suite will be empty after I move out, what if we just have a party here."

Kenny and Solomon shared two halves of a duplex that was the first purchase Solomon made with the first dividend check from an IPO that Kenny got the Four Horsemen to buy. Two months before Mareschelle passed, Kenny found a duplex for sale in Alderwood and bought it with the same intention of living in one half and renting out the other like Solomon did.

"Now that I can work with." Desmond stopped flipping

channels, pissed that he couldn't find the Knights—Monarchs' game. He asked, "What channel is this damn game supposed to be on?"

Before he could answer, Kenny noticed headlights coming down the driveway that stretched from their cul-de-sac to the garages at the back of the Hang Suite property. The house's moniker originated from Kenny's college attestations that the soulful melodies of Maxwell's *Urban Hang Suite* CD assisted in the majority of his conquests. Senior year, he vowed that once he had a place of his own, many more of Seattle's finest woman would be slayed in his own version of the love den inspired by that album. Having been roommates at Washington State University, it seemed fortuitous that the two bachelors moved into their first bachelor pad together. Kenny christened their new home the Seattle Hang Suite during a toast at a midsummer backyard housewarming pool party, then proceeded to play that CD later that night as he christened his bedroom with a set of twins. The Horsemen have called Solo and Kenny's duplex the Hang Suite ever since.

"Yo KD, I'mma go so you can check up on our boy, but keep in mind, he'll be grieving for a while. Trust me, I know." Desmond knew grief. His wife, Penny, died during an emergency C-section when she was five months pregnant. It took Kenny more than ten months to drag Desmond back onto the dating scene after a stint in alcohol rehab. Rehab that the Horsemen convinced him into after his bout with alcohol almost cost him his bar. Desmond did start dating again, but that first date didn't come until almost two years after Penny's death.

"No pressure, Homie," Kenny said, "but there will be a party."

Desmond said, "Hit me up after you check on him. Peace, Boyeeee."

Kenny replied, "Two fingers high."

~

Solomon exited the garage and found Kenny waiting on the back porch with two beers in hand. He accepted a hug and a beer from his friend, then they clinked bottles. *Cheers.*

"Good to have you home, Man." Kenny sat on the railing separating their back porches while Solomon set his bag near the door. "Hey Fam, if I could've rescheduled my movers, you know I would've been at the repast for you." To support vacating his half of the Hang Suite the following Saturday, he scheduled movers to pack out all of the big furniture, save his bed and the desk he used when he worked remotely from home. In truth, Kenny hated funerals, and the movers spared him having to offer condolences to Mareschelle's family, but more importantly, saved him from any interactions with her girlfriends, whom he despised with the same vigor he and Mareschelle despised each other.

"No worries, Bruh. LD had it all under control." They clinked bottles again before Solomon sat on a patio chair. "You ain't miss nothing except a lot of people from Schelle's church I either didn't know or didn't remember telling me how lovely Schelle was, or how cute she was as a little girl, or what they remembered about her from Sunday school. Then there were the; *how sorry they were for me—, how much they would miss Schelle—,* and worst of all, the insincere, *Just call if you need anything—,* crowds. Why would I call somebody now who I never called when she was alive?"

Kenny sensed the angst building in his friend's voice and thought it a good time to segue into the party conversation. "Check it out. Now that my place is all but empty, I was thinking about having a blowout to retire the Hang Suite. You basically retired your half when you got married, and now that I'm moving out, the name just doesn't fit anymore. Wood and I were talking, and we figured that we'd invite all our people over and give this place the sendoff it deserves. You know whoever moves in next will never be half of the neighbor I am, so before that loser comes and ruins the Hang Suite's memory, we should give it a proper sendoff."

"And how many of 'our people' will be women?"

Kenny paused, knowing he had to choose his words carefully. They'd been friends going on twenty-five years and Solo could smell a Kenny Didier lie coming a mile away. "Bruh, I am Kenny Freakin' Didier; my name alone on the invitation means that the place will be packed wall-to-wall with some of the finest females in all of Seattle."

"And how many of them have you and Wood decided that you're inviting to keep a grieving widower company?"

Again Kenny paused. In theory, pawning the party off as his moving out party worked, but since Solo popped up so soon before he and Desmond could strategize properly, he had to pay more attention to the detail in his words. He said, "Now for as long as you've known me, you've known how I am with women. The women I invite will make this party the talk of Seattle for the rest of the year. If a few of them happen to feel like they want to party with you, that ain't on me."

"I hear you KD, but I ain't ready for all that yet."

"Nahh Bruh, it's all good. If I remember correctly, you said your new tenant ain't scheduled to move in until sometime next month. That gives us three Saturdays to work out the details and get you to a place where I can make sure you're comfortable. I love you boy," Kenny paused then said, "I know your Missus and I didn't always see eye-to-eye, but I would never disrespect you, or her memory."

"Thank you, Brother. Knowing how you were the junk yard dog to Schelle's alley cat, that means a lot to me."

"For sure. And, if that means I need to forget to mail an invite to your country ass, then I'll just send my landlord a notice to let my neighbor know that there will be a party with loud music and a bunch of Seattle's finest women getting buck wild and running around half naked on the property that night. How does that sound?"

Solomon sat up and pretended to be all business-like for a moment. He mocked in a prim and proper British accent, "As your landlord, Mister Didier, I'll inform your neighbor of the potential situation. And as long as the cops don't come knocking, or I don't have to fix anything before the new tenant moves in, I don't see any reason why your neighbor would give a damn." They shared a laugh that Solomon desperately needed. "As your neighbor, I think I'm a cool enough dude that I won't mind my adult neighbor having a party on a Saturday night. But my neighbor should remember that as a church-going man, I won't want the music blasting until sunrise."

"See, that right there. That's why I need my neighbor to come and enjoy the party with me. And if he happens to let a pretty lady or two push up on him and give him some of her attention…well I damn sure won't hold it against him; widower or not." Kenny knew that Solomon's burden of betrayal to Mareschelle would weigh heavily on his decision to attend. "You my Dude Solo. I can't have a shindig without the Four Horsemen; and as far as the honeys go, I ain't expecting nothing from you. I love you boy. That's all that matters." They hugged before Solomon picked up his bag to go inside. Kenny hopped the railing back onto his side of the porch then said, "Don't worry Partna, we'll have you Flying Solo in no time," before both men disappeared into their respective sides of the Hang Suite.

Three Saturdays later, Solomon sat on his porch drinking a cup of coffee, resting his feet on the wrought iron railing and enjoying the crisp morning air as he watched his college fraternity brother and childhood friend, Kenny Didier, hop into the moving truck—his clothes occupying every square inch of cargo space inside the eight by ten trailer—to drive the remainder of his belongings toward the duplex he'd purchased two miles away. The cleaners had finished up Friday afternoon, and the caterers from Desmond's Bar and Grill would be delivering the food to Kenny's empty half of the Hang Suite around six o'clock that night. His property manager had called late Friday to tell him that Kenny had scheduled the painters for Monday, the carpet cleaners for Wednesday and that the new renter would be moving in on the first Saturday of the month. Now he hoped that the *people* attending Kenny's moving out party didn't wreck the place.

Solomon's coffee was strong and hot, but his thoughts were slow and muddled, just like his morning routine since Mareschelle's passing. As Kenny's truck disappeared into the neck of the hourglass that marked the edge of the cul-de-sac, Solo looked around at the other houses in the neighborhood and caught the eye of the woman on the opposite side of the circle who was exercising on her porch. He waved for the sake of being neighborly and faked a smile.

She smiled then exercised even harder for her newfound audience.

As the dawning sunlight streamed through the trees, wrapping them in fractured hues of reds, greens and yellows, Solomon contemplated how the gentle breeze wafting off Puget Sound on quiet nights rivaled the almost Buddhist sense of calm and tranquility early morning offered. Either way, he enjoyed his quiet little cul-de-sac and even without Mareschelle to share it with, he wouldn't trade it for the world.

CHAPTER 3

AS FAR BACK AS COLLEGE, if there was a party happening, Kenny Didier made sure the Four Horsemen knew about it. On Memorial Day weekend following Solomon's junior year in college, they attended Greek Weekend on the University of Washington main campus where their fraternity, along with seven others, would be performing in a step competition as part of the weekend's events.

Solo worked out at the University of Washington student gym on Saturday morning then ran eight miles around the campus. It was just after noon when he met Desmond for lunch at the student center. Lawrence's name appeared on the screen when Solo checked his cell. He and Kenny were caught in traffic, but on their way. Solo told them where he and Desmond had landed and that they'd be on the fourth floor inside the Wolves Den, the Huskies basketball arena, when they got there. By the time the Didier brothers arrived, the judges had finished briefing the teams on the rules of the step competition. Solomon and Desmond were with some of their other frat brothers perfecting a new step they'd just started working on the week before. Kenny, dangling a key to his new motorcycle, nodded his arrival and they nodded back.

Something hit Solomon in the side of his head when he knelt to tie his shoe after they finished practicing. He looked down and saw a rolled up piece of composition paper, When he looked in the direction the paper came from, he saw a girl smiling at him. She nodded to the ball of paper, so he picked it up.

He read, *Dear Follower, leading would suit you better. If this is your predilection, proceed to the concession stand and I will follow.*

She held his stare for a beat, then shifted her glance to the stairs leading to the porch encircling the upper bleachers.

Intrigued by her forwardness, Solomon took to the stairs. Noisy echoes of young adult excitement filled the air of the arena's bleachers porch. When Solo reached an unoccupied section of wall between the concession stand and the men's bathroom, the girl slid in next to him and put her back to the wall. When she spoke, Solomon leaned his head close so she could tell he was listening.

"You seem familiar Beta Man, but I don't recall seeing you around campus."

"That's because I go to Dub Sate."

"Oh," was her monosyllabic reply.

"You've probably seen me on campus hanging with my best friend. He is a Huskie."

"Possible."

"More likely that you've seen me on the court when we come give it to your hoop team."

The girl shrugged her shoulders, cattily replied, "Maybe."

"If you make time to come watch me hoop next time the Cougs come here to smack the Huskies maybe that'll refresh your memory."

"We'll see. I'll most likely have a volleyball match that night. But...who knows? Fall is a long way off."

"Sounds like we need to check each other out on the court?"

"I might consider squeezing a men's game into my calendar," she countered, "but only AFTER you come watch me play when the Lady Huskies go east."

They both looked to their right when an air horn blew.

He caught her arm as she lunged from the wall and started in the direction of the air horn. "Wait Slim, I didn't catch your…"

Without offering her name and before they agreed on who would watch whom play first, she broke free of his grasp and spirited her way toward her sorority call echoing through the hall.

Solomon watched her bob and weave through the crowd before disappearing behind a purple curtain. He followed and found her with her sorors. When he witnessed the satisfied look on her face, he leaned against the bleachers to watch them practice their step routine. He tried to imagine her movements on campus as he watched. He wondered who else moved in her circle. Wondered why he'd never seen her before in all the times he'd been on campus with Desmond. He watched her move through her routine with elegance, ease and a grace to her movements; a pointing of her toes, an imperial carriage in the bearing of her shoulders. A graceful elongation of her neck. The way her sorority sisters swarmed to surround her, confirmed her superiority among their ranks. He tried to figure out something cool to say to a girl so gorgeous. Better yet, something funny. Something to make her laugh, to make her want to be around him. He wondered if she was single. He liked what he saw, but was more intrigued to find out what she liked. An intrigue for which his summer would bring many answers.

From behind him, a lady called for the Kappa Alpha Tau step team. They huddled for a silent prayer that ended in their high-pitched sorority call before they moved toward the arena floor to perform. She pretended to ignore him by talking to her girlfriend when the team passed, but when he touched her arm, her eyes brightened. He held up the wrinkled paper note and she stopped and smiled brightly before a nudge from the two girls behind her kept her moving.

After her team passed, he saw Kenny standing at the curtain with his arms crossed. Without speaking, he joined his Beta Iota Gamma fraternity brothers just as her team started to perform.

Solomon's fraternity was the last to perform in the men's

competition. Like a tree transfixed in flood waters, she stood at the end of the row her sorors were seated and watched him perform. When they finished, he and Kenny sat with six of their frats three rows ahead of her sorority waiting for the judges to announce the winners.

"Hey Slim," a soft, but firm, female voice called loudly from behind the BIGs, "What's your name?"

Kenny turned around, accustomed to girls hitting on him and pointed his finger to his chest in a gesture of *who me?*. All-too-often, his good looks mesmerized women, so it was reasonable for him to think she was calling him.

When Solomon turned to see it was the girl from earlier, he got up and walked toward her. Kenny followed. The arena was crowded, noisy, and people all around them were enjoying the festive atmosphere. Kenny was right on his heels when Solomon reached her. "What was that? I couldn't quite hear you over the crowd," he pointed at his ear indicating a problem hearing her.

"She said, what's your name?" a shorter girl next to her replied.

He turned and locked eyes with the shorter girl. "Solomon."

"Excuse me," short girl yelled over the swelling din of the crowd.

He leaned in, and in a deep, strong baritone that opposed the crescendo of the crowd, he said, "Solomon Alexandré." He offered his hand to the girl who'd thrown the note. "And you are?"

"Mareschelle," she told him. In the racket of the gym, her words sounding like she'd said Mary Shelly.

"Nice to meet you Mary." He was fascinated by her frenetic graces and offered his introduction with a spirited vivacity.

"Not Mary," she said. "Mareschelle. Like Mayor Shelly"

"Mayor." He listened intently, endeared by her voice. From her diction it was clear she was sharper than her peers. "That's rather unique."

"Not Mayor, Mare like a horse," she said sternly. Her tone was deeper than he expected, more adult than her young face. "My name is Mareschelle. I prefer to use my full proper name."

"What kind of weird name is that," Kenny said.

She cut her eyes at Kenny. "Weird?" she started, "Well what kind of stupid name do you have? Let me guess, Jackass?"

"Ooooo," her friends cosigned.

"Whatever Trick. We don't have to waste our time on you, it's not like you're the only black girl at U-Dub," Kenny said. "My man don't need you heifers, he can have his pick of any girl at this school."

Mareschelle cringed, turned toward him, looked him up and down. A tear escaped her dreamy eyes and rolled along her diamond-shaped face. She quickly wiped her face with her sleeve, but no one saw her. "Black...is what you call an animal. Not a lady, you Jackal."

"Yo Man, cool out." Solomon elbowed Kenny hard in the ribs.

"Sorry, Frat." Kenny glared hard at the woman he'd offended.

Solomon read the hurt on her face. Her pain felt like his own and he wanted to touch her, to reassure her, to wipe her face but he didn't know her well enough to do that. "So, what's with the note?" Solomon interjected to draw her attention back to him. Even with all of the noise from the show, his direct tone caught her attention. She averted her eyes and once again regarded Solomon. "What made you pick me, Mary Shelly?"

"I hate jackals who can't address me by my proper name," she told him, ignoring his question. Her words were directed toward Kenny although her eyes were fixed on Solomon.

"I don't think he is aware of how unique your last name is."

"I didn't make him aware of it." And she was right. Mareschelle was her proper first name. The two men had mispronounced it, but she'd never gotten to tell either of them her last name.

"Whatever." Kenny pointed toward their frat brothers. "I'm down there if you need me."

Mareschelle scowled at Kenny one last time. He had turned and was a couple of steps away when she said, "I can't see why he would need a jackal like you when he's got me right here."

"Ooooo," her friends called out again.

Kenny flipped them his middle finger but never looked back.

Solomon absorbed the words, 'when he's got me right here.'

Mareschelle was fit to be tied. She pursed her lips and wanted to scream, but instead reached her arm past Solomon and flipped her middle finger at Kenny's fleeting back.

After a beat, Solomon removed the rag around his head and wiped the perspiration from his brow. He rubbed his hand roughly through his half-inch twists then shook his head.

"Forgot your comb this morning?" Mareschelle kidded.

Solomon offered a toothless smile in response.

"But your twists are cute," she continued.

"Cute," he cautioned in a mannish tone, "is for boys and puppies."

"So which does that make you?" she ricocheted.

"Play your cards right and you might find out," he said, coolly offering a dare he knew she was not ready to take.

"Touché," she giggled after a brief stare, thinking that the skeletons in her college closet were probably just as wayward as his. Her friend whispered in her ear and she switched the subject. "Are the rest of the boys in your frat like him?"

"Like him how?" His voice was flip, borderline defensive.

"Jackals?" the short girl shot back.

He was slightly offended, but maintained an even tone. "Maybe."

"Or are the others more like you?" Mareschelle said.

"Like me how?"

"Cute."

"I am not cute." Now his tone was annoyed.

"Take the compliment, Honey," short girl added. "You really are."

Her insistence annoyed him. Most girls his age weren't obedient, but he began to find their confidence unsettling. Mayor Shelly seemed smart, and sexy, and sure about everything she did. He wanted to know *Who she was? What she was about? Where she came from?* But he didn't want to find out standing in a circle of her friends. Fortunately for him, as the weeks and months of the upcoming summer passed, he would find the answer to these questions and many more throughout marathon conversations. He would learn her spirit and see her in a light that he liked and truly desired. She would prove strongly independent in a way much different from other women he knew. Beginning that day, she would never cease to amaze him.

The sorority leader with long legs and bright eyes was very much a new school woman. In retrospect, Solomon realized that her being so up front about her attitudes ended up making him nervous. Between his mother's array of boyfriends and Kenny's rotating door of girlfriends, he'd come to believe that relationships were manifestations of gamesmanship and an unending desire for control.

That reality of her strong personality, exacerbated by Kenny's criticisms, would lead him to almost walk out on some of the best sex west of the Rockies. But Mareschelle's confidence would subvert all of that. Make him realize that he was more traditional than he knew.

A voice came over the arena's public announcing system telling everyone to *please take your seats*.

"Okay Cutie with the nice booty," her short friend interjected. "We're about to be crowned champions, so let's wrap this up." Competition judging had concluded and the crowded Wolves Den grew quiet. The short friend interlocked arms with Mareschelle before averting her gaze toward Solo. "As much as we Laaa-dies appreciate young men fawning over us, right now is not the time." She locked eyes with Solomon and said, "If you want to waste more of her time, find her on the yard tonight, but for now, this exchange is over."

They did not get to say goodbye before Solomon watched the girl with the name that sounded like Mayor Shelly being led away. Before he could apologize for Kenny, the one called *Little Bit* whisked Mareschelle deep into the comforting confines of their sorors.

Just before midnight, Kenny and Solomon were chilling on the grassy, diamond-shaped, half-acre quad that separated the Beta Iota Gamma, Eta Theta Tau, Sigma Chi Psi, and Kappa Alpha Tau houses. They were at the weekend's biggest fraternity party watching women in summer dresses or with short shorts riding up their round bootees.

"Didn't you once tell us you had Indian in your blood?"

"Hunh?" Solomon heard the words but didn't know their meaning.

"Did you say Cherokee?" Kenny continued, "Or was it Poulsbo?"

"Navajo," Solomon shouted. His eyes were fixed across the yard where Mareschelle and her crew had just entered. His frats and her sorors, along with a hundred other Greeks were *partying like it was 1999*...because it was.

"Right, right, Navajo." Kenny shoulder bumped Solomon. "But you act more like its Savajo."

"What?" Kenny's words befuddled his friend.

"You know *Save A Hoe*," Kenny laughed out loud. "Sounds like *Nav-A-Hoe,* but acts more whipped than warrior."

"Shut up, stupid," Solomon yelled above the roar of the music.

Kenny grabbed Solomon's shoulders, pointed him toward the gaggle of KAT women from U-Dub and pushed him in their direction. "If you want her, go get her, Chief Savajo. I got you."

Solomon looked back to respond, but Kenny was pushing his way toward the DJ stand. When Solo turned back to face the KAT women, he caught Mareschelle watching him. When her crew started laughing, he manned up and traipsed toward their quintet.

Coincident to Solo's arrival, Kenny hopped onto the elevated stage and pointed for the DJ to hand him the microphone. The DJ scratched the record then faded the music down. All eyes turned toward the DJ stand where Kenny raised the microphone and started spewing lyrics made famous by the prolific hip-hop orator, Redman.

"Alphas…Gammas…Kappas…and Quuuuuuuesssssss … Let me hear you say Dirrrrrrrty!" Kenny pointed the microphone at the crowd. They weren't quite certain where he was headed with it, but a couple of people meekly said, *Dirrrty*.

Kenny pointed the mic at himself and snarled, *say Filltheee*…and pointed the mic at the crowd. This time the volume doubled when more of the crowd caught on and replied *Fillllllthyyyyyy!!*

Next Kenny rapidly snapped, *Nasty*. This time when he pointed the mic, the crowd returned a guttural growl, *Nast-aayyyyyy!!!*

Kenny realized he had them, pulled the mic back, regarded Solomon, and nodded his head toward Mareschelle and her posse. Kenny performed for a moment; rolled his hips, brushed off the shoulders of his fraternity jersey, flicked his tongue like a viper then shouted, "You know I'm nasty…Too damn dirrty to clean my act up."

The crowd responded with a loud *Oooooooo!* as the DJ scratched a couple hard beats before slowly bringing up the volume.

Right on point, Kenny continued with, "My Greek Family, if you ain't dirrrrrteeeee," the DJ started spinning Christina Aguilera's *Dirrty*, "then you ain't here to parrrt-aayyyy!" Kenny pumped his fist and in a barking noise repeated *roof, roof, roof, roof, roof, roof, roof.*

The crowd pumped their fists in return and started to gather around the stage barking along with Kenny as the speakers boomed;

Ladies (move);
Gentlemen (move);

Somebody ring the alarm...
There's a fire on the roof.

Bass pumped through the speakers, electrifying the crowd into a frenzy as Kenny led them in a back and forth of Kenny shouting: *Ring the alarm...*

And the crowd responding: *And I'm throwin' elbows*
Ring the alarm...
And I'm throwin' elbows.

Ring the alarm... And I'm throwin' elbows...was exchanged three more times before Kenny shouted, *Where my dawgs at?* And started barking again, *roof, roof, roof, roof, roof, roof, roof, roof, roof, roof.*

As Kenny single-handedly commandeered the party, Solo approached Mareschelle and her posse at the back of the crowd. The music was too loud for words, so he asked for a dance by offering his hand.

Mareschelle raised her eyebrows cautiously at his outstretched hand. She looked at her girls and, with their backing, shouted over the din of the music, "Oh no! You don't get to step to me like that."

Solo gave a chuckle as he eyed the gaggle of gorgeous, cackling hyenas decked from head to toe in their sorority colors. He regarded Mareschelle and after a beat he turned to move on with his life thinking, *if she wants to be like that, there are way too many women out here to waste my time on her.*

Mareschelle and her posse laughed at Solo.

When the crowd was as hyped as Kenny wanted them to be, he turned to the DJ and said, "Let 'em have it, DJ." And for the next four minutes, the DJ finally let the record play, allowing Christina's magnificent voice to serenade the invigorated audience of college students. After a minute or so of pumping his fist and playing the role of Hype Man, Kenny dropped the mic on the DJ stand and dove into the crowd. They caught Kenny and passed him around in a circle before letting him down in the center of a hole that had formed in the middle of the dance floor. Kenny took center stage and started his fraternity's step show routine. A moment later, a handful of his frats, including Desmond, joined him stomps.

While the DJ scratched the record to accompany the performance to *Get Dirty*, Mareschelle followed her posse as they moved to join the melee, but was stopped dead in her tracks when a rejuvenated Solomon boldly stepped in her path. Before she had a chance to challenge him with her words, he wrapped an arm around her and moved on a tangent away from her crew. She offered little resistance, keeping her eyes fixed on her sorority sisters, but allowing her feet to follow the brother from Washington State.

While her friends entered a dance battle with a rival sorority inside the circle of Greek teens, Solo stopped and pressed his front against Mareschelle's back. He put his face to her ear and asked, "Are we a game to you Kappa Tau girls, or is it just me?

She eased her face to the right until they were cheek-to-cheek. "I'm sorry Billy Dee, I thought you State boys had thicker skin?"

Solo spun her in his arms to face her, put his face to her ear. "Doesn't a lizard's tail grow back if you step on it?"

She smiled when he stole a kiss, took her hand and led her to the dance floor. They found their landing spot and he spun her twice before pulling her close. Mareschelle liked his renewed confidence and momentarily accepted his embrace before putting space between them so they could dance without bumping uglies. They danced in close proximity among fellow Greeks, close enough to maintain an air of intimacy but far enough apart for Mareschelle to keep it respectable, because she needed him to appreciate her as a lady.

Through that song and the next three, Solo learned that she was feeling him enough to touch him with a hip or leg bump when she wanted to but not enough to allow the schoolboy to put his hands wherever he wanted. Once that boundary was realized, they moved in and out of each other's bubble like Soul Train veterans. They shared a nice slow dance to Monica's *Angel of Mine*, but when a song that was apparently one of her favorites, *Lately* by Tyrese, faded in, Mareschelle was teleported into a far-off realm of her own understanding. She stepped close enough to Solo to give him a huge dose of her all-day Chanel scent, raised her hands toward the treetops and intertwined them before raising her chin to face the heavens. Like a belly dancer at half speed, Mareschelle relaxed her force field, entered Solo's personal space and with next-to-no recognition of his physical presence, seductively twisted, turned, bumped and grinded against him.

Completely enamored, Solo remained in her air and enjoyed the ride. At the beginning of the dance, he saw the girl from U-Dub as a conquest, but once the song finished and she came out of her trance, she had morphed into his obsession. However, in the moment between thought and action, before he could say or do anything to let her know what he was thinking, Mareschelle opened her eyes, kissed him on the cheek and evaporated into the crowd to join her sorors.

Solomon moved to chase after her, to find out where her head went during that dance, but Kenny appeared out of nowhere and gripped his shoulder, stopping him and quickly dousing his aspirations of inquiry. Despite his fantasy pulling him toward the attraction of his private dancer, Solo couldn't resist the force of his friend pulling him back toward the reality of hanging with their squad. After looking for a second and even a third time from Kenny toward the direction that Mareschelle disappeared, Solo eased his charge and acquiesced with a disheartening *DAMN*!

CHAPTER 4

SOLOMON AWOKE ON MONDAY MORNING stuck in the years ago memory of his first college dance with Mareschelle. After he was dressed and in his car driving to work, the radio played the same song that was playing on the night he proposed, allowing memories of Mareschelle to carry him through the rest of the drive completely oblivious to any concerns about what awaited his first day back at work.

~

Solomon and Mareschelle had spent numerous nights together since they'd first met at Greek Weekend, but had not had sex. On their second date, she'd told him she was a virgin and that she intended to stay that way until her wedding night. After a couple heavy, consensual, make-out sessions proved her steadfast commitment to her pledge, he stopped trying to get past second base. On mornings when they'd lay in bed together, Solomon marveled at Mareschelle's beauty, reveling at how lucky a man he was to have such an intelligent, attractive girlfriend.

On that particular June Saturday morning, Mareschelle turned on the television and found an English Premier League Soccer game. When they first met, she'd told Solomon about being on the volleyball team because her volleyball season overlapped with his basketball season and she wouldn't commit to going to one of his games until after he first came to one of hers. And it wasn't until spring conditioning started for her senior year that he found out she was on the Lady Huskies soccer team.

Mareschelle was a better than average, and very tenacious, midfielder who scored six goals her senior season; none of which Solomon ever witnessed. When he was able to make it to her matches, as he promised over Valentine's dinner, she either did not score or did not play because of injury. U-Dub never finished better than third in the conference during her time on the team and her senior year ended with a fourth place finish.

Having completed her undergrad degree and headed to law school in the fall, Mareschelle found herself exchanging emails with several coaches about joining a women's team in the Seattle-Tacoma adult league. It wasn't professional soccer, but it was a great way to stay in shape and offered a chance to play with some of the best amateur, female players in the state.

Solomon chuckled at Mareschelle's intense criticism of England's best pro soccer players, He had played basketball at Washington State and his numbers his senior year were the best of his four years on the team, but with no professional basketball prospects in his future, his mockery offended her.

A disagreement ensued about who was more knowledgeable about what sports and how some people should keep their mouth shut when they don't know what they're talking about. After the word *Fine* was shouted between them several times, Mareschelle turned off the television, threw the remote in the trash, stormed into the bathroom and slammed the door behind her, effectively ending the argument.

When she emerged from the bathroom forty-five minutes later, Solomon apologized for almost fifteen minutes before she accepted.

Solomon and Mareschelle had plans to attend one of the Juneteenth festivals that afternoon. It wasn't celebrated as an official holiday in Washington State, but there were several local celebrations throughout Seattle recognizing the legislation of the Emancipation Proclamation finally reaching enslaved Texans. During their courtship, they had been on dates at several parks around town. Once on a date at Marymoor Park, they ventured down to Lake Sammamish where he played his guitar and sang for her. Solomon loved to play for her and more importantly, he valued her criticisms of his musical hobby because Mareschelle was more than a polite audience, she was engaged and always seemed to listen deeply.

Mareschelle packed a blanket and a picnic basket for their lunch in the park. Unbeknownst to Solomon, she had also packed her soccer ball and cleats. Their morning tête-à-tête had left her a little salty and if the occasion presented itself, she planned to teach her beau a lesson.

The festival ended right before sunset and as their fellow patrons started to leave the park, Mareschelle rekindled the soccer conversation. Despite his repeated apologies, she refused to accept his insistence that he believed her, and the next thing he knew, she exchanged her sandals for soccer cleats, pulled her soccer ball from her bag and began juggling it in the air from right foot to left without letting it hit the ground. Solomon got up and pretended to defend her as she started kicking it around underneath the path lights in the park. As the moments passed, the competitive nature of the two former college athletes elevated, and soon they were pushing and shoving, and trying to take the ball from each other like the Premier League players on television that morning. Solomon stumbled and Mareschelle took advantage of the opportunity, kicking the ball swiftly between two nearby trees set fifteen feet apart.

"Goaaaaalllllllll!" Mareschelle ran in circles before repeating the on-field dance she had done a dozen times in college after scoring.

"Foul," Solomon called obtrusively while she danced.

Mareschelle laughed then sang, "Ole, ole, ole, ole. Ole. Ole," as she retrieved her soccer ball from the bushes behind the tree.

"I tell you what Mizz Pelé," Solomon said when she returned. "If you score on me straight up, mocha lattes from Bucks on me for the rest of the summer." He knew she relied on mocha lattes for her morning caffeine fix. He had once joked that if he cut her, her blood would ooze mocha latte brown.

"Deal," Mareschelle said confidently. "And no reneging."

"No reneging," Solomon confirmed, holding up three fingers like the Boy Scout he never was. "And if you don't score...you let me get to third base tonight."

"Deal," Mareschelle said even louder and more confidently.

This time it was Solomon who said *And no reneging* to which Mareschelle happily confirmed, *And no reneging.*

With the negotiations finished, Mareschelle walked Solomon to the invisible line that connected the two trees she'd kicked the ball through. She said, "YOU stand here," then walked off twenty paces.

"You know I won't hold it against you if you back out right now." Solomon crouched awkwardly into his version of a goalkeeper stance. "I mean, a semi-professional futboler like you not being able to score against a washed up basketball player like me might bruise your ego."

Mareschelle took her ball and smacked it hard against her palm several times. As a midfielder, Mareschelle had been one of the five designated Strikers for the Lady Huskies when sudden death games resulted in penalty kicks. "I won't hold it against you if you back out right now. Are you sure your fragile ego can handle what's about to happen?" She leaned over and tossed the ball onto the ground away from herself with a slight backspin so it would almost return to her. While it came to rest, she jumped in place with high knees three times then rolled her neck, shook the kinks from her shoulders and hips then finally her legs.

Solomon mocked her stretching by doing a couple of jumping jacks before bending from side-to-side. He waved her on and joked, "Anytime little lady," when he was finished.

Mareschelle narrowed her focus. "Just whistle when you *think* you're ready." When Solomon whistled, she took four quick, stationary steps then two long strides forward and pummeled the ball. She swung her foot with such force that the ball rocketed straight for Solomon's head, missing when he ducked and landed face down on the ground, then releasing a resounding *CHING* when it impaled the fence enclosing the basketball courts. "There she goes," she cheered herself on as the ball disappeared into the darkness. "And the crowd goes wild." Again, she repeated her circles then goal scoring dance.

"No fair, I wasn't ready," Solomon belted out as he picked himself up off the ground.

"Uh oh Mister Alexandré, you know what that means…I'm getting free lattes," Mareschelle chided while Solomon found the ball. "I like my lattes. They're gonna taste good. Gonna taste real good."

"Is that all you got?" He rolled the ball back to her hard enough to clobber twenty pins on the way to his final strike to score a 300 in bowling. "Best two out of three!" he demanded.

Instead of flinching when the ball screamed toward her, Mareschelle raised her cleat and brought the ball to rest with merely a bobble. "My Grand-Da can throw harder than that, Rag Arm."

He threw the ball harder than he meant to because he was pissed, but was sincerely surprised when she stopped it so easily. Solomon went back to the imaginary line and this time Mareschelle swung and hit the ball on a line to his left. Solomon dived after it but missed. It scraped against the tree as it screamed through the makeshift goal.

Mareschelle cringed noticeably when he rolled into the tree with a loud thud. "I don't know sports fans, but that one look like it hurt. And did you see the way Betancourt exhibited excellent ball control as she went the opposite way," she said, imitating a broadcaster. "It's nice to see a Striker who sends it to all parts of the net."

Solomon got up off the ground and retrieved the ball once again.

Mareschelle was feeling herself. She loved her boyfriend, but was having fun, so she started dancing as she waited for him to bring back the ball. She imitated a crowd roaring, and again brought back her broadcaster. "What precision. She should tour the country giving penalty kick clinics."

This time he aimed straight for her butt and threw a screamer at her as she danced with her back to him.

She leaned, but didn't fall when the ball slammed into her butt. "You can act a fool if you want," she warned. "But if you bruise it, you lose it."

"What was that? Did you say, *If I bruise it I can peruse it*?" he asked her. "Because if your butt will contuse, I'll be its masseuse," he rhymed like an erstwhile Johnny Cochran. "Best three out of five."

"Why should I?" she clowned. "I'm already up two, and you already got the two-out-of-three for free. What do I get when I win?"

"You hit this next one and I'll wash your car every Saturday morning for the rest of the year."

Solomon crouched for a third time. Mareschelle did her same stutter step routine then hit a line drive straight up the middle. He put his hands up and caught the ball before it nearly decapitating him. Trying not to drop it, he lost his balance and found himself butt down in the damp grass. When he dropped the ball and it rolled through the imaginary goal, he looked at her, amazed that she had enough ball control to do that on purpose.

"You okay, Hunny?" she pined after him innocently.

A little too innocently for Solomon's liking. "I'm fine." He got up and brushed himself off. When he thought she wasn't looking, he ran at her. She squealed and took off running. After much effort, he finally cornered her near the tennis courts. He picked her up, pinned her against the fence and pawed her ravenously.

"You Brut. You savage thug. Get your grubby mitts off me."

He put her down and stroked her cheek. "I know you did that on purpose, Schelle.

Grinning like an imp, she whined, "You trying to kill me? Why do you have to resort to violence?"

"Because I do."

The temperature had cooled significantly since they left home that afternoon and their breath was visible each time they exhaled. Solomon reached up, caught some of hers and pretended to eat it.

"You are so silly," she said, leading him back to their blanket. She pushed him down, sat in his lap and started kissing his neck. "How come you're not complaining about it being cold now?" she asked.

"Because you're starting a fire in my loins."

For some reason she couldn't wrap her mind around, she found his statement humorous. She laughed that really ebullient laugh that she did from time to time. It was that same laugh that made him find her on the quad the night they met. Of all the wonderful sensations she had given him, visually and physically, it was when she laughed like this that gave him the greatest thrill.

"I'm in love with you Mareschelle Betancourt," he said.

She abruptly stopped laughing. She tilted her head at him and with a fake British accent said, "As well you should be, Chap."

He smiled at her and said, "Come on, let's pick up this stuff and go home, Pelé."

"And stop by Starbucks for a mocha latte on the way," she giggled. "And for the record, let's go with Thori Bryan; not Pelé."

That night after they ate dinner, Mareschelle wiped down the countertops while Solomon put away the dishes. Solomon went into the basement to take a call from his mother and found the kitchen empty when he returned. The sound of Chrisette Michelle singing *If I Have My Way* wafted gently down the hallway. He paid the song no attention until it start to play for a second time. When the shrilly sung words *one day we'll make love, passion unheard of, I'll be your* *woman* bounced off his ears, he called Schelle's name, but she didn't answer. He turned off the kitchen lights and walked into the foyer. "Schelle?" he called louder this time. Still, no answer. He found her in the living room writing in her journal, oblivious to his arrival, as she stood in front of the unlit fireplace singing along with Chrisette.

When Chrisette Michelle faded into TLC's *Digging on You*, he went to her, wrapped his arms around her middle and pressed his front against her back. She accepted his embrace, leaned back into him, continuing to sing off key. They shifted to find their comfort spot and he held her until she finished writing, all the while humming in her ear and pressing his lips against her neck in small nibbles.

When she finished writing, she closed her journal, then turned and kissed him on the mouth.

Solomon asked, "Would you like a glass of wine?"

"Just one?" she chided.

"You're right, it has been a long day?"

"Even longer if you lose three-out-of-five."

Solomon hunched his shoulders and pursed his lips in mock anger.

Schelle feigned being scared then craned her neck to ward off a slight twinge. She rolled her neck when the sharp pain subsided a beat.

"Tension?" Solomon asked.

"Yes."

"I'll tell you what," he started. "Let's grab a bottle of wine…"

"And his brother," she added playfully.

"And let's move this conversation upstairs. We'll slip into something more comfortable, light some candles, toast to no more three-out-of-fives, and I'll give you a massage." Solo hurried into the dining room and grabbed two large glasses to accompany the two bottles of wine he chose.

"Candles, wine, and a massage?" she purred when they met in

the foyer. "You know all of my love languages."

Before they climbed the stairs, Schelle stepped in front of him, held his cheeks and kissed him long, deep and slow.

"What did I do to deserve that?" he asked, catching his breath.

"That little thing you did with your lips while I was writing."

They laughed, and she gave him another scintillating kiss before practically skipping up the steps in front of him. As he watched the movement of her hips, he thought that despite losing three-out-of-five, the proposition of getting to third base might actually lie ahead.

In the bedroom, they changed into a matching set of satin pajamas. Mareschelle turned on some music while Solomon opened the wine.

"Are you ready for your stress reliever?" he asked, joining her on the chaise lounge that sat in front of their bedroom window.

"After I finish this glass of this wine, you can give me whatever you think I need or deserve."

"Stress...Less...Is the best!"

"Yessss!" Schelle exclaimed, emptying her second glass of wine.

A Babyface song followed a slow Chante Moore song. When her favorite song, Jesse Powell's *You* came next, she hummed along as Solomon massaged her neck, her humming evolving to lyrics at the *forever* part. Solomon eased to the floor and she instinctively handed him her wine glass for a refill. Instead, he moved in front of her and pulled a ring box from his pocket. "Like this kind of forever?"

Schelle jerked, widened her eyes. "Are you serious, right now?"

He nodded his head and she covered her mouth with both hands.

Calling her full name, he told her, "Mareschelle Renáe Betancourt, you deserve the world if I could give it."

"I don't need the world, I just need my king."

"If I were a king, I'd command the stars to come and ask your permission to shine the way you shine in my eyes."

Tears streamed down her face in anticipation of hearing the four words that every girl dreams of. Her hands trembled, intermittently reaching for the box then stopping. It was right there where she could see it, and it was beautiful, but he hadn't actually asked her yet so she thought not to snatch it from him.

Solomon wiped gently at her tears before continuing. "I can't live without *You, Baby,* and I never want to. I want to spend the rest of my life exploring the warmth of your smile, filling your heart with joy and discovering every mystery that lies deep inside of you."

Mareschelle was in full waterworks mode, but through all of his words, her sniffles and her tears, she never looked away from the tiny velvet box in his hand.

They exchanged nervous smiles and looked at and away from each other several times. Solomon rambled incoherently for a few seconds but stopped when she asked, "What?"

He exhaled intently then said "This thing has been burning a hole in my pocket for almost a month now. I was waiting for the right time to ask you, but you always seemed too busy. I had this whole speech in my head talking about if the world ended tomorrow that I'd spend every moment loving you today and ..."

"And you'll promise to give me your all when life gets me down and I need you the most," Mareschelle said talking over him. "That you'll take care of me and show me that I'm your everything even when we have nothing but love to keep us together."

For a moment, they were talking over each other instead of to each other. His voice trailed off a bit and his eyes fell to the floor, but he snapped back to attention when she yelled, "Boy if you don't give me my ring already."

Solomon took a deep breath, pulled the 3-carat band of yellow diamonds from the box with his right hand and held Mareschelle's left hand in his. As the ring crossed her fingernail he asked her in a strong, clear, confident voice, "Mareschelle Betancourt, will you marry me?"

"Yes. Yes. A thousand times Yesss," she shouted as he rested the ring squarely at the base of her finger. She squealed at the realization of what had just happened then leapt off the chaise and into his arms, knocking him backwards onto the floor.

The pain from falling into the tree at the park returned and he groaned miserably when she landed on top of him with all her weight. A pain that quickly subsided when her lips met his. Maybe it was the alcohol, maybe it was the ring, but whatever it was, Mareschelle kissed him like her life depended on it. When they stopped to catch their breath, they laid there for a good minute while she marveled at her beautiful new engagement ring. When she seemed calm enough to actually comprehend his words, he asked her, "Are you still interested in that massage?"

"Yesss, Baby! Yes I am." Mareschelle raised up onto her knees, straddled him and waved her hand back-and-forth admiring her ring.

"Now *Yesss*, your tipsy butt across the bed, Young Lady."

She followed her man's instructions, climbed off of him and laid sideways across the bed on her stomach still marveling at her ring.

Solomon drew the shades, dimmed the lights, retrieved a leather bag from his closet then momentarily disappeared into the bathroom and returned with a bowl of hot water. He pulled a bottle of massage oil from the bag and placed it in the hot water to warm while he proceeded to take off her pajamas, leaving her in only her bra and panties. He covered her bottom with a warm towel then lit an Egyptian amber scented candle. He loosened her pigtails then proceeded to massage her scalp with his fingers. When she sighed heavily, he pulled the warm oil from the bowl of water and squirted a pool in his palm then rubbed his hands together.

Wine warmed her insides. Strong hands applied warm oils, warmed her outside as Solomon touched her neck, shoulders and her back. From her head to her toes, Solomon vigorously massaged every inch of his bride-to-be's body.

"Oooh, that feels soooo goooood!" Mareschelle moaned.

"Tell me where you want me to touch you and that's where I'll touch."

"Everywhere, Baby." Schelle's words were slow and deep. "I want you to touch me everywhere."

"I'm warning you Schelle, I'm about to lay it down in here."

"Lay it down, Baby...and don't let it get back up."

For as confident as she presented her professional self, Solomon's girlfriend-turned-fiancée, Mareschelle Renáe Betancourt, was a pushover when it came to affairs of the heart.

CHAPTER 5

THE GONZAGA UNIVERSITY PSYCHOLOGY CONFERENCE was Solomon and Mareschelle's first time apart as a married couple. Hesitant to leave his bride of less than a year, he booked the last flight on Sunday night from Seattle to Spokane. In order to be home before Mareschelle's bedtime, his return flight required him to skip the final session on Friday afternoon.

To avoid being in her house alone, Mareschelle spent her Monday, Tuesday and Wednesday evenings at her U-Dub sorority house. When she talked to Solomon on Wednesday night, he convinced her to accompany his mother to her church after work on Thursday to help setup for that Saturday's neighborhood garage sale. Mareschelle agreed and packed a comfortable outfit to change into at Viv's house after work when she picked her up to go to the church.

As Mareschelle pulled into the church parking lot, Brother Patrick Armstrong directed her toward the back away from where they were cordoning off the main parking lot to accommodate sales tables. Two years younger than Vivienne, Brother Armstrong could pass for Cary Grant. Not only was he one of the few Caucasian men Vivienne found attractive, but whenever she found herself in his presence, he caused her quite a bit of female unrest.

Vivienne felt warm. Her seat felt sticky, so asking Mareschelle, "Is it hot in here to you?" she turned up the fan on the air conditioner.

Mareschelle rolled down both front windows as Brother Armstrong approached from the passenger side.

"Hello, Missus Alexandré." His eyes paralyzed Viv, and for a long moment she didn't take a breath. "What a pleasant surprise."

"Evening, Brother Armstrong." Vivienne wasn't sure how much he still suffered from the emotional loss of his wife four years ago to a massive stroke, but no matter how much she flirted, he never seemed willing to cross that line.

"Ms. Vivienne, I've asked you a hundred times to call me Patrick."

"Okay Patrick, but only if you call me Viv."

With that, the Cary Grant doppelganger opened Viv's door and offered her his arm. He loved when she'd squeeze his hand and once he grabbed it, he never wanted to let go.

Viv grabbed her purse and exited the car. She wasn't a beautiful woman by industry standards, but she was intriguing to regard. Straight, white teeth that rarely stayed hidden behind full lips. Oval eyes with halos in the slightest tint of green surrounding soft grey irises. A girlishly feminine woman who manicured and polished her own nails with bright shiny colors, and kept her curly, dyed-black-twice-a-month hair, cut short. Gold words stacked one atop the next across her blue t-shirt read: COUGAR DREAM TEAM. The single gold word on the back read: CAPTAIN.

Mareschelle listened to parking directions from Patrick then watched Viv practically float back to his post with him.

An hour and a half later, forty-eight rectangular tables were setup to form eight rows across the church parking lot. Mareschelle was talking to Sister Minzy Wright when her phone rang. "Hello? What? Calm down, Mama, I can't understand a word you're saying." Mareschelle excused herself from the church elder and moved away from the gossipers so she could hear her mother. In the moments that followed, she listened to her mother explain that her father had collapsed while cutting the lawn and was in the hospital. She had moved the phone away from her ear and was searching the parking lot for Vivienne as her mother's words, "Come now" went unheard.

Mareschelle interrupted Viv's conversation without explanation, picked up her purse and told her they needed to go. "I'll make sure she calls you, Brother Armstrong," she called over her shoulder.

"Stop pulling on me," Viv challenged as the stronger, younger woman ushered her toward her car. "What's wrong with you, girl?"

Mareschelle gave her a rushed explanation, but Viv missed most of it as she struggled to keep her pace. She practically shoved her mother-in-law inside then slammed Viv's door before hurrying to the driver's seat. When she opened her purse to throw her keys inside, Viv noticed an OB/GYN letterhead on an envelope in Mareschelle's purse. Her desire to be a grandmother was stronger than her dislike for her daughter-in-law for taking away her only son. The thought of Mareschelle being pregnant with her first grandchild excited her. As much as she wanted to dive right into an inquisition about the contents of that letter, Viv relegated the thought for the time being.

Brother Armstrong waved Mareschelle out of the parking lot and she wordlessly maneuvered out into traffic heading toward Tacoma.

When they were steady on the highway Viv spoke for the first time. "Don't kill us in this car, young lady. Driving all crazy like you're possessed."

"Yes, Ma'am." She kept her words short and her eyes on the road.

After more silence, Viv said, "You were saying something while you were dragging me to the car, but your lips were moving too fast for me to understand. Do you think you can drive like a bat out of hell AND tell me what's going on at the same time?"

Mareschelle's eyes darted back-and-forth evaluating a plan to maneuver between the cars ahead of her. A moment later, she settled in the left hand lane, took a deep breath and forced it out. "I didn't mean to be rude back there, but my mother called and said that the ambulance was taking my father to the hospital. She said he collapsed and wasn't talking, and she wasn't able to tell me anymore."

"Well, I'm sorry to hear that," Viv said. "But if you needed to leave in that much of a hurry, you should've left me there. My church family would've gotten me home."

Mareschelle was curt. "The thought did cross my mind." A song came on the radio that reminded Mareschelle of her high school sweetheart, the guy who betrayed her and slept with her college roommate freshman year. She slapped at the buttons until the radio went silent. Two miles later she exited Route 167 onto Route 18.

The combination of riding in silence and the mystery of what was written within the OB/GYN envelope, forced Vivienne to belt out, "I don't mean to pry, but I didn't realize you and I went to the same OB/GYN. Which doctor do you see?"

A long silence passed before Mareschelle said, "Doctor Branch."

"Oh," Viv replied, "Doctor Violette has been my doctor for as long as I can remember. He knows me inside and out."

"I bet," Mareschelle mumbled.

"That was rude," Viv huffed. "Let's chalk that one up to you worrying about your father."

"I'm sorry." Mareschelle's apology was louder than it was sincere.

"I've told my son for the longest time that I've always wanted a bunch of grandbabies." Viv and Mareschelle both looked straight ahead as she merged onto interstate I-5 headed south. "I don't mean to pry but was that letter your pap smear results, or something else?"

Stifling a queasy sense of déjà vu, Mareschelle said, "I went to the doctor because I missed my last three cycles. I took three pregnancy tests and they were all negative."

"Well," Viv expelled, "everybody's menstruation isn't regular."

A hot flash swept over Mareschelle. The steering wheel went slick in her sweaty hands. She wiped them on her pants one at a time then calmly said, "They don't know how it happened. Maybe I was exposed to radiation and didn't know it. Maybe it's because I got my period so early in the first place."

"Cancer?"

"No, not cancer. And not lupus either, they checked for that."

"Is it HIV?"

"Ms. Vivienne," Mareschelle paused. "I'm menopaused already."

"Menopaused? But you can't be but twenty-five, right?"

"Yes, Ma'am."

"Unless you're one of those heifers that looks really good for her age and you lied to my baby?" Vivienne called Mareschelle's name three times without an answer. The only thing convincing Viv that she was alright was that she continued to drive like she was auditioning for NASCAR.

"Ms. Vivienne, don't worry about what I just said, it's not that important. We can talk about it later. I just need to concentrate on getting to the hospital and checking on my daddy."

Vivienne was quiet for a solid five minutes thinking the worst about her daughter-in-law but knowing that Solomon would berate her if she said half of the bad things she was thinking. Once her son entered her thoughts, her point of view regarding her daughter-in-law shifted. Viv had given birth to Solomon after two failed pregnancies. Neither of his older siblings survived the gestation period. The first was stillborn. The second miscarried just before the end of her first trimester. Vivienne wanted children, but lost the will after the miscarriage and, much to her husband's dismay, fell into a bout of not wanting to have sex with him. Three years, and a lot of therapy later, Vivienne was pregnant with Solomon. Those 8-1/2 months were physically the roughest of her entire life. Braxton Hicks, Gestational Diabetes and severe bloating of her ankles and calves left her bedridden for the majority of her third trimester. With him, she prayed and got a lot closer to God. Despite the doctor inducing Vivienne at 34 weeks, her reward for her newfound faith was being strong enough to deliver Solomon without a C-Section. Unfortunately, after his miraculous birth, the doctor told his parents that if she tried again, carrying a baby to term could kill her. With that unfortunate news, Viv proceeded with a hysterectomy before departing the hospital, leaving Solomon to spend his life as an only child.

Mareschelle heard Viv repeatedly kissed her teeth while she stared out the window contemplating her thoughts. When she passed a strip mall and reached her exit in Tacoma she said, "Ms. Vivienne…"

But before Mareschelle could finish her thought, her mother-in-law blurted out, "He will leave you." She made the unexpected pronouncement as if she was predicting rain because she could see the clouds and feel the first sprinkles on her forehead.

"If you truly think that, then you have no idea who your son really is." Mareschelle had weathered extracting Solomon from his mother's clutches, but her Vivienne's words were caustic and shone a bright spotlight of doubt on her relationship with her husband; who would unfortunately, always be this lady's son. She wanted to stop the car and tell her to get out, but she loved her husband too much for that. But she would give him a verbatim repeat of his mother's words when he came home.

Mareschelle didn't say another word to Vivienne as they raced toward Tacoma. She exited the highway and slammed on the brakes at an intersection two blocks from the hospital. She considered running the yellow, but had done that as a teen and a police cruiser sitting adjacent her in the intersection pulled her over and ticketed her. She loved her father, but the moment of patience required to wait for the light was better than the possibility of an extended delay to receive a ticket.

When the light turned green, Viv found her voice. "The problem with young women today is the way you carry yourself."

"Excuse me, Ms. Viv, but I said I'm sick. Are you listening to me? What does being sick have to do with the way I carry myself?"

Without acknowledging her, Viv continued. "I've seen it for years, girls like you staying out all night in high school, and then when you get to college, you flat out lose your minds, all in the name of finding yourself. How did you think things would end?" Vivienne's voice splintered with tears. "Girls like you think it's cute to run around with this boy and that one. That's why nobody is on their knees for you. Because you're always on your knees for them."

"I don't know what the hell you're talking about, Lady. I get on my knees for no one," Mareschelle fired back. "Including your precious son. And my problem is not my fault."

"Nothing ever is," Viv said. "That's all girls like you ever say."

Mareschelle sat stunned, focusing intently on the car ten feet in front of her to keep from backhanding her mother-in-law. Vivienne's words hurt, cut her like a samurai's sword and left her gutted like a fish. She knew she wasn't the kind of girl Viv was talking about, but she couldn't help but wonder what prompted her to think that way.

When Mareschelle finally arrived at the hospital, she pulled right up to the emergency room door. To keep from throwing her mother-in-law out on the side of the road, or better yet, to keep from saying words she could never take back—because at that point she knew anything she said to her husband's mother would be highly disrespectful—Mareschelle leaned across Solomon's mother and opened her car door from the inside. "Would you please go inside and see if your nosey ass can find out where my mother is?" After Viv snatched her purse, stepped out the car and slammed the door, Mareschelle ordered her car's Bluetooth to, *Call Solomon on cell.*

CHAPTER 6

THE CENTENNIAL TRAIL STRETCHES THROUGH the center of Spokane from the Gonzaga University campus to Riverfront Park. Solomon had told Mareschelle that he'd always been interested in photography growing up, so when she received her sign-on bonus for joining her law firm, she surprised him with a thousand-dollar camera for his birthday. Solomon packed the camera for his trip to Spokane and decided to try it out for the first time during his nightly walk through the park. Near the west end of the park's trail, he heard the distance buzz of reggae music and thought pictures of a band would make great images to start his portfolio.

Adozen or so people were huddled around a street band and he identified the song as a cover of the Shabba Ranks classic *Mr. Lover Man*. Further in, he stopped to people watch. People-watch and sway to the rhythmic island sounds. Across the far side of the gaggle, perched on a small, empty platform raised two feet off the ground, he saw three women dancing to the beat of their heart's contentment. The woman who first caught his attention wore a pink, silk baseball hat with a matching pink and white scarf. The lean, curvy figure of the woman swayed and bounced with all of the exuberance of a Jamaican Carnivalé dancer. Her flowy blue and white dress was respectable, cut high in the neckline, yet tight enough to reveal the bouncy roundness of her pert, braless breasts. The music stopped ten minutes later and the crowd disbursed when the leader of the band announced they were taking a fifteen minute break.

Solomon watched the intriguing female dancing trio from across the street as they walked south toward center city. When the street light changed, the three women joined four others who crossed.

At the corner, the woman in blue looked in Solomon's direction. She hesitated when their eyes met. In the light of the evening sun, the fabric of her dress clung to her, and revealed the swell of her hips and the length of her thighs. Continuing their journey deeper into center city, the dancing trio turned in the direction of an old monastery.

Solomon crossed the street in their direction. Not certain if their pace had slowed or his had quickened, he found himself stopped, looking lost, in front of an outdoor cafe on the far side of the church at the same time as the women. He lost sight of them in the crowd, but that was only momentarily until he heard a questioning on his left.

"Excuse me, Sir. Are you following us?"

Her eyes were on him when he turned. Mesmerizing eyes the blue of a limpid pool of water. A challenging, flinty gaze that he wouldn't have expected from a woman her age burned through him. Something in it made him slightly ashamed of himself. Placid, killer-blue eyes, deep and inviting like a warm Caribbean lagoon drew him closer to her. In the candor with which they regarded him, they were like the eyes of a child. And yet there was also something in that scrutiny which was not childish at all. Solomon felt his heart pound once, hard against his chest.

Then she smiled. And when he didn't return her smile in earnest, she came to him and playfully gestured, "You look like you're lost out here all alone, Mon." Her native Spokane, Anglo-Saxon Protestant contained as much Caribe heritage as his native Seattle, African-American Baptist. "So ya like da Ray-Gay, Mon?"

"Yeah, Mon," he said after a beat. "It's Irie!" His forced attempt at a Caribbean accent equally as terrible. "Ya don't meet many 'round here who dance to reggae with the fire, Mon."

They laughed at their collective bad accents, then she reached out her hand to introduce herself and he took it.

"I'm sor…" he stopped when he heard the ringtone he had set for Schelle's cell phone. "Excuse me, I need to take this."

She asked, "Can I look at your pictures?" still holding his hand.

She loosed her grip when he handed her the camera and he turned his back when he answered. As he listened to his unexpected call, the woman scrolled through the two dozen photos Solomon had taken that day. His back was to her when she finished, and with a mischievous smile, she opened the flap on the bottom of the camera and removed the SD card containing the digital images—including those of her and her friends. Then the blue-eyed beauty tapped Solomon on his shoulder, handed him his camera, pointed in the direction of her two friends, mouthed, "I'll be over there," and then retreated to join them.

Solomon nodded then placed the camera strap around his neck. After listening for almost a minute more as Mareschelle informed him about her father being hospitalized, Solomon forgot about the dancing trio and took off running toward his hotel.

~

Mareschelle hung up the phone as she rushed through the Emergency Room doors and hurried to the admission's counter. She saw Vivienne demonstratively talking to the poor soul who was unfortunate enough to answer her call. Mareschelle only hoped that the woman had not called her husband. In that moment, she hated that she had chosen to confide in Vivienne. What Solomon's mother had said to her was foul, and for the life of her, she couldn't think of anything she'd done to warrant that from her. Reaching the counter she said, "Hello, my name is Mareschelle Betancourt Alexandré. My mother called and said my father, Darnell Betancourt, was being brought in."

The admission's nurse agitated her mouse for a moment before telling Mareschelle that her father was still in the ER.

"Well do you know if my mother is back there with him? Her name is Rachel Mae Betancourt."

The nurse looked up at Mareschelle. "Short lady with hazel eyes?"

"Yes, that's her."

"She's back there. Let me call and have one of the nurses in the back let her know you're here. If you want to take a seat, I'm sure she'll be out in a moment."

Mareschelle paced the lobby until her mother emerged through the Emergency Room doors five minutes later. She wiped away the last of her tears, rushed to her mother and as quickly as she did, her tears returned. They hugged, kissed, and after a moment of uncontrolled sobbing, the elder Betancourt told her daughter that her father had suffered a stroke—but he was alive and being treated. She told her everything that she could remember, then told her that she would go in the back and bring the doctor out to talk to her because they would only allow one person in the back with the patients.

As Rachel Mae disappeared to find her husband's doctor, Mareschelle saw Vivienne anxiously awaiting the report. As a churchgoing, Christian woman, she knew she needed to suppress her anger and tell her mother-in-law what she knew, but at the same time, she wanted to call Solomon and tell him about his mother's nasty attitude and hurtful words. But just before she pulled out her phone to call him, Vivienne touched her wrist and, in the softest voice she ever heard from her, anxiously asked, "Is he going to be alright?"

Mareschelle struggled to understand her. Vivienne sounded confused, disoriented, her voice quaked and she seemed rattled for some reason that Mareschelle was completely unaware.

"Mareschelle, I've been foolish. Both of our doctors are very good. They'll figure out how to fix you. Don't you worry about money or anything like that, we will get you all fixed up."

"Ma'am?" Mareschelle asked her, uncertain what she was talking about. *Worry about money? Why would I worry about money when Solomon and I each make more than her?*

"Oh baby," Vivienne said. "What happened?" Her tone was soft and sugary. This was the way mothers were supposed to be. Warm and omniscient at the same time. Her words were like kind hands; soft and scented. Mareschelle wasn't used to this type of affection from Vivienne. Tears pricked the corners of her eyes. When Viv hugged her, she let her tears fall freely as she relayed her mother's words.

Having received her message, Vivienne fought back tears of her own as she, still holding her hand, dragged Mareschelle to the seat next to hers. "Does my son know?"

"Yes, Ma'am. I called him in the parking lot." Mareschelle pulled out her cell phone and cradled it next to her ear. "I told him I'd call him back once I had more information about Daddy."

"Does he know about the letter from the doctor?"

Without responding, Mareschelle dropped the phone to her lap and openly sobbed. She had read the letter from the doctor eight times in the two days since she'd received it but had not told Solomon about the letter because she didn't want him to worry while he was out of town. Children were a huge part of her and her husband's future plans. Mareschelle and Solomon had first mentioned having children two weeks into their engagement. Although they differed on a number—her ideal number of children being two, and his being four or five—they both agreed that they wanted to start having children as soon as she finished law school and passed the bar exam. Vivienne didn't know it, but what Mareschelle wanted from life more than anything was not to be the girl Viv described. She wanted to star in her own fairytale love story, to be a loving wife and doting mother and live the happily-ever-after of two people forever in love—just like her parents.

CHAPTER 7

THE SUMMER BEFORE SOLOMON STARTED his guest lecturer stint in Spokane, a whirlwind of drama blew through the Hang Suite. His neighbors, Majac and Tessa, spent their final week as fiancées together before their flight to Pennsylvania for their wedding. On Thursday, Solomon met Majac, Tessa and her sister, Leona, at the Huskie Café inside the student union building on the campus of the University of Washington where Tessa had given a lecture earlier that morning.

Leona brought a surprise with her in the form of her and Tessa's long lost father whom she'd found earlier that day when a Hummer almost ran him over while crossing the street a couple of hundred feet behind her. That meeting quickly devolved into an active shooter situation when two men drew and started firing their guns. Stray bullets hit Tessa, Leona, Majac and several other customers inside the café, and instead of getting on an airplane to fly east for Majac and Tessa's wedding, the trio spent the next two weeks in the hospital.

Tessa lost her baby.

Majac, determined to marry the love of his life, married Tessa in the hospital's chapel two days later on the day of their wedding. It wasn't her dream wedding, but all she wanted was to marry the man of her dreams, so despite losing his child, she was happy to finally get her man and be able to spend the summer with him as newlyweds recovering from injuries.

Solomon was the only one of the four who was not shot during the melee, but he'd spend his time at the hospital checking on his friends and fretting over Leona who had her kidney destroyed when a piece of shrapnel found its way into her abdomen. He and Leona had been dating for just over six months, but both agreed that they were in a committed, monogamous relationship. Still reeling in the guilt of losing Mareschelle a year earlier, Solomon decided that if he was going to lose another love, that love would be his wife; so with their collective family and friends gathered in the family visiting suite, Solomon got down on a knee, pulled out a ring and proposed to Leona.

She accepted without letting him finish his question. Her joy sent her over the moon, but a realization made the next day, brought her crashing back to earth.

While watching the news report about the homeless man who foiled the robbery at the Huskie Café, Leona's sister, Jennifer, and Solomon's mother, Vivienne, both recognized the picture of Leona's father on the TV screen. In a private conversation, they deduced that Leona's estranged father and Solomon's missing-in-action father were in fact twin brothers. Their disclosure to Solo and Leona devastated the couple. As quickly as they'd found true joy in their relationship, that joy was snatched away.

Two weeks later, a series of blood and DNA tests confirmed their relationship—Solomon and Leona were first cousins. The silver lining in their doused marriage proposal presented itself in the form of Solomon being —courtesy of the strong DNA match from their fathers being twins—a perfect donor match for Leona's damaged kidney. Leona would not become his wife, but a part of him would live inside her forever, giving her a better chance at a healthy future.

~

Columbus Day Weekend was a sports fan's wet dream come true that year in Seattle. The Mariners were hosting playoff games Friday and Sunday nights. The University of Washington Huskies were playing their homecoming football game late Saturday afternoon. And on Monday night, the undefeated and division-leading Seahawks were hosting the undefeated 49ers. But more important than all of that, the second Saturday of every month was reserved for the Horsemen and friends poker game. A game that had originated in college with Kenny, Solo and their roommates then later joined by Lawrence and Desmond after graduation, and now with them in their late thirties, the tradition has stood the test of time.

After spending the day furniture shopping with his mother, Solo dropped Vivienne at church for bingo night, then hurried toward North Seattle. It took him all of thirty minutes to iron, shave, shower and dress. Boot cut jeans, a rose-colored tie around the neck of a white shirt and a bronze blazer was his outfit. Majac didn't answer the door when Solomon knocked, so he sent him a text to inform him that the hostess would be expecting him when he made his way into town. Majac sent a thumbs up emoji in response to Solo's *just tell her you're the 'Magic Man' and she'll bring you straight to the party* text.

Majac parked at the public garage a block south of Woody's instead of the valet parking Jaz would've paid for had they been out together. The clear, sixty-degree night made the walk comfortable. As he passed the alley behind the buildings that included Woody's, Majac saw the figure of a man down the alleyway and immediately hoped it was the homeless guy from the Huskie Café—Tessa and Leona's father. He jogged in the direction of the man, but the man was gone by the time he got to where he saw him. Baffled by the guy's disappearance, Majac checked every opening in the alley as he backtracked his way out of the alley. Just like his fruitless summer efforts following his release from the hospital, he and Solomon had spent weekends in July and August trolling alleyways, missions, freeway underpasses and shelters searching for him, Majac was once again unsuccessful in finding Courtney Franklin. Had he ventured another twenty feet down the alley, he would have found the man he sought crouched at an outdoor cleaning station drinking from the faucet.

Woody's Bar and Grill had been the Four Horsemen's Saturday night hangout since Desmond opened it six years after they graduated from college. It wasn't anything exceptional, just a small local bar, but it was their sanctuary. A place they could go and be away from the stressors of their everyday lives, share drinks during good times, and work out solutions to their problems during bad. In the upstairs meeting room that overlooked the main dining area, two dozen people ate, drank and watched the undercard of the boxing match on a giant one-hundred-inch curved screen TV.

"Alright fellas, who's your daddy?" Kenny blustered. Lawrence, Solo, and Desmond were used to Kenny's theatrics, so none of them were holding their breath. After puffing his chest out a time or two and doing his *Kenny Dance*, he pulled four slips of paper from his breast pocket, slammed them on the table and yelled, "BAM!"

Looking to see what all the fuss was about, the fellas finally gave him their attention.

"Soooo…?" Kenny picked up the tickets and waved them in front of his fellow Horsemen. "Who wants one of these 40-yardline Skybox tickets to watch our Hawks whip some 49er ass Monday night?"

Lawrence replied first. "I'll check my calendar, but I should be good."

"I'm in," Desmond said.

"What's the date for that game?" Solomon asked, his face buried in his cell phone. "If it's this coming Monday, I'll be at a conference in Spokane; but if it's a week from Monday, I'm good."

Kenny checked his phone intently. After a beat, he said, "Yeah, this coming Monday, not the Monday after."

"Damn, I'll have to pass," Solomon rolled his eyes for a moment then followed with, "My neighbor Majac is coming through later. Why don't you ask him? I think he's in town for a while?"

"Cool," was Kenny's one word answer.

Kenny shoved the tickets back in his pocket as two of their friends, Marshall Townsend and Overton Sinclair, joined the table. Desmond greeted his guests then excused himself stating, "Duty calls."

Inside Woody's, Majac blushed when he told the hostess that he was *The Magic Man* she was expecting. She smiled at his embarrassment, her thick, strawberry-blonde twists shaking as they shared a laugh. She liked tall men and he was five inches taller than her. She checked out the fine line of his shoulders beneath his suit jacket. When she noticed his wedding ring, she feigned, "Maybe someday you'll be free enough to tell me how you earned that nickname."

"Hopefully not," Majac retorted as she escorted him in. Just before they reached the steps, Majac saw Desmond near the kitchen chastising his shift manager.

"Excuse me, Boss," a man called from behind them.

Desmond spun on the sous chef he'd hired only two weeks prior. When he saw the fear in his eyes, he paused before asking, "What?" in a much less intimidating tone than he used for his shift manager.

"The delivery bell rang at the rear kitchen door, but Chef Miles didn't tell me to expect deliveries tonight, so I checked it." When Desmond didn't yell at him, the Sous Chef seemed to gain a little confidence in his tone. Woody's head chef was off for the night and since he was new, the sous chef figured he should involve the boss instead of acting on his own this early into his employ. "I didn't recognize the man at the door, but he asked for you personally. Said you'd be expecting him. I let him in and had Chad, the busboy, wait at the back door with him while I found you. I thought it best to find out what to do from you."

Desmond patted the young man on the shoulder. "Come on, let's go see who it is." Despite the stern look on Desmond's face, he was pleased that the bar was so busy. He shoved the inspection report into the shift manager's chest and growled, "Fix it!"

At the back door, Desmond saw an older man with thick, salt-and-pepper ropes of hair. He carried a backpack and wore a weathered Army jacket, khaki fatigue pants and badly worn Army boots. The nametag on the jacket read FRANK.

When he first met the old-timer in the park across the street from the Binders and Spines bookstore near the Alderwoods Mall, something about the old man struck Desmond as interesting. Assuming he was homeless, he bought two drinks and two sausage sandwiches from the nearby hotdog stand and invited FRANK to join him for lunch. Desmond did most of the talking because FRANK was too busy stuffing his face to answer Desmond's questions. When they were finished, Desmond gave FRANK one of his cards and told him if he wanted to make a little pocket cash, to come to the backdoor of the address on the card around eleven pm and ask for the owner. Once or twice a month since then, FRANK banged on the backdoor of Woody's between eleven and midnight. Desmond would bring him in, give him a plate of food and offer him a spot in the hundred-square-foot supply closet off the kitchen to eat. He'd also instructed his kitchen manager to pack FRANK a bag of leftover food to take with him when he left.

Once the restaurant closed, FRANK would emerge with a broom, dustpan and a mop bucket full of hot water. With a tune on his lips, he would gleefully wipe down all of the tables and chairs then place the chairs upside down on each table before sweeping the floor. Then he'd grab that mop bucket handle and tow it around the room like it was the leash tugging along an untrained puppy. When he finished cleaning, the shift manager paid FRANK one hundred dollars in twenties. It was substantial enough to keep a couple of dollars in the elderly gentlemen's pockets and minimal enough that

Desmond could avoid hiring an extra person to clean up.

Desmond had heard Solomon's recap of the U-Dub shooting and was aware of Solomon's relationship to Leona, but somewhere in there, he had not made the connection that his cleanup guy, FRANK, was the Leona's father in Solomon's story. Had he known, he would've called Solomon the moment FRANK arrived.

Once upstairs, the hostess walked Majac toward the back corner where the Horsemen, and two fellas Majac didn't recognize, waited for Desmond to return and fill the empty seat at their poker table.

Solomon noticed the hostess and stepped away from the table to greet his neighbor when he saw Majac.

Majac was excited to join the group although he didn't know what to make of the conglomerate of strangers. Once the noise subsided, Solomon made a swooping introduction. "Fellas, you all remember my neighbor, Anton Charles? He's the submarine commander who lives in the other half of the Hang Suite. Majac, you know Kenny and Lawrence, and those two are our boys Overton and Marshall." Each of the men Majac didn't know nodded or waved in recognition. "Make him feel at home, and save some of his spare change for me."

Marshall chimed, "If he sits down at this poker table, his spare change will belong to me."

"LD, take care of my friend."

"Yeah, LD," Overton added. "And we'll take care of his money."

"I know that's right," Kenny laughed.

Majac laughed as loud as the others.

"And if I were you," Solo warned Majac. "I'd leave enough money in my wallet for cab fare."

"Gone, Solo. We got him," Lawrence urged Solomon to leave then pulled out Desmond's chair. "Have a seat, Commander."

Majac sat in the chair between Kenny and Lawrence. "Hey Rev." Majac greeted Lawrence, then extended a hand to Kenny. "Nice to see you again, Partna."

"Yeah, I remember now," Kenny harrumphed. "We met at the art auction, right?"

"Yeah," Majac confirmed. "That's right."

Kenny and Majac shook hands. "But I could've swore Solo called you by another name."

"You probably remember him calling me Majac?"

"Yeah, that's' what it was." With a little too much bravado, Kenny said, "Well Mister Majac, you ready to partake in on some of this?"

"The more pertinent question," Majac said in reply, "Is how much of this do I want to take?"

Overton dealt and everyone picked up their cards.

"Welllllllll," Kenny said, exaggerating the word as he poured Majac a glass of the same brown liquor that filled the rest of their glasses, "I say we raise the ante a bump in honor of our new friend."

"Don't take stock in anything that comes out of his kickball sized head," Lawrence guffawed. "Kenny's been losing money to us for years, and I'm not sure he don't like it that way. For somebody that good with money, I can't see how he's that terrible at cards."

When Majac realized his arrival was not an intrusion, a feeling of fraternity swept over him. In that instant, he felt like one of the fellas, despite not yet finding his place among them.

When Desmond returned a half hour later, a waiter followed him with two trays of hot hors d'oeuvres for the table. He sat with a huff, his cell phone to his ear, in listen only mode. "Being married was way easier that this dating stuff."

"What's up, Wood?" Lawrence asked.

"Last night Sharet and I got into of those *truth moment* conversations," Desmond said, "and she told me that she was a stripper in college. Said she did it to help pay for tuition."

"What's wrong with that?" Kenny asked as Solomon dealt.

"Nothing," said Desmond. "She's pissed because I made a face when she told me. I wasn't judging; I was just surprised. I explained myself, but since then she's been going on about how no woman worth a damn wants a man who judges her."

"I warned you about holding women up to ideals that aren't realistic," Kenny said.

"Putting women on pedestals seems good in theory, but you can't do that stuff in a relationship because then they have no room to maneuver," Solomon said. "No room to grow."

"Pedestals are for statues," Overton added. "Put a woman up there and when you hit a little turbulence, she'll eventually fall off."

In the silence that followed, Desmond hated that Sharet thought he somehow thought less of her despite him telling her he hadn't for the past twenty-four hours. He feared that if she did, then she'd get rid of him and he'd be back to languishing in the solitary existence of bachelorhood. He knew that being alone took strength. Since his wife died, he knew that being alone didn't prove anything except that he could be lonely. "Damn," he said quietly resting his head in his hands. Not having Sharet around was something he didn't want to imagine.

"Hey Wood, in order to win your woman back, you have to go that extra mile. We don't always know how far that mile is, but we have to keep going until we find ourselves at the end." That was Majac. "If she is worth the anger, then she is definitely worth the effort."

"Don't sweat it Wood." Kenny laid a pair of jacks and tens on the table. "Give her tonight to cool off. Cook her breakfast in the morning then take her shopping tomorrow and buy her some stuff you wouldn't normally get her with all of the money your taking from us."

Overton, and Majac laughed. Desmond grinned at Kenny who went right back to stuffing his mouth with food.

Marshall said, "Money can buy you love."

"No it can't," Lawrence objected.

"Love is overpriced," Kenny retorted with a mouth full of food.

"It doesn't matter how well you treat them," Solomon added, "some woman always find something to start trippin' over."

"Unfortunately my brothers, we are taught that the best way to move on from a relationship is to discard the person we once claimed we loved." Lawrence didn't normally bring out his preacher-isms when he was with the fellas, but the topic made it necessary. "I won't argue with the fact that all kinds of relationships find endings, but I do question how they end."

"Hey man," Kenny blurted out, "hold it down however you have to. That's all we can do out here."

Solo said, "Leona once told me that a man could be intelligent, entertaining, progressive, studious, and silly, as long as he was never immature. Once I realized she was all of that, I chased her like no other woman in my life." Solomon thought about how lonely he'd been and realized that Leona was way too vivacious to ever be lonely.

"You see," Kenny chimed, "the major difference between men and women is that a man sees a woman for who she is right now, what she looks like right now. A woman sees a man's potential; not the man that he is now but the man only she can change him into."

"God is easy compared to women," Lawrence said. "They are truly the ultimate mystery."

"Man, miss me with all that nonsense, LD." Kenny laid down a hearts flush before he continued. "Let me tell you that if God wanted to remove the mystery of how to completely satisfy our women in bed, he would have built a vibrate function into our dicks."

The table erupted with laughter. After a moment's hesitation, Lawrence burst out laughing too. When he gained his composure he said, "Now that my idiot brother, who thinks with his little head instead of his big one, has blessed us with his infinite wisdom, can we get off the philosophy and get back to playing cards?" Lawrence wasn't usually the most ambitious of the group, but tonight, for the first time since they could remember, he was up twice his buy-in and didn't want to lose his edge.

When the boxing match main event started, Lawrence, being two-hundred fifty dollars up, would be the night's big winner. Desmond and Majac would be each be sixty dollars richer. Kenny would be down one hundred dollars and Solomon down fifty.

CHAPTER 8

SOLOMON KNEW THERE WAS NO way he'd be able to sleep after his fighter's 4-to-1 odds won him more than ten grand, so instead of going home, he went to his office and reviewed transcription notes. His adrenaline ran so hot that the sun rose before he realized that he'd been up all night.

On his drive home, he decided to stop at Eddie and Jack's Good Sign Bakery, a hole-in-the-wall spot that was quickly becoming his new favorite. He figured he'd pick up some pastries to share with his Mom when he picked her up for church. And if they had coffee, he'd grab a cup to ensure he finished the drive home. When he switched into the left-hand turn lane and slowed to a stop behind the two cars already waiting at the red light, he noticed her exit the Magnusson Building and stop at the corner. The turning lane light was red, and the crossing hand changed from red to white so that she could cross. Images of his wife crowded his mind, crashed down and overpowered his thoughts. Everything about her told him that the woman crossing the street was his Mareschelle. He blew his horn and she turned toward the noise, confirming she was real. Their eyes met and she smiled a golden ray of sunshine right at him. The light went green and three seconds later while he stared at the back of her stepping onto the sidewalk to his right, the horn from the car behind him began blaring. He snapped out of his trance and turned left. She peeked back at him as he turned the corner and let traffic push him away from her. He tried to watch her in his mirrors while simultaneously avoiding crashing into someone.

Solomon made a left at the next intersection. "Come back, Baby." Two more lefts brought him back to the intersection where he saw her. "Come on, Baby. Come back to me." This time he stopped in the right turn lane. He wasn't sure if it was good or bad, but the busy intersection had a 'no turn on red' sign that allowed him to loiter at the intersection without being harassed to turn by other drivers. He waited at the red light, panning the streets front, right and back looking for that vision of loveliness he believed to be Mareschelle. "Come on, Baby, I'm right here. Come back to me." But no such luck. When the light turned green, he didn't move, hoping that she'd emerge from a nearby store, but after five seconds, incessant horn blowing behind him prompted him to turn. After a second horn blare, he crept around the corner, driving as slowly as he could without causing an accident and all the while searching the store front windows for the woman with the amazing smile. "I know you're out there Schelle. I can feel you. Come on, Baby. Come back to me"

At the end of that block, he made three right turns to bring him back to that beginning intersection. He figured that enough time had passed for her to finish her business and emerge so he could see her again. When she did, he'd double park and go to her, and find out who she was, confirm she was real and not an apparition. But again, no such luck. Solomon circled that block two more times in both directions and after a half hours' worth of gas was spent, he ended his search and headed home to get some rest. He was frustrated, agitated, so obsessed with finding his wife's ghost that he forgot to go to Eddie and Jack's.

~

Haunted by a Mareschelle sighting, church was not an option. He called Vivienne and cancelled, but told her that Lawrence would come get her if she wanted. Once home, he slid the blinds in his empty bedroom closed, peeled off every stitch of clothing, showered then turned on the radio before climbing into bed. In a few hours, he'd get up and pack for his 7pm flight to Spokane, but Memories of his Schelle mixed with the images of the woman from that morning stood between him and the pleasure of sleep. He closed his eyes and hoped the lyrics of a Dru Hill song could soothe him to sleep.

Sorry, didn't notice you there ...
Then again you didn't notice me,
So we'll remain passersby ...
Until the next time we meet.
I'm hoping I can make you mine ...
Before another man steals your heart,
And once your beauty is mine ...
I swear we will never be apart.

By the end of the first chorus, he had slid into a restful state, but despite closing his eyes, the lyrics of the song played on his mind.

'Cause my eyes have seen the glory ...
In the coming of your smile,
So I swear if you ever come 'round again ...
Please stay for a while.
You are so beautiful ...
When I'm down and out (when I'm down) ...
I never seem to get tired (I never seem) ...
Tired of your love, oh tired of your love
'Cause you are wonderful ...
You're wonderful (and I'm dying) ...
I'm just dying to make you see (to make you see) ...
Anything you want inside your heart ...
You can find right here inside of me!

*Walks by me every day ... Her and love are the same
(oh oh ohhhhh ... oh),*

*The woman that's stolen my heart ... And beauty is her
name.*

*I'm hoping I can make you mine ... Before another man
steals your heart ...*

*And once this beauty is mine ... I swear we will never
be apart.*

Solo tossed and turned for almost an hour before sleep finally
came, when an image of Mareschelle snuggled against his sleeping
back. She bent her knees to match his angle as though he laid
horizontally in her lap. "Solomon?" he heard her say into the space
between his shoulder blades. When he didn't answer, she snaked an
arm under his and hugged him across his chest. "Solomon?"

"You okay, Baby?" He imagined knocking her in the chin with
his shoulder when he turned over. He went to touch her face but she
rolled away. Recognizing her smile in the shine from the outside
light, he burrowed against her and draped his leg across her hip. "Is
this your way of saying you need some attention?"

"I have to tell you something." Although a dream, the tone and
depth of Mareschelle's voice were pitch-perfect.

"Okay," he said, withdrawing his weight. "Do you need me to
turn on the light?"

"No, don't. I said I have something to tell you, not show you."

"Is it serious?"

"Yes."

"Bad news, or good?"

"News that I've wanted to share since before the last time you
left for Spokane."

"Sounds like we need the light on?"

"No," she said. "Please." She felt braver in the dark, where they
could hear each other, touch each other, but not quite see.

Solomon found sleep and his dream brought his Schelle to him. Brought the memory of the night after he returned from Spokane and Schelle shared the same news that she'd earlier with his mother.

"Okay, Baby. You can't see me, but I'm listening." He spoke in an endearing, comforting tone intended to relax his bride. He dreamed about Mareschelle's explanation of her doctor's visit, and the early menopause revelation that would leave her womb barren.

The streetlamps outside his window made his bedroom more dim than dark. Her eyes glowed greenish in the yellow light.

"So they're certain there's nothing that can help you get better?"

"He told me the condition is irreversible in ninety-eight percent of women."

"Well then we'll pray that you are special enough to be in that two percent of all women."

The light reflected off his eyes while he waited for her to continue, but she didn't. She curled into him and let her tears tell him how scared and unhappy she was about never being able to give him a baby.

Solo wrapped her in his arms and let her cry until her tears ran dry. He quieted her ever so often, holding her tight to comfort her, telling her how much he loved her whether they made babies or not.

Mareschelle heard her husband's every word, found comfort in his love and wanted him to know that she appreciated his love. When she was all cried out, she wriggled out of her panties then freed him from his pajama bottoms. She wrapped her arms around his shoulders and pulled him on top of her. She exhaled *Make love to me* before covering his mouth with hers. The kiss lasted a lifetime, each of them searching for all the love they could find in a kiss.

When he came up for air, she dug her heels into the mattress and pushed herself toward the middle of the bed, his knees pushing against the back of her thighs to aid her progress. She rolled him over, assuming the dominant position, sat her middle on the front of him and guided him inside of her. She made love to her husband with an all-consuming passion. She was energy itself; simultaneously beautiful and powerful all at once.

After she reached her nirvana, she cradled his head in her neck and called his name as she absorbed the final brunt of his climax. His chest and stomach heaved against hers. He was far off somewhere trying to desperately reach his place of great emotion. She slumped on top of him when he finished, rubbed his head, quieted him and pressed kisses against his face and neck, repeating, "I love you, Solomon Alexandré. I love you, Baby."

~

Solomon woke just before noon with an aching deep in his stomach. The memory of Schelle telling him they'd never have children conflicted with the intense dream of them making love. He leaned across the side of the bed to vomit, but his stomach was so empty that only dry heaves came. When he could stand, he went to the bathroom, drank some water, used the toilet then went back to bed. But now, he couldn't sleep. Each time he closed his eyes, her face, and more specifically, her smile appeared on the back of his eyelids as vividly as the picture on an IMAX screen. Only now, he wasn't certain if it was his wife's face or the woman crossing the street that morning. She was real and he knew it, but he also knew that he really did bury his wife. He tried to convince himself that maybe he missed his Schelle so much that he conjured her face on that woman. He looked and the clock read 11:48, so deciding that he'd catch a nap on the plane, he got out of bed knowing that his thoughts were the demons preventing him from the pleasure of sleep.

His phone rang an hour later as he sat on the balcony overlooking his backyard listening to his favorite satellite music channel. He saw the caller ID and answered in a thick, rumbly, "What up, Preach?" presuming Lawrence hadn't gotten much sleep either, having to be up at the crack of dawn for the early morning service.

Lawrence's deep baritone was surprisingly upbeat in response.

"Nothing much, Bruh. Mom Viv chatted my ear off about you cancelling on her when I picked her up for service today. I just dropped her off and promised her I'd check on you."

Solo and Lawrence chatted it up for a moment, confirming the time that Kenny was picking him up to meet the Horsemen at 13 Coins Restaurant for dinner before dropping him off at the airport. After ending his call with Lawrence, Solomon lit a wine-flavored cigarillo, took a deep puff of the tobacco, gazed at the thin cigar wedged between his first and middle fingers, and thought about Mareschelle. It was she who had introduced him to cigars. Her love for the smell of scented tobaccos grew from her father's avid pipe smoking. It was amazing how much he still loved her, and he was grateful to her for so many things. There'd been so little in his home life since she died. When she was alive, his world was full of vivid colors. After his intense grieving had ended, Solo was shocked to find that his return to everyday life was just like it was when Mareschelle was alive, with one big exception: life was boring and everything around him seemed to appear in dull shades of grey.

He thought about the women he'd encountered after her passing. He thought he loved them, but later discounted them as distractions of mutual convenience. A convenience that he wanted for a while. Then he met Leona and dared to hope for happiness again. Now that feeling was gone too and he didn't feel that he knew *how* to move on. And he was even more uncertain about *where to* and *who with*. *What if Tessa hadn't been shot?* he thought. *Would Leona and I have made it to the altar? Would she have become the next Missus Solomon Alexandré without either of us knowing that we were paternal first cousins? First cousins who didn't know our estranged fathers were twin brothers?*

CHAPTER 9

DESPITE THE INDIAN SUMMER TEMPERATURES, autumn was in full bloom in Northeast Washington State. After the stroke scare with Mr. Be, Solomon thought Spokane cursed for him and didn't return for over a year. Now three years removed from that dreadful first trip, this was his fifth speaking engagement in Spokane and the third since Schelle had passed. At lunch Wednesday, his Dean of the Psychology department at Washington State, who was now provost at Gonzaga and one of the pageant judges, invited him to the Miss Washington pageant planning dinner. Thursday night at the Spokane Promenade, Solomon excused himself from a spirited debate with two colleagues to get a drink from the bar.

"White wine please," answered a woman over Solomon's shoulder right after the bartender asked for his order. "Hopefully the gentleman will be kind enough to put it on his tab."

Solomon did not recognize the voice, so he turned before ordering to see who was so audacious. When he saw the reggae-dancing girl with the killer-blue eyes, his tongue went mute. Three years had passed since he'd first seen her and her two friends, but in that moment, she was just as mesmerizing as that day in the park. He tilted his head in recognition, but couldn't recall her name.

She smiled an, *I think I know you* smile.

Not wanting to look like a fool for not remembering her name, he said, "Well if it isn't the SD card thief?" She smiled a guilty acknowledgment before he asked, "How are things in the world of kleptomania?"

Killer-Blue Eyes peered at the bartender waiting for Solomon to confirm that he was covering her tab. "Very parched."

The bartender looked from Killer-Blue Eyes to Solomon and asked, "Anything for you, Sir?"

Solomon regarded the bartender before returning to meet her gaze. "I guess it's a good thing that generous men are still chivalrous enough to buy pretty ladies a drink."

She said, "Then I guess I should be thankful that now is one of those thens."

Solomon cocked his head, stared deep into those killer-blue eyes trying to find her angle. But no matter how hard he looked, he couldn't find the devilment. He widened his aperture to take in her entire face. She appeared to be a simple human being; pretty, sexy without trying to be, and seemingly unpretentious. In a single word, everything about her was…innocent. And in acknowledgment of that perfect innocence, Solomon turned and ordered himself a glass of port wine.

The bartender regarded Solo, raised his eyebrows in query and asked, "And the lady's white wine?"

"Well," Solo began, "we can't let the lady get too parched, she may dry up and blow away."

Drink in hand, Killer-Blue Eyes eased her free hand into the crook of Solomon's arm and escorted him back into the ballroom where they circled the floor sharing polite conversation as she spilled the tea on the women in the room.

Solomon knew he was easily charmed, but he hoped it didn't show. He asked, "And what exactly makes you the expert?"

"I'm no expert, but when I won the crown three years ago, I had to endure all of the snide remarks from these jealous crumbs talking about me behind my back."

Killer-Blue Eyes was energy itself; charming, beautiful and

powerful all at once. For the first time he could remember, time stood still. It felt so right that it couldn't be wrong. Could it? Her fruity scent permeated his nostrils and gave him fever. At that very moment he knew he wanted her. Her vibe told him she felt the same way.

"Funny thing you should mention that SD card," Jordyn began.

"The card was almost empty," Solo said. "I just started using it that day."

"Yeah, only pictures on it were of me and my girls," she said.

"SD card only cost ten dollars. If your little sticky fingers had stolen the battery, that would've set me back more than fifty bucks."

"I had those pictures printed if you ever want to see them," she continued. "Melanie and Savannah loved them."

From the corner of her eye, Killer-Blue Eyes saw the two men Solomon was seated with when she first noticed him. They were on a beeline in their direction and she wanted to avoid the canned, 'So who's this lovely lady?' or the 'Are You going to introduce us to your friend?' one-liners that the older men at these events always opened with trying to get close to the younger ladies. So as the odd pair of sexagenarians closed in on her and her companion, she clutched Solomon's arm tighter, and with practiced subtlety, she sneezed, and in doing so changed the direction they were facing. With hopes that Solomon hadn't seen them coming, she quickly acknowledged his *God Bless You* with a *Thank You* then picked up her pace as she escorted him away from the two old geezers.

"So tell me again where you're visiting from?" Her interest seemed genuine. " I don't think I caught that last time we talked."

"Seattle."

"Oh, big city man out here slumming in the country. You here by yourself? How long are you staying this time?"

"About four days on this trip; and yes, I'm flying solo."

"And who have you met so far in my fair city?"

"Just you."

"Really? I find that hard to believe." Killer-Blue Eyes peeked over her shoulder for the old geezers, but they had given up their chase.

"Why do you say that?" Solomon asked.

"Because the first time we met, you made it plain as the nose on my face that you were watching us. And if I noticed you noticing us, I can imagine that you have noticed others as well."

"Well, the people in my working group are not the most sociable. And most of our nights have run late, so by the time we finished work there was time for dinner, a glass of wine and then back to the room to get ready for the next day. No time to notice anyone."

Killer-Blue Eyes guided Solomon around the conference room pointing out some of her former Gonzaga professors, other former pageant winners, and several local politicians including the Mayor. "So tell me sir, if you haven't had time to notice anybody since you've been here, what have you been doing? I mean, what makes tonight different? Is being here your dinner and a glass of wine, or is out looking for young women how you and your people run late?"

Solomon noticed subtle signs and patterns in people that most people missed. A trait he had a hard time turning off courtesy of professional training. With Killer-Blue Eyes, he noticed that when she used words that ended in 'ing', a hard 'kay' sound ended the word. The first time she said it, he paid it no mind. Having heard her use 'ing' several more times, he recognized the dialect. He'd travelled to Warsaw and Kiev as part of an Interdisciplinary Studies course during the summer between his college junior and senior years, and was able to recognize the trait in her speech as Eastern European. His first thought was definitely Russian, but after careful consideration, he realized that her heritage could've stemmed from any of the Baltic States. With her height, build and dialect, Killer-Blue Eyes could have easily passed for a brunette sibling of the tennis star Maria Sharapova. As he absorbed her dialect, Solomon enjoyed the way her trademark 'ing-k', deeply rooted in Eastern

European heritage, added to her charm. He said, "Chairman of the conference bailed early. Story is his wife got sick. Our deputy director is a judge for this year's pageant, so he invited us to tagalong. So, there you have it, and here I am."

She nodded her acknowledgment as they walked for a beat listening to the banter of the people at the tables they passed.

"So since you said you don't get out much, how much of my city have you seen, Mister Spokane Virgin?"

"Spokane Virgin?" he started.

"Yes, Spokane Virgin?" she repeated. "Not experiencing something makes you a virgin. And from what you've told me, you haven't experienced my city, so that makes you a Spokane Virgin."

Solomon contemplated a retort. "Well if the Gonzaga Campus, Centennial Trail and my hotel aren't enough of an experience for you, then Yes, Miss Spokane, I accept being a Spokane Virgin."

"See, I told you so."

"So riddle me this Batgirl, are you a Seattle Virgin?"

Before she answered, they stopped at the table she vacated to follow Solomon to the bar. She ignored the dozen eyes staring at them and casually asked , "Hey girls, what did I miss?"

The woman immediately to Solomon's left said, "Oh hell no, where have you been for the last hour?"

The woman in a gold suit directly across the table from her eyed Solomon before she responded, "From the look of it, we're the ones who missed something."

Killer-Blue Eyes shifted her gaze from the gold suit woman to Solomon. "Oh, how rude of me, this is my friend …" Killer-Blue Eyes paused realizing that in their haste to banter, neither she nor her gentleman friend had offered their names. She guffawed loudly once the realization hit her. "Umm, I actually don't know this gorgeous man's name, ladies."

"Excuse me?" said the woman to her right in a red and green dress.

"I don't know his name because I never asked."

"What do you mean you never asked?" she said. "Since when do you walk around arm-in-arm with strangers?"

"Well, he's not exactly a stranger. We met a while back when he was downtown taking pictures of me, Mel and Vannah."

The woman two seats to Solomon's left said, "You mean the creep who ran off without saying goodbye? So rude!" He surmised that she was either Mel or Vannah. "Punk didn't give his name back then either."

Then the lady in the red and green chimed in, "If he ran off on you before, why would you be walking with him now?"

Killer-Blue Eyes giggled as the women trained their eyes on her waiting for an answer. "Well ladies, I don't know what was wrong with him before, but tonight he has been the perfect gentleman. And I'm certain, if we ask him nicely, that he would gladly tell us his name." Killer Blue Eyes joined her sextet in eyeing her escort.

A bead of sweat sprouted on Solomon's forehead under the heat of a dozen staring eyes. He cleared his throat then said, "Good evening ladies. You all look wonderful tonight."

"Yeah, yeah, we didn't ask for all of that, Homie," Red and Green Dress interjected. "Get on with the name giving."

"Nice to meet you ladies. I am Doctor Solomon Alexandré."

Killer-Blue Eyes said, "Nice to officially meet you, Doctor Solomon Alexandré." She pointed to the woman immediately to Solomon's left, then one-by-one introduced the five women by first name. "And my name ..." she smiled, batting her long lashes like a genuine belle raised of the antebellum south. She placed a hand over the plunging neckline of a silk blouse that fluttered when she moved. "My name is Jordyn."

Solomon met Jordyn's gaze. It took everything within him not to stare at her ample cleavage. He extended his hand and she took it. "Nice to meet you all." He felt the heat of his audience, but maintained his gaze fixed on Jordyn. Her eyes were blue and bottomless. Filled with both curiosity and intelligence. Mesmerized by those deep blue eyes, he repeated, "I'm Solomon. Solomon Alexandré."

"You already said that," came from the woman in dark blue.

When he noticed the grumbles emanating from the table, he forced himself to look away.

Jordyn removed her purse from the chair back in front of her. "Excuse us ladies, Doctor Solomon Alexandré and I are going to get some air?"

Two minutes later, Solomon and Jordyn heard a woman calling her name as they neared the hotel entrance. Mel and Vannah were rushing their way. "Excuse us, Sir, we need a word with her before you go."

"Not a problem," Solomon stood awaiting his interrogation.

"If you don't mind," Savannah furled her brow when he didn't walk away and offer them their privacy. "She won't be but a minute."

Catching her drift, Solomon exited the lobby and checked his email, sent a couple of text messages, and accepted two Facebook friend requests while the trio chatted. Through the window, he watched Jordyn pull a plastic clip from her purse and use it to raise her hair off her neck.

Ten minutes later, after the women hugged, kissed and said their goodbyes, Jordyn joined him wearing not quite a smirk, not quite a smile, but more of a devilish grin.

Solomon asked, "You and your posse good?"

"Right as rain," she said.

Then they stood for a beat, unwittingly waiting for the other to address the valet before Solomon said, "If you give me your valet ticket, I'll have him pull your car around."

Jordyn laughed. "I didn't drive. I rode with Melanie and Savannah. I thought I was riding with you?"

"I didn't drive. I rode with one of the professors from Gonzaga. He lives a couple of blocks from my hotel."

"So what now?" Jordyn asked.

"Now the Spokane Virgin walks the Spokane native down this street until she finds someplace she'd like to eat." Solomon offered his arm. Jordyn latched on and they walked east for two blocks before stopping in front of RJ Murphy's Bier and Brasserie. He asked, "Is here good?"

"I think Savannah's eaten here, but I've never. But, we're here, so it's probably as good a place as any."

"Well then, we should go in."

She looked for an empty sidewalk table outside but they were all full. After she looked over the half-wall into the café and saw she'd be the only woman in the place, she said, "Not here, it's too crowded."

"Well, I'm on your time, so let's find someplace less crowded."

For two blocks down the street and across the street, all of the cafes they considered were crowded. He heard her stomach grumble and suggested, if you don't see any place out here that looks good, come back to my hotel with me. They have a fantastic restaurant and the bartender serves a mean margarita."

"Well Doctor Solomon Alexandré, where is this hotel of yours?"

"I'm across the river at Hotel RL."

She tilted her head in a kind of weary, waiting surprise. "Isn't that kind of far just to get something to eat?"

"Not far for me, but then again, I don't know how far it is from your native Spokane home."

She stared at Solomon with a bright, suspicious bafflement as if she was thinking, *I'm willing to play your game my friend, but what are the rules? And more importantly, what are the penalties?*

"And to make sure you don't go missing, I'll call us an Uber when we're done and make the ride with you."

He looked at the Uber/Lyft/Taxi stand across the wide expanse of Hollister Boulevard and offered her his hand to cross.

She hesitated for a beat before sliding her hand into his. Holding his hand felt natural. His warm hand surrounding hers made her wish that Hollister Boulevard was miles more than six lanes wide. When they made it to the opposite sidewalk he let her hand go. It had been awhile since a man had held her hand so gently. She missed the sensation of being touched in that way. Unsure of what to do next, she picked at her finger nails.

Solomon pointed from one car to the next. "Your chariot awaits."

Jordyn's slender, 160 pound, five-foot eight frame was perfectly tanned courtesy of a recent Labor Day weekend in Mexico. When she dropped her purse entering their Uber, Solomon stepped back to better admire her legs as she bent over to pick it up. Tight calves stemmed from a fitted skirt accenting her lithe physique. She was bow-legged at the knees and he found the curve of her round hips enticing.

Jordyn climbed inside the backseat of the minivan and sat facing forward, legs crossed at the ankles. Solomon pulled down the folding seat and sat facing backward so he could admire her face full of light-brown freckles. She put her hand on his knee and watched the city pass in silence until they reached Hotel RL.

As they passed the park where he'd first seen her, he thought how if not for that drummer and his reggae, he might've never met Jordyn.

Their first meal together lasted three hours, enough time to size each other up, so to speak. Solomon did most of the talking, and Jordyn grew more comfortable with every funny story the good doctor told. Her heather brown hair hung down past the front and back of her shoulders. Her almond-shaped eyes bordered a bulbous nose. He grew to like her beyond the pretty of her face and the curves and edges of her body. He'd tell a joke or a story, pause, wait for her smile, wait for her laughter, then proceed right into the next story.

When the waiter brought dessert, Jordyn asked, "I love the way you enunciate every word. Like an attorney." Jordyn twisted her lips. "Or maybe you're a con artist. A grifter out to take advantage of me."

"Is there a difference?"

"Not that it matters right now." Her face brightened then she said, "Hell, for all I know, you could be a serial killer waiting to get me alone and stuff me in a box out in the woods never to be seen again?"

Solomon was stone quiet considering the morbidity of her statement. He blew air then swallowed half his glass of wine.

As he drank, Jordyn burst out in laughter. "Gotcha!"

Solomon swallowed, put down his glass and joined her laughter.

When Solomon summoned the waiter, she placed her hand on top of his. She smiled, "I like the way your hand feels on mine. I like touching you."

"Are you flirting with me Jordyn?" He enjoyed her candor, and found himself attracted to Jordyn more now than when he watched her dance. He wanted her to know that he liked her. That he was interested in experiencing more of her company, but not trying to take advantage of her youth. That buying her dinner had no pretense, no manipulation toward an encounter that she'd regret.

Jordyn decided over the course of the evening that even though she had only officially met him earlier that day, if he asked, she would spend the night. The empty second bottle of wine shifted the witty, informal dialogue compelled Jordyn toward innuendo.

Solomon checked his watch and hinted that it was late and he didn't want to keep her any longer than she wanted to stay, so After dinner, desert, and two bottles of wine, they found themselves standing inside each other's personal bubbles on the sidewalk outside Hotel RL. She stared intently, her eyes boring into him. Inspecting him. The night was cool, but she felt his heat. His energy made her heart race, her skin tingle when he stroked her hair. "Remind me again why you are trying to get rid of me so quickly?" she said, cupping his hand in both of hers. She stared at him with a look of control rather than fear; and just beneath that look, there was an odd sort of exhilaration playing in her eyes. She liked the thought of flirting with danger. She liked it a lot. "I mean you just found me after three years."

"No," he said, trying to not sound indignant, and failing on purpose. "That's not it at all." He grinned, brought his eyes to hers and licked his lips.

In a brazen gesture she stepped all the way inside his personal bubble. "So then you wouldn't mind me breaking your curfew?"

"I figured suggesting that may seem rather presumptuous," he said. "Since we just met."

A moment later when she felt his erection push at his pants and touch her, she laid a hand on his pants and said. "Maybe, but that sure feels presumptuous," to confirm her meaning.

He barely moved as she increased the pressure from a touch to a firm grip before she kissed him just because she could.

And he kissed her back with hot, eager, passionate kisses.

She was drunk from the food, the wine and the kisses. "I really like you," she said trying to catch her breath after he broke the kiss.

They eyed each other in provocative silence.

"I…barely…noticed," he said in ragged spurts before she lifted her hand from his pants and moved it to caress the side of his face. "I love it when a big strong man can be vulnerable."

Her forwardness blew him away. He smiled, unable to conceal his pleasure with her flirtatiousness.

Ten minutes before midnight, the same Uber driver from earlier pulled up to take her home. Jordyn walked to the driver's window and knocked on the glass. When he lowered the window, she handed him forty dollars, thanked him for his time and let him know that she no longer needed the ride.

Solomon's 11th floor corner suite offered sweeping views of the city to the south including the outline of the Clock Tower in Riverside Park. The Promenade illuminated the Spokane River in the distance to the west.

Jordyn sat on the window seat overlooking the courtyard below.

Solomon stood behind her, caressing her shoulders. "Would you like a drink?"

"Water would be nice. And a drink," she chuckled.

He stepped away, turned on a cordless speaker and brought up a music playlist on his tablet. The smooth, vibrant sounds of Al Green's *Let's Stay Together* filled the air with a romantic vibe enticing Jordyn to sway to the seductive melody.

"Try this," he said, offering her a glass of honey infused bourbon. "It's my favorite. I bring a bottle with me in case the hotel bar doesn't carry it," he said, and sat two bottles of water on the table next to them.

She sipped the brown liquor and although he could see she tried not to, she winced when it hit her throat. "Smooooth," she grimaced.

He chuckled. "I've got some wine if you'd prefer."

Her tongue said, "No. this is good," but her eyes said different.

"There," Solomon poured an equal amount of water into her glass without asking. "That should help out a honey-bourbon virgin." He laughed when she winced again after taking a second sip. "I had a good time tonight," he said sitting next to her. "I definitely need to see more of Spokane's more interesting offerings."

"Other than me?" she joked. She wanted to say, *The most interesting thing in this town is sitting right in front of you.* But instead, she lifted her glass and took another sip. This time the diluted drink went down a little smoother.

"I'm sure I'll enjoy everything interesting you want me to see."

"Nothing interesting ever happens here," she laughed.

"You live here. I'm just visiting. Visitors always find different things interesting than the people who live somewhere."

Jordyn turned to the window. "I will give it to the little town; it is definitely peaceful living here." Then she thought, *I could get lost in him right here and now. And we could be gentle with each other, right? This view and this hotel and a man as gorgeous as him. We could have a moment together, right?* When she turned to face him again, her eyes were clouded and her face was vulnerable. After a moment, she purred, "You will be gentle, won't you?"

And then they were both frightened. And the king-size bed seemed to be the only noticeable object in the room.

Solomon felt his hands shake and his heart began to race. He felt that Jordyn was waiting for him to make a move. That every action from here forward would be his to promote. And he felt, that he could do nothing. Then they both took a large swallow of their drinks…and the red dangerous shadow of uncertainty lifted.

Their shared moment of angst passed and they shared a smile. In that moment, the gap between them closed and an irrefutable current surged through them, urging them to quickly and absolutely fulfill that promise. And they sensed it simultaneously. And for that reason, they hesitated, they dawdled, they smiled and stared, and they deliciously put it off.

After midnight, a light rain moved in from the west. For some reason the Clock Tower and the lights from the Promenade seemed closer through the rain. Solomon leaned into Jordyn and looked through the window at the sky.

Jordyn walked away from the window and confessed aloud, "I don't know about you Mister, but I only see midnight on the weekends. My Monday through Friday requires eight hours of sleep."

When she turned the deadbolt and dimmed the lights, he saw his reflection in the window. He watched a frown darken his face. He hated the rain. More than anything, he hated driving in the rain. Two years after Mareschelle passed, he was driving home in the rain after having dinner with Mareschelle's parents. Later that night, Mr. Be suffered another stroke. Torrential rains slowed his return drive to Tacoma and Mr. Be passed before he reached the hospital. Since then, driving in the rain brought about anxiety, sometimes to the point of panic attacks. He was anxious now. He heard the light murmur of water and watched raindrops slither down the window. He took deep breaths to try and relax, to calm himself and prevent the onset of panic.

When he heard Jordyn call, "Hey Mister Midnight, may I borrow a T-shirt to sleep in?" from the far side of the king-size bed, his face illuminated with the jubilation of a child. When she said, "I'm sorry, I should have asked, do you prefer to sleep on the right side or the left?" he heard the non-thinking brain in his little head answer, *Your Middle*. The he swallowed hard, shifted his eyes, hoping the voice he heard came from inside his head and not from his mouth. He stood for a beat longer without answering; the look on his face told her that in that singular moment he was genuinely perplexed. Then he finally answered, "A gentleman always sleeps between a lady and the door."

Around four-thirty, Jordyn woke in a terror that gripped her throat. She screamed, but the sound was buried so deep inside that the only place it could be heard was within the tomb of her own head.

Her flailing arms awakened him. Put Solomon in a reflexive fighting posture until he realized nobody was hitting him. "Jordyn? Jordyn?" He called as he reached for the bedside lamp. Once he could see her face he called again, "Jordyn, are you alright?"

She gasped for air to the point of almost hyperventilating.

He sat her upright and grabbed her shoulders. " Talk to me, Jordyn. What can I do? Are you alright?"

In the dimly lit room, her big blue eyes looked black with terror.

He shook her gently until she finally focused on him. When she recognized he was not the man choking her in her dream, her breathing eased and she fell forward and sunk into his chest. A moment later when her voice came to her, she murmured, "Some water please."

Solomon grabbed a bottle of water from the fridge.

Jordyn drank half of the bottle's contents then sank back into the tender comfort of his arms, hoping for the pleasure of sleep as her newfound guardian lay beside her, frantic, like he'd not known sleep for weeks. He watched her, watched over her and tried to rest as the frightened beauty queen from Spokane told him about her nightmare.

~

Six months after she ended their engagement, Glenn Zimmerman showed up with a dozen roses at Jordyn's apartment to apologize. Prayer and counseling after he attacked her in a drunken rage following his draft party, helped he forgive him. After a dozen requests she finally agreed to have dinner with him. Glenn waited while Jordyn got dressed in her sexiest black dress for their date that fateful Friday night. Glenn promised her a fancy dinner, but didn't tell her that he had cooked it. When they arrived at his—formerly their— old apartment, the anticipation of a nice dinner in a restaurant as an appropriate apology went by the wayside. Glenn showed her the food he prepared, but didn't talk to her making the first ten minutes extremely awkward. He hadn't said more than three words since they left her apartment and the unsettling way he stared at her made her self-conscious about her appearance. Not certain of the look on his face and with him not offering any words, she asked, "May I use your bathroom?"

Glenn returned from his trance and whispered, "Yes," after another beat of silence. "Let me show you where it is."

His choice of words surprised Jordyn, considering she'd once lived there too. Finished in the bathroom and she dried her hands. Her heart jumped when she opened the door. Glenn...was still standing there. "You didn't need to wait for me, I can find my way back down the hall."

"You were gone a long time, so I came to check on you."

Her heart raced. Glenn's odd behavior her think back to the night of the draft party.

He smiled at her, putting her slightly more at ease when he asked, "Would you like some Ben & Jerry's?"

"Yes," she chirped and forgave him for acting so strange when he returned with a pint of ice cream and two spoons.

"Oh my God, Karamel Sutra Core is my absolute favorite. I used to buy a pint every Friday after my kinesiology class as a reward for staying awake. The sweet old lady at the corner store near my apartment always kept a pint stashed for me.

Glenn smiled knowingly, scooped some and fed it to her.

Finally a romantic moment, she thought. They kissed; softly at first, and then with an intensity that made her tiny panties wet with anticipation. Glenn stood, took her hand and led her down the now dark hallway to a door that had been shut since she arrived.

Despite their engagement Jordyn and Glenn had not physically consummated their relationship. Inside his bedroom, she noticed it was practically bare, save a dresser, a bed, and a camera lying on its side. Before she could ask about the camera, he pulled her close, kissed her and peeled her out of her dress. He removed his shirt, sat on the bed and she straddled him. Glenn kissed her neck and stroked her full breasts. She purred and clung to him. His hands explored her body; caressing her nipples, her back, her ass, and her thighs. She moaned softly, eager to feel him. He touched her inside her panties and could barely contain himself. Just as she reached to undo his belt buckle, he ejaculated.

She snickered but didn't outright laugh at the endearing situation. "Oh my God, you umm…you, oh my God." Then she met his gaze and saw he was visibly embarrassed. "Are you alright, Baby?"

Certain she was trying to humiliate him, Glenn snapped. It was her fault he embarrassed himself. If she hadn't been teasing him all night, he wouldn't have done that. He shoved her off him angrily and she tumbled to the floor hard.

Now she was pissed. "What the hell is wrong with you?" she demanded, scrambling to her feet.

"Don't ever laugh at me," he yelled.

She pulled her panties up and looked for her dress.

Glenn was enraged. He hadn't taken his anxiety medicine in a couple weeks; he thought he had it under control. He looked away from her and tried to calm down. "Why are you acting different all of a sudden?"

Jordyn couldn't believe her ears. "I'm acting different? You've been acting funny all night."

"I thought you were different, this is all your fault."

"Tell me how tonight going wrong is my fault."

"You laughed at me. Made fun of my things and the way I live."

"Made fun of you? I barely giggled, and that was to lighten the mood about you losing it before we even got started good. I wasn't trying to hurt you."

Glenn grimaced. "Oh, so now you feel sorry for me?"

Jordyn found her dress.

Glenn saw his mother, not Jordyn, about to leave him.

She picked up her dress and turned to face him.

"Shouldn't I?" Then she realized that he interpreted her joviality as mockery and the fury in her eyes quickly turned to fear when she noticed Glenn's crazed expression. She was in trouble. He looked like a mad man. She turned around, grabbed her shoes and made a beeline for the bedroom door.

Glenn's mind flashed in and out of the present moment. At ten years old, he saw his mother walk out the door on him and his brother. Saw her leave them behind with their monster of a father. Now he saw Jordyn leaving him and snapped. He snatched her by the hair and pulled her roughly back inside the bedroom then.

Jordyn tried to pull away. "You freaking nut!" But he held her, slapped her, punched her in the mouth. She scratched and punched him back. Screamed for help.

The more she fought back, the angrier he became. He punched her again, then picked her up and slammed her against the cold, hard floor, silencing her. When he looked down at Jordyn's silent, motionless body, he immediately realized he had gone too far this time. He thought about her face, the face that resembled his mother's. He sat down on the bed crying over what he'd done and knew that he was in serious trouble. He hadn't meant to hurt Jordyn, but he couldn't change things now.

Glenn lied to her about his status as a college student. Told her he was still taking classes despite not being on the football team. He didn't want to lie to Jordyn, but he had fallen for her the moment he laid eyes on her at physical therapy. She signified everything he wanted in a woman. Jordyn had become his obsession. Now he looked down on her bruised face and cried even harder.

Two days later a neighbor found Jordyn bloody and beaten sitting in the front passenger seat of her car outside her apartment building. The police arrested the following day after Jordyn's father told them Glenn's name. Courtesy of his father's high-priced attorneys' manipulation of the legal system, Glenn plead guilty to the lesser charge of Assault in the Second Degree, instead of the original, more serious charge of Aggravated Assault in the First Degree and went to jail.

Jordyn recovered from her physical injuries, and—eventually—moved on with her life.

~

By five o'clock, they were both sound asleep. At seven o'clock when his alarm went off, a narrow shaft of sunlight breached the blinds ensuring him that morning had come. He looked at her and blinked, took a deep breath and let her scent permeate his nose. He held her, and the tighter he did, the deeper she nuzzled into him.

Enamored with one another but knowing that the morning meant journeying to separate destinations, they showered separately, dressed, then ate breakfast at the buffet before leaving the haven they had created in the night.

"I wish today wasn't my last day here, I really enjoyed last night. Thanks for hanging out and introducing me to your city."

"My pleasure. Anything for a Cougar. Do they call men that?" They laughed. "Oh well, if not, then anything for an honorary Zag professor. Look me up next time you're in town so I can give you the homegrown tour of the Zags' side of the river."

Solomon kissed her once and then once again. "It's a date." His kisses were gentle, said that he enjoyed her, that he liked her, and that he could possibly love her. Her skin was butter soft, and for a few moments, he rubbed it like a tailor fingering fine silk. He released her face and put his hand on the door of the taxi, prepared to shut it when she entered.

Jordyn turned away, paused, then turned back and, plunging into him, kissed him with more passionate energy than she had ever mustered into a kiss in her twenty-six years of life. That wonderful kiss from the beauty queen with the killer blue eyes would carry him smiling all the way back to Seattle.

Jordyn climbed in and her dress rose up above her knees before she settled in the seat and crossed her legs.

Once again, Solomon's attentions were drawn to her legs. Toned, healthy legs with delicate ankles and soft, curvy calves. Words failed him as he thought about how he'd describe those big pretty thighs to Kenny when he got home. He started to shut the door, but stopped abruptly. He leaned down to see her face and asked, "Hey cutie?"

"Yes, Sir?"

"It might be easier to look you up if I knew your last name."

"And here I thought you had a sense of adventure." Her purposely haughty voice made both of them laugh out loud before she answered, "Last name starts with an H. Not too many of us spell their name with a Y, so look for a Y and an H. I shouldn't be hard to find."

"Jordyn H?" Solomon repeated. He shut her door, and like a stiff breeze crossing the Puget Sound, the car vanished down Cataldo Boulevard whisking Jordyn H. away to destinations unknown, and concluding the most exhausting, exhilarating, and refreshing night he'd enjoyed in half a year.

CHAPTER 10

THE WORK WEEK FOLLOWING EASTER, Solomon and his business partner Desirée attended the Resiliency symposium at the University of Seattle where Psychology Department students and faculty shared what they learned outside the classroom. A range of activities including a virtual poster session, data talks and workshops, a panel of clinical professionals, and a graduate student-led Q&A preceded the Dean of the Department's keynote speech on Thursday which concluded the event for students.

On Friday, Solomon joined several of his symposium colleagues for cocktails and hors d'oeuvres in the solarium atop the Magnusson Center. While watching a storm cloud eclipse the peak of Mount Rainier from the fifth story window during the final break, he noticed a woman on the sidewalk with the same hairstyle and color Mareschelle wore. He immediately thought of the mystery woman from downtown the morning after the boxing match. He excused himself from the conversation, hurried out into the hallway then sprinted to the stairwell; the elevator would have taken too long to come. On the ground floor, he bolted past the security guard and through the front door. He located the flower stand, but didn't see her. Jay-running, he darted through moving traffic, narrowly avoiding being struck by two cars and a tow-truck. Reaching the opposite sidewalk, he ran to the flower stand and asked the owner where the young lady with the black hair went, but she said she didn't remember seeing her. He thought hard about his view from the meeting and remembered her scarf, he blurted out. "Which way did the lady in the red scarf go?"

"I'm not sure sir," she replied, "I have other customers to serve."

Solomon frantically surveilled the street hoping to catch a glimpse of her walking somewhere, but didn't see anyone resembling her. He asked the florist, "Can you tell me what kind of flowers she bought?"

"Yes sir. She bought Lilies."

"What color?"

"White."

"Thank You." Solomon hurried to the end of the block and looked in every direction hoping to see her. Ten minutes later, when the crossing hand changed from red to white, he used the crosswalk to return to the same side of the street as the Magnusson Building, the same building he'd seen her appear from that Sunday morning many months ago.

~

"Beats me, Solo." Desmond placed three beers on the table at Woody's Saturday night. "We all see somebody who looks like someone else every now and then."

"But it's not the first time, Wood."

"Well they say everybody in the world has a twin. You've seen all of the Elvis and Prince imitators out there," Lawrence added. "Maybe her resemblance to Schelle combined with you missing her so much makes you see someone that's not actually there."

"Yeah, I get the whole everybody has a lookalike thing, but what are the odds that they'd both live in the same city?" Desmond pushed them menus. "You guys want anything from the kitchen?"

LD Said, "I don't know about you guys, but I've been eating leftovers from Mom Viv's Easter dinner all week, so I need a salad."

"Right," Solomon added. "I thought it was just me."

"Well I ain't starving, but I hit the gym yesterday and today, so I need a little something," Desmond said before opening a menu for himself. "You guys got enough room in you to help me knock off a nachos platter?"

"Yeah," Lawrence replied, "but have them put the salsa and sour cream on the side."

"And the guac too," Solomon added.

"But what I really want to know Solo," Lawrence asked when the appetizer order was confirmed, "What happens to you emotionally if you ever find this woman and she's neither a ghost nor Mareschelle?"

"That, my brother, is what I ask myself every time I see her."

The three Horsemen sipped their beers and crowd-watched in silence after the waitress departed to submit their nachos order.

~

Despite the late hour and the four Mexican cervezas he'd consumed with the nachos, Solomon was still amped when Lawrence dropped him off. Inside the Hang Suite, he made his way down to his man cave, poured himself two fingers of Basil Hayden's and racked the pool balls. Two hours later after five games and consuming half the freshly opened bottle of bourbon, the third yawn convinced him to go lay down. Fifteen minutes after finishing his last drink and setting his alarm, he'd showered and slipped into bed. Seeing his wife's image around town several times in the past months had stood between him and restful sleep the past two nights. Now, staring at the ceiling as midnight approached, he wrapped both arms around Mareschelle's pillow, inhaled the faded scent of her perfume and welcomed the pleasure of sleep.

~

Solomon's last day with Mareschelle started as one of the happiest of his life. He awoke shortly after 6a.m. and reached for his wife, but felt her empty pillow. He pulled the pillow to him and inhaled her essence in her absence. A moment later, Mareschelle entered the bedroom with a wonderfully prepared breakfast. After they demolished the delicious plates of grits, pan-seared fish and soft scrambled eggs, she climbed on top of him and served up a good old-fashioned stack of hot loving as his breakfast dessert. A troubling thought had kept him awake half the night and despite his desire to share his feelings, Solomon didn't want to risk ruining the moment. "Aaahh, now that's the kind of stroll through the garden a man won't soon forget," Solomon cooed, unable to see her face as she rested her head on his chest. He failed to notice that she'd nodded off a moment later as the troubling thought nagged at him while he relaxed beneath the sheets running his fingers along the contours of her ample curves. "Schelle, something's been on my mind for a while now and I need to share it with you."

Oblivious to the conversation, Mareschelle sleepily inhaled the musk of his thick, dampen chest hair as the heat of their passion cooled. In her sexually sated mind, she grunted *Hunh?*

Mistaking her noise as confirmation of his statement, Solomon unburdened himself not realizing she had dosed off.

When his post-coital aroma had morphed into the stench of sex funk, she awoke, unaware that she had missed the confession that troubled him. She sat up, her elbows denting the pillow as she stared into his eyes then confirmed the smell that awakened her with two small sniffs. She shook her head, frowned at his body odor, grabbed his hand and pulled him to his feet. "Come on," she purred before leading him through the house, out to their backyard and into the swimming pool wearing only their smiles.

After a refreshing skinny dip, Solomon and Schelle climbed out of their pool and hurried inside to avoid offering any early rising neighbors a peep show. On the way up the steps leading to their bedroom, Solomon couldn't keep his hands off his wife's bare body. When she stumbled from his pawing and tickling, and he came tumbling down on top of her, she released a deep, beautiful joyful sound. He loved her slightly nasal laugh. A laugh that preceded a kiss, then led to a quickie right there on the hallway floor. From the moment they ran out the back door naked, Solomon harbored the morose thought that Vivienne would somehow magically appear and scold him like he was still a teenager. Afterwards, and with no surprise visit from his mother, they showered and dressed to continue an unimaginable day.

Before she traveled the five short steps to the yard, Mareschelle stood on the back porch looking through the haze of an unseasonal, late morning, ground-level fog that had rolled in and blanketed their north Seattle neighborhood while they showered. Her man was out there somewhere in the vastness of their fog-covered, half-acre of a backyard; she just had to find him.

Their journey's destination was her childhood home in Tacoma for a dinner celebration of her parents' 29th wedding anniversary. But first, they picked up two mocha swirl, turbo iced coffees for their planned detour of a midday trip up Mount Rainier for lunch and sightseeing.

Seventy-five miles into the one-hundred mile drive from their Longwood, Seattle home to the Mount Rainier National Park, Solomon stopped at Manipon Winery Garden Resort. They were ready to be out of the car and had twenty minutes before their noon tour of the winery started. Solomon dropped Mareschelle off at the entrance then parked. Inside, she confirmed her reservation for the tour and wine tasting. At exactly high noon, a myriad of chimes exploded from a massive grandfather clock. When the music ended, the sommelier guiding the tour introduced herself and led them out the back door toward the vineyard.

The resort grounds were lovely, small hills, lush greenery and the ever-present vision of spring blooms providing brilliant color in every direction. A half hour into the tour Mareschelle was glad she had worn her favorite walking shoes. The hills weren't steep, but the terrain was not ankle friendly. That, combined with the fairly odd couple steps ahead of them who seemed to be on a trek of their own, made for a challenging journey.

The large man's heavy, slow and deliberate gait exacerbated the torture. On the other hand, the youthful gait of the small, eerily beautiful woman with him was so lighthearted that she seemed to be floating next to the big brut like Tinker Bell next to Captain Hook.

Solomon and Mareschelle attempted to pass the odd couple and distance themselves at each apparent opportunity, but the unfortunate combination of his girth and the narrow rows between vines made passing impossible. Throughout the tour, the woman would swing one hand back and forth while the other was constantly in contact with her lover's waist. The odd couple navigated the vineyard paths like a blindfolded drunk driver in an obstacle course and seemed to be working through a lingering argument, stopping at times to enter a battle of words while the rest of the group kept moving. Then they would end each short bout of disagreement with a kiss-to-make-up session complete with unrelenting apologies for upsetting the other.

A half hour later, Solomon and Mareschelle were pleased to be back inside listening to the sommelier describe the first of seven wines they'd be tasting. Her demeanor was pleasant and for Mareschelle, the best part of her presentation was the explanations of the differences between champagnes and sparkling wines. Solomon sipped the whites because he paid for the tour, but his interests lie in tasting the various reds. Following a myriad of questions, mostly by the women in the group, the sommelier suggested they all sample a variety of the vineyard's crackers and chocolates to clear their pallets before they progressed into the reds.

An hour after they finished the wine tasting, the Alexandrés were where the clouds met the earth, seventy-seven hundred feet above sea-level at the Mount Rainier West Summit Lodge. They ate lunch, then wished they had worn heavier jackets as they trekked the mountain side taking pictures because the air temperature at that elevation was twenty-five degrees colder than it was at home.

Mareschelle got a sick stomach, so Solomon stopped near the entrance to Lake Mowich as they were leaving Mount Rainier so she could use the bathroom. But he didn't stop soon enough, and she didn't make it quite clear of the car before she got sick. "Dammit," Solomon cursed when he saw vomit on his car door, then stifled his anger because they were having a wonderful day. Five years married and the romance still seemed new and blossoming every day, and he was pleased to be of service to her, so he gathered himself, helped her out of the car and escorted her to the bathroom to clean herself.

Mareschelle sat on a park bench after she came out of the bathroom while Solomon finished cleaning the car. She was eating crackers and drinking a bottle of water when her phone rang. "Hello," she answered with more zeal than normal when her caller ID read that it was the lady from the *They're All Angels* adoption agency.

Solomon heard her enthusiasm and glanced back at her.

Mareschelle smiled. Felt her pulse flutter at the very idea of giving her husband a child, even if it didn't come from her womb. She tempered her tone and said, "Hello, Miss Abernathy, how are you today?" trying to conceal her excitement. Mareschelle had contacted the adoption agency after a third doctor confirmed that she'd never be able to sustain a natural childbirth.

"Hello Missus Alexandré, I hope I didn't catch you at a bad time?"

"No ma'am, I am happy you called."

"Great," Miss Abernathy continued. "I was calling to ask if you and your husband could come meet four children next week between Tuesday and Friday.

"Yes!" Mareschelle shouted with enough enthusiasm that people near her stared. She smiled pleasantly and blew Solomon a kiss when he turned to see why she was shouting. "Yes Miss Abernathy," she said, normalizing her tone. "We will make time to be wherever you need us."

Miss Abernathy proffered times for their visit to the agency.

Mareschelle asked Miss Abernathy to email her the dates and times so she could confer with her husband. After she hung up, Mareschelle decided she would wait until after the party was over and her parents' guests were gone to share the great news with Solomon and her parents, all at once.

Once he cleaned his car to his satisfaction, he joined Mareschelle and they sat for a moment enjoying Mother Nature's music. Although they couldn't see the ducks from where they were sitting, the quacking sounded like an entire flock had settled down for the night in the pond.

"Come on," Solomon said, leaving their park bench and dragging Mareschelle over the embankment toward the lake. "Let's go feed the ducks." At the water's edge they could hear the ducks, but couldn't see them behind the tall grasses along the lake's edge. Solomon took off his shoes and socks, and waded into the water toward the quacking.

"Solomon come back. You don't know how deep the water is."

He stopped when the water was ankle deep. In an arcing motion, he threw Mareschelle's crackers into the water as if lobbing them over a short wall. A squawking ensued before Mareschelle saw the birds flutter across the lake. She removed her shoes and waded out to Solomon's side with more crackers. The flock of birds lifted above the brush then dove to the water some ten feet in front of the bird-feeding couple. Five minutes later, ducks surrounded them, snapping fiercely at the water as they consumed every morsel. Other park patrons remained oblivious to Solomon and Mareschelle's raucous laughter and splashing because their sounds of joy were drowned out by the birds quacking.

~

Solomon and Mareschelle arrived at her parent's home just before five that evening. The party was scheduled to start at seven, but Mareschelle wanted to be early just in case some guests arrived early. After warm greetings, Missus Be went back to barking orders at her husband, now adding her daughter and son-in-law as subordinates in her chain of command. Because the submissive trio knew how much the party meant to her, they carried out her demands without objection or opposition.

Miss Abernathy's phone call left Mareschelle floating on cloud nine. She loved her parents and was looking forward to their celebration, but her focus was fixed on breaking the news to Solomon after the party.

Solomon played the dutiful son, moving tables and setting up chairs under Mister Be's direction. He watched his bride flit around the house joyous and happy, a little too happy for someone who'd been ill two hours prior. He didn't hover over her, but he did keep an eye on her whenever she came into view. When Mister Be sent him out to the garage for a hammer and wrench, Mareschelle followed. As she watched him rummage through his toolbox, she imagined telling him that they would soon be parents. She imagined his face would be sober and serious. But then he'd look at her, searching her face for his cue. She'd give him a smile to let him know that it was okay to be happy. That this was a good thing. He might not say right then that he was excited, that he loved her, but there is more to life than what you do and don't say to one another.

The screwdriver he dropped rolled under the toolbox. "Dammit."

"You alright, Sweetie?" She rose from her perch on her father's riding lawnmower and knelt beside him as he hunched in front of the toolbox looking for the missing tool. Fawning over her husband, she traced her ring finger across the downy hairs at the base of his neck. When the time was right, and all of her parents' party guests were gone, she'd tell him her plan.

"Ahh, there it is," Solomon said retrieving the tool and standing to face his bride.

"My Hero." Mareschelle kissed him before they went inside. Solomon enjoyed the kiss, but there were dynamics happening around him that he was unaware. Namely, that if he agreed to the adoption, their life would be different by month's end, and their little household would be one person larger.

Just before ten, as her parents were saying their goodnights to the last of their guests, Mareschelle felt a sudden wave of vertigo. She took a seat at the dining room table then waved Solomon off when he looked her way. A few minutes later, she felt better after she finished a glass of water so she went back to the business of straightening up.

Once the last guest drove away, Mareschelle invited everyone into the family room before excusing herself to the kitchen. Solomon's cell phone rang as she returned from the kitchen with a bottle of sparkling wine. He excused himself into the hallway while she placed the bottle and wine glasses on the coffee table. Mister Betancourt opened the bottle and they made small talk about the party as Solomon emanated a flurry of *Unh-hunhs* and *I understands* and *okays* from the hall.

Solomon saw the four glasses of sparkling wine when he returned. "Oh, I can't." He walked toward Mareschelle and held her hands in his. "I'm sorry, Baby, but we need to leave."

"Why? Was that your mom? Is she in the hospital? Is she alright?"

"No, it wasn't the hospital, and as far as I know, Vivienne is okay."

"Why then? Why do we have to leave? It's ten o'clock on Saturday night. We are celebrating my parents' anniversary and you are with your wife. Why do *you* have to be anywhere else?"

"That was one of my clients' attorney. The couple has been arrested. He said the magistrate said she'll release them both, but only after they talk with me in her chambers."

"But you're a psychologist, Baby, not a psychiatrist. You do crazy marriages, not crazy people."

"But Schelle, I…"

"NO!" Mareschelle glared at him desperately. "No, no, no, no, no! If they're not dying or in the hospital, then you don't need to go. Not. Now!"

"Look Schelle, it shouldn't take long. You can wait in the judge's reception area for me, and then we can head home."

"Reception area? You have lost your damn mind. I'm celebrating with my parents. I'm not going to some courthouse so I can sit in some reception area until all hours of the night while you pretend to fix the broken marriage of some people who probably don't belong together in the first place."

Mareschelle felt his hands slacken before he let go.

"Wow!" She looked down to where his hands were no longer touching hers. When he tried to touch her, she pulled further away. The look of regret on Solomon's face was so apparent that it hardly needed to be stated. But then again, every argument contains statements or actions that a person immediately regrets as soon as they pass from thought to action or spoken word. "Well, Doctor Alexandré, it's obvious that your job and those people mean more to you than your wife; so just go ahead and leave."

She watched his jaw shift and his lips clamp together. He tried to catch her arm but she pulled away, sat and poked her lips out.

Agitation and excitement filled his voice. "Mareschelle please, I'll be back as soon as I can and we'll talk about it then."

"Don't bother coming to get me after you're finished with your big important job. I'm good right here." Mareschelle crossed her arms, poked her lips out even harder then turned away and glared out the window.

Their day together had been perfect from the moment she woke up. In her eyes, despite the stomach sickness, sharing the adoption news would complete her perfect day. But now her husband seemed determined to destroy that perfection.

Rachel Mae slid across the sofa to comfort her daughter as

Darnell went to Solomon. "You go on and help them people, Son. We got her. Once she calms down she'll be alright. And in the morning after you've gotten some rest and put yourself together, bring yourself back down here and get your wife. I can't promise that she won't still be mad, but she'll be right here waiting for you." Without waiting for a response, Darnell escorted Solomon toward the front door then locked it behind him after he left.

CHAPTER 11

ANGER MIXED WITH SORROW AND needled at Mareschelle's soul as she watched Solomon drove away through the living room window. When his car was out of sight, she ran for the steps, rushing toward the sanctuary of her childhood bedroom. She stopped when her mother called her from the opening to the dining room. Rachel Mae smiled to ease her daughter's tension then went to her and kissed her on the forehead. "Now you listen to me, Rennie Betancourt," she called out her daughter's pet name then cradled her in her arms and rocked her, trying to calm her. "If the man has to work then you can't fault him for that. You know he has to pay the bills around that nice place you all have."

"Mama, all that man does is work. Even when we went on vacation, he took his computer and stayed up at night reviewing patient files. It's like he's here, but he's not here."

"Sit down, Rennie." She cupped her daughter's face in her hands and gently pulled her taller daughter's face to hers. When their foreheads touched, she said, "As a woman, you have to learn to be a little more understanding and supportive. Solomon is a good man. He's not out in the streets all times of night. You have a lovely home and a rental property to supplement your income."

"Buying the duplex was my idea Mama."

"Be that as it may; fact is, you own it as a couple."

Mareschelle sighed because she knew her mother was right. She wanted to say *whatever*, but she knew from experience that the comment would warrant a smack upside her head.

"You know that boy loves you more than he loves himself," Rachel Mae continued. "So if things aren't going exactly the way you want them to right now, give him some time. He'll figure it out."

"When Mama? This has been going on forever. Work. Work. Work."

"You can't make him into the man you want him to be to suit your needs. You have to accept him for who he is."

Mareschelle exhaled a long agitated sigh then grabbed the wine bottle and poured herself a second glass.

"Has he ever hit you?"

"No, Mama!" she exclaimed, slamming the bottle down onto the table.

"Cheated on you?"

"No!"

"What about letting you go without food, shelter, clothes?"

"No, Mama. He hasn't." The two women stared at each other, both wanting the other to concede and see her point. Mareschelle spoke first. "But it's more than food, shelter and clothes Mama. It's his inconsideration that drives me up a wall."

"It's a remarkable thing, the mind is. If you let it control you, it will drive you up the wall. But if you commit to happiness, then your mind will find a peaceful place. All those years your daddy was on the road with his job, who do you think kept you clothed and fed? I did that. Because that was my role. We all have a role to play. Play your role Mareschelle Renáe."

Mareschelle cringed. The sound of hearing her mother so calmly use her full name instead of her nickname blanketed Mareschelle with the weight of pure guilt. "What's my role Mama? Should I sit around and wait for Solomon to tell me what to do? Or should I just wait until he has a minute in his schedule to fit me in?"

"Now Baby, don't be like that. I may not know the everyday ins-

and-outs of your relationship with your husband, but I know the boy you brought in here to meet me and your Daddy, the one who hasn't stopped gushing over you every time he comes near you, has not devolved into as terrible a man as you are making him out to be."

Mareschelle sighed. "This is not a knock on you Mama, but I'm not as docile as you. It's not in my character to sit around and wait to voice my opinion only when I think I have a point to prove. You didn't raise me that way."

"Be careful, girl. Winning the fight, may mean losing the war."

Mareschelle angrily wiped away a single tear before she said, "I'm not saying Solomon is a monster, Mama. I'm just saying that sometimes I get lonely. He's a workaholic and I get tired of playing second fiddle to his job and all of the problems he brings home from the people he sees every day."

"But you knew what he was before you married him, Baby. Has he really changed that much." Mareschelle opened her mouth but the words didn't come. "Now I want you to think about that before you answer me Rennie, because I want your answer to be from your heart and not your head." Rachel Mae took the bottle of wine from her daughter and poured the remainder of the bottle into her own glass. She hugged her daughter long and tight then kissed Mareschelle on the forehead. "Well, these dishes aren't going to clean themselves."

"See Mama, that's what I'm talking about. Daddy's in there watching TV ..."

"No Ma'am. You stop right there. That is my husband and this is his house. You shut your mouth right now before I really have to put you in your place." Before Rachel Mae turned to walk into the kitchen, the two women stared hard at each other, communicating more with looks than any words could say. "Now if you don't feel like helping me in the kitchen, I suggest you go run a bath and try to relax. You know where everything is, I haven't moved it."

"I love you, Mama," Mareschelle called to her back.

"I love you too, Rennie Bear."

Just as she got ready to go upstairs, Darnell walked into the dining room. Mareschelle gave her daddy a huge bear hug. Over her shoulder his eyes asked his wife 'what is this for'? Rachel Mae shrugged, then entered the kitchen to keep her husband from seeing her own tears.

"Schelly Baby," Darnell started, "your mother and I have had a thousand fights over the years. Most, worse than this. I know it hurts right now, but give it a minute to cool off. You two will be okay."

"I hate him so much right now, Daddy. He had no right."

"Maybe not, Baby, but neither one of you is in a mind to talk sense to each other right now. And we don't hate nobody, you hear me?"

"I just want to lay down, Daddy. I've had a sick stomach all day."

"You go on up to your room. I'll have your mother bring you something to help you sleep."

"Thanks, Daddy." Mareschelle laid her head on her father's chest, wrapped her arms around his middle and squeezed him tighter than a blood pressure cuff. She whispered, "Love you forever, Daddy," before breaking her embrace and heading upstairs to run a bath.

Twenty minutes later, Mareschelle felt like a hundred pounds of lead had settled in the bottom of her stomach. She tried to sit on the ledge of the tub, but the room began to spin and the floor slid out from beneath her. Her mouth became dry and itchy, as if acid was prickling her tongue. Wind splashed in her face, then she was on a high-speed elevator hurtling down so quickly that the lead in her stomach was now in the roof of her mouth. Streams of light stabbed at her eyes. Greyness blinded her. Water flooded into her mouth, her nose, her ears. Then…darkness. Then…stillness. Then…absolute quiet.

Darnell heard a thunderous thud on the ceiling above the dining room. He made his way to the bottom of the stairs and hollered, "Schelly, are you alright up there?" but Mareschelle didn't answer. "What'd you break this time?" her father asked, remembering the time his pretty, but clumsy, teenage daughter broke the bathroom mirror while wildly swinging her hairbrush in the middle of a private dance session. "Schelly," he called forcefully while making his way up the stairs. She was no longer a teenager living in his house, but she was still his baby girl. When she didn't answer his call from the top of the stairs, he made his way to the bathroom door. He knocked firmly on the wooden door, then called in a gravelly baritone, "Schelly, are you alright, Baby?"

Mareschelle didn't answer. And she never would again.

When Darnell couldn't get his daughter to answer, he shouted for his wife to come upstairs. Out of respect for Mareschelle as a grown, married woman, he waited in the hallway as Rachel Mae entered the silent bathroom to check on her daughter. That wait wouldn't last long. The fragile seconds of silence were shattered when Rachel Mae shrieked as if she'd seen a ghost. Darnell bolted into the bathroom. In the tub, shower curtain pulled down on top of her naked body, Mareschelle's head and shoulders lay submerged beneath the water.

Darnell's repeated shouts of *No, no, no, no, no* crescendoed as he pushed past his howling, trembling wife to rescue his daughter. He pulled Mareschelle from the water, shouting her name over and again. He slapped her face several times to try and wake her, but that didn't work. He turned her on her side, slapped her hard on her back and scooped water from her mouth. A panicked moment passed before he yelled at his wife to *Call 911*. When Rachel Mae didn't move, he yanked a towel from the bar, laid it between Mareschelle and the floor then rushed past his catatonic wife and out into the hallway. Downstairs he called 911, pulled the front door handle and left the door wide open before hurrying back up the stairs.

Thirty minutes later, Darnell and Rachel Mae Betancourt sat

huddled on the hallway floor as the EMTs exited their bathroom. The female EMT said, "I saw she still had on her Epilepsy alert bracelet. It appears she had a grand mal seizure that took her into the water. I'm sorry, but there's nothing further we can do for your daughter."

Rachel Mae expelled a blood-curdling scream as Darnell wrapped her tighter in his arms, their arms wrapped around each other like brown ropes pulling them tightly together. When the realization of her daughter's death overcame her temporary mania, Rachel Mae struggled to escape her husband's grasp and get to their daughter, but Darnell held firm. He thought back to when he first knocked on the bathroom door and called to Mareschelle asking her if she was alright. She wasn't alright then. She wasn't alright now. She would never be alright, ever again. As her parents, having found her the way they did in their bathroom, he and Rachel Mae would never be alright again.

When the EMT asked if there was anyone that he could call for them, a sorrowful realization hit Darnell like a ton of bricks. Just two hours earlier, he told Solomon not to come back to the house. As a fellow husband, his heart broke that Solomon did not know anything of his wife's condition, and even worse, that he and Mareschelle had been arguing when he left. Now the thought of Solomon receiving the phone call to come back to Tacoma and bear witness to the nightmare that had just unfolded sent him into a fit of loud, deep, sporadic sobbing. And then, amidst the tears, Darnell thought that, as his daughter's husband, just like he and Rachel Mae, Solomon too would never be alright again.

CHAPTER 12

SOLOMON WOKE WITH A START, sweating and gasping for breath. The nightmarish memory of Mareschelle's passing had almost sent him into a full-blown panic attack. Vividly recalling losing his wife hurt like staring into the sun without eyelids. He needed a distraction. Needed something to get her off his mind.

And then the ringing wouldn't stop. *Why won't it stop?* he thought, as he sat up, trying to focus. The illuminated numbers on the digital clock read 6:42. The lack of a red dot meant it was a.m. not p.m. The alarm shouldn't have been ringing for another thirteen minutes. Then he realized the ringing wasn't his alarm. It was the telephone. "Hello," he answered groggily.

"Well good morning, kind Sir. How are you on this bright and beautiful Monday?"

"I'd be better if I was still asleep." He flopped down onto the bed and closed his eyes. He exhaled then said, "I'm sorry, who is this?"

"Wow, you don't even recognize my voice. What a shame? And here I thought I was somebody special."

Nobody who hasn't spent the night is special before 7am, he thought; but knowing the delicate sensibilities of a woman, he kept his words to himself. He said, "I'd take a guess, but since I was unconscious and dreaming two minutes ago, and…I haven't had any coffee to shock my brain into any state of reasonable alertness, I'm going to need you to be gracious enough to gift me an answer about the identity behind the mystery voice."

"Interesting," she said. "If I'm that forgettable, I may as well ask the conductor to turn this train around and take me back to Spokane."

He sat up. "Jordyn?"

"Yes, Doctor Solomon Alexandré. Jordyn H. Remember me?"

"Yes, of course. Of course I remember you, Jordyn." He stifled a yawn. "It's just, well; I didn't sleep well so I'm a little tired. My apologies for not catching your voice, I don't quite have myself together yet." His eyes were open now, but his voice was still groggy.

"No, Sir. Now that I think about it, it's me who should apologize for calling so early. A little overzealous I guess. It's just that I had to catch this early train to Seattle and I wanted to catch you before you got into session with your patients and didn't have time to talk."

"No. No. It's fine. I need to get up and get ready. Tell you what, since you're already on the train, let me get myself together, and I'll call you once I'm dressed. That way we can talk about your arrival."

"Sounds good. According to my itinerary, I've got time to kill, so hit me back when your conscious mind can remember my number."

"Yeah, no problem. Let me get dressed then I'll call you back."

"It's a date." Jordyn hung up without a goodbye. She had escaped her Spokane haven and was travelling to Seattle for a pageant function with her fellow Miss Washington pageant alum, Savannah Grimes. Their return trip to Spokane was scheduled for Saturday morning.

When Solomon called her from his car phone, Jordyn's first question was if he had dinner plans. When he said he didn't, she told him she'd feed him if he'd pick her and Savannah up from the train station and take them to their hotel. Solomon agreed and Jordyn texted him her train information.

~

Solomon sat on the hood of his Audi A8 and watched Jordyn and two other high-heeled striding, former Miss Washington pageant winners bolt through the door of Benaroya Hall Monday evening after obtaining their interview and rehearsals schedules. The stems on that six-legged stallion were perfectly wrapped, stretched and highlighted in three distinct shades of denim. Jordyn's silk shirt was tucked into jeans that disappeared into ankle boots. Her hair artfully tousled and her makeup was perfect for an audition. When she turned to exchange air kisses, Solomon saw the perfection of her high, round butt, and tried not to stare while the three beauty queens hugged their goodbyes.

"I'll catch you at breakfast," Jordyn called to her friends' backs.

Solomon grinned a wide, toothy smile. Now that she was coming straight at him, there was no point in faking the impossible.

Jordyn took his wrist and pulled him along. "We need to hurry."

"Where?" Solomon asked, not getting the greeting he anticipated.

"Please just, come on," Jordyn said without explanation.

Solomon moved to keep from falling. "Where are you dragging me?" Six paces down the block, he matched her accelerated stride and fell into step with her.

"I have to get to the Moore Theatre to see Damien Carter. He's holding auditions for a narrating gig."

"Narrating what?" he asked.

"Nothing big," she said keeping two steps ahead of him. "It's a history biopic series about Women Warriors."

"Women warriors? Sounds like a Nat Geo thing?"

"No, not Nat Geo," she spat as she power-walked down Virginia Street. "The Smithsonian Channel."

Once they arrived at the Moore Theatre, they stood facing each other, almost eye-to-eye thanks to the tall heel of her boots. She folded her arms across her chest and hugged herself, anxiously tapping her foot, as they awaited her turn with the casting assistant. She introduced herself and was told that Mister Carter had stepped out to make a phone call, but she would be next once he returned.

After the audition, Jordyn felt like she'd flubbed the audition and wanted to get very far away from the theatre, very quickly. As they walked toward no named destination, she took his hand in hers. "Anything special you'd like to do tonight?"

"If you're game, I know something we could do."

"What?" she asked, taking his hand again.

They walked toward Puget Sound, fingers interlaced. A block before they reached the water, Solomon retracted his hand for a moment to wipe away the sweat. Something about her made him nervous and he hoped that she didn't notice his hand sweating as profusely as he felt it was.

"What's this?" she said, stopping at the gate to the landing.

"The Bremerton Ferry." Solomon let her hand go to pay at the kiosk, then recaptured it to walk her to the bottom of the boat landing. They waited under an expansive awning as the ferry unloaded forty-ish passengers and about twenty cars. Then the passenger entry door was pushed open from the inside by a slim, fifty-something woman.

"Great," Solomon guffawed as they reached the top of the stairs. On the lido deck, there were lots of wooden benches and a small concession stand that was closed for the night. An arced, clear Plexiglas roof provided protection from precipitation. Solomon dragged Jordyn to the end of the ferry facing the western side of the Sound. Fewer than a dozen cars loaded up before they left. One other couple came up to the lido deck, but they settled at the aft part of the boat, their backs to Solomon and Jordyn. A few minutes later, Jordyn jumped when the horn blew and the ferry started moving west.

Solomon wrapped an arm around her. "I used to love this when I was a kid. Thanks for letting me drag you down here."

They sat and looked out across the placid Sound for a couple of moments. The sky was clear and the stars twinkled above them like a million Christmas tree lights. Jordyn was enjoying him. She'd never had a man pay such close attention to her before.

Solomon was just about to say how great hanging with her was when she kissed him. What he thought most about during the kiss was how her small, velvety, muscular tongue moved slow and deliberate, as if mapping out the contour of his mouth for future reference.

Both the kiss and the ferry ride were smooth as glass. It wasn't the quite the intimacy he'd shared on the Edmonds Ferry with Mareschelle when they'd taken it to Kingston for a night out at the Indian reservation casino, but it was equally as sensual.

Jordyn laid a hand on his thigh, their kiss invoking the beginning of an erection before they broke it. "Aren't the stars beautiful?" she asked, neither moving her hand nor squeezing, but just letting the weight of it rest right there. Was she lying to herself that attempting a relationship with a man this wonderful was too hard? Or was she being realistic in thinking that whatever they were doing had to be limited to being nothing more than their guilty pleasure whenever their schedules permitted? After a moment, they were back to kissing. Each time her tongue pushed into his mouth his tongue pushed back. Jordyn caressed the back of his neck with her other hand. When deep sounds came from his throat and his erection started to throb, she eased the weight of her hand away from him, but kept kissing.

Solomon could see the other couple in his peripheral vision. They were far enough away that the ferry's engine noise muffled his struggle to keep quiet. With Jordyn's hand moved, he shifted in his seat to ease his tension.

"Nice form, Doctor." Jordyn eyed the front of his pants as she stood when the ferry slowed for landing. "And even better control. I was afraid we were heading for an embarrassing moment."

When the ferry bumped against the fender boards on the pier,

Solomon asked, "Where are you going?"

"Aren't we getting off?"

"No, Ma'am." He patted the seat next to him for her to return. "This experience is about the ferry ride, not exploring what's on the other side of the Sound."

Head cocked, Jordyn raised an eyebrow. "We're not getting off?"

"Not here."

"So we're just riding the ferry in circle all willy-nilly?"

"Yep."

She sat and ten minutes later the ferry left the pier headed back to Seattle. Jordyn cuddled into Solomon's arm. Again, that hand came to rest on his upper thigh, but he was relaxed now and grinned broadly at her touch. And just like that, there it was, the intimacy and the closeness he so desperately sought.

A stiff breeze that stopped as quickly as it came, shot across the deck. Jordyn curled up beside him, put her hand on his chest and her head on his shoulder. Amid the purr of the ferry's engines, Solomon watched her fall asleep beneath the star laden sky above Puget Sound.

Operation Roundabout Ferry returned them to Seattle just before ten. Once clear of the pier, they found seats at the sidewalk café of the Nijo Sushi Bar and ate dinner. The restaurant was conveniently located one block west of the Kimpton Hotel Monaco where Jordyn was staying and two blocks west of where he'd parked his car. They drank Saké and ate appetizers—beef tataki, sashimi, dancing shrimp, and Jiaozuo dumplings with a ginger, mushroom, duck and cauliflower filling. For his entrée, Solomon had Peppercorn Softshell Crab. Jordyn ate Katsu Curry chicken.

While they contemplated dessert, Jordyn said, "Can I ask you a favor?" Plaintively she pulled her lower lip under her front teeth in an attempt to look innocent, the way beautiful girls sometimes inadvertently made goofy faces. Unlike the threats he endured from his grandmother when he cried or made weird or ugly faces as a child, Solomon was certain that nobody ever threatened her with the promise that her face would permanently freeze like that if she kept doing it.

"Another one already?" His smile told her he was just joking.

"That is unless you have plans with someone else," she mused.

Solomon smiled his answer. "I probably do. But ask me anyway. I enjoy having options." Being with her opened him up to ideas, possibilities, and arguments that he would have normally rejected.

She scrunched her nose playfully. "Smart-aleck comments like that will get you uninvited before you get invited."

Solomon peered into the depth of her forever blue eyes. Her golden-brown hair had recently been braided. Now that it hung loose, it was wild, with kinky waves wrapped around all of the pretty skin on her oval face. Her features were small and ladylike, yet her warm aura was abundant and overpowering. In thirty-seven years, he had never set eyes on anything like her. "Gets me out of the decision-making process," he said sarcastically.

Jordyn punched him playfully in the chest. "Okay look Doctor Alexandré, Sunday is the annual Gonzaga Booster dinner. My sorority has reserved a couple of tables, and as a chapter president, I'm required to host one. The dress is semi-formal," she continued, "and actually, it's rather convivial. There dinner is buffet-style, and there's usually a long, dull booster's speech. Then once the oligarchy of rich alums get all liquored up, the ties loosen, the ladies slip off their high heels and all of those drunks start acting like they're auditioning for Dancing with the Stars. Other than that, it's quite chill."

A dark, heavy cloud passed over sprinkling the ground with a handful of raindrops. The café's awning had been retracted once the sun dipped below the horizon of downtown. Jordyn shifted her gaze to the top of his head when he moved to wipe away the few drops that sat like morning dew on a smooth flower. Solomon noticed how the drops of rain glistened on her hair like gold dust.

"Obviously," she continued after sticking out her tongue to taste a handful of God's tears, "if it's not the sort of thing you enjoy, then just say no and I'll suffer through that misery all on my own."

"Misery, huh?"

"I mean, I don't know. It's my first time hosting. In the past, as soon as dinner and *the speech* ended," she raised her hands to show air quotes, "our departure came in the form of an unspoken, extended trip to the bathroom. Now that I'll be hosting and expected to stay and mingle, I would like someone there I enjoy talking to."

Solomon smiled, bringing his eyes to meet her gaze as Jordyn made every effort not to meet his. "So you enjoy talking to me, huh?"

"Just thought I'd ask," she said, her eyes boring a hole through the menu as she refused to look at him. From behind the cover of the menu she shrugged her shoulders and said, "No harm in asking."

When the waiter came, Jordyn ordered the grilled pineapple and strawberry shortcake kabobs.

Solomon ordered the blueberry and lemon pound cake parfait. "And two glasses of Port," he called to the waiter. "Oh well, I mean, if you'd like me to go, I can search my calendar and see how many hearts would be broken if I wasn't available this weekend."

"In that case, I'd better run for the hills now before the women of Seattle break out their pitchforks and torches." Jordyn playfully drew away from him. "Good thing my Scarlet A is covered up. I don't want to spend my week in the big city burning at the stake."

"Are you sure you wouldn't feel better served asking a fellow Zag alum? I wouldn't want to step on any toes. What if they find out I'm a Cougar alum? Then who would be burning at the stake?" Solomon's inquiries started a volley of laughter. They clinked dessert wine glasses over their dessert plates then asked the waiter for refills when they were empty. Then they talked, shared smiles, laughed out loud, ate their desserts and drank port wine until Nijo closed at midnight.

CHAPTER 13

JORDYN PEEKED THROUGH SOLOMON'S HALF open office door just before noon on Tuesday wearing a rainbow-colored dress that stopped mid-thigh. "Mind if I come in?"

Solomon smiled his concurrence.

Jordyn entered and closed the door. He walked toward her and her to him. She put her arms around him and he held her as tight as he did when he was ten and his mother told him his father had left them. They may have kissed, but he really didn't remember.

"You're crying," she said.

He didn't realize the thoughts of Mareschelle had made him cry before she knocked on the door. Now he was sitting on his desk. Jordyn had settled between his legs and wrapped his arms around her middle, making him hold her like her father used to when she was young. His tears had stopped, but the grief still stung his insides. "How did you know where I worked?" he asked.

"I needed to see you, so I asked Siri."

"Are the Seattle women after you with pitchforks?"

"Nahh," she said taking in his office decor. "I'm after you."

He took a deep breath to quell his pounding heart as the beginning of an erection—that he was sure she could feel—started in his pants. His mind tuned in and out like a radio receiver ranging through his feelings and the things on his to-do list. He didn't want foreplay, just sex with that gorgeous woman right there on the desk.

She noticed his discomfort and in the absence of words, she turned, pressed against him and kissed him for a full minute, encouraging his erection into full bloom.

"I have an appointment coming soon Jordyn, there's no time."

"I don't mind waiting." They both looked down to where his nature searched for hers. She bumped her pelvis against his playfully as she spoke. "But are you sure there's not something you want to get off your…mind?"

"Ummh, that…was incredible!" He pulled her arms from around his neck and stood. "What did I do to deserve that?" He ran his hands along her arms to her elbows and walked her to the chair where his client would sit in ten minutes. Her hem fell toward her hip and gravity revealed most of her outer thigh when she crossed her legs.

His heart thrummed. He needed a woman so much right then that he probably would have gotten excited over her scratching her head. "I don't know if I'm ready for something that intense yet, Jordyn," he said. "If I sleep with you, then I'd have to give up something."

"I'm not asking for that."

"But I would. You know I would."

"Well, what if I ask you to give up your evening and let me treat you to dinner and a movie? And I promise to behave when the theater goes dark."

Her smile was like sunshine and he wanted to bask in it for every second that Vivienne would allow before announcing the arrival of his next appointment. He asked, "Out in public or back at your hotel?"

Jordyn covered her bosom and gasped. "Why Doctor, your words embarrass me. Must I remind you that I invited you to dinner and a movie, not to Netflix and chill. *A Lady* knows the difference."

Solomon said, "You can read me like a first grade nursery rhyme."

She cracked a grin and perused his office. "That's why I like you. You're a simple man."

He looked at her inquisitively, uncertain of her choice in words.

"Uncomplicated is what I meant." They shared a smile. "And you're so smart, Solomon. I can't wait to get to know you better." She stood and kissed him again, but for only three seconds this time.

He moved toward his chair when she broke the kiss.

"Well if you're not going to satisfy that hunger…" She left her words hanging. "Have you eaten lunch? Do you have time to grab something to go? I don't want you up in here all day without eating."

In the elevator, she pulled him close, put her head on his shoulder and chattered about the morning events at her pageant. In the deli situated in the lobby, they ordered sandwich wraps and two aloe vera waters. He pointed out his patients when they entered the lobby. She knew her time with him was over for now, but she'd left her purse in his office, so she accompanied him back upstairs—but only long enough to retrieve it.

Solomon met Jordyn later that night. He parked at a free garage just off the Alaskan Way and walked the two blocks to the Kimpton Monaco. They ate burgers at Red Robin then walked a block to the 5th Avenue Theatre and took in the seven o'clock screening of the latest Marvel movie.

After the movie, Jordyn followed Solomon back to her hotel with an air of dutiful submission. When they arrived at the Kimpton, she called, "Solomon?" in an unfamiliarly diminutive voice. Like flecks of cinnamon on an alabaster counter, an imperfect scattering of freckles highlighted the smooth skin across her nose and cheeks. The bulk of her beautifully ribbed and rippled mane of golden-brown hair fell on her chest in waves. "It's still early, and my first session doesn't start until eleven tomorrow morning. I know it's probably too late to Netflix and chill, but is it too late for you to show me where you live?"

Solomon marveled into her indecipherable eyes, smiled and

pecked her lips gently. "I'd love to, but I live a couple miles north of downtown. And," he stretched out that single syllable, "Getting you there and back would make for a late night."

"And back?" She'd never been to his part of town, so she wasn't certain where he lived, but she was interested in the destination.

"Yeah, I have my annual physical tomorrow morning at seven, so I'm trying to get to bed early tonight. But my afternoon is free, if you'll accept a raincheck?"

She told him that pageant commitments—a rehearsal, a mandatory press conference and dinner—occupied her entire Wednesday. He told her that he had Bible Study following a late counseling appointment. Since other engagements prevented their comingling on Wednesday, he offered, "How about I cook you dinner Thursday night and give you a proper tour of the Hang Suite?"

"Does the tour include an explanation of why you call it the Hang Suite?"

"For sure."

"Then I'm in."

Solomon kissed her first this time, not as time-consuming as the minute-long kiss in his office, but longer than their departing peck on the lips. As she walked up the hotel stairs, he said, "Call me Thursday and let me know when to come pick you up," then smiling ear-to-ear, he practically skipped back to the garage.

~

Knowing that you only get one chance to make a first impression, Solomon did some light housekeeping before going to bed Wednesday night. He had promised Jordyn a home cooked meal but hadn't made groceries, and a Thursday afternoon traffic jam left little time to cook following his delayed arrival at the Hang Suite. He wanted to make sure everything was correct before she got there, but from her last message, he only had an hour before he needed to leave to pick her up.

By six o'clock, Solomon had navigated his way downtown, picked up Jordyn and drove her to the Hang Suite. Because she was a first time guest, he parked curbside and walked her through the front door instead of taking her around back and parking in the garage. Over the winter, he'd had the downstairs and his master bedroom remodeled and redecorated because the old floorplan contained too many painful memories of Mareschelle. The original Hang Suite downstairs floorplan featured from front to back, a separated living room, dining room, and kitchen with a side-entering hallway that contained stairs that rose from front to back. In the remodel, he had a couple of walls removed to transform the downstairs into an open-concept great room floorplan with a view straight from the front door to the back of the kitchen. Half-walls and columns delineated the three new areas. The kitchen was still at the rear and the picture room featuring all of his mentors was still on the front, but the fireplace was moved to the center of what used to be the dining room halfway between the front and back doors. Directly across from the fireplace was a split staircase with a middle landing rising to the middle of the upstairs hallway. The third bedroom was converted into a loft-style office at the top of the stairs, and the guest and master suites were still at opposite ends of the hallway. When it was finished, Solomon's new floorplan gained him sixty-eight additional square feet of living space in an open, beautifully-flowing floorplan.

"Life goes on," Vivienne had told him at dinner every Sunday after church for the year following Mareschelle's death. As far as Solomon was concerned, life had stopped for him just as surely as it had stopped for Mareschelle on the day she died. When the New Year came, Solomon took those three words and hired a contractor to remodel his wife and former lover out of the Hang Suite so that he could try to make his *life go on*. He even went as far as removing the painting of Mareschelle when the fireplace was excavated and giving it to her mother, who placed it in her daughter's bedroom which was more like a shrine.

Jordyn marveled at the vibrant colors and intriguing choice of decorations throughout his house. For a bachelor, Solomon was extremely neat. "Very nice," she purred, running her hand across the clean lines of the matching loveseats set on opposite sides of a gray-and-white marble coffee table in the picture room. Five books sat between two white, marble bookends—one shaped like a heart, and the other like a brain. White letters spelled out *Books feed your heart and your brain* on a grey plaque protruding from beneath the books. Jordyn stopped to peruse the titles—*Ms. Etta's Fast House; The Five People You Meet in Heaven; Curves, Edges and Perfect Imperfections; Chemistry Matters, and The Book of Night Women.* She said, "Have you read all of these?"

"Absolutely."

"Your favorite?"

"All five, that's why they're out here instead of hiding on the shelves with my other books."

"But what if you were stranded on a deserted island and could only have your one all-time favorite?"

Solomon contemplated choosing just one book as his favorite. Of the more than 300 books on the shelves throughout his house, what about these five made him segregate them for display? After a beat he told her, "Ms. Etta's Fast House is most vibrant and the most fun. *The Five People You Meet in Heaven* is no doubt the most endearing. *Curves and Edges, and Chemistry Matters* are part of a series that explores male-female intimacy through the lens of several different relationships. I liken those two to a fictional representation of my job as a marriage counselor. But if I am going to pick an absolute favorite, then it has to be *The Book of Night Women.* It's thought provoking, exciting, and is without a doubt the best page turner I've ever read. I started chapter three one night, and when I put it down around ten the next morning, I'd finished the book. I've never before or since read anything that captivating. So to answer your question, *The Book of Night Women* is my all-time favorite book."

Jordyn smiled at the look of pure joy on his face. "So then that's the one I want to borrow."

Solomon pushed the book toward her. When she reached for it, he snatched it back. "Do you have a library card, young lady?"

Jordyn purred, "I'll show you mine if you show me yours."

They laughed as Solomon laid the book on the coffee table. "It'll be here when you're ready for it."

Next he showed her the remainder of the first floor, then the basement. Jordyn enjoyed her tour of his man cave the most, especially the wine cellar and cigar parlor, but for some reason couldn't figure out why the basement seemed larger than the first floor. And it wasn't anything like she expected when he announced having a man cave. Then again, what did she expect? Some secret chamber with a gaggle of two-way mirrors and freaky stuff hidden behind a fake, moving wall where he videotaped everything. Who was she kidding, this guy was too refined for that R. Kelly, *Trapped In The Closet* crap. But then again, it was still daytime, and she was old enough to know that the freaks come out at night.

She took inventory of the decor and layout during her tour of the three second story rooms. The two dressers in the master were a pleasant shade of mahogany that matched the wooden frame of the king-size bed. She thought for a minute and then realized that for his height, a king-size bed made sense. The bronze painted room, paired with the burnt orange, brown and tan comforter, was a perfect shade match for the dresser and carpet. The orange gave the perfect pop of color to keep the room from being dull. Four king-size pillows anchored a half-dozen colorful throw pillows atop the comforter. The bathroom was normal enough; a row of bronze-colored tiles set at chest level accented tan tiles throughout, while two sets of burgundy towels matched the rugs in front of the shower, sink and toilet.

After the tour, Jordyn sat at the massive kitchen island nursing a glass of Rosé from a local winery while Solomon finalized the meal.

He pulled four boneless pork chops from the freezer when he got home. He had grilled eight on Sunday night for dinner with Viv, Desmond and Sharet. He ate two. Viv ate one, then took one home. Desmond and Sharet cancelled last minute so he froze the other four. He sliced then sautéed portabella mushrooms with oregano and olive oil. When the chicken was ready, he'd throw them on top of Linguini noodles with some chopped chives. He pulled out some bacon and steamed some asparagus. He butterflied the boneless chops, then stuffed them with the asparagus, fresh herbs and a mixture of Havarti, Gouda and spicy cheeses before wrapping them in the bacon.

Jordyn cheered, "Bravo," when he stuck the chops in the oven.

Solomon bowed, then sat next to her. They clinked glasses then sipped their wine while the chops roasted.

Jordyn asked, "So how many patients do you have on average?"

"I normally work with about twelve to fifteen couples at a time. I think the most I've had on the books at once was twenty seven."

"I know you have patient confidentiality rules, but tell me a story about one of your more interesting couples. No names, of course."

Solomon drank the rest of his Rosé, then refilled both of their glasses. Before he started, he pulled some garlic bread out of the freezer to compliment the pasta, set it on a baking tray, and then came back to her. "There was this one couple I'd been seeing for about a year but didn't seem to be making any headway with. So one week, instead of having them together at their session, I scheduled them for consecutive sessions. In each of the sessions, I basically gave them advice on how to entice one another. At the end of the session, I gave them identical exercises to try with each other because they had both told me that the other was being distant. In order to give the exercises sufficient time to develop, I extended their return session a week past normal."

"I don't get why they couldn't be in the same session if you gave them identical advice. Seems to me that you could've saved yourself the duplication," Jordyn said between sips.

"Separate sessions with the same counseling was something my favorite professor taught in one of his seminars."

"Sounds excessive to me, but I'll go with it for the sake of conversation." She took another sip of wine. "Please continue."

"The husband came in first," Solomon started. He was intrigued that Jordyn seemed so interested in his work. He wasn't a narcissist, but he enjoyed being able to talk about work in a relaxed setting. He told her, "For the first ten minutes, I asked him some generic questions about sports and his job to get him in a talkative mood. I gave him a white paper with some exercises written on it that he was to try with his wife before our next session. Then I gave him a notepad and told him to write down everything that happened after the exercises.

Jordyn averted her gaze to the oven timer. The aroma of the food was invading her nose and distracting her attentions.

"When his wife came in," Solomon continued, "I read through the exercises on the white paper the exact same way I did with her husband. And just like her husband, I told her to turn off the television and their phones, and find a quiet place to talk. I recommended they light some candles to set the mood for an intimate conversation. Then they were supposed to tell each other five things they liked about each other and then five things they didn't like about each other. There was also stuff on there about naming people in their lives that they thought they should get rid of and some questions about their closest family and how those people were affecting their relationship."

"So how'd they do?"

"Not as well as I'd hoped." The oven timer beeped reverting Solomon back into chef mode. He reset the timer so the garlic bread could warm, removed the baking dish and set it on the stovetop to allow the chops to rest while he finished his story. He offered her more wine but she deferred, so he continued. "Three days before their next joint session, Security called me to the parking garage in my building because the husband had busted out the windows in my car."

"What? Why?"

"Turns out, the wife took my sheet of suggestions and used it on her co-worker instead of her husband. When the husband came home a day early from a business trip, he found his wife and her co-worker having sex on the theatre room sofa in their basement. After he finished beating up the co-worker and dragging him out to his car in his underwear, he came to my office garage.

He and his wife had argued that they both followed my advice and since he was using the advice on his wife and the wife was using the advice on someone else, he concluded that I told her to do it in her separate session, so he destroyed my car."

An elongated, "Wowwwww!" was all Jordyn could manage.

Solomon uncorked a bottle of Viognier to accompany dinner, then lit the two candles on the table. He always left his dinner table set, so all that was necessary to prepare the table was to light the candles.

"So are you still seeing them?" Jordyn asked as Solomon escorted her from the kitchen to the dining room.

"No, the husband filed for divorce once he got out of jail for vandalizing my car."

"Did you have to buy a new car?"

"No. After my lawyer got finished with him, his insurance company totaled my car on paper and bought me a brand new one."

"Nice."

"Yeah, nice about the car," Solomon co-signed. "But not nice that I lost clients and couldn't help them save their marriage."

"You can't save them all."

"It's my job to try."

"Huh," Jordyn guffawed. "Some people don't need saving. And that kind of crazy right there is why I haven't given any serious thought to marriage. I don't need that kind of crazy in my life."

With dinner concluded, Solomon acquiesced to Jordyn begging him to teach her how to play pool. But first, he led her into the cigar parlor which featured an eight-foot-wide, floor-to-ceiling humidor, two six-seat sectionals that sat around wooden tables topped with butane lighters, cigar cutters and ashtrays. "Are you a bourbon or a whiskey girl?"

"Bourbon," she answered while he grabbed three cigars from the humidor. "Bulleit, if you have it."

"Well alright now," Solomon chimed before venturing out to the bar.

Solomon poured two fingers of Bulleit for her and two fingers of Blanton's for himself. When he returned, Jordyn had already cut the ends off all three cigars using the silver cutter prepositioned on the table. Solomon set her drink in front of her then slid in beside her on the sectional. He held up a lighter and asked, "Shall I?"

"It's your man cave."

Seeing that she obviously knew her way around a cigar, he said, "I only asked because you already sliced them open."

"I really didn't know what I was doing, I was just playing with the stuff on the table while you were gone." Her smile told she was lying.

He inspected the cigar cuts. "Yeah, and I'm just a squirrel trying to get a nut."

"Aren't we all?" she replied gaily.

Over the next forty-five minutes, they sipped bourbon, swapped college stories and sampled all three cigars. Jordyn's favorite turned out to be the Excalibur by Hoyo de Monterey. It bit on the front end and made her cough, but after her third toke and exhale she crooned, "Ummm, that's really smooth."

Solomon couldn't help but laugh, and when Jordyn joined him another short coughing fit ensued. He was enjoying her company. Despite it being late, and Friday being a workday, he never once thought to check the time. When their glasses were empty, he invited her to accompany him into the wine cellar.

Jordyn pulled out random bottles asking the price of this one and that.

Solomon disappeared around the back of the divider in the middle of the vault to search a section of reds. 'Tell me again what year you were born."

"One-Nine-Nine-Four," she started singsonging and rocking her head from side-to-side.

When Solomon returned from wine Neverland, he opened a seventy dollar bottle of 1994 JOSEPH PHELPS Insignia Napa Valley. He poured two glasses, handed one to Jordyn and said, "A toast...to the Naughty Nineties." They clinked glasses then both drank the entire two ounces of wine he'd poured in each glass.

"Cough. Cough, cough." That was Jordyn. She looked at the glass as if words should be written on it. She kissed her teeth twice then said, "I know it's my year, but do you have something a little less hmm-umm ... earthy?"

Solomon returned this time with a 1994 CROFT Vintage Port that had won first place with a score of 94 points.

Jordyn sipped the CROFT more apprehensively than she gulped the Insignia. When the fruity vino pleasured her tongue, she exhaled a long *Aaahhh.*

"What do you think?"

She sipped. "Now this right here could be a girl's best friend."

"Good, now didn't you say something about a pool lesson?"

Solomon quickly figured out that the pool lesson inquiry was a ruse. The food, cigars and alcohol had relaxed Jordyn to the point where her competitive nature kicked in and instead of allowing Solomon to show her the ropes, she asked to break after he finished racking. After he chalked her tip, Solomon spooned against her back to show her how to hold the cue for maximum power in her break.

But Jordyn was more interested in flirting. As he hovered over her talking pool, she kept backing into him, rubbing her butt against the front of his pants. When she finally shot the cue ball and broke the rack, she turned to him without watching the break, leaned back against the table and asked, "How'd I do?"

Solomon looked at the aggressive break. "Looks like you might've already had a lesson or three. But you didn't sink anything."

Before he could move to take his turn, Jordyn grabbed his belt and pulled him into her. She dropped her cue, slid back onto the table and asked, "You want to sink something?" then pulled him in for a kiss.

Solomon flinched when the cue slammed onto the tile floor, but he didn't break the kiss.

Jordyn squealed between kisses, slid her hands from his waist to his chest and began unbuttoning his shirt.

Solomon couldn't refrain from taking her in his arms and kissing those tender lips as she pressed her tender body against his. He hiked her skirt up enough to allow him to settle between her thighs. Her body held the scent of fresh roses and being wrapped in her arms had a more intoxicating effect than the liquor.

When his shirt and belt buckle were undone, she leaned back onto the felt tabletop, pulling him down on top of her. When their bodies met, a shock of electricity pulsed through her. They were caught up in their passion, their immediate excitement exceeded all bounds, and the billiards lesson was over.

When excessive foreplay advanced to the point of removing underwear, Solomon stopped, lifted his weight off her and struggled to catch his breath.

"What's wrong?" Jordyn asked nervously.

Solomon swallowed hard and looked at the pool table beneath

them before meeting her gaze. "As much as I would definitely like to sink my cue into your center pocket, I don't want to do it like this."

"Do you want me on top? Or are we going back to taking it slow?"

Solomon smiled at her candor. "Come here." He straightened and she followed. After he buttoned his pants, he lifted Jordyn from the pool table and headed for the bedroom. At the top of the basement stairs, he stumbled and accidentally bumped her shoulder against the door frame. "I'm sorry."

She smiled but didn't respond. She was too sexually aroused to let his clumsiness distract her. She leaned forward and kissed him. Held it for a long breath, then whispered, "I'm alright," when she broke the kiss. "Now take me upstairs and show me why you call it the Hang Suite."

CHAPTER 14

FRIDAY MORNING WINDS WERE LIGHT, the air fresh and crisp. The sun was bright in the sky when Jordyn's taxi arrived at the Hang Suite. "I'll call you tonight after the pageant, Pretty Boy, so we can work out tomorrow's escape plan?" She left his house barefoot. Her shoes hanging in her hand. Blood-red streaks surrounded her blue irises making her eyes appear as an abstract artist's concept of an American flag. Solomon and Jordyn were both still slightly hung over, so she insisted on calling for a ride share instead of requiring him to drive her to her hotel. Solomon insisted too—on paying for the ride.

"Now that's a plan I can get behind." Solomon's goodbye kiss lasted for a long second before she pulled away. Wanting more, he took her face in both his hands and kissed her like she was leaving for war. For the briefest of moments the weight of his life had lifted.

There must have been some kind of hesitation in her kiss or her body language because after the kiss ended she laughed and said, "Don't worry. I'm not asking for any more than I already have." Jordyn turned, put on her sunglasses and smiled as they walked to the car hand-in-hand.

By the time she reached her hotel, she had a full blown hunger and hangover headache, and after last night's follies, she realized her dress desperately needed dry cleaning. She tried to tip the driver, but was refused when he informed her that the tip had already been covered in the reservation. Jordyn shrugged it off, smiled at the thought of Solomon being so chivalrous, then stepped out of the ride share as the doorman opened her door and welcomed her back to the Kimpton.

Savannah stood outside Jordyn's door and dialed her cell number for the fifth time. She hadn't heard from her friend since 3 o'clock Thursday afternoon when rehearsal ended and now it was approaching noon on Friday. Savannah had called before she went to bed to find out what time Jordyn wanted to meet for brunch, but left a message when she didn't answer. In the morning, she'd called her cell and her room phone, and then knocked on her door before she went down for brunch. Jordyn didn't answer. She called again once her food came to see if Jordyn wanted her to order something and bring it up to the room for her since brunch was about to end. Again, Jordyn didn't answer. Savannah was concerned, so instead of going back to her room, she headed to the elevator to go find the pageant director. When the elevator door opened, Jordyn stood inside. "What the hell, Jordyn Hoffman?" Savanah was livid. "I've been calling you for almost twelve hours. You ain't dead, so you better have lost your phone!"

"What's wrong Vannah?" Jordyn whispered her words, but they sounded like shouts inside her head. She had on sunglasses and her hair looked like she'd finger combed it at best. When Jordyn removed her sunglasses, in the hallway, Savannah noticed her bloodshot eyes.

"Dang girl, did you get any sleep last night?" Savannah asked, also noticing that she was still in her outfit from the night before.

"Not much, "Jordyn replied. "Solomon and I were up late...talking."

"Well you look like you need a shower and some breakfast."

"What I need, Mom, is a nap." Jordyn put her glasses back on and walked toward her room. "When are we supposed to be downstairs?"

"The shuttle leaves at five."

Jordyn waved her key card across the magnetic pad to unlock her room, cracked her door then handed her card to Savannah. "I love you, Vannah, you know that right? But right now all I need is quiet and sleep." She kissed Savannah on the cheek. "Come get me at three-thirty. And after the pageant I'll answer any and all of your questions while we eat." Then she retreated into her room.

~

In the Belltown neighborhood underneath the Humphrey Apartments is the 39-seat speakeasy, Bathtub Gin & Company. This Prohibition-themed cocktail bar was opened in 2009, but its unpretentious décor and intimate setting are sure to throw visitors back to the 1920s. Guests enter through the alleyway behind the brick building, between 1st and 2nd Streets. Once inside, they can take a load off at the six-seat bar or on one of the small couches and enjoy a finely crafted smoked Old Fashioned or Cosmo.

"Speak your peace." Solomon answered without looking at his caller ID.

"Well good evening, Doctor." Jordyn's commitment to the pageant was over. She and her three-headed entourage were ready to end their final night in Seattle with a bang. Calling to arrange their Saturday rendezvous was why she'd promised to call, but wanting to see him was the goal. "We're all finished with the pageant. What are you up to?"

"Me? I'm chilling at the Bathtub."

"In the tub? So are you in for the night, or getting ready to go out?"

"No Sweetheart, not in the bathtub, AT the Bathtub."

"You're out? In somebody's bathtub, and you answered the phone?" Jordyn heard jazz playing in the background and pictured him in another woman's hot tub. Her next conclusion jumped straight to silent name calling. But instead of cussing him out and making a fool of herself, she decided to take the high road, and simply said, "I'm sorry, I should just hang up."

"Jordyn, no, wait." Solomon giggled before he continued. "The Bathtub is a bar I occasionally frequent. It's a Speakeasy. I hadn't heard from you, so I decided to go out and have a drink and mingle with friends."

"Oh," was Jordyn's mono-syllabic retort.

"Bathtub is chill. You should come through. I think you'll like it."

"But I'm with my girls. I don't want to abandon them."

"Bring them. If they're anything like you, they'll find a way to have a good time."

"You going to come get me?" Jordyn put her cell on speaker.

"Where are you?" he asked.

"Still at the Benaroya."

"Cool."

"So you're on your way?"

"How many of you are there? Parking was a mess tonight."

"Three of us.

"Three's a safe number. I'll tell you what, if you walk, Bathtub is less than ten minutes away. So here's what we're going to do so we don't lose two hours looking for parking. You and your girls walk west to 1st Avenue then head north, and I'll leave here and head south. As long as you don't miss 1st Avenue, we'll see each other in about five minutes. Deal?"

Jordyn looked at Savannah and Shonne who shrugged their shoulders at her inquisitively. They were ready for some fun and her phone call was delaying their progress. She pressed the mute button and asked them, "You two good with a five minute walk to chill with Solomon and his friends?" After her friends both expressed their eager concurrence, Jordyn took Solomon off mute and said, "Deal, Doctor Alexandré. 1st Avenue in five minutes; and you are giving us a ride back to our hotel afterwards."

After the call, Savannah, Jordyn and Shonne, another pageant winner, strolled arm-in-arm on Union Street headed west. Savannah pulled brownies from her knapsack and handed one to each of her friends. "A little something extra to get the party started right. Go ahead, I made them myself." she said, stuffing a brownie in her own mouth to ensure her girls that they were safe.

The extended–stay rooms at the Kimpton Monaco Hotel were furnished with full kitchens. Thursday night while out at a party with Shonne and another friend from the pageant, Savannah bought an ounce of marijuana labeled Howling Hyena that her friend swore would have her cruising smoother than a Bentley. Before she went to bed that night, she chopped up the weed and baked it into brownies in her hotel room. Since Friday was the last night of the pageant and the hotel was smoke-free, she figured the cannabis infused dessert would make for a great post-pageant celebration for her and her girls.

Since the tainted brownie didn't kill Savannah immediately, Jordyn and Shonne followed suit and tasted theirs. By the time they met Solomon, all three woman had each consumed two brownies. As they covered the half mile from the Benaroya to the club in a basement of a hotel Solomon said was called the Bathtub Gin & Co, Jordyn's friends minded her business.

"Okay slut," that was Savannah. "Now that Miss Washington is over, let's get back to you staying out all night and half the morning."

Shonne turned to Savannah and asked, "Ooooh, what I miss?"

"Vannah is trippin' because I didn't answer my phone last night, and apparently she's not satisfied with me telling her that the reason I didn't answer was because Solomon and I were deep in conversation."

"Since when did a *deep conversation*," Savannah made air quotes with her fingers, "require condoms?"

Shonne ooohhed again, and Jordyn laughed.

In the bathroom of the Benaroya Hall Thursday afternoon, Savannah had asked Jordyn to borrow her lipstick and Jordyn, forgetting about the condoms, had told her to get it from her purse.

She had a headache when they returned from the photo shoot at the zoo, so before going to lie down, she stopped by the hotel pharmacy. Her stated purpose was to buy aspirin and a couple other toiletries, but the first thing she went for when she got there were the condoms. She had a strong inkling that if Solomon played his cards right, she was gonna want to screw his brains out that night and she wanted to be prepared just in case he wasn't. She had liked the idea that he would not be prepared. Solomon had shared very little about his relationships, simply stating 'I don't have anyone special'. He did however tell her that he wasn't sleeping with anybody. And *if that is true,* she thought, *why would he have condoms?* And Jordyn would've felt some kind of way if he had presumptively bought some just for her. Nothing turned her off quicker than a man who expected her to put out. She had thought about leaving them in her hotel room instead of putting them in her purse, but she knew better. They had dinner plans at his house Thursday night and although she wasn't so sure about his spontaneity, she knew herself. If he said and did the right things, and they got caught in bad traffic and couldn't make it to his house, what's to say that she wouldn't have him pull the car off the road and put the top down so they could do it under the stars; or in a park up against a tree. If the feeling hit her and it felt right, she could be unconstrained like that.

"So just because a woman has prophylactics in her purse, doesn't mean she used them," Jordyn spouted in her own defense.

"True," Shonne cosigned. "But if you did use them, was the bait you mastered, a really good, all night Friend U Can Keep?" this time Shonne did the fingers quote thing, then said, "or simply a Minute Man?"

Jordyn furled her brow at Shonne's question. "I don't get it, Shonne?"

"Read between the lines, Hunny. I'm trying not to be crass."

"I got nothing, Shonne."

"Damn, Jordyn. Do I really have to spell it out for you?"

"Yes, Shonne. I don't know what the hell you're talking about."

"Hell with all that," Savannah interrupted, "if that's the same purse you had last night, let me see those pristine, unused Trojans?"

"Go to hell, Vannah," Jordyn snapped with a smirk.

"That's where you're going, you hoochie mama. You ought to be ashamed giving it up already." Savannah was irritated. "And Shonne's anagram is asking if you just gave him head, or did you smash? And if you smashed was it good or did he cum quick?"

Shonne chided. "And were they Magnums or just Trojans?"

"Ha Ha," Jordyn laughed at Shonne then deflected back to Savannah. "It's not *already*? I've known him since last year."

"No, you met him last year...in November...now it's April and this is the first time you've seen him since. That qualifies as *already*."

"The hell with all that;" Shonne interrupted. "So what if you gave him some, I want to know if it was good?"

Jordyn smiled so hard she thought her face would tear. "TREMENDOUS!"

"Tremendous?" Shonne challenged. "I'm going to need a little more definition than that. So are we talking like Clydesdale tremendous? Energizer bunny tremendous? Or, let you be in charge and rock his world tremendous?"

Jordyn laughed out loud at the mental images Shonne's words left behind. "I'm not some kind of perverted control freak. I don't have to always be in charge. I can be...submissive," she chuckled at the choice of words she knew weren't true. "The entire night was tremendous. I'm talking homecooked meal, smoking hand-rolled blunts in his cigar parlor, hundred dollar bottle of wine, gorgeous bedroom with a skyline view, king-size bed with 1000-thread count sheets, made me cum, then spooned and talked to me until I fell asleep in his arms...kind of TREMENDOUS."

The three women shot glances between each other absorbing Jordyn's words and starting to feel the effects of the brownies. "Soooo, are we confirming Clydesdale or Energizer Bunny?" Shonne asked, still confused by the context of her last statement.

Jordyn stared straight ahead and recognized Solomon's silhouette more than a block away. She thought to check her watch, but knew she wasn't wearing one, and he was close enough for her to see him, and their condom conversation had easily consumed more than five minutes, so she was good with him coming to rescue her from Savannah's Seattle Inquisition. "Like I said Vannah, the conversation and everything that went with it was tremendous! I'm a lady," she drew out her words, "And a lady doesn't kiss and tell."

"It ain't the kissing I want to hear about," Savannah countered.

Jordyn waved as Solomon approached.

Shonne sized him up and said, "Unhh, you may not, but I'll tell you what tremendous things that man right there can do to me!"

The women laughed out loud as Solomon stopped before them. He looked at Jordyn hoping to learn what was so funny, but when she didn't offer anything, he said, "Now I know her," he opened his arms to hug Savannah then said, "but who is this?" after Savannah released him.

Before Jordyn could introduce her, Shonne grabbed Solomon's right hand in both of hers. "I'm Shonne, but you can call me Shonne, or anything else you desire you beautiful man you!" Shonne was a slim, small-chested woman with big round eyes who rocked a super-short haircut. Her delicate skin looked dewy and flushed as if she were near tears. But she was not a crier.

"Down girl," Savannah chided, "Don't scare him off before he feeds us and buys us drinks."

"What?" Shonne feigned confusion. "I was just introducing myself to the fine gentleman."

Jordyn and Savanah exchanged knowing smirks. The quartet

laughed before Solomon offered Jordyn his arm. Savannah slid in before Jordyn could accept the proffered arm and Shonne grabbed ahold of him from the other side.

"Here Jordyn," Savannah offered her elbow. "You can escort me."

At the speakeasy, a short, Filipino bouncer with jet black hair and black eyes that looked like sparkling jewels had the whitest, most perfect teeth she had ever seen. Blocking the entrance, he looked like a miniature version of the wrestler The Rock in his black-and-white, two-sizes-too-small *Brahma Bull blood, sweat, respect* T-shirt. Solomon showed him a bracelet and he let them pass without objection. Inside, a three-piece band was playing on a small, raised platform, and two of the ten tables were unoccupied. Solomon nodded to the hostess who waved for them to follow.

As she turned and led Shonne and Savannah to his table, her blue hair shining bright under the clubs' soft florescent lights, Solomon took Jordyn's elbow and walked her toward the bar for drinks. To their right, they passed a dozen or so young men who all looked like models and were sitting, smoking, and whispering in small groups along the steps of a wide, oak staircase. Their glamour dazzled her. Small votive candles set among the banister rails of each step illuminated their faces. They all talked with their hands. Their bodies cut sharp profiles in tight t-shirts and tailored pants. Glittered faces. Mascaraed eyes. Tinted lips. Wet hair sculpted with gel. Clove cigarettes and strong cologne overwhelmed her.

Jordyn didn't go out much in Seattle, but she felt safe here with him. She was emotionally sated to be chilling on the low, in a remote location with her girls and her Seattle Boo away from the pageant people because she didn't want them seeing her getting faded. They were driving to Spokane on Saturday, but that would only last four hours before he dropped her off and checked into his hotel, but for now she was happy that he had asked her to come through.

With drinks in hand, he held her elbow until they passed the staircase and entered the main room of the Bathtub. The din of conversations rose and fell all around them. Most of the guests were speaking English, but she could discern a mingling of Filipino and Spanish. Jordyn tried to keep pace with her escort, but he kept getting pulled into conversations and was soon in a heated discussion about the senatorial run-off election with an architect from Everett. On his arm, but feeling left alone, she tried to introduce herself to three women speaking French and wearing identical outfits, but all three ignored her as they strained to only show interest in the man with the French accent who was trying to describe to them how he'd just signed a deal to design a limited edition line of Turkish chapeaus.

At their table, six appetizers arrived, interrupting the quartet's conversation about sports, their favorite teams and their favorite players. From the context of the meal's discussion, Shonne was 29; Jordyn and Savannah were both 27. They had already discussed what schools they attended and their majors. Jordyn shared some of her childhood endeavors, expressing how fond she was of having spent most of her summer's on her uncle's farm in Windsor, Idaho.

Jordyn bragged about her Zags beating his Cougars in basketball seven of the nine times they'd played during his college years. He challenged all three women to extend their boundaries and come explore *the big city*, as Jordyn had called it earlier. They promised to visit again, then questioned him about his conference the following week, where he lived in Seattle, and what he'd take them to do the next time they visited. Of all the facts that were revealed throughout their ramblings and endless banter, two stood out to Solomon. The first and most interesting was that not only did Jordyn and Shonne share the same birthday, two years apart, but they were the same age when they each won the title of Miss Washington State, and they both finished as second runner-up in the Miss America pageant. The most depressing fact was that Solomon's wife had died of the same disease that killed Savannah's father.

The women kept returning to jokes about condoms and shared some others that they didn't expect him to follow because of their age difference, but he did. As a counter, he posed intellectual questions with erotic undertones. After three drinks, they seemed drunker than he thought they should've been, but he wasn't aware of the marijuana brownies they'd eaten beforehand, so he contributed their intense giddiness to being light drinkers and their huge appetites to not eating since long before the pageant started.

Jordyn asked, "What time should I expect you tomorrow?"

Savannah turned to Solomon and asked, "You're taking us to the train station? Well aren't you the perfect gentleman."

Solomon averted his gaze from Savannah to Jordyn. "I'm so sorry Solomon. In all that went on today, I forgot to tell Vannah that I was riding home with you instead of taking the train with her."

An awkward silence shrouded the table for a beat.

"Would somebody pass the potato skins?" That was Shonne.

"No worries," Solomon countered. "If I drive the Audi, there will be more than enough room for all of us."

"And I'll still be riding Solo back to Olympia," Shonne said taking a second bite of her smothered potato.

"No Jordyn, you two go and enjoy your road trip. I have my computer, and I can use the time to work on my masters' thesis."

Jordyn was embarrassed that she'd made plans with Solomon, abandoned her friend for a man, and most importantly, had forgotten to tell Savannah for going on eight hours since she woke her up from her nap. The shame on her face was not half as terrible as the shame she felt. Savannah read the genuine hurt in Jordyn's eyes and said, don't worry about it, baby. The quart of Chunky Monkey ice cream you're going to buy me every Friday night for the next two months when we get home will put you on a good start to making up for it. Tears welled in Jordyn's eyes and the two women eyed each other wordlessly for a long moment before Shonne pointed to Solomon's plate and asked, "Are you going to eat that teriyaki chicken?"

Solomon picked up his chicken-on-a-stick, inserted the entire portion in his mouth then pulled it out and dropped the chicken on his plate. Laughter erupted when he looked Shonne in the eye and said, "Help yourself, babe."

And without a care or a concern, she did. When she was done stuffing her mouth with Solomon's saliva covered chicken, Savannah tapped Shonne with her left hand, pinched her right thumb and forefinger together then nodded toward the door.

Shonne correctly interpreted Savannah's meaning and said, "If you two love birds will excuse us, we're going to step out real quick and grab some fresh air."

"Take your time ladies," Jordyn said, "I'm not going anywhere."

Solo averted his eyes to Shonne and Savannah who were watching her in the periphery. They excused themselves and disappeared outside. A glint of solemnness in her eyes replaced the comedy that resided there before. "Not me and my girlfriends all night, Silly; just me. Can you handle that?"

Solomon smiled wide enough to brighten the dimly lit room.

The band returned from their break during Savannah and Shonne's absence. The first song they played was a cover of Jill Scott's *Long Walk*. There was only one couple on the dance floor when Solomon asked Jordyn to dance, so she happily accepted. Solomon twirled her and pulled her into his space where she fell into his arms like it was the softest place on earth. "I didn't expect to see you tonight," Solomon said. "I figured you'd be busy with the last night of the pageant, but I am glad you decided to come through."

"Pageant's over." Jordyn pressed her face deeper into her chest. "And I'm right where I want to be."

"I like your friends," he said. "That Shonne is a real character. But should I know something about all of the condom jokes?"

"No baby," Jordyn cooed, "Nothing for you to worry about

there." She sunk deeper into Solomon and offered no reply to his next two questions. Solomon stopped talking and slow-motioned her around the dance floor through the end of one song and then the next. As they danced, Jordyn reminisced about Thursday night and how the three pack of condoms came to no longer be in her purse. As the band covered Prince's *Scandalous,* she thought about how his eyes went to her breasts when she stripped to reveal her burgundy bra and panty set in the man cave. She realized that he thought she was braless, then giggled that he had been fooled by the shear silk of the bra.

Later, in the bedroom, she wanted to prove to him that she was unlike any of his previous lovers and that she was willing to pleasure him in every way he desired. She unbuckled his belt and ran her fingers back and forth along the skin under his waistline. She lifted his shirt, leaned her head down and pressed her lips against the skin of his stomach. He ran his hands through her hair as she placed her open mouth on the exposed skin of his stomach and tongued his belly button. Her prowess and rhythmic movements left him both breathless and speechless. She removed his pants, and although she couldn't remember when or how, he removed her underwear.

She reminisced at how the sex went on and on, all night long. How she cried out in joy while riding Solomon's undulating body, and how she begged for the pain of satisfaction. He had experienced her cries as some sort of inner ecstasy when she urged him to keep going, whispering that she had not felt this good, in a very long time.

During the refractory period after he had cleaned her and disposed of the first condom, she remembered laying on his chest and telling him how beautiful he was and how caring and gentle a lover he was.

In the dead of night, sometime well after midnight, Solomon took her out onto his bedroom balcony and made love to her. They sexed long and hard with that second condom under the cover of a new moon and the stars dotting clear skies. Barely able to contain herself, Jordyn was louder out there than she'd ever been before. The harder and faster he pushed into her, the louder she got. Deep into their throes of passion, they saw a light come on in a house across the way. They sat still when someone opened a curtain, then laughed and retreated into the dark, shadowy refuge of his bedroom.

Forty minutes later, she lay wrapped in his arms, staring at the clock. Jordyn was scared and confused. On the ferry ride, she told him that she was enjoying him, but she lied when she said she had no room in her life for a relationship. That their *Friends with Benefits,* or whatever they were doing, could be their guilty pleasure whenever their schedules permitted. The numbers on the clock changed as she laid still, listening to him breathe behind her.

Sometime later, she eased her body from underneath his arm and walked into the bathroom. She turned on the shower and stood in the mirror naked as the steam began to slowly fog. When the mirror was fully covered with steam, she twisted her hair in a sloppy ponytail and stepped into the shower. When he knocked and asked could he come in, she met him at the door, uncovered and soaking wet. He closed the door, gently lifted her by her waist, and softly loosened her ponytail as he walked her back into the shower until they were both drenched beneath the stream of hot water. She kissed him passionately while massaging his shoulders. "I thought you'd left me," he whispered between kisses. "Then I thought you being here was a dream."

"I'm not a dream baby, I'm right here."

He eased her against the wet shower wall and slowly pressed his weight into her. She accepted his weight and wrapped her legs around his waist. They kissed as the shower head rained hot water on them.

"Remember," she whispered as she shifted her hips to the perfect angle for him to enter her. "You said you wanted to go slow."

"Yes. Slow. I remember," as he softly kissed her neck. He entered her slowly, stroked her gently and murmured, "Friends with

Benefits."

She turned away from the water and breathlessly purred, "Slow."

Sex in the shower brought about their third set of orgasms. Afterwards, he dried her, kept his silk pajama bottoms and gave her the top. The radio serenaded them as they fell asleep entangled in each other's warmth.

Right before dawn, he lay lightly snoring as she snuggled against the back of him. There was nothing stopping her from a relationship with him. She felt the least bit guilty at the time, because after making love to him on consecutive nights in his house, she speculated on why she told that lie. She wanted to sleep, but her excitement about their road trip was barely containable. As much as she yearned for Saturday morning to come quickly, she didn't want that perfect moment of being awake and experiencing his restful sleep at the hands of her love making to ever end. For her, knowing that she wanted to watch every second of his slumber meant that actually achieving any measure of restful sleep was probably outside the realm of possibility. Jordyn inhaled his masculine scent, nuzzled her nose into the middle of his wide back and let her tears cascade down into his pillows until she fell asleep.

CHAPTER 15

AT TWELVE THIRTY SATURDAY AFTERNOON, Solomon arrived at the Kimpton Hotel Monaco. He'd slept alone for less than six hours before getting up at 9am, packing and then going into his office to gather his laptop and files for the conference.

Jordyn waited in the lobby with her pink-and-black, polka-dotted roller bag luggage. She wore jean shorts, flat thong sandals with faux diamonds on silver leather, a pink satin ball cap with matching pink and white scarf, Wayfarers and a powder blue T-shirt with a white and pink unicorn print. She greeted him with, "Now that's a road trip car!"

He'd driven his royal blue 1968 Ford Mustang Shelby GT 428 Police Interceptor. The mint condition, $118,000, V8-powered convertible sported an automatic transmission with rear-wheel drive, power steering, air conditioning, and satellite radio in the glove box. "Style, and speed. The only way to take a road trip." Dressed in jeans, a suede fiddler's cap and an SFD T-shirt, Solomon lifted her three bags into the trunk next to his two and they were on their way east, riding I-90 away from the overcast Seattle skyline toward Issaquah and ultimately Spokane.

When the sun broke through the clouds they were 29 miles east of Seattle and 250 miles from Spokane. Jordyn stopped singing, peeped over her shades and saw a sign for a road that led from their current unofficial middle of nowhere toward Mount Rainier. She pointed at the sign and, executing a poor imitation of Doctor King, said, "I've never beeennn to the mountain top."

He coughed a laugh, then attempted an equally poor imitation of the late martyr, "And talking crazy like that, you never will."

Jordyn wished his car was smaller so they could be closer. She slipped off her sandals and nervously asked, "Doctor Alexandré?"

"Yes?"

"Can I ask you something, at the risk of offending you?"

"You can ask me anything."

She asked, "Did you tell anyone you were going away with me?"

"I told my mom not to expect me for church on Sunday because I was heading up to Spokane for the weekend to hang out with friends. And of course my business partner knows I'll be at your alma mater all week."

"I didn't know this was a business trip. I thought we were going to hang out and chill while you were here?"

"We are," he said. "From now until noon on Monday you have my full attention. And if you're available in the evenings, I will be at your beck and call." Again, his eyes slipped down to her short shorts. "But as far as this weekend goes, I am just going to chill out and be a man in the company of a woman enjoying those things that a man does when in the company of a woman."

"Oh really?"

"Yes, really?" he said.

"Great," Jordyn beamed. "In that case, I have the whole weekend all planned out." She turned to face him, right leg folded on top of left, feet tucked under her butt. "Tonight we'll head out to the Casino for the dinner buffet then play blackjack. If it's not too late and you still have energy, *The Black Panthers: Vanguard of the Revolution* is playing at this single screen theatre I go to watch eclectic stuff. Most of the films they show turn out to be really interesting. And after that, we can critique the film while we walk the promenade holding hands before we spend the night kissing. If the *Black Panthers* isn't your thing, we can eat shrimp and crabs at Terrapin and take in the blues show.

Jordyn sat practically bouncing in her seat. "And then tomorrow we can order pancakes, lay around in our jammies and watch movies until we have to get dressed for the gala. But if you absolutely want to get up, we can grab a café at the Union and I'll give you a proper tour of the entire campus. This weekend is going to be absolutely perfect." She was ecstatic that she and her *Friend with Benefits* were taking a trip together. This weekend would be their first time spending both days and nights together. She saw them showering together. She saw them sharing her bed. And best of all, she saw them not rushing off to some other commitment—at least for the next 48 hours.

When the familiar sound of a stomach rumbling filled the car, Solomon peeked at the beauty queen, who blushed and kept staring out the window. A half mile later, she cleared her throat. "Maybe it's time for a quick pit stop? Not long. Just enough to, you know…fill the tank."

"And I'm sure both of us could benefit from some food." Solomon turned his head to throw a smile her way but jerked his head back toward the front of the car when something caught his eye. Without warning, he slammed on the brakes. Jordyn was thrown forward into the restraint of her seatbelt as Solomon's behemoth came to a screeching, sliding halt.

"Are you alright?" Solomon reached to her frantically.

"Yes, I think so," she said between heavy breaths.

When they looked past the car they'd almost rear-ended, they saw the beginnings of a traffic jam that seemed to stretch for miles. Right before where the cars stopped moving, Solomon saw the sign for a roadside travel center and decided to pull off. "Yeah, lunch sounds like a great idea right about now."

"Exactly," Jordyn agreed.

"And I might need to check my shorts."

Despite the near tragic event, Jordyn exploded with laughter when she caught the joke.

The travel center cashier explained that the traffic jam was leading to the concert at The Gorge. Jordyn looked up the event on her cell phone, saw that one of her favorite bands was playing that night and asked Solomon if they could stop. Since his only firm commitment was on Monday at noon and they were on the back side of their trip east, he agreed. Jordyn bought tickets on her phone while Solomon paid for their snacks and drinks, then they were on their way to their detour destination, the Gorge Amphitheater.

The energy in the place was indelible. No rain, no lightning, just dirt, three bands, ten-thousand energetic people, and madness.

Jordyn gyrated to the music from the moment they arrived. They found a spot on the hill exiting stage right and spread the blankets he'd bought at the travel station because his car wouldn't hold lawn chairs. Jordyn fangirled—and totally lost her mind her for favorite artist, Colbie Caillat—but nothing compared to her excitement when Sam Hunt took the stage after Gone West.

A lifelong Washingtonian, Solomon had been to a couple of concerts in the decade after graduating high school but he couldn't recall ever hearing anything about The Gorge,. He couldn't relate to her level of excitement, but he appreciated her enthusiasm, and after observing the beauty from Spokane's apparent out of body experience, he couldn't wait to attend another Gorge event.

The former beauty queen ten years his junior joined Gorge partygoers and danced nonstop near and around Solomon until the music stopped just after eleven. He enjoyed her youthful exuberance, but he'd never seen anyone exert so much energy in a dance. An energy that she'd carry to the bedroom later when they made love.

Midnight was twenty-four minutes in front of them when they arrived at The Cave B Inn. They'd reserved a cabin near Sagecliffe for after the concert, knowing that a two-hour drive separated them from Spokane. He parked the Interceptor, grabbed their smallest bags and she followed him, still singing and dancing her way down an arcing path past a dozen cabins identical to theirs—cabin number 24.

Moonlight streamed through the floor-to-ceiling bay window situated on the back of the cabin to offer occupants complete privacy. Enough light that they didn't bump into anything, but opaque enough that it blurred dimensions offered by the sharp clarity of manufactured bulbs. When the morning sun rose, they'd learn that the powder-colored roofs were translucent to enhance cabin illumination. The interior cabin decor was minimalistic and there were no apparent wall switches that he could find to turn on a light. At first glance it could have been mistaken for the bedroom of a camper or survivalist. Solomon used his cell phone flashlight to find the red, white and black candles lined up across the timber sticking out above the bed as a headboard. Once lit, their flames licked toward the ceiling and illuminated a table lamp on the far side of the bed. When Solomon turned on the electric light, he noticed a bistro table with two cushioned chairs by the window. A queen-sized bed and a cherry wood armoire completed the furnishings.

Jordyn danced around the room before tossing her polka-dot bag onto the bed. "I need a shower." Her hips and shoulders never stopped moving as she pulled out a negligee and her toiletry bag, then turned toward the bathroom. "I'd invite you to join me, but I'm tired and I won't be in there long." And she wasn't. Within ten minutes of shutting the bathroom door, Jordyn emerged freshly showered, smelling of lilac and jasmine in her panties and negligee, her damp hair pulled into a loose ponytail. Still gyrating from the energy of the concert, she sang, "Bathroom's all yours."

When Solomon emerged from the bathroom ten minutes later, Jordyn sat straddling one of the cushioned chairs in front of the massive bay window, arms crossed, elbows resting on the chair. She had turned off the electric lamp, but left the candles burning. She'd placed their remaining snacks on the table and was sipping on a bottle of lemonade. "Better?" she asked, still admiring the midnight view.

"Tons," Solomon replied.

"Good, then join me." Jordyn stood and offered Solomon, a bottle of water before she walked to the window. The wide-open curtains allowed a brilliant view of the darkness below and the clear sky above. When Solomon approached her, she reached back and pulled his arms around her middle.

Cabins at the Cave B Inn were situated high enough up on the cliffs to overlook both the Gorge and the Columbia River. Mirrored windows prevented outsiders from seeing in. Unless you were right up against the inside of the window, your view from the cabin was limited to sky and hilltops, but nothing below.

Solomon turned her to face him, cocked his head and stared deep into those forever beautiful blue eyes. His facial expression should not have surprised her but it did. Because even though she knew she liked him, it seemed impossible until that moment that he was liking her too. He raised his hand to her lips. Touched her like a child touching a stranger's face. He wanted to translate what was happening between them to his fingertips, make sure he could trust what he was feeling by taking her in through his hands. *Are you a kind person?* His fingers moved across her cheeks and she closed her eyes; he was like a blind man creating her for himself. A simultaneous smile broke the trance and Jordyn gave him her back.

For almost ten minutes, Jordyn excitedly reaffirmed how much she enjoyed the concert. When she moved his hands to hold her this time, he lifted the hem of her negligee and rested his hands inside the waistband of her panties, exposing her panties to the window. A spark of heat ignited, then grew in her in widening circles when he started fidgeting his fingertips.

"Don't start something you won't finish." Their eyes met in the reflection.

He said, "Yeah, people shouldn't start things they can't finish."

"Yeah, I just hate that."

"Yeah, hate not being able to finish THAT right about now."

Jordyn responded, "For real though."

Kissing the back of her head, he said, "Damn, you're gorgeous."

After she finished his water bottle, Jordyn turned to face him, leaned her weight into him and eased him back toward the chair. The Miss America finalist purred in a new voice, "Let's take our time tonight." She stared with those bright, splendid blue eyes, and admired him topless. His good natured smile, his broad chest and strong arms had her melting in anticipation of being held. She'd experienced his gentle hands so she knew they felt just right against her skin. Her anticipation lay in the feeling of the rest of him.

Just when he was about to speak, she pushed him onto the chair. In the next motion, she straddled him, not in a seductive lap dance kind of way, but in a tender, sensual way. Although seated, Jordyn stretched up onto the balls of her feet. Something about that position made her feel sexy, like when she wore her stiletto heels. Then she leaned in and kissed him gently.

For the next two minutes, they tasted each other's lips, tongues and necks like they were forbidden fruit on a deserted island. Kissed each other as if they were the oxygen that was keeping the other alive. In the short breaths between kisses, they watched each other in the fantastic mixture of candlelight and moonlight and smiled like juvenile co-conspirators. When their desire outweighed the joy of sight, they kissed for another five minutes.

For the first time, Solomon saw how the face of a stranger becomes the face of a lover. He lowered his face and kissed her on the curve of her neck. He made a circle with his tongue on her neck and Jordyn swallowed her breath. A hot wave of lust rippled through her, filled her with a long since visited sensation. He kissed her breast through her negligee. When he tried to remove it, she stopped him with a shy grunt. He obeyed and kissed her breast through the soft material. Her nipples tightened, rose and showed their appreciation for his obedience. Made her realize how she longed for a man kiss her softly without wanting to immediately enter her. That latent heat of passion…that…fire within her, was finally truly ignited.

She seemed tentative and tremulous. When their eyes met again, empathy erased any skepticism she may have harbored. She exhaled deeply and said, "Kiss me. Please." It felt like a dream to her as he kissed his lips up her cheek, found her mouth, cupped her chin in his gentle hands and gave her a powerful kiss that made her whole body shake. She submitted and pressed her middle into his.

Everything in him from his heights and depths to his tragedies came rushing together like a great flood barely channeled in a narrow mountain stream. And it chilled him. Roared in him like an icy river. And he shook with a violence that exuded a powerful energy.

An energy that flowed through Jordyn. As the passion of their heat grew, she pressed her lap into his sex stiffening against her thigh. A bead of sweat formed on her neck and tickled as it trickled down her spine. She squeezed her thighs tight around his legs to hold him close. A moment before she thought she'd pass out; Jordyn broke the kiss. She inhaled deeply, trying to maintain control, panting long, hard breaths in and out for a time she couldn't measure. She felt him shift his hands until her butt was seated in the palms of his hands and he gently pulled her pelvis flush with his. She rubbed up and down his arms, then across his shoulders, then inward and down across his broad chest before finally coming to a stop on his firm abs. He didn't quite have a six-pack but there was enough definition to remind her that he was all man. She leaned in close and ran her hands around his sides to the bare skin on his back. She wanted this guilty pleasure to last for every piece of time that they could allow to hold on to. She took a deep breath then sucked hard on the sweetness of his neck like it was a honey-dipped strawberry.

She breathed, "Make love to me, Solomon," and tried to stand.

While both hands held her firmly against him, eight fingers slipped inside her panties and massaged her butt while two strong thumbs applied gentle pressure to the inside of her hips. Solomon's handsome mouth opened and closed on his lover's body.

"Please Solomon," she begged.

Despite his best efforts to remain stoic, she noticed a slight smile creep onto his lips. "You're funny," he answered, flashing a full smile.

"You heard me Mister Spokane Virgin, I need it good like the lady in Monster's Ball! Can you do that for me?"

"Yes," he groaned, then released the pressure on her hips. He pinched her satin panties. Pulled them down and off as he allowed her to stand up and out of them.

Jordyn pulled back the sheets closest to the window and retreated to the center of the queen-size bed, allowing sufficient room for him. In some marvelous way for her, this moment in this bed obliterated a sea of doubt, regret, introduced a beautiful yielding. Tonight she was yielding to a lover who had not betrayed her.

Solomon crossed the room and sat on the bed. He saw the faint smile on her lips. The terrifying innocence residing in her face. That look, in that moment, would remain with him forever.

They locked arms then drew into another kiss. That guilty pleasure took them to the pillows, her mane sprawled across her shoulders framing her face. He grew against her. She bit her bottom lip, squirmed until he was in the right spot and moved against that growth. They loosened their hold on each other, allowed their hands to join the symphony of their kissing mouths and orchestrate the sounds of sweet, passive intimacy.

He eased kisses down her stomach to the ring in her belly button. He would have gone lower but she pulled him back to her and kissed him. Another blistering kiss and everything became... ethereal...

haunting. Heavy breathing created evocative sounds. She rubbed his head, his shoulders, his back. Her heartbeat moved from her chest, down her stomach and into her lap. That steady rhythm causing warm waves of wetness to flow. She took his hand, moved it between her thighs, met his gaze and whispered, "Good like the lady in Monster's Ball!"

He pushed her legs opened as wide as he could. Strummed that magical button, his thumb playing her like she was a one-key piano. Sent her to a wonderful place with no issues. A place where she had no hardships. No overdue rent. A place where reservations and constraints didn't exist. A place free from worry about abusive former lovers.

She licked her lips. Squeezed her own breasts before he grabbed her hand, then squeezed one nipple and rubbed his bald head with the palm of her other hand. Pushed his head down to where his hand imitated Donald Shirley, her hips dancing to their own rhythm.

His tongue replaced his thumb and gave her good head. A moment later, she lost control. He paused. Backed away. Stared, watched her tremble, watched her try to regain control. Hovered over her as she fought to catch her breath.

When her writhing slowed, she moved her hands up his arms, over his shoulders and chest, down his strong back and wrapped her hands around his waist then pressed his hips onto hers. She kissed him hungrily as he sank his sex into hers. She gasped. Shifted. Accepted his weight and let him find his rhythm.

She shifted until that rhythm caused her to dance. Sent her back to that promenade where he'd first laid eyes on her. Closed her eyes and let the memory of reggae wind her into a frenzy. Held her arms around the doctor from the big city and made love to him like they were the only two people in their own tropical paradise.

They labored together for a long time, slowly, violently, both dreading the end of a love making session that would leave the two of them spent and refreshed. She came first. An intense rhythmic orgasm like she'd never felt before. Through it he slowed his pace, allowed her to ride that wave from Spokane to Seattle and back. When her tide had ebbed, his flow sped up. Stirred her until she rolled him over and rode him to his own finish line. Made him shiver and shake like he was on a bed of hot ice. Took all of his energy and gave some of hers in return. Remained in his arms and accompanied the arrival of her second orgasm before collapsing on top of him.

She had flipped him and he had flipped her so many times that even though she knew they weren't moving, she was flying so high that she didn't quite know if she was lying on the bed or floating on the ceiling. "We are a mess," she cried, showering his chest and neck with a flurry of wet nibbles and soft kisses.

For the next half-hour they would lie in the haven of that bed talking, giggling, kissing and experiencing the foreplay that should've happened before the sex. She didn't bother to cover herself when she got up, glided across the room and disappeared into the bathroom. Guiltlessly he watched her—more round than wide—high booty and strong, slender thighs. Thighs honed by miles of running that tapered to taut, well-defined calves.

When she returned, they talked, laughed and made love twice more, then showered. After the shower they ate their sandwiches and talked until almost three. Both feared the morning. That time when the moon and stars would be gone. When the room would be harsh and sorrowful with sunlight. And the bed would be dismantled, waiting for more of the flesh to be absorbed in it. How long would this night have to last them? What would the morning bring? The imminent morning, behind which were hidden so many unknown mornings. So many lonely nights.

"Tell me something sweet, Solomon."

He thought for a moment then whispered in her ear, "The world may think you're pretty on the outside, but I know your true beauty resides in your gorgeous spirit."

Exhausted, sated and riding an endorphin high that few people ever experienced, Jordyn laid atop the bedspread, joined him beneath a throw blanket taken from the settee and fell asleep in his arms

CHAPTER 16

THE TRANSLUCENT CEILING FILLED THE quaint cabin with daylight Sunday morning. Jordyn blinked herself awake just before ten, stretched and yawned, but did not move any more until he awoke. Solomon awakened minutes later. The surprise in his eyes showed no memory of her being there. In no hurry to leave his bed, she kissed his cheek then squirmed beneath the covers to offer him a good morning.

The landscape shifted as they drove away from The Gorge. Despite the exuberance of their love-making the night before, they found themselves quiet with the new day. The palm of her left hand rested in Solomon's lap as he silently listened to his music. Jordyn focused on the landscape, thinking that she saw movement in the hills as the valley widened and the trees thickened into an overwhelming fortress of towering Redwoods. She searched for a few minutes unable to identify what she thought she saw. She didn't see anything, but that didn't mean there wasn't anything out there. There was always wildlife, big and small, moving through the Washington forests.

Solomon broke her concentration when he asked, "So what interesting things do you have on your after work calendar this week?"

"Nothing serious," she replied. "What do you have in mind?"

Friday afternoon while Jordyn slept off Thursday night, Solomon used the time to research restaurants, theaters, and popular places to go and things to do. "Well, when my Friday afternoon client canceled, I used that free time to see what touristy things I could get into in Spokane to help rid me of my infamous *Spokane Virgin* status. I never schedule anything for the first day of the conference, so I bought us tickets for a couple of interesting looking things to do Tuesday through Thursday after work. I figured that if you don't mind squeezing me in, you could be my tour guide and teach me as much about Spokane as a week would allow."

Jordyn laid her head back and asked, "And what fascinating adventures did your research yield?"

"Did you know there's a black cowboy film festival playing this week. Tuesday night is a film based on the tale of the Rufus Buck Gang, Wednesday night Denzel stars in a remake of *The Magnificent Seven*, and on Thursday, Danny Glover stars in *Buffalo Soldiers*."

"Well to be honest, I recall the name Buffalo Soldiers from one of my history classes, and everybody has heard of Denzel, but I haven't heard of any of those movies. But if you want to go, I'm game."

"Well, Denzel and Danny movies are always going to be playing somewhere, so how about we do the Rufus Buck thing on Tuesday."

"That works. There's normally a Poetry Slam on Wednesday night, and I can give you my personal tour of the GU campus."

"I can work with that, but since I run to the campus every morning, then shower and change there for my conference, can we just meet on campus Wednesday?"

"No problem." Jordyn slipped off her sandals and propped her feet on the dashboard. "And after the poetry slam, we can walk the waterfront and ride the Ferris wheel. The view from the wheel at sunset is so beautiful."

"And maybe dinner at Bruggino's. My host professor told me their Italian wild mushroom and gnocchi dish is to die for. And they pair it with a five year old Sangiovese. I can't wait to taste it."

"Sounds like a plan. So what about Thursday?"

"Thursday's easy. My buddy Kenny got me two tickets to Bumbershoots. He said Outkast will be there as part of a small venue tour. Do you like Outkast?"

"I love Big Boi," she returned. "Andre 3000 not so much. I can hear his words, but I can't always grasp the innuendo in his lyrics. Will there be dancing?"

"I don't know. I'll call Monday and find out about a dance floor."

"If there's a dance floor, then count me in."

"Who sounds like the Spokane Virgin now?"

"Oh no Mister. Not knowing the layout of one club, does not make me a virgin. I'm Spokane born and bred, and don't you ever forget it."

Solomon guffawed at her mini-rant. "Well I guess you told me, Miss Spokane Born and Bred." He loved how animated she could be before instantly dropping back into a calm demeanor. That bipolar switch-on/switch-off thing that really dramatic actors did before annoyingly ending with the words 'and scene'. *Maybe she minored in Theater and just hasn't told me yet*, he thought. "Dinner and Outkast at Bumbershoots it is."

"And that just leaves Friday?"

"Well, Conference ends Friday at noon. I figured with good traffic, I could be home by dinner."

"And abandon me for the weekend?"

"Not abandoning you, just trying not to be on the road too late Friday night. Besides, you have me all to yourself this weekend."

"So why should next weekend be any different?"

"Because I pushed this weekend's plans to next weekend when I agreed to join you this weekend and be your dinner date."

With that, Jordyn dropped her feet to the floor, shifted her hips so her back faced Solomon and returned to gazing out the window.

Solomon asked *What's wrong* and *Are you alright* several times.

When she didn't answer after the fourth try, he turned the radio up.

The lack of conversation, and the mellow jazz in concert with the soothing symphony of tires humming on asphalt lulled her to sleep. An hour later, squalls of wind-driven rain intermittently pelted the car. When she opened her eyes, she yawned, "Where are we?"

"Hello there Sleeping Beauty." They were less than hour west of Spokane on a tract of two-lane freeway where cars normally did at least ninety miles per hour in the slow lane. A stretch of road where bladders filled to the brim before finding sanctuary; gas stations were at the fill-up-here-or-go-empty mile-marker, and signs said BEWARE because moose and reindeer ran rough shot over that part of the state's terrain. "Have a good nap?"

Jordyn sat up and rubbed at her face, blinking hard and shaking herself to full wakefulness. "Why'd you let me sleep so long?" She shifted to peer out the window. They were gliding through a forest she didn't recognize. As she continued to gain her bearings, she noticed brutal storm clouds blowing in from the north.

"You needed it. You were up late last night."

"Thanks to you," she blushed.

He chuckled.

"Traffic was light, my music was good and we were making good time so I figured it wouldn't hurt." Lightning strikes illuminated the sky with the brilliance of a holiday fireworks show. Southwest of Spokane, they took the State Route 904 exit toward Cheney. Before they could reach the travel station at Tyler, a torrential squall of rain and hail pelted the windshield rendering the wipers virtually useless, but Solomon still managed to land a parking spot without a scratch.

With no place to be until six, they waited out the storm inside the travel station. While Solomon used the restroom, Jordyn ordered two drinks and a platter of nachos.

"Have you always liked old cars?" she asked when he returned.

"I've always loved old and fancy cars. Especially those that cost as much as some houses."

"Always?"

"Well, at least as far back as I can remember. My mom was a big fan of cops and robbers shows when I was a kid and they always had cool cars that no matter how fast the bad guy drove, the tough detective's car was always faster. That, and I loved the real fancy cars that the bad guys and cool cats in the Blaxploitation movies drove."

"So I just heard you say that you secretly want to either be a bad boy, a cop or a pimp?"

"None of the above," Solomon laughed. "All of them eventually get shot. I don't really care for guns too much."

"But you love fast and fancy cars?"

"Yes I do."

"Since the one outside qualifies as fast, and you've chauffeured me around Seattle in your Audi, does that mean you have a pimp car?"

Solomon pulled his cell phone from his pocket, pressed a couple of icons and opened his picture gallery. "When I have the time, I enter them in car shows." He handed the phone to Jordyn. Their road trip vehicle, the Shelby GT Interceptor, was the first of three antique cars in his collection. The second car was a hugger orange 1974 Ford Gran Torino he found at the Lake City Summer Festival vintage car show and had restored. It had a supple white leather interior and a white vinyl convertible rooftop. White, hockey-stick shaped side stripes ran along the door handles to the front bumper and across the hood, outlining the grill.

"Now that's what I'm talking about," she beamed when she saw his 1938 Avion Voisin C28 Cabriolet Saliot. He named it Fay Francis, in honor of his grandmother. "That's the kind of car that impresses a girl when you pick her up for a date!"

"That exquisite automobile only comes out of the garage to grace the streets of Seattle with its beauty when the chance of rain is zero."

"Where did you get it?"

"I won her in a poker game."

"Really? You play high stakes poker?"

"The game didn't start out high stakes, but egos and alcohol pushed it to that level. It was getting late, and I mean well after midnight, and there were only two of us left in the hand. I was sitting on a Hearts Flush, and two aces had been discarded. I would say I was feeling confident, but the alcohol and my cards had me outright cocky. Dude went all in with his chips, and to cover, I dropped my Rolex in the till. Dude wanted to call my bet but was out of chips so his drunk ass was foolish enough to put the pink slip for that beauty on the table."

"And you won."

"And I won."

"I'll drink to that." Jordyn raised her glass of ginger beer soda and they clinked glasses. "Cheers."

"And I stopped gambling after that," he said laughing. "The only poker I've played since is no-stakes poker with my boys at Woody's."

Solomon returned with two ice cream cones. One chocolate and one vanilla. "I didn't know which flavor you preferred."

"I think I'm in the mood for some chocolate on my lips." She flicked her tongue as she accepted the cone. "Too bad they don't have dark chocolate." As intended, she made Solomon blush. "FYI, my fav is Ben & Jerry's Boom Chocolatta."

The clouds cleared, the rain stopped, and just like God promised Noah, a rainbow appeared. It was the brightest, most beautiful rainbow he'd ever seen, but unlike normal rainbows, this rainbow didn't arc from one unknown point to the other, formed a colorful halo around the mountain. Just then, he knew a God existed. A God's existence he doubted when his wife died.

Jordyn wanted to be sexy for Solomon, so she changed into jean shorts before they left the road stop. She asked him to let down the roof; allow the sun to *provide some vitamin D* were her words. Her sunglasses were on, sandals were off and right foot was on the dash. Her head and her seat were all the way back, her left leg folded Indian style, splayed enough to give her pilot a glimpse of her Paradise as he drove toward what felt like their honeymoon destination.

Struggling to keep his eyes on the windy, two-lane State Road connecting Tyler to South Spokane, Solomon chanced a quick sideways glance. A glance that lasted a beat longer than he expected once he saw the hem of her Daisy Duke shorts exposing hips thick and sweet like honey, and the opening to the valley of her ecstasy.

Jordyn smiled and laughed and flirted over the music as they passed another fifty more miles of forest in the final hour of their road trip. She drew quiet as they breached the horizon and thoughts of life in Spokane entered her mind. She had always played life safe. Never taken any risks. That was before she chose to drive across state with a man she barely knew. A man she'd only been on one official date with. A man she bedded twice in a week on the other side of the state.

She'd taken a taxi to the train station; left her car parked in front of her home. If she'd gone missing, nobody other than Savannah would have a clue where to start looking for her. Jordyn's cellular rang. The caller ID showed it was her girlfriend, Melanie Crawford, calling. She had called Jordyn a dozen times since she'd left for the pageant. They'd planned for Mel to take her to the train station and pick her up. They had argued before she left so Jordyn took a taxi. Now, seven days later, the two women still hadn't spoken. *What were we arguing over?* Jordyn couldn't exactly remember at the moment. She rejected the call. She'd call her, but after her time with Solomon.

Jordyn reached for Solomon's right hand, put his fingers between her legs at the edge of her short shorts, dropped her right leg and closed her legs around them for a moment so he could feel her heat.

With the Spokane Valley thirty minutes ahead, he wasn't quite *doing 15 in a 30*, but he wasn't *in no hurry*, he was moving *slowww—just as fast as he could*. His fingers fought against the tautness of her thighs in search of her spot. He eased when she resisted, pressed forward toward her valley when she relaxed. Learned how to touch her the way she wanted to be touched.

As they twisted northeast along the 904 back road at a forty mile an hour pace, he rubbed her heat. Eyes closed, right foot out the window, left foot on the dashboard, the beauty queen twisted her necklace and shifted in her seat to accept his touch. The jeweled star on her necklace dancing like a puppet on marionette strings. "Take me home, Doctor Alexandré," she sing-songed. "Take me home."

~

Solomon's GPS read that they were five miles from her house when Jordyn asked him to stop by her pharmacy. Just over a mile from her house, they walked past a parked car with its engine running. Music blared behind darkly tinted windows where the driver sat smoking a blunt while a woman orally pleasured him.

The driver from the parked car recognized Jordyn. He approached them on the sidewalk with a woman by his side when they exited the pharmacy. He gave Solomon a fake 'Whassup' before attempting to give Jordyn a hug then scowled when she balked it off.

"I'm sorry to hear about your dad passing, Greg." The woman glared when Jordyn placed a hand on Greg's forearm. Jordyn and Greg had graduated a year apart from the same high school. They were not friends, but they were familiar through mutual friends, and their parents attended the same church. "Let me know if I can do anything."

Misinterpreting the intention in Jordyn's tone, the woman with Greg reached over and pushed her away. "You better back down before you get slapped down, Tramp."

Jordyn snapped, "Don't trip, Ho. Nobody wants him like that."

The woman jumped straight into ratchet girl mode. "You don't know me Tramp, I'll snatch a knot in your ass right here!"

Greg grabbed her as Solomon stepped in between the ladies.

"Whatever, Trick. I'm right here." Jordyn shouted and cussed as Solomon refused to let her go so she could fight.

"Let her go. I'll whoop that ass!" The woman continued her verbal assault as Greg pushed her into the car then pulled out his cell phone and made a call.

~

Jordyn's sidewalk confrontation filled her with an energy she needed to burn. Still worked up when they arrived at her house just after two o'clock that afternoon, she pressed Solomon against the inside of her front door. Somehow she managed to close the door and slip into his arms in the same smooth motion. Her tongue felt like a hot, flaming spear slipping around inside his mouth. Everywhere it touched, it aroused erotic emotions. They had kissed many times, but nothing like this. Her mouth was hot. Her body heat radiated through her clothes. She slipped from his embrace and led him to her bedroom by his shirttail where they both rushed to get undressed. She finished undressing first, pulled him out of his pants before shoving him onto the bed. "Make me feel good, Doctor."

Instead of preparing for the Gonzaga Alumni Gala, they had sex—a nice, slow, twenty-minute, bare-chested, cheek-to-cheek, arms hugged tight around each other's shoulders, missionary groove that brought them both to climax and left her sheets soaked with sweat. The smile on Jordyn's face told that even with the rain, she couldn't have planned a more perfect day. After a jovial tête-à-tête, she fell asleep in his arms three hours before the start of her alumni dinner.

CHAPTER 17

JUST BEFORE SIX SUNDAY NIGHT, a chauffeured car picked them up from Jordyn's townhouse and drove them downtown to the gala.

"Shots... Shots... Shots... Shots... Shots... Shots... Shots... Shots... Shots... Shots... Shots... Shots... Shots... Shots... Shots... Shots... Everybody," Solomon chanted along with the radio as they arrived at the Spokane Convention Center.

"Slow down, Doc. Or are you telling me that what you're trying to do is get me drunk so you can take advantage of me later?"

Solomon looked out the window at the people waiting to enter and said, "I wouldn't think of anything that dastardly."

The driver stopped so they could exit.

"Dastardly?" she snorted. "What are we, cartoon characters?"

They laughed at the memory of childhood cartoons before he exited and extended his hand. His jaw dropped when she slid across the seat and her hip-ending slit opened to reveal both thighs. He stared, conjuring adjectives to describe the beauty of her voluptuous legs.

"Thank you."

He stretched his face into a smile and nodded. "Of course."

With his aid, she stepped out like a princess exiting a royal carriage. Outside, she inhaled the smell of pine and something fruity.

He tucked her arm in his as they entered. "No my Dear," he said referring to their conversation in the car a minute earlier. "We may get a little tipsy tonight, but I don't want you drunk. I want you lucid enough to enjoy and remember everything that I plan to do to you!" His voice grew as he emphasized the word everything.

Jordyn pressed her lips hard against his then turned, smiled and walked away arms waving, head bobbing side-to-side, chanting, "Shots... Shots... Shots... Shots... Shots... Shots... Shots... Shots... Shots... Shots... Shots... Shots... Shots... Shots... Shots... Shots... Shots... Shots..." to herself all the way to the hostess table.

Jordyn and Solomon met the three couples sharing her table taking pictures in the foyer. They joined the pictures before Jordyn proudly escorted Solomon into the main banquet hall, intent on introducing her handsome date to every booster who crossed her path. They grabbed complimentary champagne and strutted about the banquet hall hobnobbing like seasoned professionals, Jordyn showing off the good doctor from Seattle to those she knew intimately, and to those who knew her because of her pageant status. She was confident, and just as comfortable issuing a challenge as she was receiving one. She imagined knowing him in every way that a woman could know a man—especially since they'd covered almost all of the physical ways in the past 72 hours—but she knew that she couldn't promise the kind of commitment he had inferred.

Jordyn asked Solomon to dance with a conniving, "Dinner doesn't start for another half hour until dinner and the band is already playing, we wouldn't have to keep up this forced mingling charade if we were dancing."

Solomon agreed, twirled her then drew her close when they arrived on the dance floor. Cheeks pressed together, stomachs tight against one another, they were inseparable as they glided around the massive ballroom. All eyes in the room were on them, their entanglement juicy and inviting as they navigated the dancefloor the way seafarers sailed their boats, whirling to the sounds of strings and their own heartbeats.

Both simple and sophisticated, this woman truly fascinated him. Lost in thought, Solomon continued to dance even after the music stopped. But why he didn't know.

Jordyn kept dancing for two reasons: first, he was leading, and as long as he kept leading, she would follow; and second, she missed the comfort in a man's firm touch. Someone to hold her and tell her everything would be alright. Someone to laugh with and to whisper her heart's dreams and sweet nothings.

When there was no music playing...just them moving...he realized they weren't just dancing to music, they were dancing to dreams. Right then and there, he knew he could fall in love with her. And she with him.

A half hour after they first graced the dance floor, the music stopped and the band leader requested everyone move toward their seats so the dinner service could commence. They headed toward the restrooms, almost colliding with one of the three loud couples in the foyer.

The sextet stopped, their raucous behavior immediately attracting the attention of those within earshot. A man who appeared to be the leader of the group took a menacing step toward Solomon wearing a bright gold suit. The loud color shouted Easter Suit from every inch of fabric. "Hey Hoffman." he stared at Solomon and puffed out his chest. "Nice to see you again, Doll Face,"

Jordyn smirked, then said with fake solicitousness. "Didn't think these kind of events were your style."

Solomon noticed a frown shape his brow for a moment, then the man met Jordyn's eyes and the frown became a smile. The woman standing next to him looked at Jordyn and said, "Hey Girl, long time."

Jordyn averted her gaze to the woman, then curled her lips into a frown. Her eyes were definitely not smiling at Easter Suit.

Easter Suit averted his gaze from Jordyn to Solomon, eyed him from head-to-toe and said, "Well ain't this 'bout nothing?"

"Whatever, Glenn." The look on her face said she wasn't happy to see him. She didn't want Solomon to see her anger, so she turned and said, "Give me a minute to freshen up and I'll be right back."

Solomon locked eyes with the man then reached to shake hands. At first impression, he reminded him of a clean-shaven, more muscular version of the white singer who served as one of the four panelists on the TV show, *The Masked Singer.*

Easter Suit ignored Solomon's outreached hand. He feigned a toothless smile, then nodded in Jordyn's direction and told his date. "Why don't you and the girls go powder your noses."

When the women were out of earshot, Easter Suit extended his hand to shake Solomon's. Once they held each other's grip, he tightened his grip on Solomon's hand and turned his smile to a sneer.

Solomon gripped harder in return. Asked Easter Suit, "Something I can help you with?"

"I doubt it," Easter Suit replied, looking over Solomon's shoulder and locking eyes with his associates. The two men with Easter Suit had flanked Solomon and posted up behind him like bodyguards. They were so close, the warmth of their alternating deep breaths washed back-and-forth across his neck. Solomon recognized one of them as Greg, the guy outside the pharmacy earlier that afternoon.

"Don't know your face, boy. What part of Spokane you reppin'?"

"I'm not," was all that Solomon offered. He looking down and tried to free his grip, then squeezed harder when he couldn't. He looked back up at Easter Suit and when their eyes met, neither one smiled. Solomon balled his left fist. Outnumbered three-to-one, the odds of him winning a fight were slim.

"So since it's obvious you ain't none of my peoples, what set you from, boy?" Despite being in the proverbial bad situation—a native of Seattle dining in his rival city of Spokane with a Spokane woman—he wasn't about to let someone whoop his ass without sending them home with their own bruises. Not quite sure of Easter Suit's mindset, Solomon's third eye corrected itself about throwing the first punch and made him loosen the fist in his left hand. He just wished his third eye would have told Easter Suit because he definitely didn't appear to be a believer.

Solomon yanked at his hand, but Easter Suit tightened the grip. The two punks with him leaned into Solomon arms. From a distance, they looked like four guys sharing an intimate confidence. He couldn't remember being this scared in a long time, but it was the situation that scared him, not the man.

"I asked where you was from." Easter Suit said, making a fist of his free hand and faking like he wanted to punch Solomon in the face. When Solomon didn't respond, Easter Suit said, "This must be that punk from Seattle." He spat air and stomped on Solomon's foot like he was killing a roach.

Solomon jumped back, about to scream from the pain, when Easter Suit clamped his free hand over Solomon's mouth and kneed him in the groin. Solomon took a shot between the legs so hard that he shrieked like a teenage girl and buckled over. His body wanted to carry him to the floor, but Easter Suit still maintained a grip on his hand and the two punks held him up by his arms. Solomon was in so much pain that he thought he would pass out. He couldn't scream. He couldn't yell. He couldn't beg for his life. He was too pre-occupied with breathing. When he finally got to the point that his knees were about to give out, Easter Suit looked down at Solomon and laughed.

"The look in your eye said you thought you were going to kick my butt. I knew you Seattle boys were soft. Now I'm going to give you one warning, stay your punk ass away from my girl."

"Your girl?" Solomon grimaced then thought, *Who is this guy? How did he know I was from Seattle? Had Jordyn talked to him about me? If so, why?*

"Shut up bitch." Easter Suit glared at the people near them, who, turned away when they saw the menacing look on his face.

Solomon wondered why someone from the Alumni Committee hadn't shown up to investigate the commotion. Why the people around him didn't call security. He wondered if the people who hadn't helped him knew who he was and didn't want to be the next person joining him in the hurt locker.

Solomon looked up and said, "Well then, who did Jordyn go to the bathroom with?"

The punks released Solomon and he fell to his knees. Easter Suit lifted his foot like he was about to stomp Solomon. When Solomon raised his hand to protect himself, Easter Suit lowered his foot back to the floor. "That's my piece of ass for tonight. But that ain't none of your damn business." He tightened his grip, emphasizing his point.

"Look brother, I don't want no trouble," Solomon whimpered.

"Didn't I say shut up?" Easter Suit raised his foot again. This time kicking Solomon in the ribs.

Solomon groaned, tried to protect himself from another attack.

The two goons laughed like they were at a comedy show.

When Solomon finally looked back up, Easter Suit looked him in the eye and quietly pronounced, "If we were outside I'd stomp your ass 'til you stopped breathing. I don't know what you think you know, but know this; Jordyn is now, and will always be, my girl. Got it?"

Solomon saw the seriousness in his eyes. He knew that anyone who could get away with stomping him at a public gathering and have everyone too scared to call the police was somebody he wanted nothing to do with. For Jordyn to abandon him and go to the bathroom without introducing or explaining to him who this man was, she must be afraid of him too. And if he considered her, *his girl*, why hadn't she mentioned this guy before. After all of the bad luck he'd had with women in his life, he'd never been some woman's side piece. In that moment, he didn't care about explanations, he just wanted his ribs and balls to stop hurting. After suffering a humiliation like this, he knew he didn't want to see any more of Jordyn Hoffman.

Easter Suit was accustomed to kicking ass. He recognized the acceptance in Solomon's eyes and loosened his grip an ounce. "Now, when she gets back, finish up your little dinner date quick like, tell her you don't feel good and take her home. And you bet' not go inside her place. Drop her off and beat feet back to that sorry ass town of yours. You feel me?"

Solomon stared his pained acknowledgment.

"And don't let me see you out here again, you Emerald City fag."

The two goons laughed.

Again Solomon wondered how he knew he was from Seattle.

Easter Suit finally released his grip on Solomon's hand. The trio of Spokane bad guys walked away victorious, the two pseudo-bodyguards exchanging high-fives like they'd just won the Super Bowl. Along the way, Easter Suit shot intimidating sneers at any of the gala's patrons who dared lift their eyes in his direction.

Solomon stood and fixed his suit. His slow sluggish motions brought to mind visions of zombie movies as he sloughed past people who had watched him be assaulted and dragged himself to the bathroom where he grabbed napkins and wiped the mucus, slobber and tears from his face. The only cogent thought in his head was how differently that conversation would have gone if he hadn't been flying solo. If the Horsemen had been with him. But they weren't.

When Jordyn returned to the foyer and didn't find Solomon, she went to her table where the waiter had just brought their entrees.

Despite the incessant conversation at the table, Solomon ate his food in silence, not once replying to any questions or comments. When his plate was empty, the long-lost waiter finally re-appeared. Before he could ask if they wanted dessert, Solomon told Jordyn he was leaving. That he'd send the limo back for her once he'd gotten to his hotel. Once Jordyn realized that he wasn't going to give her an explanation and was truly leaving without her, she grabbed her bag, excused herself from the table and hurried after him out the front door toward the valet station.

CHAPTER 18

WHEN THEY ARRIVED AT JORDYN'S, she slid off her shoes and put them in the basket just inside the door, then walked straight over to her sofa and flopped on it as if she'd passed out. Solomon shut the door she'd accosted him against six hours earlier after their trip to the pharmacy, walked past her prone body and straight up to her bedroom.

Twenty minutes later, as their first weekend together neared its end, Jordyn emerged from the main bedroom closet garbed in a White House/Black Market hip-length sleepshirt, sipping on an amaretto sour that she poured before joining Solomon in her bedroom.

Solomon hurriedly packed his clothes in his weekender bag.

Jordyn walked up behind him and burrowed her head between his shoulder blades, and with much effort, managed her hands underneath his shirt. "Solomon, what's wrong with you?" she asked, playfully tweaking his nipples with her thumbs and forefingers. "You haven't said more than a half-dozen words to me since dinner."

Solomon and Jordyn had just begun to know each other. Past a weakness for romantic comedies, the only thing they really had in common was their shared appreciation for a good bourbon—and mind-blowing sex. He spoke eight concise words; *I'm sorry Jordyn, but I have to leave.*

"What did I do to make you lose your mind and have to leave me like this after the wonderful weekend we just shared?" She lifted the back of his shirt and pressed the warmth of her bare chest against his, wide back. "Would you stay if I promise not to wear clothes for the rest of the time you're here?"

The earthy aroma of her patchouli body cream invaded his nostrils. Despite his anger, Solomon felt instantly aroused. "No."

She caressed his stomach, loosened his belt then shoved her hand down his pants. "My favorite ice cream cone feels like he'd like it."

Solomon looked to the ceiling, refusing to make eye contact.

"What's wrong, Solomon?" she begged. "Can't I kiss it better?"

He chuckled, sniffed again and looked away.

She sniffed near her shoulder and asked, "Do I smell?"

"I can smell you, but it's not too bad."

"Maybe you need to scrub me in the shower until I smell good."

They both paused to listen to the not so distant rumble of a train passing along the tracks that separated the back of her neighborhood from one of the city parks. She held him tight, her taut nipples pressing into him as she laid a line of kisses across his back. Not achieving the response she desired, she exerted much force in turning him around to face her against his will. She lifted his shirt, kissed his chest and gently bit his nipples. Jordyn continued kissing down his stomach until she reached his belly button, but stopped when he put his hands under her shoulders and lifted her to halt her progress. "Jordyn, please stop."

"Are you sure?" she asked, glancing down at his engorged pants. She put her hand in front of his face, extended a single finger and playfully pointed downward. "Does he get a say in this?"

"Not right now he doesn't."

She grunted. "Well, he needs to be."

"No he doesn't, and I need to go."

Frustrated by his rejection, Jordyn pushed stiff arms into his chest. He fell back onto the bed and then she mounted him, straddled him and playfully sank her teeth into his nipple, then laid her full weight on him, trapping him, her elbows propped on the bed just above his shoulders, her soft, doughy breasts resting on his chest. The only sound he could hear over her panting was the roar of a train passing in the distance. A sound intimately familiar to her. She wedged her cold, bare feet behind his calves. The look on her face said she wasn't letting him leave without a fight. "What did I do wrong?" she asked, breathing the delicate scent of amaretto over his face.

His expression hardened. "You didn't tell me that you had a psychotic boyfriend." He shifted his eyes directly onto hers, fretting this being the last time he'd look into those deep blue eyes pools of beauty. Solomon inhaled. The inflation of his chest further compressing her breasts. "A psychotic boyfriend that showed up at the alumni dinner and threatened to kill me if I didn't leave you alone. A psychotic boyfriend who, with the help of his two goons, kicked my ass in front of an audience while you were in the bathroom all chummy with his new girl."

"He's my ex, not my boyfriend." Her eyes watered with guilt. "Why didn't you say something, Solomon? I didn't know."

"What did you want me to say? *How'd your talk go? You girls all caught up now? And oh by the way, your boyfriend, that I didn't know existed, said he'd kill me if he ever saw us together again.*"

"Solomon?"

"No," he said forcefully. "I like you Jordyn. I like you a lot. But I am not going to be part of some twisted love triangle. Maybe a dozen years ago, but not now. I'm sorry, but I can't!"

Their eyes remained locked on each other. Tears dripped from her face to his. Hard cries followed. She wrapped her arms around his neck, dropped her head next to his and collapsed on top of him. They lay there for almost ten minutes as Jordyn repeated, "He's not my boyfriend," and cried harder than any woman he'd ever heard, her warm chest heaving atop his, her tears soaking his face and neck.

He didn't bother to wipe them away, just stared quietly at the ceiling and waited. When her crying eased, he rolled her over onto her side and gently loosened her arms from around his neck.

Jordyn asked, "Do you love me Solomon?" Her makeup calcified by tear stains.

"What?"

"Do you love me?"

Once again he stared wordlessly into those brilliant blue eyes.

"I guess I'll take that as a no," she sobbed and pressed her forehead against his temple. "But if you don't love me, why are you with me?"

He sensed her good nature. She just happened to be in a bad situation. A situation he couldn't be party to. He had to tell her the truth. If nothing else, he owed her that much. Probably for the first time since his wife passed, he was one-hundred percent open and honest with a woman. "A couple years ago, you caught my eye dancing with your friends in the square. You captivated me, and I wanted to know who you were. And lucky for me, you turned out to be a nice person."

"Then why are you leaving?"

"Because it looks to me like you still have some things to work out with this man. And until you do, I cannot, and will not be a part of something that doesn't concern me, and more importantly, something that threatens my safety." Solomon stood and Jordyn pulled his arm.

"He is no longer a part of my life."

"Well the beat-down and his threats make me think otherwise."

She raised her hand and he flinched, anticipating a slap. Instead, she stroked his face as softly as she ever had, almost whispering, "As much as I hate it, that's a reasonable answer." Jordyn blew air then laid back down on her bed.

Solomon walked into the bathroom, returned with a cool, wet rag, wiped her face and neck, closed the zipper on his bag then leaned over and pressed a long hard kiss on her forehead. "I'll let myself out."

Jordyn scrambled from the bed, followed him into the living room and playfully tackled him onto the couch. Solomon's weight caused her to lose hold of him and he slid onto the floor. They laughed, but before either of them could speak, the window shattered.

She screamed and rolled back into the couch. Solomon shot his hands up in front of his face as shards of glass flew toward him. He saw her on the couch when he uncovered his eyes, her hands covering her head. Broken glass covered the floor and the bottom of the curtains danced with flames. He yelled, "It's a fire Jordyn, you gotta get up!"

She screamed, crawled over the back of the couch and didn't stop moving until the wall hit firmly against her back. Fear covered her face as she sat cowering in the corner.

Solomon spun on the hardwood floor, yanked the flowers from the vase on her coffee table and tossed the water at the baseboard to douse the flames. When the fire didn't go all the way out, he refilled the vase and doused the fire again, this time fully extinguishing the flames. When he made it to the front porch looking for whoever busted her window with the flaming rock, there was nobody in sight.

Jordyn's smoke detectors alarmed and within twenty minutes, the fire department and police arrived. She couldn't stay in her house that night, so she asked Solomon to take her to Savannah's after he declined her request to go with him to his hotel. Her heart of hearts told her that her ex-boyfriend had thrown the firebomb, and even though she told the police she thought he did it, she had no physical proof aside from her gut instinct.

CHAPTER 19

IF YOU ASKED ANYONE IN Spokane about Glenn Zimmerman, most would offer similar opinions: crook, scum bag, thug, and all around bad guy. Unless of course, you were a sports fan, then you might hear: has been, tragedy, or guy who caught a bad break. Riding All-State status as a high school quarterback, Glenn Zimmerman arrived at Gonzaga University like a rock star. A status he would maintain until the homecoming game of his junior year when the Heisman candidate suffered a shattered ankle bone and torn Achilles that would end his football career. When he spiraled out of control on pain medications he moved out of the football team dorm and in with his older brother Larry, a part-time construction worker, part-time strip club bouncer.

A once-promising athlete who ruined a career in baseball, Larry rode Glenn hard about rehab and getting his sports career back. He drove Glenn to the rehab facility every day for two months straight before Glenn conceded and finally went inside. That would turn out to be the best day of Glenn's young life. At rehab, Glenn met his future college girlfriend, Jordyn Hoffman, a kinesiology major and sports fanatic who recognized him immediately. Over the next three months, she would become his therapist turned girlfriend and the one bright spot in Glenn's post-football life.

Jordyn and Glenn had known each other for almost five months when he treated her to a fancy dinner and told her that he'd decided to forego his senior year, accept an invitation to the NFL combine and enter the NFL draft. He proposed that night and asked her to move in with him—and she did. For the three nights of the NFL draft, a small crowd gathered at Glenn's apartment—his brother, his closest friends and Jordyn. When the draft ended, it appeared rehab and his performance at the combine were not enough to convince a team to draft him. His brother gave him his condolences, and his girl and his buddies took him out to get the draft off his mind.

Pissed off at the world, Glenn drank an entire fifth of vodka that night and started fighting any and everybody who wouldn't agree with him about why he didn't get drafted. When his newly engaged fiancé tried to calm him, he yelled at her, then strangled her before three guys managed to pull him off of her. But by the time they did, she had passed out. The bar manager called the police and four days later when his brother bailed him out of jail, Jordyn had cleared her stuff out of their apartment and left her engagement ring behind. The next day Glenn dropped out of college.

~

Now in his late twenties, Glenn Zimmerman goes by G-Z, a low-level drug dealer known around the streets of Spokane for having a football team full of young thugs who handle the pills he sells to high school kids and college students. After serving a year in prison and more than five years since his relationship with Jordyn ended, he was wary enough to heed the restraining order against him and keep his distance on the two or three times their paths crossed since he'd assaulted her.

Shortly after midnight, more than two months after the Zags Alumni dinner where he saw Jordyn and the guy from Seattle, G-Z and his goons hit a strip club on the rough side of Spokane and partied until just before dawn. After the five of them ate breakfast, the goons dropped G-Z off at his apartment building just before six Sunday morning. He walked into the lobby and pulled out his cell. Horny from the lap dances, drunk off vodka and full from breakfast, he called his ex-girlfriend, hoping to catch her in a friendly mood. Although he knew they weren't together anymore, and ignoring the restraining order that was a condition of his parole, he told his drunk self that he could convince her to come be his company.

After the fourth ring, Jordyn answered with a groggy, "Hello?"

"Hey Babe, what you doing?" said the voice on the other end.

"I'm sleeping," she replied angrily. "Who the hell is this?" If she had opened her eyes instead of reaching out blindly to pick up the phone from where she habitually kept it on her nightstand, she would've seen *Unknown Caller* on the ID and not answered. She had blocked his old number, the one with the ID she had entered as *Total Asshole* before blocking it.

"Come on girl. You ain't too tired to not know your man."

"I don't have a man," she countered. "Who the hell...?"

"Look Babe," he interrupted, "I just finished breakfast and I'm wide awake. It's been a long night and I was thinking you should come keep me company. You know, come put your man sleep the right way. Know what I'm sayin'?"

"Glenn?" Jordyn asked, finally recognizing the voice. She turned her head toward the alarm clock and saw 5:50 in blue numbers. Hoping it was a nightmare, she blinked and tried again to focus.

"You still there," he asked, unlocking his apartment door.

"Glenn Zimmerman, I don't know what kind of drugs you are on, but you have lost your sociopathic mind calling me this early in the morning. Matter-of-fact, why the hell are you calling me at all?"

"Look Babe, are you ..."

"Stop calling me Babe," she interrupted angrily. "I am not your Babe. You lost that privilege, and the privilege of calling me."

"Come on, Babe, don't be acting like..."

"Are you freaking deaf?" She pulled the phone away from her ear, yelled loud enough to wake the dead. "Stop calling me Babe!"

"Alright. Alright Cool. Ease the drama already. Look, what are we doing Jordyn? You coming through, or you want me to jet out your way?"

"Hear me and hear me good Glenn, there is no you and me. I'm not coming to you, and if you come over here, I will cut your balls off and run them through the garbage grinder!"

The silence on the line made her think her words convinced him how serious she was, but just before Jordyn decided to slam the phone down, she heard him say, "Oh I get it. You still mad about old boy at the alumni dance?"

"You know this has nothing to do with the dance." She hesitated. "Wait. What. What happened at the dance?"

"Damn, old boy didn't tell you?" Glenn hesitated, then laughed out loud. "Huh, I guess he's more of a rider than I gave him credit."

Solomon had summarized his trauma for her that night, but despite her hatred for Glenn and her desire for him to get off her phone, she needed to hear him confirm Solomon's story. "Glenn what the hell are you talking about?" she demanded. "On second thought, I don't want to hear anything you have to say. I just want you off my phone."

"Yeah," Glenn boasted, "I probably wouldn't want to hear how my punk ass wannabe boyfriend got his ass kicked in front of a room full of people and didn't do squat about it either."

"What?" she yelled. "What the heck did you do?"

"I handled my business," Glenn blustered. "He was with my girl. I kicked his ass and sent him on his way. Since he didn't tell you, I guess he heeded my warning and got the hell out of dodge."

The day Solomon left, she was angry enough to call Glenn and cuss him out over what he'd done to Solomon and accuse him of throwing the flaming brick through her window, but that would require her to talk to him and invite his crazy back into her life. So at Savannah's, instead of the amaretto she'd been drinking after the gala, she drank straight Bulleit Rye whiskey until she cried herself to sleep.

After a beat it finally clicked. "Oh my God," she shouted when

Glenn further justified her hatred for him. She'd been upset when the phone rang before sunrise and it wasn't an emergency. She'd been mad when she recognized Glenn's voice, knowing that she never wanted to hear from him again. Now she was incensed. She laid there in the dark, infuriated, thinking, *How the hell could I have been that blind? That naïve? That stupid?* Tears slid down her face and she began to shake. "You sorry son of a bitch. If you ever call me again, I will have you arrested," she yelled into the phone then pressed the red receiver image to end the call. She held the power button and turned off her phone before slamming it down onto her spare pillow.

When Jordyn turned on the bedside lamp, her alarm clock read 6:09. She didn't want to be awake this early, but she didn't know what to do with what she'd just heard, and with all of the adrenaline coursing through her, there was no way she could go back to sleep. Every fiber in her body told her to pick up the phone, call Solomon and apologize. Tell him that she was sorry and beg him to allow her to make it up to him. Then she remembered waking him at just before seven when she called from the train. That was later on a weekday and he was asleep, so she knew for sure that he was asleep this early on a Sunday morning. So she decided to go for a run. The campus exercise trail would be empty this early and the cool morning air would help clear her mind. Then she'd call Solomon and apologize, and thank him, and tell him everything else she'd wanted to for the last two months. *Yes, that's what I'll do*, she thought before she jumping out of bed and padding barefoot into the bathroom.

~

Solomon woke at six o'clock Sunday morning without the help of an alarm, threw his feet out from under the covers and pressed them against the cold floor. Unlike Monday through Friday, getting an early start on the weekends satisfied him. The timer on his coffee maker was set for five-fifty. In boxers and a t-shirt, he padded across his hotel room to the kitchenette, removed the cup of hot coffee from the machine and stirred it to ensure the two teaspoons of honey had dissolved. He took long gulps, then set the empty cup on the window ledge before chasing the rich, Hawaiian flavored coffee with a full bottle of water to ensure he was fully hydrated for his run. He opened the curtains and dressed by windowlight and synchronized his Bluetooth earbuds to the built-in music player in his watch.

At six-thirty, dressed in jogging pants, a hooded, long-sleeve dri-fit shirt, dri-fit socks and running shoes, Solomon turned on his music, left the lobby of the Spokane Downtown Courtyard, pulled his hoodie over his head and stretched lightly before entering the asphalt extension that led from the back of the hotel parking lot to the Spokane River Centennial Trail running path. Normally when he ran in Seattle, his muscles would be heavy with sleep for the first mile, a sensation he'd shake off as the caffeine kicked in and he eased into the rhythm of the run. But he'd slept well Saturday night and his legs were looser than normal. Jogging north on the Centennial Trail, his route would take him approximately four miles away from the center of town, along the Centennial Trail, and across the Spokane River to the campus of Gonzaga University. On Friday, he'd stayed on the south side of the river, allowing his five-and-a-half mile run to encompass the Spokane campus of Washington State University. At dinner Friday, a colleague suggested that if he wanted to stretch himself for a good distance, he could follow the Centennial Trail across the river to the less-densely-populated Gonzaga exercise trail. The air was crisp and his pace felt good. Moving faster than normal he considered doing eight miles, instead of six as he crossed the Spokane River en route to Gonzaga.

Having run the route from her condo to the campus trail more than a hundred times, Jordyn ignored her immediate surroundings and concentrated on the tempo of the Tchaikovsky symphony blaring in her earbuds. A mile from campus she heard the sound of church bells marking the seven o'clock hour. The untamed din of the bells, geese honking near the lake and weekend morning soccer or flag football games were a regular feature of campus life that helped her feel alive.

Still full of adrenaline and angst from Glenn's phone call, she practically sprinted the final hundred yards reach campus and the exercise trail. The three-quarter mile, sixteen-foot-wide trail offered exercise stations every fifty yards. Jordyn routinely stopped at every other one, completing all of the eleven stations before she finished her workout, but with today's extra energy, she stopped at every exercise station on both laps around the track.

At the beginning of her third lap, Jordyn finished a set of five chin-ups and was catching her breath when out of the corner of her eye, she caught the vision of a tall, lanky, figure taking long, strong strides down the trail toward her. He was over six feet and about 220 pounds. From the speed of his pace, he had to be an athlete or an ex-athlete. She took a deep breath and stepped back onto the trail, jogging toward the next station. Twenty yards before she reached the sit-up bench, she could feel him bearing down on her. She veered right giving him plenty of room to pass her. As he passed, she instinctively looked his way, searching for a glimpse of his face. No luck. The hoodie he wore pulled over his head was too low and his pace was too fast. His 'Hi, how you doing?' rang out loud as he pounded past her, expelling light puffs of air from within his hoodie.

Thrown off-stride, self-conscious and stumbling, she stammered, "Fine. I'm fine," to his back as if the stranger blasting past her was actually expecting a reply. As he ran away from her, she stopped, stepped off the trail and laid on the sit-up bench. A pang of excitement coursed through her as she turned to watch him disappear down the trail; or could it have been dread?

Jordyn finished her sit ups and proceeded through the next six stations. She was back on the trail when the stranger veered onto the path and into her line of vision fifty yards away. She picked up her pace and when she saw his shadow overtaking hers, she turned to face him. Glistening white teeth grinned ominously as he exhaled heavy puffs of hot air from within the shroud of his hoodie. He passed her and a slight odor of male sweat, mixed with a fragrant peppery undertone, left a favorable impression in his wake. Searching for the scent, she realized her pace had slowed. She sped up again and watched the man with the broad back open his lead on her to five and then ten yards.

Why does he seem so familiar? Is it his shape? His tone? No, it's his scent. Buried beneath the aroma of sweat that invaded her nostrils, she inhaled the guilty pleasure of a familiar cologne. He stepped in a puddle, and the splashing water jolted her out of anxious thoughts. She recognized the scent of the cologne and she unconsciously called out, "Solomon?" loud enough to scare a couple of birds into flight.

The runner in the hoodie slowed and turned his head to look back just as she raised her sunglasses onto the brim of her hat to reveal the brightest of blues eyes. Sparkling eyes that reflected the brilliance of her soul. When that light of recognition shone in his eyes, he pushed the hoodie back, revealing his bald head and called, "Jordyn?"

Jordyn ran to him. Her off-white running outfit glowed around her as if the sun was illuminating her in the cool morning air. She leapt into the greeting of his strong arms with the excitement of just coming home from war. They hugged for a while before he set her feet down on the trail. Their smiles masked their shared uncertainty of what to say first. His face and head glistened with sweat. Dreamy sexy thoughts about the last time she'd made him sweat like that crossed her mind. She smiled wide, her eyes beaming like two blue beacons.

Captivated in the sparkle of her brilliant baby blues, he paused his run tracker and pulled out his earbuds.

Uncertain of where to begin the conversation, she reached down to grab his earpiece and asked, "May I?"

He looked down to see what she was reaching for and they gently bumped foreheads. A beat passed as they both rubbed their foreheads. When her gaze met his, they both laughed hysterically. Her radiant blue eyes sparkled even more when she laugh. A full, innocent laugh like she was being poked in her ribs or relentlessly tickled.

"You're looking very well," Solomon said when he regained his voice. Exercise had given a brilliant hue to her cheeks, and heightened the effect of her slightly tanned skin. He took in her running suit, remembering how she said she loved to jog. Sheer panels from mid-thigh to mid-calf showed the definition in her legs. From the looks of her taut frame inside the form-fitting jacket, she'd been doing a lot of running since they'd last been together. Twenty pounds lighter than in high school, her frame was now that of an athlete, a model, or he thought laughingly, a beauty queen. "What I meant to say is, I didn't expect to run into you out here. I thought you told me that you were a sleepy head on the weekends?"

She laughed, saying in a lowered voice, "Yes, sometimes I do enjoy hibernating on the weekends, but the phone interrupted my rest this morning and once I realized I wasn't going back to sleep, I decided to get up and see if I could run off some of my angst."

"Angst?"

"You know what, don't worry about it," she said. "The real question is, what are you doing here?"

"Me? I've had a twelve-pack or two too many over the past couple months and committed to burn off some of those calories before this growler grew into a full-blown keg," Solomon chuckled, patting his stomach.

"No silly," she asked. "What are you doing in Spokane?" Then she said, "I take it you've found somebody else to visit since you didn't call to let me know you were coming."

Months had passed since the incident with Jordyn's ex at the Gonzaga Alumni dinner. They'd attempted to call each other on several occasions, all of their attempts going to voicemail. More than two months had passed since the last time she'd left a voicemail. Since he'd taken so long to get back to her, she figured he was intentionally ignoring her.

In his opinion, the ball was in her court. They had both been hurt—him physically, her emotionally—but if possible, he would like to remain her friend. If anything more than friends was to be a consideration, he would have to know that her ex understood that he—Glenn—was, without a doubt, out of the picture. Solomon had been caught out there once, but if anything like the alumni dance incident ever happened again, the four horsemen would be riding on Spokane. And Jordyn would be nothing but a fond memory.

"I left you a voicemail about two weeks ago," he said.

"I remember a text, not a voicemail; but it didn't say you would be in Spokane. And it definitely didn't say you were coming to see me." Jordyn rubbed her forehead again and absorbed the image of the man before her. He was as handsome as he was serious-minded. A strong jaw and full lips with the face and body of a fashion model. But she hadn't fallen for his pretty face. It was never his looks with her. It was his energy. And right now, she felt a soulful, high-frequency current surging between them. And she knew he felt it too. Once or twice before she had felt this sexual energy pass between them, but never this strong. She placed her hands on her hips, looked him dead in the eye and tried to look stern. "I'm waiting."

Solomon stretched his shoulders and looked up, thought about her words, took a deep breath and then blew air. She was right. Two weeks before he came to Spokane for this upcoming conference, he texted her to say he'd be in town, but he didn't provide dates. When she didn't reply, he chalked it up as her not wanting to see him, and left it alone.

Solomon enjoyed their time together. Loved the energy in being with such a vibrant, younger woman. Hanging with Jordyn was his way of vicariously reliving the twenty-something, single life he missed, having married at the young age of 24. Other than his wife's untimely passing, there were no regrets to his marriage; however, Solomon took full advantage of being be single and dating a woman with Jordyn's youthful exuberance.

"I'll tell you what, Jordyn," Solomon said as he stopped his run tracker and saved his workout. "I've gotten six miles in so far and that's enough for me. If you're not finished, then I'd love to continue your workout with you. If you are done, can I buy you a cup of coffee."

"Come on then." She grabbed his hand and held it as she exited the exercise trail into a corridor of oaks, birch, pines and elms. She ran and he followed, his heavier weight slowing her pace. Her feet caught, pulled and kicked against the earth as she attempted to drag him along.

Admiring her determination, he eyed the course of the path ahead, sped up, and passed her easily before they fall into a comfortable pace.

She watched his elegant stride as he passed her, his hands like blades knifing through the air.

Five minutes later she yelled, "Halfway," as he turned a corner onto a dirt path and started up an incline. Her breaths came hard as she pushed out the words, "Now comes the hard part," in his direction.

They pass the campus cathedral at the top of the hill and she yelled, "turn left," when he signaled which way with his hands. When they come to the edge of the clearing three minutes later, he stopped in five short paces.

She stopped four paces beyond him, sank to her knees, leaned forward and buried her face in her hands, leaving only her mouth and nose exposed to breathe. The crisp air of the early morning made for a pleasant run. The blank texture of the campus park had been the perfect canvas to paint their aggression. Every fiber in her body burned from the obstacle course and the finishing sprint with Solomon. She could feel sweat dripping off her everywhere, but no longer felt her angst, no longer felt the anxiety of a call from a troubled ex-boyfriend that started her day in torment.

Five minutes later they were both breathing near normal. After helping each other through a cooldown stretch to slow their heartbeats, Solomon said, "I don't know about you, but I could eat."

She agreed, then leaving the exercise trail behind them, they slow-jogged one block north of the Gonzaga campus to her favorite coffee shop.

CHAPTER 20

JORDYN'S HOUSE WAS LOCATED IN one of the quieter sections of the city: light volumes of car traffic, several child and pet friendly parks, and very few bars. She had used the $25,000 grand prize for winning the Miss Washington beauty pageant as a down payment on the quaint, three-bedroom townhouse.

Solomon entered through the open front door promptly at six o'clock. When they left the coffee shop that morning, they agreed that they each had left words unsaid, so he accepted Jordyn's invitation to dinner at her house. "Hello," he called. "Jordyn, it's me, Solomon." Quiet answered him. "Jordyn, it's me, Solomon," he called again. "Are you in here?"

A ceiling fan whirred in the living room. The vibrant colors of her furniture reflected her artistic mood. Scented candles burned throughout. Fresh-cut, yellow tulips from a small, meticulously tended garden at the back of the house were in a vase on the dining room table. Salvador Dali prints from Home Goods stores hung on textured green and blue walls.

On his way to the kitchen to put the wine he'd bought in the refrigerator he saw what looked like a trail of blood on the hallway carpet. The trail ran up the stairs, and just like that, so did he, repeatedly calling Jordyn's name. He found her in the front bedroom, her head and body slumped over the side of the bed like a puppet whose strings had been cut. Blood covered her bruised face.

Her half exposed left breast shone through the shreds of her torn shirt.

He checked her pulse. She was alive. Unconscious, but alive. Solomon lifting her head onto the mattress, shook her forcefully then yelled, "Wake up, Jordyn!"

He heard a faint voice ask, *Hello? Is someone there?* before he saw her cell phone and picked it up from under the corner of her bed.

"Hello? This is Doctor Solomon Alexandré. Who is this?"

This is the 911 Operator. Police are on the way. Can you tell me what's going on?

Solomon saw her eyes moving slowly behind their lids. He told the operator of his recent arrival and discovery of Jordyn. Her head moved and her eyes rolled open, briefly revealing the whites. He held her in his arms, patted her cheeks to wake her and repeated her name several times. "She just opened her eyes," he said nervously.

Good. Police are minutes away. Try to keep her conscious. I've dispatched an ambulance, but I'll stay on the line.

Jordyn slowly raised her hands to stop him from slapping her face as he regarded her injuries. "What happened?" he asked.

"I don't know." Her tongue moved lazily in her mouth. She'd forgotten the events of the past few hours, and when she looked up to see Solomon standing at the side of the bed she wondered how he had gotten into her bedroom. *How long has he been standing there? Where did he come from?* "Oh My God," she started shaking and asked in a croaky voice, "Is he still here?"

"Who?" Solomon looked around the room. There was no evidence of anyone being there but he wanted to make certain. "Let me check." Solomon laid her head gently on a pillow, then checked her bedroom and closet. Nobody. He ran into her guest bedroom, but there was nobody there either. He cradled her in his arms when he returned "There's nobody here."

She jerked at his touch, the fastest movement she'd made in hours, and sat up quickly. She felt sick, then stood, unsteadily and rested against the wall as the sickness grew stronger. He reached to help her, but she pushed him away. She entered the bathroom, unaware if he followed her. Leaning on the sink and looking at her reflection, regarding her torn, blood-stained clothes, tension registered in her shoulders. Again she felt sick. She leaned down to the sink and ran the cold water; first to take a drink, then to splash on her face. The nausea came and went, then returned even stronger than before. Taking three more sips of water and straining to keep her eyes open, she managed to control the nausea.

Solomon entered the bathroom after he heard the water stop running. "Do you remember what happened? Who were you thinking was still here? The police will be here in a minute. Did he," Solomon paused, "rape you?"

When he escorted her back into the bedroom, Jordyn drifted toward the bench at the foot of her bed and sat down hard. She thought of how the intruder had violated her house, recalled the venom in his voice and started crying.

~

Three hours earlier, Jordyn was still beaming from her morning run and chance meeting with Solomon. She told her home assistant to *start my Vibes playlist.* She was so excited about her dinner date that she turned the volume way up and bounced around her bedroom as she picked out a dress, underwear and shoes for the date with Solomon before undressing to take a shower. Once out of her running clothes, she noticed they were a little more pungent than she liked to leave in her hamper, so she threw them in a basket, slipped on a knee-length sleepshirt and took them downstairs. Her plan was to throw the load of clothes in the washing machine and look through the freezer to decide what to cook for dinner, but downstairs, she noticed her back door was open. She'd gone out to fill her bird feeder before heading upstairs, but was certain she had shut the door afterwards.

She set the basket in the laundry room then noticed broken glass on the floor when she returned to the kitchen to shut the door. She paused, called *Hello*, then jumped when a man dressed in all black and wearing a Donald Trump mask burst out of her pantry. He punched her in the face, splitting her lip and knocking her down. Blood spilled onto the floor tile and cabinet doors. She pushed herself up onto her hands and knees, and crawled behind the kitchen island.

"Come here, whore," the masked man called rounding the island.

Dazed, confused, crying, and scared for her life, Jordyn stumbled to her feet and ran toward the front door. She unlocked and opened the door just as the intruder reached her. He pushed her and the door shut as they struggled, but Jordyn held onto the lock and knob, managing to turn the deadbolt to the extended position before he kicked the door loose from her hands trying to shut it. The deadbolt was out, causing the door to slam against its frame then drift ajar as he turned her and punched her again. The glancing blow propelled her back into the room. She got up, and headed toward the stairs this time.

"Oh, hell no!" Donald Trump yelled, tearing at her shirt as he followed her up the stairs. "Come here," he called reaching for her.

She kicked him and he lost his grip. "Get the hell out of my house." She grabbed a vase with glass flowers off the plant ledge on the landing and threw it at him. The vase crashed into his forearms as he blocked it from hitting him in the face.

He tripped her at the top of the stairs, grabbed her and she raked her nails across his face. "Damn it bitch; now I'm really gonna hurt you," he shouted and tore at her nightshirt as she scrambled on all fours. He swung wildly and knocked her to the floor with a punch in the side, then kicked her in the ribs once she was down.

Jordyn wrapped her arms around her sore ribs and rolled onto her back. The music stopped when her phone rang through the speakers and her home assistant announced, *Call from Savannah Grimes*. When he turned to look in the direction of the automated voice, she kicked him. He fell and tumbled down eight steps back to the landing.

The phone stopped ringing and the house went silent again. Just before the assistant turned the music back on, Jordyn fought through the pain in her aching ribs and yelled for her home assistant to *Call 911*. Then, she got to her knees and started toward her bedroom while her intruder recovered.

Before she had moved a full body-length, Donald Trump bounded up the stairs, lunged and clipped her ankle. She fell again and he pulled at her until he reached her shoulders. "Come here, bitch," he yelled, ripping at her shirt. He pulled, she kicked, and her shirt tore even more. One desperate, well-placed kick hit him in the testicles; left him flat on the floor. Jordyn fell to her belly, crawled into her bedroom, slammed the door behind her and flopped her weight back against it.

Donald Trump stumbled his way to her bedroom, and tried to push her door open. When he couldn't, he kicked the door twice with all of his might, but Jordyn's dead weight was enough to keep the door shut.

911, What's your emergency? rang loudly through Jordyn's home speaker. The 911 operator read the address aloud then urged her to, *Stay on the line, I'm sending the police.*

Angry, sore and not wanting to be there when the police arrived, Donald Trump limped down the stairs and into the kitchen. He paused at her back door long enough to ensure nobody saw him rush out, then kept his mask on until he reached the grove of trees behind her house.

Jordyn—groggy, bleeding and in pain—laid against the door until she couldn't hear anything moving on the other side. When she heard a car start and speed off, she crawled to her bed and passed out.

~

Solomon's first impulse was to tend to her and address her open wounds. He thought. *What caused her head wound? What if she had a concussion?* His second impulse was to take her to the hospital. Having seen plenty of television crime shows, he knew that the police needed to see her wounds. He knew she'd need to remember what happened. Her house was in a serious state of disarray. *Was this a home invasion? Was an intruder in the house when she came home? Did she know who did this to her? Had she been raped?* A million thoughts flooded the handsome psychologists mind. He thought to get her out of the bloody, sweat-soaked nightshirt, but he didn't know if he should remove her clothes before the police could take pictures as evidence. He knew he needed to do something soon, but wasn't certain what to do first if she couldn't remember what happened to her. "Do you know who did this to you?" he asked, praying for an answer.

Jordyn struggled to keep her eyes open. She nodded and agreed unknowingly. Mumbling, twitching, and drifting in and out of consciousness, she watched as he tapped her cheek to keep her awake. After a fifth, harder slap, her brain registered the sensation of pain.

He held her head in his lap as he confirmed her address with the 911 operator. "Hang in there, Sweetheart, help is on the way." He went through a series of questions the operator gave him to ask Jordyn, most of which she answered incoherently. Within ten minutes, the doorbell rang and he heard EMTs calling from downstairs.

When they entered her bedroom, he stood back while the EMTs tended to her. As they prepared to transport her to the hospital, he asked the 911 operator to call Savannah because she was the only person he knew who should know how to contact her family. Once the EMTs took her to the ambulance, he worried about locking up her house. He saw the broken glass on the floor when he locked the back door. He found her keys in her purse thrown in a downstairs corner. He picked up her purse and carried it with him, locked her front door, hopped in his rental car and followed the ambulance to the hospital.

As Jordyn lay sleeping Sunday evening under the influence of heavy sedation, Solomon checked for flights back to Spokane from Seattle. He had a minor medical procedure scheduled for Friday morning that he'd already rescheduled twice and was wary of how his doctor would react if he rescheduled a third time. He planned to fly home for his procedure, then catch the first flight back to Spokane either Friday night or Saturday morning.

But that wouldn't be necessary. An hour before visiting hours ended, Savannah rushed into a sleeping Jordyn's hospital room with Jordyn's father. A nurse explained Jordyn's condition and told them that she was sedated, but should be alright. After Savannah promised to call him daily with updates and her father thanked him for taking care of her, Solomon conceded to forego his return trip, save the return airfare and stay at home the following weekend.

CHAPTER 21

LAWRENCE DIDIER IS ONE OF two associate pastors at Mount Sinai Greater Gospel Church. Saturday evening, the senior pastor called and told Lawrence his brother-in-law, a fellow pastor at South Seattle First Baptist Church of God in Christ, went into the hospital that afternoon and wouldn't be able to preach Sunday. He spoke of Lawrence's aspiration to one day head his own church and asked him the favor of filling in at his brother-in-law's church in South Seattle. Lawrence initially hesitated, nervous about having never preached anywhere other than seminary and at Mount Sinai. After agreeing, he called the Horsemen for moral support and asked them to attend the service.

~

The service at South Seattle First Baptist opened with three riveting selections by the music ministry before a praise dance team performance preceded Lawrence's entry into the sanctuary. Once he reached the pulpit and the praise team exited through the side doors at the front of the sanctuary, an usher escorted a teen mother and her newborn baby to the altar for dedication.

In the pew behind Lawrence's three Horsemen friends, a late forties woman in an orange dress whispered, "It's such a shame. She was one of the good girls in the church."

Her gossip partner, a woman her age in a tan dress, whispered, "The apple really doesn't fall far from the tree." She was talking about the teen girl's mid-thirties mother sitting in the front row. "You know her momma had her in high school."

Orange Dress said, "If the no good daddy would just be a man and step up, she wouldn't be up there by herself."

Tan Dress surveilled the sanctuary for the boy rumored to be the father. When she couldn't locate him, she quipped, "He probably knew about the dedication and decided to skip service today."

Orange Dress' son, a teen in a brown suit next to her said, "He's a punk and she's a thot. They deserve each other."

A lady to Desmond's right turned and shushed the gossiping trio.

The three women stared at each other defiantly for a beat. When their mean-mugging battle concluded, Brown Suit boy proclaimed, "Word around school is that she's not sure if he is the daddy."

Tan Dress interrupted, "Mama's baby. Papas maybe. Been that way since the dawn of time."

A boy seated next to Brown Suit boy said, "Baby Girl is bangin'. If I'd have known she was giving it up, I would've put my bid in."

Brown Suit boy and his friend were unaware that the teen mother's first cousin, a nineteen year-old who'd spent two years in juvenile detention for assault, sat in the last seat of the row directly behind them listening to their every word. When he'd heard enough of them bad-mouthing his cousin, he growled, "Y'all busters need to shut up," and punched Brown Suit boy in the side of his head. Then he jumped out into the side aisle, grabbed Brown Suit boy's friend by his suitcoat, pulled him into the aisle and slammed him into the wall. Bigger, stronger and twenty pounds heavier than both of the younger teens, Teen Mom's cousin alternated his assault, throwing lightning quick punches between Brown Suit boy and his friend.

Desmond turned toward the commotion and Solomon followed when Desmond pulled Kenny to help him stop the fight. Lawrence called for the church to remain calm when the commotion drew the congregation's attention away from the service. Solomon nodded toward Lawrence once Desmond and Kenny corralled Teen Mom's cousin. Then he helped the usher's drag Brown Suit boy and his friend out the sanctuary's rear doors. After the other boys were gone, Teen Mom's cousin let Desmond and Kenny peaceably escort him out the sanctuary's side door. Security called Seattle Police, but when they arrived, the senior deacon told them that they needed to wait for the pastor, Lawrence in this case, to confirm that he wanted them detained and charged for their disturbance.

From start to finish the altercation lasted less than ten minutes, but regaining control of the congregation and resuming the dedication took Lawrence another ten minutes. Because of the delay, Lawrence would have to curtail his sermon to much shorter than the prepared sermon senior pastor emailed him Saturday night.

Following the dedication, the music ministry accompanied the choir's entry through the side sanctuary doors for the main service. Lawrence returned to the dais for their second song and narrated like Kirk Franklin foreshadowing the lyrics for God's Property.

Lawrence commenced his sermon and was deep into sanctified preacher mode by the time the three Horsemen returned to the sanctuary. When the ushers admitted them through the sanctuary's rear doors, they heard Lawrence profess, "Not everyone who is good looking; looks good. Come on now somebody. You don't have to be good looking in order to look good in the eyes of the Lord."

Desmond absorbed Lawrence's words and cut his eyes toward Kenny. He loved his friend for life, but couldn't help but think those words were meant for his ears. Solomon entered last, nodding at Lawrence to signal that things with the boys were alright. When they arrived at their pew, it surprised him that the choir sat in the choir stand with the hoods on their choir robes pulled over their heads humming softly as Lawrence preached. Since it was his first visit to an unfamiliar church, he paid it no mind and settled in for the remainder of the sermon.

Lawrence continued with, "I know it's getting to be afternoon and some of you may be thinking about getting out of here and home to your television to watch the game. Kicking off your shoes and letting the shows on whatever channel tell you what others want you to here."

His words charged the crowd and the congregation responded with a hearty applause, and a chorus of approving shouts and screams that soared to the church rafters.

"But before I let you go," Lawrence sipped some water before continuing. "I want you to think about letting your mind run wild on more positive things than you might be normally used to. Let your mind run wild and see yourself owning your own business or writing your own book. Let you mind run wild and see your children graduating from college." He paused, wiped his brow then said, "Somebody should have shouted right there." Those who caught the joke chuckled. Wary of a similar lack of response, he led them to the rest of his sermon carefully, like a wife leads her husband to believe he originated her great idea. "I encourage you to change the channels of your mind and factor out all of that negativity everyday life places before you. See yourself weathering the storm and living the life that God wants you to live. And once your mind is clear, let your mind run wild with God as a starting point. Remember," he paused one final time, "so as a man thinketh, so he is."

With that, the organist struck a shocking chord and the choir stood. The band played softly and the choir swayed side-to-side as Lawrence retreated from the dais to the pastor's chair. The soloist for the closing song walked to the front corner of the choir stand and removed her hood before the rest of the choir followed her lead and removed theirs.

Solomon gripped Annette Didier's wrist and sprang from his seat when he saw the soloist's face. The face that belonged to the mystery girl he saw at the art auction, in the crosswalk downtown and once again from the fifth story window of the Magnusson building. The face that belonged to his wife, Mareschelle.

Expression filled with awe, he faced Annette when she touched his wrist just above where his hand gripped hers.

Annette squeezed and said, "It's okay Baby, I see her too."

Solomon eased his grip on Annette's arm, looked to the statue of Jesus Christ hanging ten feet above Lawrence's head, folded his hands and whispered, *Thank You, Jesus.*

Both Kenny and Desmond were checking their phones. They heard him call Jesus' name and turned to see him praying. Kenny shrugged it off, but Desmond's intuition told him something strange was happening.

When she started singing, Kenny looked up and realized the soloist's resemblance to his nemesis, Mareschelle. He slapped Desmond hard on the arm, pointed at the soloist and said loud enough for everyone within six feet to hear, "This church is better than Springer AND Maury!"

After the sermon, Kenny led the charge to the front of the church as members of the congregation gathered to meet the guest pastor. Solomon followed, but his focused remained on the doors to right of the pulpit where the choir exited. Solomon's distraction piqued Desmond's interest as the three friends posted up opposite the greeting line giving Lawrence space to meet interested congregants.

Some choir members returned to the sanctuary after disrobing. Solomon allowed his mystery woman to greet Lawrence and after she finished, followed her towards the rear of the sanctuary, Desmond trailing anxiously in his wake. He watched from a distance as Solomon caught up with her seven pews shy of the rear church doors.

"Excuse me Miss," Solomon called eagerly. She stopped and he moved closer, expecting her to evaporate into thin air before he reached her. But she came closer and she was real. He recognized her face—from her hair to her skin, from her mouth to her unbelievably light brown eyes— an exact replica of his dearly deceased wife. It was her. His Angel. His Mareschelle.

They were two pews away from her when she raised her head from checking her cell phone and skeptically regarded them as if expertly examining goods for barter.

Desmond stopped just short of running into Solomon and regarded her over his best friend's shoulder. Solomon looked at her so intently, she had to look behind her to make sure he had actually called her and she wasn't preventing him from getting to someone behind her. She cleared her throat when she turned back to him. "Can I help you?"

"Mareschelle?" Solomon asked when their eyes met. His heart was in his throat, beating rapidly as he waited for her response to confirm he was not dreaming.

"Excuse me?" she inquired.

"Is your name Mareschelle?" Desmond asked as Solomon stared.

"No brother, my name is Amari." Her reply were the sweetest words he'd heard since he'd last heard his wife. "Have we met?"

"Amari?" Solomon asked in a puzzled tone. He wanted to believe he was dreaming more than he wanted to hear she was someone else.

"Yes, Amari Favors," she replied gently, greeting him with a smile more stunning than the diamond necklace around her neck. Her wavy hair was down. Long and curly like she had washed it right before bed then slept with it in one long single braid. "And you are?"

Capitulating to the disappointing reality that the mystery woman was neither a dream nor his Mareschelle, Solomon cleared his throat and said, "Excuse me for being so rude, I'm Solomon Alexandré."

"Hello Brother Solomon. Is there something I can do for you?"

Solomon noticed Amari glance at his left hand.

"Yes." Solomon cleared his throat again, then said, "Amari Favors, I've seen you around before and I was wondering if you'd be willing to share a cup of coffee with a guest to your church?"

Amari looked at Desmond over his shoulder watching them. "Do you think your friend will forgive you if you abandon him for me?"

Desmond had watched the entire transaction. Being a widower himself, he thought Solomon had been hallucinating. Desmond knew a widower's pain, and the more he watched, the more he remembered the fun times he and Penny had shared with Solomon and Mareschelle. Now that Solomon had finally found the woman who had distracted him for so long, Desmond empathized with how seeing her must be torturing his friend.

Solomon turned to face Desmond. Kenny had joined them, heard her question and nodded his approval. Desmond shrugged nonplussed.

Solomon turned to Amari and offered a satisfying smile. "I think they're good."

"Well then, Brother Solomon, I'll join you for that cup of coffee."

"Call us," Kenny yelled as Solomon and Amari exited the church.

~

Amari followed Solomon two blocks to a burgeoning community of shops plentiful with open air markets, restaurants with overpriced menus, and pricey condo mazes. The cafe situated on a corner of two four-lane streets, had solid panes of glass twelve feet high on both its east and south walls. Walls that stretched forty feet from the heavy glass doors housed in weathered frames to give them a rustic look.

A dozen people were ahead of them in the line, but Solomon caught the eye of Daphne, a macadamia-hued woman with a small wiry frame who'd waited on him several times and knew the regular orders of most coffee house patrons. He raised two fingers and pointed to the far corner. She nodded before he led Amari to the window overlooking Puget Sound, which he thought offered the best view of the area. He held Amari's chair before a waiter quickly bussed their table then brought two glasses of water and offered them a basket of fresh caramel and cinnamon biscotti.

Amari studied the single-page coffee house menu as Solomon removed his suit jacket and settled across from her. Her eyes skimmed the various offerings, but her thoughts were focused on Solomon, who at that time, sat impatiently staring at the hostess station, willing their server to come over. She asked, "Are you a regular or decaf man?"

An overwhelming sensation of joy shot through him. "Regular," he replied, a little more at ease since she felt comfortable enough to initiate conversation. "Their coffee is too good to ruin it with a decaf."

Amari chuckled and said, "I guess we'll see."

Their eye contact became a stare and an unsettling feeling reminded him of many a Saturday night or Sunday morning spent in that same café drinking coffee and talking for hours with his Schelle.

Amari noticed his discomfort look and asked, "Are you alright?"

Solomon's thoughts were focused on Amari and her remarkable resemblance to his wife. He swallowed, blinked a couple of times then closed his eyes. His heart raced as he imagined her as his Schelle, then just that quickly felt embarrassed to no end. He opened his eyes and met her nut-brown stare. He looked away, only to be drawn back toward the gorgeous shade of brown in her eyes.

"Yeah, I'm..." He blew air and stuttered again. "I...I was just thinking..." was all he managed to say before Daphne arrived with their drinks and the rich, fragrant aroma of fresh brewed coffee. She set the drinks down and asked, "Would you like anything to eat, a salad or a Panini maybe? And our sausage rolls are to die for."

"Maybe later," Amari answered, letting Solomon off the hook.

Daphne left and they mixed in their desired amounts of sugar, cream and syrups then each took small sips of the piping hot coffee before letting it sit to cool.

They shared the power of a glance. She held his gaze, gave him an innocent smile, the kind that could turn an honest man into a cheating fool. On the drive from the church, he considered a dozen different openings which had all since vacated his mind. Now seated before her with his wife's eyes staring into his, Solomon fidgeted in his chair, exhaled and dropped his shoulders.. How was he going to tell Amari that the reason he asked her here was because she was the spitting image of his dead wife. She'd think he was crazy or a nut job. He'd never had such a conversation before and was struggling to conjure a non-threatening way to initiate the topic. He half wished that he could leave and let someone else have this conversation with her. But who? As the lines of worry eroded the smooth skin of his forehead, Amari touched his hand. "Solomon, are you sure you are alright?"

The phrase *Don't ask questions if you can't handle the answer* ricocheted in his mind. Not only did he not know if he could handle the answers, he wasn't certain what the questions should be.

Her cell phone's ring tone interrupted them. She checked the screen then swiped left to ignore the call.

He asked, "Do you need to get that?"

"No, I'm good. Now where were we?"

Solomon cleared his throat. "Amari can I be frank for a moment?"

Without looking away, she quipped, "Frank? You could at least give me a chance to meet Solomon before introducing me to *Frank*."

Solomon caught the joke and appreciated her sense of humor.

"I'm sorry. No, seriously, please go ahead and be Frank or Solomon or whoever it is that best suits you right now."

"It's rather funny that you should say it like that because the reason I approached you in church is because I thought you looked like someone I used to know."

"Umm, Solomon, if you're trying to score points here, you're going to have to come a little harder than that."

"No creativity necessary Miss. I really do mean it." Solomon fished his wallet from his jacket pocket. "Can I show you something?"

"Is it decent?"

Solomon chuckled as he opened his wallet and pulled out the picture of him and Mareschelle from their engagement party. He also had a picture of the two of them from their wedding day, but the engagement picture more clearly showed her face. "This is why I asked you here," he said handing her the picture with the back to her.

Amari's eyes bulged and her face went flush when she saw the picture. She couldn't believe what she was seeing and didn't appreciate the joke. The woman in the picture not only shared her face, but her eye color and her dimples. Wild thoughts of stalkers and other crazy people ran through Amari's head thinking that Solomon was some kind of psycho.

"What is this?" she asked. "How did you get my?" Amari threw the picture onto the table. "Is this supposed to be some kind of joke? Who put you up to this? Philip? One of his stupid friends? Probably Daniel. I hate him. Wait, are you a paparazzi?"

Solomon went into panic mode. He wasn't sure how she would react, but he wasn't prepared for the picture to upset her like this. "Amari, please let me explain."

The lady in the picture was Amari, but she knew it couldn't be real because she'd never met this man before. She felt her stomach roll. She thought, *What's his angle? What kind of game is he playing? What does he want?* She said, "I am sorry if I misled you in anyway Brother, but I don't know who you think I am." Feeling trapped, she lifted her purse from the empty seat and decided it was time to leave.

"No. No. I," Solo urged. "Please Amari, sit back down and let me explain," he pleaded for a second time. "That is not a picture of you. If you sit down, I will explain everything."

"You know what," Amari started. "This is way too creepy for me."

Solomon had hoped that if he gave her some space, she might let him say more. "Wait Amari please."

Amari stood, and gathered her jacket. She had heard enough and wasn't staying for anymore crazy explanations. "NO!" she said, extending her palm like a police officer for him to stop. "Solomon or Frank or whatever your real name is…" She stepped away from the table. "I don't know what kind of sick game you are playing, but I will not be a part of it."

"No games, Amari, I promise." He placed a business card on the table in front of her. "I have a reasonable explanation if you'll just grant me time. If not now, then please call me when you calm down."

Daphne had seen the entire episode unfold and came over to ask if everything was alright.

Amari regarded her, then looked at the card but did not touch it. She turned and hurried from the café to her car parked four doors down the street.

Solomon didn't chase her. Didn't try to further the issue. From the beginning, he knew it was a long shot but he had to try. He was familiar with the saying that everyone has a twin, but figure the odds that Mareschelle's doppelganger lived in the same city.

Solomon sat for a long time wondering how he could have better made his case to Amari. When he ran out of excuses for not saying the right words, he looked down and realized that both coffee cups were still full. He loved his coffee house, and not wanting to let his favorite brew go to waste, he drank his cup of coffee and Amari's too. When he got up to leave, he left Daphne a twenty dollar tip.

CHAPTER 22

TWO MONTHS AFTER HIS TRIP to Spokane, Solomon was home getting ready for a night out with Kenny. After meeting Amari, he took two weeks away from the office. He initially left, headed to Reno to do some gambling. After three straight days of losing, he realized lady Luck was not riding with him. Instead of going straight home, he detoured through San Francisco because Savannah told him Jordyn was there visiting her mother. When he couldn't connect with her, he stayed in the City by the Bay and went to all three games of a series between his Mariners and the Giants. The final leg of his trip back to Seattle included a four day pit stop in Portland to attend a fraternity brother's bachelor's party and wedding.

Dressed and waiting for his ride, Solomon checked his wristwatch. He flirted with the idea of wearing his necktie knotted loosely with the top button of his shirt undone. He'd never been to the Train Station, but Kenny raved about it. Now that he would see first-hand what all the noise was about, he made certain to dress for the occasion.

"What's up Kenny,?" Solomon answered, expecting his friend to already be there.

"I'm good," Kenny said. "I wanted to make sure you are good."

"Getting dressed," Solomon said. "I'll be ready to roll when you get here."

"Yeah, that's why I'm calling."

"Traffic moving slowly?"

"Nahh Bruh. I'm parked."

"Dang, it's that bad."

"I ain't talking about traffic. I'm parked in front of your place."

"Oh, I thought I heard a car." Solomon stepped to the round, manhole-sized window in his closet to look outside. Indeed, Kenny's car was sitting at the curb. "Door's open. Come on in."

"Are you sure about that?"

"Yeah I'm sure. Why you keep asking?"

"I asked 'cause I ain't trying to get into the middle of something ain't none of my business."

"What the hell is that supposed to mean?" Solomon asked.

"That is supposed to mean, I don't want to be in the middle of whatever's got this white girl crying on your porch."

"The *who* crying on my porch?"

A half hour before Kenny called, Jordyn Hoffman arrived at Solomon's. She saw lights on in the second story window as she approached his doorstep and wondered if he was home, or if he was just one of those people who left the lights on for security purposes. She stepped onto the porch; hesitated as she reached for the doorbell. She thought she heard footsteps and rapid thudding just inside the door, a sound similar to the one her heart was beating inside her chest. Jordyn imagined his hand on the doorknob as he looked through the peephole. She thought everything would be okay if he turned the lock hard and answered quickly. That would mean he saw her arrive and immediately wanted her to come in. She told herself that if he hesitated and turned the lock slowly, then he didn't want her there.

She had not called him in almost two months and questioned how she would be received after all the time that passed since he last saw her in the hospital. Unable to find the courage to press the bell, she pulled out her cell phone and dialed his number, but didn't press send. She was afraid of being rejected. Afraid that the terrible endings of his last two trips to Spokane had filled him with feelings of distrust, anger, or even worse resentment. Tears welled in her eyes as she stood staring at the phone screen, teetering about which decision was best.

She heard his Bruno Mars *24 Carat Magic* ringtone came to life inside the house, slid her phone into her purse and sat down on Solomon's front stoop. She wrapped her arms around her shins, dropped her head to her knees and started crying. Her sobs and her dilemma over whether or not to knock engulfing her such that she didn't even notice Kenny park his car and walk toward her.

Kenny tapped Jordyn softly on the shoulder. "Can I help you?"

She jumped, her eyes wide with fear as she scrambled to her feet.

Not wanting to alarm the weeping woman more than he already had, Kenny took two steps back and raised his hands in surrender. He should have felt secure, being on his best friend's front porch, but this was America, and if a hysterical woman, especially a crying white woman, made the wrong accusation, he could quickly find himself in a world of hurt. "Just asking if you were all right," he said softly.

Jordyn wiped her eyes, looked Kenny from head to toe, then brought her eyes back to meet his. His outfit was the latest fashion. She could tell that he was meticulous about his looks and most likely considered himself a ladies' man. With the weakest of grins, she finally asked, "Kenny? Right?"

"And you are?"

Solomon opened the door because she could answer. She turned, met his gaze and he smiled. "Jordyn?" he asked softly.

Her heart leapt with joy. Despite his questioning tone, the tenderness in his tenor comforted her. "Hi," she whispered, her lips wet from tears. She waved meekly. Offered a quivering smile. Despite what she thought earlier, she was now certain he was happy to see her.

"Jordyn?" Kenny asked as both she and Solomon regarded him. "Like the girl from Spokane—Jordyn?"

Solomon and Jordyn laughed lightly.

"Yes, Kenny," she said, extending her hand to shake his. "Jordyn. The girl from Spokane."

Solomon stepped out onto the porch to greet his company—both expected and unexpected. He reached for her without hesitation.

Now Jordyn knew coming to see him was the right decision.

In the two weeks following his return from Spokane after the Fourth of July when he found her beaten and unconscious, he called and talked to Savannah every day. When she was awake and released from the hospital, he considered flying from Reno to see her, but her father asked him to give her some time to recover. Through the remainder of his road trip, he called to check on her recovery but his interest met waning reciprocation. He altered his roundabout Reno vacation when he heard Jordyn was in San Francisco, but once he got there, Jordyn made no effort to return his calls, so he stopped reaching out to her. He enjoyed his time with her and wished her nothing but the best, but he refused to chase a woman who didn't desire him.

Solomon took her into his arms, hugged her tight. "What are you doing sitting out here?" Over her shoulder, he looked at Kenny, then followed his best friend's eyes to the suitcase sitting against the wall.

"I needed to get away. Everything is crazy back to my place right now. I promise that I'll explain everything. I just…" Tears returned to replace her words. "…Please?"

"Please what? Of course you can stay here. Come on in. Besides, I have a surprise for you." He nodded toward her luggage.

Kenny nodded, blew air, then picked up the oversized suitcases, followed them inside and sat them in the foyer. Like an intelligent third wheel, he felt the enormous space in their unspoken words crowding him out. He realized their need for some time alone and yielded, "Hey Frat, I'm going to get a drink," tapping on his wristwatch before gliding smoothly down the hallway to raid the bar.

Solomon took her things to a guest bedroom, and told her that he'd make some tea while she freshened up.

"What's the surprise?" she asked.

"I'm not telling yet," he said exiting into the hallway. "But from the looks of those bags under your eyes, you could use a nice surprise."

"Pleasssssse?" She stretched the word out for several seconds.

"Look, Kenny and I are heading out for dinner and drinks," he said, one hand still on the doorknob. "They normally have a great band, and when they don't have a band playing, they either have poetry slams or open mic nights. Since you claim to have an ear for music, I bet you'd probably enjoy yourself."

"Oh, I've got an ear," she said, slipping out of her shoes. "My Grams used to say I have an old soul," she added.

"And a pretty one too," he said.

"Thank you." The comment seemed earnest, unlike a pickup line and she smiled. "And my surprise…?"

"Your surprise will be here when we get back."

She glanced at the time on her phone. "Is there time for me to take a quick shower?"

"Certainly," Solomon offered before closing the door behind him.

Jordyn stripped away her clothes and jumped in the shower. She thanked God that Solomon was home. She needed a safe place to get away. A haven away from her life, her ex-boyfriend, and everything else wrong in her life in Spokane. Solomon's place was comforting. She could stop and think, understand the things happening to her.

Downstairs, Kenny said, "All right then, since our duo is now a trio, and the third is coming back here with you tonight, I'm going to head out and get us a table. I'll meet you there."

"Sounds like a plan," Solomon agreed then they exchanged fist bumps before Solomon locked the door and Kenny jogged to his car dodging rain drops.

Jordyn padded down the stairs twenty minutes after Kenny left, the alluring scent of her Daisy perfume softly announcing her return.

When she posed on the stairs, Solomon stood still, entranced by her heavenly visage. "Damn, you clean up nice."

Black sequins and crystal beads embellished the white, crepe, sleeveless blouse beneath her collarless black panel jacket. The bulk of her mane was pinned beneath a cute, floppy, teal and white Channing hat. Like the curled tail of a cat, a single tuft of hair escaped the hat, cupping the sleek jawline of her left cheek. The 4-inch heel on her black, cutout, suede sandals was the same teal in her hat. Although probably not the most comfortable for walking, the shoes gave her casual outfit an elegant appeal. Super-sheer, black hose climbed her 32-inch inseam to disappear beneath the dangling hem of her shirt. She definitely showed like a model, beauty queen, or whatever gorgeous creature she was trying to be.

Solomon howled like a cartoon wolf and they laughed aloud before leaving through the kitchen and out the back door. He pressed a button on his keychain and the garage door opened. Inside the garage, he bowed, opened the door and waved her into his 1938 Avion Voisin C28 Cabriolet Saliot. "Your carriage awaits madam."

Jordyn stopped in the door opening and turned to face him. The enchanting scent of her perfume filled his nostrils, her eyes glistened in the pale fluorescent light. In that moment, she wasn't a superficial beauty queen, she was simply a woman, and she was simply beautiful.

He leaned over the window and brushed his lips against hers; softly at first, and then with a hunger that built with each passing second. There was tension in that kiss. Longing. Fear. And twenty seconds later, when they broke the kiss, there was relief.

CHAPTER 23

WHEN SOLOMON REACHED HIS BLOCK, he noticed a set of headlights in the rearview mirror make the same turn fifty yards behind him, but paid it no attention assuming it was one of his neighbors returning home. Instead of parking in his garage, he parked at the curb behind Jordyn's car just as her Uber pulled off. He left the keys in the ignition, hopped out of his car and raced to stop her.

She had unlocked her car and was about to pull the driver's door open when he leaned his weight on her door. She was still angry with the horrible way their unexpected date had ended a half hour prior, but Solomon didn't budge when she spat, "Move!"

~

The Train Station was packed when they arrived three hours prior. A band from Olympia was on the marquee for that night, but shortly after they found seats and ordered drinks, the club's emcee announced that the band would be late because of car trouble. He came back ten minutes later and announced that in the interim, they were going to host an open mic competition with a five-hundred-dollar prize.

Five people signed up including Solomon. He played the piano and was one of the two finalists along with a woman who provided her stage name as Decadent Red. They saw that same lady sitting on their frat brother's lap earlier when Kenny took Solomon and Jordyn upstairs. He didn't call her name, just referred to her as *this gorgeous lady*. Jordyn noticed a hint of recognition in her eyes when her date introduced Solomon and Kenny as his frat brothers, but she dismissed it as nothing more than familiarization between people who lived in the same city. Neither Solomon nor the woman made a production of it, so Jordyn continued on.

Decadent Red was walking on sunshine when she reached the side stage after being declared the contest winner. Behind her, the crowd was still clapping, whistling and chanting *Red* over and again. She kissed the emcee on the cheek then practically leapt into Solomon's arms. He held her there for a moment as she squeezed her joy into him. "Ahhhhhhh!" she screamed. "That. Was. So. Awwesome!"

Kenny and Jordyn were behind Solomon when they rounded the corner. She had asked Kenny to take her to see where Solomon had disappeared since he hadn't returned to their table after performing. As if she'd been struck a violent blow on the head, but hadn't fallen, Jordyn stood stock still. Her eyes open, stricken with disbelief.

Kenny whispered shit then grabbed Jordyn's hand when he saw his best friend and Decadent Red, known to him as Leona Pearson, embrace in a bear hug. "You want me to kick his ass," he deadpanned.

Everyone backstage stopped when Jordyn screamed, "Dammit!"

Leona met the angry gaze of Solomon's date as he loosened his grip on her and turned to find Jordyn's voice.

"I guess I should've known," she started. "since you couldn't take your eyes off of her upstairs."

Solomon was caught in a bad place. Although he hadn't initiated the hug, he didn't stop it either. And she felt so good in his arms that he did not hurry to let her go.

"I knew coming here was a mistake," Jordyn spat, staring at him long and hard the way a scorned woman could stare right through a man. "I should've figured that out when you dropped me off at the hospital and never came back." Jordyn snatched her hand from

Kenny's. She was a lioness in a cage, mentally pacing, searching for an escape path before rushing toward the entrance.

Solomon hurried after her. Called her name several times.

She was distancing herself from him, but for her, it was neither fast nor far enough. On the sidewalk, she searched left and right, frantically looking for a taxi or some type of ride service to facilitate her escape. "Where the hell can I get a cab," she yelled at the bouncer.

"Jordyn wait." Solomon emerged through the door in full stride. "Please, let me explain."

"Nothing to explain Mister Lover Man." She avoided his eyes. "It's obvious you want to be with whoever that is. It was obvious upstairs and it was obvious backstage."

Solomon touched her hand.

"Don't you touch me," She yelled.

Solomon raised his hands in surrender as the bouncer and a dozen people waiting to enter the club watched the sidewalk drama play out. He watched her face go through a range of emotions. Her eyes showed uncertainty, then apprehension, then anger.

"What does it take to get a flipping cab in this town?" she asked to no one then turned and shouted, "Taxi!"

Solomon spoke to her back in a more subdued tone to prevent their impromptu audience from any continued eavesdropping. "Jordyn, I'm sorry for what you thought you saw. Leona and I are friends. We're cousins. I didn't introduce you to her upstairs because it wasn't the place or time. If that was wrong, then I apologize. I'm glad you're here and I'm glad you cared enough about me to come all this way to see me, but if you want to get away from me, let me get my car. I'll take you back to my place to get your bags and then I will drive you anywhere you want to go," he said, irritated by her capricious words.

"No, you can mail my stuff to me," she spat venomously as she opened the back door of an Uber. "I don't ever want to see you again!"

~

After Jordyn checked that the door handle didn't break any of her nails, her expression moved from anger to pain.

Desperate to explain the misunderstanding, Solomon said, "Look Jordyn, it's not like that, she…"

"Don't you dare say she doesn't mean anything to you. I don't know how long you've known that woman, but I'm grown enough to know that there's something between the two of you."

"Come on, Jordyn. I didn't mean to sound…"

"You sounded like how you felt, like I was annoying you." Then she continued, "Oh wait, I'm sorry. Maybe I misunderstood. How did you mean to sound?"

"The hug was innocent. She was excited and it just happened," Solomon pleaded. "It had nothing to do with you."

"Obviously," she snarled. "From where I was standing, it had everything to do with her and whatever it is you share with her."

"Some of it was, and some of it wasn't," he said. "Most of it was not. She was excited about winning and our familiarity probably made her comfortable enough to hug me."

"Just probably, hunh?"

"Look, nothing happened. It…was an innocent hug between friends."

"If you're such friends, why didn't you introduce me to her upstairs?"

"It wasn't the place.

"No, because you have a history with her, and because of that history, you waited backstage hoping I wouldn't see you with her."

"The fact remains," Solomon said forcefully, "that I am sorry."

"All I ever wanted to do was please you," she sobbed. "I tried to show you a good time in Spokane and you abandoned me. Then, being the idiot that I am, I come all the way to Seattle hoping to make up for whatever you think I did wrong and end up being treated like dirt again."

Solomon stepped closer and began explaining 'the nuclear family' in black neighborhoods and his learning of his relations to Leona after the shooting at the University of Washington. He explained how they dated before they found out they were cousins. How they didn't know because both of their fathers were estranged from their mothers and they'd never met because their mothers never took them to their fathers' family functions.

Despite his convincing tone, Jordyn was still mad. She could tell there was more to their relationship than just a couple of dates. More than just an innocent hug between friends, or cousins, or whatever. She knew there was nothing platonic in the way they hugged, and for that reason there was no way she was going back into his house with him. Even if that meant she had to get on the first train back to Spokane and return to that nightmare.

Solomon stepped further into the street to face Jordyn, the light from his porch forming a halo behind her head. "If my hugging Leona was wrong, then I apologize."

She could feel his energy when he reached over and touched her arm. First it tickled the fine hairs on her arm. Then it spread like a morphine itch, making her resort to her nervous habit of raking her fingers through her hair. "Solomon, I just turned twenty-seven and you're ..."

"A little older!" he said abruptly, but softly.

"Right, but, my thing ain't here in Seattle, and yours ain't in Spokane. And from everything I can tell, you don't want me here."

"That's not what I meant, Jordyn."

"I understand that there's no future in whatever I think this is? Hell," she guffawed, "I can't even say what *this* is. Don't know how to address it because there's nothing to address. So you're right, Solomon, it's nothing. I was tripping." She pulled away from his hand and walked to the passenger side of the car.

"You weren't tripping, Jordyn. I was."

Then she screamed, "Solomon watch out." As the car that had turned onto his street shortly after he did, sped up and quickly closed the gap between them.

Solomon turned to see the car's headlights flash on less than ten yards away. When he realized he was about to be the meat in a car sandwich, he leaped onto the hood of Jordyn's rental car just as the speeding car swiped the driver's side, leaving a broad swath of black paint stretching from the front fender to the rear.

Jordyn's scream pierced through the sound of crashing metal.

The impact of the black sedan pushing her car up onto the curb bounced Solomon off the hood and onto the sidewalk. As the black car sped off into the night, Solomon scrambled to his feet. "Are you alright?" he asked, wrapping Jordyn in his arms and pushing her toward his front door.

"I'm fine," she said. "What the hell was that?"

"I don't know."

Solomon's Neighbors—some concerned, some nosy—were in their windows and on their porches watching. After the police left, Jordyn still insisted that Solomon take her to a hotel. The drama of the hit-and-run had shaken her, but the anger of him hugging Leona was still prevalent enough for her to maintain that she did not want to spend the night with him. Whatever he'd done to cause someone to want to run him down was too much drama for her to be involved.

Solomon unlocked the front door so she could grab her suitcases, promising to take her to the hotel after taking care of her rental car.

Jordyn called for an Uber before she rolled her suitcases from the front door to the curb—a walk she'd excitedly taken in reverse four hours prior. Taking that stroll felt like a death row inmate walking the Green Mile. She stopped and stood near, but not next to Solomon as the tow truck pulled off.

With his hand on the door handle, he said, "No matter what you think, I did not mean to sound dismissive of your feelings earlier."

"How did you mean to sound?" she asked, her fingers loosely wrapped around the handle of the luggage.

"All I ever wanted to do was get to know you. But unfortunately, drama seems to follow us everywhere we go." He sighed heavily and pressed his palms against his temples.

"So I'm a burden?" she blurted out. "Is that what I am to you?"

He recomposed himself and reached for her.

She stepped away.

"Right now, I don't know what this is," he confessed. "I just don't."

"Putting myself out there like this isn't easy for me Solomon. You may not know what it is like to be young and lose that younger self at the hands of another only to find yourself within a newer older self. My ex hurt me something terrible" she said, starting to cry. "I thought you were different."

Handing her a handkerchief, he said, "Please don't cry. I'm sorry."

"What else is there to do?" she tried to hide her feelings, but failed miserably.

"You could hug me," he said with a little more bravado than she cared for. "I'm still here for that."

"Just like you were there to hug that other woman?" Her eyes flashed angrily. "No thank you, asshole."

When he met her gaze again, his eyes went hard. "I don't care how you feel. Or what you think I've done to you, but I am a grown man, and this is my home and you are not going to disrespect me like that."

She teetered, shifted her weight.

"You know what? Maybe you should leave."

"If I leave, I'm not coming back," she said.

Solomon grumbled. "If you don't want to stay, then I'm not going to beg you. I'll miss you. And I'll regret not asking you to stay, but I won't beg. I'm done begging." Solomon turned and strode up the walk to his front porch. He didn't look back, but he could feel her eyes boring into his back.

As Jordyn stood on the sidewalk waiting for her ride to arrive, Solomon watched her from the stoop of his front porch. He'd gone inside and poured himself a drink, and even though their conversation had ended, the protector in him wouldn't let her stand outside alone. The rye whiskey bit as he swallowed, but it was a bite that he enjoyed when he was mad.

When a red Toyota Camry arrived, Jordyn verified the plates, compared the face of the male driver to the picture of the driver on the app, then got in without saying goodbye. When the little red car pulled off with Jordyn sitting in the back seat openly sobbing, Solomon finished his drink then threw the glass and watched it smash on the sidewalk where she'd been standing.

CHAPTER 24

IN THE TWO WEEKS FOLLOWING the Train Station debacle, Solomon had left seven messages on Jordyn's cell phone but none were returned. He considered visiting her on an upcoming trip to Spokane, but thought better of showing up unannounced after a long conversation over three bottles of wine in which Desmond convinced him to leave his thoughts of Jordyn long behind. After that, everything ran smoothly until the day he was arrested while hosting his neighbor's retirement celebration in the backyard of the Hang Suite.

"And then they arrested me," Solomon said, finishing his story for Trey. They had met with the District Attorney for four hours that Monday. Trey argued several strong points including the woman was still missing, there was no significant physical evidence that indicated Solomon had perpetrated a crime against her, and there was no body to warrant a murder charge, therefore, all of the charges were circumstantial. The meeting ended with no official charges being filed. Solomon was required to surrender his passport, released into Trey's recognizance and required to report to the Seattle police department any plans to travel outside the greater Seattle area.

Trey Thomas didn't have an opening in his calendar to meet with Solomon for four days. Now they sat in his office, having concluded a marathon, three-hour Q&A session about Solomon's involvement with the missing woman from Spokane. Trey excused his secretary, wished her a nice weekend and asked her for the transcription notes on Monday afternoon since it was already late on Friday.

Once the two men were alone, Trey poured two glasses of bourbon, handed one to Solomon then asked, "So if my math is right, tomorrow will be three weeks since this woman left your house in an Uber?"

"Yep." Solomon replied flatly.

"And all you know is that the Uber was a red Camry?"

"Yep."

"Did she call you once she got to the hotel to let you know she had arrived safely?"

"Nope," Solomon said. "I asked her to, but she didn't call or text."

"And you have no idea what was going on with the black car that almost ran you over?"

"I never saw the car. Only reason I know it was black was because that's what Jordyn told the police when they came."

"And you are sure you haven't seen her since she left your house?"

"Nope," Solomon said, after emptying and motioning for a drink refill.

Trey nodded for him to refill his own glass, then pulled out a copy of the police report the Spokane police department provided and slid it across the table to Solomon. "Here's a little light reading for you this weekend. Call me Monday if there's anything in here that sticks out to you, or if you remember anything that can help us figure out anything about this woman disappearance."

Instead of going to his office Monday morning, Solomon was sitting in Trey Thomas' waiting room when his attorney arrived. "Can you go to Spokane with me?" Solomon asked when Trey shut his office door. "I know I can't leave Seattle without informing SPD, but I want to talk to Jordyn's girlfriends face-to-face and see what they tell me."

"You're right, you can travel, and you'll have to check in with the Spokane police when you get there." Trey opened his calendar. "When are you talking about going?"

"I cleared my calendar for this entire week," Solomon said excitedly. "I would have driven up this weekend, but I wanted to clear it with you first and I didn't want to interfere with your weekend."

"That was smart, and considerate, of you."

"I want to leave as soon as you can go. I need to find out what's going on. I'm no angel, Mister Trey, but I could never physically hurt a woman."

"I believe you son, but my calendar is full. I can't leave town this week." Trey and Solomon stared silently for a beat, both carefully considering their next words. As Solomon thought of what to say next, Trey said, "I have a trusted colleague in Spokane who owes me a favor. If he is available, I'll ask him to go to the Spokane Police department with you in my stead."

"That's awesome! When can we call him?"

"Well, since you walked in here unannounced this morning, I need a little time. I have a full slate this morning, but I'll have my secretary get him on the line after my partners' meeting." Trey watched a smile of acceptance creep onto Solomon's face before he pushed a button and asked his secretary to get Detective Chrystopher on the line.

~

Attorney Josh Ventura was Trey Thomas' colleague in Spokane. After Detective Foreman of the Spokane Police department agreed to meet at three o'clock Tuesday afternoon, Solomon ate breakfast at sunrise Tuesday morning then hopped in his Audi A8 and drove to Spokane. He arrived at Josh Ventura's office as the morning expired and they were on the phone with Trey right at one o'clock. After a thorough conversation, Josh felt sufficiently briefed to meet with the detective.

When Detective Foreman arrived to meet with Solomon and his stand-in counsel, Jordyn's townhouse was no longer considered a crime scene, but police tape still hung across the front entrance and a padlock secured the broken door. He handed Josh and Solomon rubber gloves, told them, "Put these on and touch as little as possible inside," and waited for their agreement before he unlocked the door. The living room was dark when they entered. Detective Foreman instructed them to open curtains as he searched for a light switch. Once the room was illuminated, Josh saw several piles of mutilated photos strewn throughout. He noticed that if there was a man's body in the pic, the face was cut out.

Detective Foreman picked up an envelope and waved it around. "An envelope just like this one was found during our initial search. According to my notes, you were identified in most of the mutilated evidence."

That reminder put a sour taste in Solo's mouth.

Detective Foreman moved into the garage while Josh moved toward the kitchen. Solomon went upstairs. The glass table in Jordyn's bedroom was smashed, her mattress turned upside down, and her pillows ripped apart. There didn't seem to be anything missing or moved from her walk-in closet and her bathroom was pristine. Her guest bedroom closet, which she used to hold the overflow of her extensive wardrobe, was empty, all of its contents strewn about the guest room floor. The search of Jordyn's townhouse yielded no clues about her whereabouts or any leads as to who may have taken her.

"Jordyn and her girlfriend Savannah are close as sisters. Have you talked to her?" Solomon asked when all three men returned to the living room. "What about her other girlfriend, Melanie?"

Detective Foreman pulled out his note pad and thumbed through a couple of pages. "Yes. I interviewed Miss Hoffman's father and a

Miss Savannah Grimes, but I don't have anything in my notes about a Melanie."

"Well, I don't know everything about their dynamic," Solomon replied, "but every other time I saw Jordyn out with friends, Melanie and Savannah were joined at the hip."

"Maybe Melanie knows something that Savannah may have missed," Josh Ventura offered. "Now that everybody has had a chance to let the emotions of Miss Hoffman going missing subside, I think it might be prudent to conduct another round of questions that Mister Alexandré and I could observe."

"Sounds like a great idea to me," Solomon added.

"Do you think we could arrange those interviews before week's end?" Josh asked.

Detective Foreman checked his cell phone when it buzzed. "I have to get back to the precinct. Let me see what I can do about these women, but I don't want you approaching them on your own." Detective Foreman handed Josh his business card and huffed, "Call me later," before ushering Solomon and Josh out of Jordyn's house, securing the padlock and driving off in his unmarked police car.

On Wednesday afternoon, Solomon and Josh stood outside the interrogation room behind a two-way mirror watching Detective Foreman interview Jordyn's girlfriend, Savannah Grimes. Savannah answering the questions Solomon had prepared for Detective Foreman for more than thirty minutes. Then her thanked for coming in and escorted her from the room.

Solomon and Savannah locked eyes when they stepped into the hallway at the same time. "I don't know what you did to my friend, you bastard, but I hope you rot in hell for it," she growled before slapping him with an open palm.

Solomon rubbed his cheek. The fury in her words cut him deep. He and Savannah hadn't been overly chummy, but she'd seen him interact with her friend and never thought she'd consider him capable of hurting Jordyn. "I don't know what happened to her Savannah, but I will do everything possible to find out! My words may not have merit right now, but I promise I did not hurt your friend," he said to her back as she walked away. The stinging sensation of Savannah's slap reminded him of the humiliation he suffered at the hand of Jordyn's ex-boyfriend and his goons at the Alumni Gala. "Detective Foreman, has anyone interviewed a man named Glenn Zimmerman? He's Jordyn's ex-boyfriend, and he was visibly irritated when he saw me out with Jordyn once."

"Irritated how?" Josh asked.

"Irritated to the point where he sucker punched me before he and his goons practically kicked my ass in front of a handful of people who all looked the other way when they recognized them."

"I know Glenn Zimmerman," Josh proclaimed. "My son played football with him in high school."

"Yeah, I know the name. He's a petty crook around these parts. I've seen him in here for a couple of misdemeanors, but nothing significant enough to warrant any serious jail time."

"Check his record. I recall Jordyn telling me he assaulted her once."

"Hmmmm," Detective Foreman grumbled. "I'll have to pull that file."

Five hours later, Solomon and Josh were back in the observation room. This time they were watching Detective Foreman interview Melanie.

"Miss Crawford, I'm Detective Foreman and I'm leading the investigation into the disappearance of Miss Jordyn Hoffman. According to reports, you and Miss Hoffman were very close friends."

Something in Detective Foreman's speech struck Melanie as odd. "Excuse me, but you said 'were'." Her eyes got big. "Is Jordyn alright?"

"Truth is, Miss Crawford, we don't know. A couple of weeks

ago we got a phone call from the Seattle police. The manager of the hotel Miss Hoffman checked into called the police when a disturbance was reported in her hotel room. When Miss Hoffman didn't let hotel staff in, they entered on their own and found her room ransacked—and Miss Hoffman was nowhere to be found. Spokane police checked her house and it too was ransacked. Her father hasn't seen her, and her friend..." Detective Foreman checked his notes despite having interviewed her only a couple of hours earlier, "a Miss Savannah Grimes told us that the last time she saw Miss Hoffman was the night the three of you shared dinner at your house before she went to Seattle. According to Miss Grimes, Miss Hoffman was still at your house when she went home that night. We're hoping that you can fill in some of the blanks in the timeline for us so that we can bring your friend home."

Melanie took a deep breath and panned the room. "But..." she started. Then, "What else did Savannah say?" Beads of perspiration appeared on Melanie's brow. "I haven't seen Jordyn..." she got quiet and squinted.

"Miss Crawford, other than Miss Grimes, who else do you know was close to Miss Hoffman? I mean, did she have a boyfriend or an ex-boyfriend, or do you know if she was dating anyone?"

Melanie's brow furled when Detective Foreman said ex-boyfriend. Both Josh Ventura and Detective Foreman noticed, but the detective didn't let on that he did. He maintained his demeanor as he asked "If she was at your house before she left, do you know why Miss Hoffman went to Seattle? I mean, did she go to see someone? Was it a business trip?"

"When I woke up the next morning, Jordyn was gone."

"So she spent the night at your house?"

"Yes."

"Had she ever left in the middle of the night before?"

"NO. She never did anything like that before."

"Do you have any idea why she would do something so out of

the ordinary?"

"I don't know."

"Think hard, Miss Crawford. Your friend is missing. Possibly dead. If there's anything you can tell us, I'm sure as her friend, she'll be grateful if you help us find her."

Melanie's hands were shaking when she began talking again. "Jordyn's been dating some guy in Seattle named Solomon. I only met him a couple of times. I don't know how serious things are between them, but she talks about him often."

Detective Foreman wrote down his first name then asked, "Do you happen to know this Solomon's last name? We'll have Seattle PD bring him in for questioning if we can find him."

"Umm, I would have to think about his last name, but I remember that he's a doctor."

"Alright, well while you think about that, I want to go back to Miss Hoffman leaving your house in the middle of the night. Are you certain she actually went to Seattle? Did you talk to her while she was there? Do you know how she would've gotten there? By train, bus, did she drive? Is it possible that someone picked her up from your house?"

Melanie tried to answer each of Detective Foreman's questions, but each time she started to talk, he injected another question. Josh Ventura told Solomon that it was a technique police used to frustrate interviewees.

"Miss Crawford, you mentioned that Miss Hoffman wasn't serious with the guy in Seattle. Was she serious with anyone here in Spokane?"

Melanie didn't respond.

"Are you dating anyone Miss Crawford?"

"He doesn't. I mean, what does that have to do with Jordyn being missing?"

"Just routine questions Miss Crawford. Maybe the person you're dating might have seen Miss Hoffman. We have to explore all avenues. If you are dating someone, can you give us their name?"

Melanie's legged bounced beneath the table as she seriously contemplated omitting the part about Jordyn leaving her house because she was angry that Melanie was dating Glenn Zimmerman. Melanie had been in love with G-Z since middle school and with Jordyn missing, it seemed like a great opportunity to permanently insert herself in G-Z's life. She said, "I spent the entire day alone after Jordyn left. I called her six times, but she didn't return any of my calls. I called Savannah and she said she hadn't heard from her. She said she'd call her and that she'd call me back after she talked to her. When Savannah called me back Sunday night, I had company and we didn't talk long. She said she didn't talk to Jordyn and that whoever heard from her first should tell her to call the other. I agreed and I went back to my date."

"I'll need the name of the person you were keeping company with so we can confirm your story with them and Miss Grimes.."

After an almost two minute journey through silence, Melanie whispered, "Glenn. His name is Glenn."

Detective Foreman asked, "Does this Glenn have a last name?"

Again whispering, she said, "Glenn Zimmerman. He wasn't at our girls' dinner before she left. He and I were together from Sunday morning until he left my house Monday morning, so I don't know how he can help."

"Like I said Miss Crawford, we are covering all bases. If this Glenn Zimmerman is a friend of yours, then he may be a friend of Miss Hoffman's, and you never know, he may know something about her that you don't, or you may not remember. Something that can help us find her. We'll ask him all of the same routine questions we asked you."

Melanie was visibly perturbed. She scratched nervously at the back of her hand as Detective Foreman wrote in his notebook. Paranoia set in through the eternity of the three minutes that passed while Detective Foreman finished writing his notes.

When the detective kicked his chair back and quickly stood up, Melanie jumped. "Thank you for coming in today, Miss Crawford. The officer in the hallway will see you out." Detective Foreman walked Melanie to the interview room door. "As soon as we hear something about your friend, we'll be in touch."

"Thank you detective. Please find my friend."

Detective Foreman handed her his card. "If there's anything you think of that we didn't talk about today, please call me at this number."

Solomon and Josh were invited back Thursday afternoon to observe the interview with the street thug known to Spokane police as G-Z. Glenn Zimmerman showed up with a lawyer and, when his attorney allowed him to speak, every word out of his mouth was hostile toward the detective. He corroborated Melanie's admission that they were together all day Sunday and into Monday, but neither of their stories accounted for the time between when Savannah Grimes left Melanie's house and when she called.

G-Z lied to the police that he'd been out partying with his crew Saturday and got home just before midnight. A lie the two goons who burned his car later co-signed. His telling them that he called the police to report his car was missing after he woke up was consistent with the time stamp of the report Detective Foreman later looked up. He told them that he called Melanie after he showered, and invited her to brunch Sunday if she could come get him because it looked like someone had stolen his car.

He had been sleeping with Melanie on and off for a couple of months. He knew she had kept their little secret from Jordyn since he was Jordyn's ex-boyfriend and he couldn't think of a better person to establish an alibi with than Jordyn's best friend. G-Z had Melanie pick him up around noon and was still with her when Savannah called at 10 o'clock Sunday night to tell her about Jordyn's house being broken into. When Melanie regarded him while listening to

Savannah's story, he shrugged his shoulders in inquiry, to which she waved him off, ignoring her initial sense that G-Z had something to do with the break in because she had the man she wanted ready to share her bed with her that night.

"If you don't mind me asking Mister Zimmerman, what happened to your ear?"

G-Z fingered the gauze wrapped around is earlobe. The white cloth tinged red because the stitches had bled earlier when he didn't do a good job cleaning it. "Yeah," G-Z started coarsely, then guffawed as he finished with, "Ear piercing gone wrong. You should see how bad I made the piercer look."

Detective Foreman escorted G-Z and his attorney out into the hallway as they exited the police interview room. "Don't worry Mister Zimmerman, if we have more questions, we'll be in touch."

"All I'm worrying about de-tec-tive, is what movie to watch while I eat my pizza, and what woman to poke on after my belly is full."

Josh Ventura listened to the off-color comments made during the Glenn Zimmerman interview and didn't let Solomon leave the observation room until he was certain Glenn had enough time to leave the detective's floor of the precinct. He noticed the tension in Solomon's face and cautioned him to stay away from Glenn after hearing Solomon's repetitive negative comments about the man during Detective Foreman's interview. "Let's go get something to eat," he urged Solomon, trying to keep him in his presence and prevent him from following Jordyn's ex.

Solomon agreed with no more than an, "Okay." Now that he knew G-Z was involved with Melanie, he didn't need to follow him. That *what woman to poke on after my belly is full* comment was more than enough to let him know where he could find G-Z once he convinced his stand-in Spokane counselor that he was calm, collected and not going to do anything stupid.

When Melanie answered her front door that night at just before ten o'clock, he was wearing a baseball cap pulled down to cover his eyes. He shoved the pizza box toward Melanie but she didn't take it. "Nineteen sixty eight, ma'am." Solomon strained to disguise his voice as, hoping that the box would distract her from recognizing his voice and paying enough attention to his face to recognize him,

"But we already…" Melanie started before a man's voice called from the living room. Instead of arguing with the pizza man, she called back, "Glenn, did you order another pizza?"

Solomon's mask, nylon gloves, hat and the dimly lit exterior outside Melanie's front door were the perfect cover for his disguise. Before she could continue he broke into, "Look lady, I just deliver them. If you don't tip me, then I only get five dollars an hour delivering this crap to you people. I didn't order it. If it's not what you ordered, then you need to call and ask for the manager, he can fix this not me. All I do is drive the box out here and give it to you, you feel me?" Solo knew he could take Glenn in a fair fight, he just needed to get him alone. His little charade worked exactly as he anticipated.

A moment later, a pissed off Glenn Zimmerman jumped off the couch and stormed toward the front door to chastise the pizza delivery boy. When he pushed Melanie out of his way, Solomon slammed the pizza box containing four bricks into his face. As Glenn stumbled backwards from the blow, Solomon stepped in the door and lead with a field goal kick to his groin. Glenn fell to his knees and before the pizza box could hit the floor, Solo punched Glenn with a left cross. The brass knuckles inside his nylon yardwork gloves crashed hard into his jaw and took him to the floor.

Solomon shouted, "Shut up," when Melanie screamed. He raised his fist, but knew he'd never hit her. When she cowered and stumbled back, his feigned assault had accomplished its intent. His bluff hinged on his hope that Melanie knew Glenn had enemies, but she'd never considered they'd bring their street drama to her doorstep.

As Melanie sat on the floor crying, Solo turned his attention back to Glenn down on all fours. He kicked Glenn in the ribs causing him to roll onto his side. When his body hit the floor, he kicked him in the ribs again, then twice more before raring back and kicking him across his chin with what would leave Glenn lying unconscious on Melanie's foyer floor. He stood over Glenn, waiting ominously for him to move as Melanie whimpered in the background. When he was confident that he was out, Solomon turned to exit. He pulled his mask down and held one finger in front of his face as he passed Melanie. "No police," he said, making eye contact so that he was certain she fully recognized who he was before he left her there crying on the floor for the man who had jumped him at the Alumni Gala.

CHAPTER 25

HAVING SEEN JORDYN'S HOUSE RANSACKED and still not knowing what happened to her, Solo dreaded the idea of being alone for the drive back to Seattle with nothing to think about except the memories of their time together, and more specifically, the wonderful memory of their road trip via The Gorge. His visit to Spokane may have yielded no answer about what happened to Jordyn, but he felt great about kicking Glenn Zimmerman's ass. Had their first go round been a fair fight, Solo knew he would've won both fights against Jordyn's ex instead of taking that first L. In his heart, he prayed that idiot would round up his goons and ride to Seattle so the Four Horsemen could give them a proper North Seattle ass whipping. Hoping and praying for the satisfaction of that dream coming true kept a smile on his face through the majority of his journey.

Twelve miles east of the exit to The Gorge, Solomon made a pitstop at a Big Rig Haven rest stop on Interstate 90. Bladder empty, Mentos candy and a drink in hand, Solo stood at the counter deciding what type of wing sauce he wanted. He grew impatient watching the clerk repeatedly fail at ringing up the person two people ahead of him and looked to the other side of the service enclosure hoping another register was open so he could check out and be on his way. The second register was closed, but another cashier fixed the problem and got the line moving. Behind him, a stout, fifty-something woman, stepped in line. Her truck company badge read Brandi, and she beamed a pocked face full of freckles at him, apparently anxious to enter into conversation. The stoutly built woman with bright red hair twisted into unkempt Pippi Longstocking braids regarded Solomon's cup and asked, "Hot chocolate?"

"Not today, but I like it on occasion." He noticed the greenish yellow tinge to her teeth and was thankful she was far enough away that he couldn't smell her breath. He almost choked on his drink when she said, "Too bad, because Brandi goes well with hot chocolate."

Brandi was wide in the hips from sitting behind the wheel of an eighteen-wheeler. That width staying constant right up to her shoulders.

"Probably too sweet for my palate," he replied calmly. "I need something a little stronger to help me get down the road."

"I love something strong on the road with me." She kept licking her lips, doing a north Idaho version of the LL Cool J flirting thing. She asked, "Heading my way, Handsome?"

Solomon saw Coeur d'Alene, Idaho under the name on her badge and took a chance with, "I am, if your way is west toward Puget Sound."

"Too bad I'm cranking my engine all the way to Idaho," Her eyes traveled the length of him. "'Cause I'm sure your handsome ass could've kept everything in my cab purring right along."

"Sounds like fate crossed our paths for no reason." Solo blew air after laughing off the frightening mental image of being enslaved in Brandi's eighteen-wheel love wagon. "But can I at least buy your drink?"

"If you insist, Sexual Chocolate."

Solomon paid then turned to leave. "Pleasure meeting you Brandi."

Brandi cocked a sinister smile. "If you change your mind, it definitely would be," she said, grabbing Solomon's butt as he passed.

Solomon jumped.

"Oops, my bad," Brandi laughed.

"Yeah, I guess I need to watch where I'm walking." Solomon laughed away his flattery as the lady trucker's advances brought about images of the hilariously funny, overbearing housekeeper Berta from the TV show *Two and a Half Men* trying to seduce Martin Sheen's character.

Wanting to make sure Brandi didn't have any ulterior motives, Solomon exited the front door, turned left and stood at the end of the building twenty feet from his car pretending to fiddle with his phone for the next ten minutes while he watched Berta's twin sister, Brandi from Idaho, climb into her big rig and thankfully drive off headed east. Once he was certain the danger of being Brandi's big rig love entanglement had passed, Solomon hopped in his car and rode a smile of relief and the thoughts of Jordyn dancing at The Gorge all the way home. A dance he would kill to watch just one more time.

CHAPTER 26

SOLOMON DRESSED FOR SUNDAY SERVICE, but between missing Mareschelle and speculating about Jordyn's disappearance and possible murder, he couldn't focus on worshipping. Lawrence was preaching in South Seattle again, but had not requested The Horsemen's presence. After her refusal to take his card personified the botched ending of their first meeting, a second attempt at winning over the ghost seemed ominous.

So instead, he took off his suit jacket and traded a seat in a church pew for the seat in front of his computer. He went to the City of Tacoma website, found the hall of records page and looked up birth records. After every combination of names for Amari and Mareschelle proved fruitless, Solomon stared at his computer and rolled his pencil between his fingers like he always did when he was deep in thought.

The phrase *adoption records* came to mind when a pet adoptions advertisement popped up on his screen. The Betancourts adopted Mareschelle when her mother died shortly after giving birth. Solomon remembered that adoption records were open to the public, so instead of calling Mrs. Be, he decided to searched the internet for adoption records. There it was—Mareschelle Betancourt, born September 17, 1980. Solomon opened the record and read the Betancourt's names and her place of birth, St. Bonaventure Memorial Hospital. Unfortunately, the adoption agency and the name of her birth parents were both left blank.

Rolling his pencil again, Solomon searched the St. Bonaventure Hospital website. He searched birth records for September 1980 and came up with a set of girl twins born on the 17th, but both the birth parents' and the babies' names were blank.

Solomon printed the records from St. Bonaventure and from the Seattle Hall of Records, and drove to Tacoma. "Hello Missus Be," Solomon practically sang when Mareschelle's mother answered.

Surprised to see him standing in her doorway, and considering it rude that he showed up unannounced, Rachel Mae sternly asked, "What are you doing way out here?"

Solomon had gotten along fine with Mr. Betancourt, but for some reason, he never understood why Mrs. Betancourt never cared for him. "If you're not too busy, I'd like to talk to you about Mareschelle?"

Unsure of his intentions, Rachel Mae remained stoic in the doorway. It had been almost two years since the two of them had spoken face-to-face. Solomon called every Mother's Day, and always sent birthday and Christmas cards. After Mareschelle passed, he maintained regular contact with his in-laws, but after her husband died, Rachel Mae no longer felt obligated to entertain him. Especially since she blamed Solomon for her daughter's death and moreover, never wanted her to marry him in the first place.

He had made the hour-long drive from north Seattle to Tacoma, so whether it be on the porch or inside the house, he wasn't leaving without speaking his peace.

With a reluctant wave of her hand, Rachel Mae relinquished the guard on her front door and let him in.

Inside, Solomon showed her the documents he had printed. He told her about meeting Amari and explained her remarkable resemblance to Mareschelle. He told her about the twin girls that were born on his Schelle's birthday and that the hospital birth record for the twins' parents listed the father as unknown and the mother as deceased. He asked if she knew anything of Mareschelle's birth parents and if she would please share any details about the adoption.

Rachel Mae told Solomon that she and Mareschelle's birth mother, a woman named Bonnie two years younger than her, were college dorm mates. That they remained friends after she graduated, which is how she found out that Bonnie had been raped at a campus party. That Bonnie couldn't tell her mother about the pregnancy, and as a devout catholic she refused to abort the baby. Then she shared that Bonnie died the morning after a complicated childbirth without her mother even knowing she was pregnant.

She told Solomon that she and Darnell agreed to adopt the baby but never saw Mareschelle at the hospital and despite knowing that Bonnie had died, the agent never mentioned a second baby when they went to take Mareschelle home from the agency. She told him that the agency had gone out of business, but she gave him the company's name and the name of the agent who handled their case. That, if Amari and Mareschelle were in fact the same twins born that day, she never knew it. And she confessed that had they known, she and her husband would have adopted them both.

Once the business of his visit was complete, Rachel Mae mellowed, offered him a glass of iced tea and shared a cherished memory from Mareschelle's childhood. That offering started a sharing of stories about Mareschelle that allowed them to maintain their civility for the majority of their three hours together. Similar to Vivienne harboring negative opinions about Mareschelle, Solomon knew Rachel Mae resented him marrying Mareschelle so young. She had plans for her daughter that included a judgeship by forty, not a husband by twenty-five. Regardless, her reasons didn't matter if this woman was her baby's twin and in meeting her, could bring the joy of Mareschelle back into her life.

Solomon thumbed through a photo album while Rachel Mae used the bathroom. Marveling at her pictures, he considered that maybe introducing Amari into Rachel Mae's life might be too much for her to handle. Might not be something she wanted. She hadn't asked him to find Amari, he forced this information on her. He knew how traumatized he felt the first time he saw Amari and thought that maybe he needed to reconsider. Maybe Rachel Mae didn't want that trauma.

When he couldn't think of anything else nice to say, Solomon thanked her for her time and got up to leave.

"Listen boy..." Rachel Mae called from the doorway as he stepped off the porch. "if this girl that you found does turn out to be my Rennie's sister, you bring her to me so I can see her."

Solomon's heart leapt with joy. He said, "Yes Ma'am," as she shut the door before he could say anything else. Anxious for Monday to arrive so he could hunt for Mareschelle's adoption agent, Solomon practically skipped to his car.

CHAPTER 27

THREE TRIPS AFTER HER SEMI-INDECENT proposal to a fine black man heading in the opposite direction, Brandi, the woman truck driver from Wolf Lodge, Idaho, slowed her rig just after dusk when she spotted a deer crossing sign on the two-lane country road that ran parallel to Interstate-90 just east of Spokane. She had detoured from the interstate to avoid a multi-car accident delaying eastbound traffic. She had lived her whole life along the Washington-Idaho border and always slowed down when she travelled the local roads through Liberty Lake County. The city dwellers, who only ventured out to Liberty Lake a few weeks a year in the summer, usually ignored the animal crossing signs along that dimly lit, heavily forested stretch of road. But the virtue of experience made Brandi cautious. At eight years old, she was in the backseat when her father slammed into a three-hundred-pound buck that bounded out of the forest. Everyone inside the vehicle was alright, but the massive deer totaled the family car.

When a burst of static from the radio momentarily distracted her just as something staggered out of the forest and into the road, Brandi jammed on her brakes. Her tires screeched, slid, and her rig fishtailed. Had she not already been moving slow, she might not have been able to stop in time. As it was, the truck ended up jack-knifed across both lanes of traffic. Brandi lay slumped over the steering wheel, her heart beating in overdrive.

She closed her eyes for a second to calm down. When she peered out the windshield to see what had scared her, the pitch-black wilderness hid whatever was out there. She put on her warning lights and straightened out her truck, and as she did, her headlights panned over a body sprawled on the bank off to the right of the road. Once on the shoulder, she jumped out of the cab and saw a woman laying on her stomach, her legs bare and the tail of her blouse barely covering her torn, soiled panties.

"Are you okay, Miss?" Brandi asked walking cautiously toward her. She panned the darkness, looking for other signs of life. She jumped when something stirred near the trees, but nothing came out.

The woman stirred, then weakly pushed herself up onto her hands and knees. She lifted her head and stared at Brandi through strands of long, unkempt sandy-brown hair. "Help me," she begged weakly.

"It's okay," Brandi said, as she drew closer and got her first clear view. There was duct tape around the woman's wrists and ankles, her face was caked with blood, and her legs were scratched and bruised. Her torn blouse hung open. Brandi took off her jacket to cover her, but stopped her in her tracks when she inhaled the stench of urine, feces, and body odor.

"Please," the woman pleaded, urging Brandi to come closer.

"Don't worry, baby," Brandi assured the dirty, disheveled woman as she draped the jacket across her shoulders. "I'll get you somewhere safe," She grabbed her under her arms, helped her stand and as she rose, her blouse parted, revealing burn marks and cuts on the woman's ribs and breasts. Brandi forced herself to see her wounds as she eased the woman into the passenger seat. After she shut her door, the woman slumped against it. Brandi got in, speed-dialed her cousin and headed toward town.

"Hey Brandi," the burly voice answered.

"Harry, I'm heading to Providence Saint Patrick with a girl."

"What happened?"

This girl... She's hurt, Harry. She came out of the forest and... I think someone did something to her. Something real bad. You should meet me at the hospital.

Five minutes short of a half hour later, Brandi parked her semi near the emergency room entrance at Providence Saint Patrick hospital. "Wake up, Honey. We're here." Brandi hopped out of the rig and ran through the sliding doors to find help. She returned a moment later with a nurse leading two interns pulling a gurney. She climbed into her truck through the driver's side, unlocked and opened the passenger door and wrapped her arms around the half-naked woman before she lowered her down to the gurney. After Brandi transferred the battered woman to the care of the emergency room team, she walked beside the gurney holding the woman's hand as they rushed her inside. When the bright white hospital lights shone on her face, the woman briefly opened her eyes, looked squarely at Brandi, mouthed, *Thank you*, then passed out.

~

Liberty Lake in Spokane County is located just south of its namesake town. Just over a mile west of the Washington–Idaho border, Liberty Lake is both a suburb of Spokane, Washington and a bedroom community to Coeur d'Alene, Idaho. The population is artificially inflated to nearly ten thousand during the summer when the rich city folks who own the cabins that ring the lake and the tourists who stay at the Liberty Lake Resort come to town. But when school starts, the population plummets back to seventy-two hundred and the only tourists who remain are the avid fly fishermen who troll the lake, and the hunters who stalk the woods during deer season.

Law enforcement in Liberty Lake is a slow occupation most of the year. If it wasn't for the alcohol induced staples of lawlessness—speeding, domestic arguments, and bar fights—the deputies in the Spokane County Sheriff's Office would do nothing but sit around playing card games or talking sports. But Brandi's call induced an adrenaline rush in her cousin, Sheriff's Deputy Harry Kennedy.

When Harry met Brandi at the hospital, doctors were in the back evaluating the woman. He asked, "You all right?"

"Not really," Brandi replied.

"What happened?"

Brandi was still shaken, and it took her a few minutes to explain what had occurred on the country road.

"You stay in the waiting room," Harry told her. "Stan's on the way and he'll take your statement. Okay?"

"Yeah."

Harry laid a hand on his cousin's shoulder and gave it a squeeze. "You done a good deed tonight. Don't worry, they'll take good care of her here." He passed through the emergency room door and showed his badge to the desk nurse. "I'm looking for the Jane Doe the trucker brought in."

The nurse looked at the room charts before pointing to her left. "She's in trauma four."

When she blurted out, "I know her," Harry was halfway down the hall to the trauma rooms. He paused, considered her words, then rushed back. "What did you say?"

The nurse recoiled from the intensity in Harry's question. "I don't know about you sheriff, but I've lived here all my life. I may not have an exciting life, but local celebrities are one of the things that people like me notice."

"Celebrities?"

"Yeah Sheriff," the desk nurse built like a high school linebacker said. "I only got to see her for about ten seconds, but I got a good look at her face. She may have been bloody and bruised, but I'd recognize her anywhere. She's not only a celebrity, but we both went to Gonzaga. She was a couple of years behind me, but I'd recognize a famous Zag anywhere."

Harry's first instinct was to stop the blabbering nurse, but if the woman's condition was as bad as Brandi described, he didn't need to rush the nurse into finishing her story. It hadn't been an hour since

Brandi called him and if the Jane Doe was still in the trauma room, she wouldn't be leaving the hospital any time soon, so Harry checked his watch and considered how long he'd have to wait to call and wake up the Sheriff.

"I wouldn't bet my paycheck because I can't afford to lose the money, but as sure as I'm born and raised in Spokane, that woman is the Miss Washington State beauty queen, Jordyn Hoffman." After the nurse told him her name and why she was so confident in her identification, she continued to ramble about the Jane Doe beauty pageant career and her opinion of why the woman didn't win the Miss America crown; and that even though she didn't know her personally, she was proud of her as a fellow Zag alum. The only reason she stopped talking was because the phone rang.

Harry asked, "How is she, doc?" when the doctor finally exited trauma room four a half hour later.

"Not good. It appears she's been beaten, drugged, raped, and starved. She's in pretty bad shape. Her body's suffered a lot of trauma. We're sending her upstairs for x-rays, imaging of her torso to check for internal bleeding and a cat scan. All of that will take a couple of hours. Her body will heal with time, but I'm worried about her mental state. We'll know more once we have her test results."

"Is there any permanent damage? Did she tell you her name?"

"No she didn't. She cried when we woke her up, but she didn't say anything coherent. The sedative we gave her will keep her groggy for a while, but we won't know more until her tests come back."

"If she can't tell you her name, can you fingerprint her?" Deputy Kennedy urged. "That way I can send her prints back to the precinct and get working on identifying her while you figure out her injuries."

"That sounds doable," the doctor agreed. "I'll have one of my interns bring you her fingerprints at the nurse's station."

Harry watched interns roll the Jane Doe—the woman the desk

nurse called Jordyn Hoffman—down the hall and into an elevator. The emergency room doctor shook Harry's hand then excused himself and walked into trauma room six to care for his next patient.

~

Two mornings later, the Jane Doe that the woman trucker Brandi had brought into Providence Saint Patrick hospital after being found along the side of a dark country road awakened. She was sore from two broken ribs and surgery to remove her spleen and fix her broken left wrist. It was after noon when they wheeled her into recovery and after dinner when they moved her to an empty, semi-private, two-person room. That was thirty hours ago.

Deputy Kennedy waited until morning to report everything he knew about the Jane Doe to the Sheriff instead of calling him in the middle of the night without all of the facts. After repeating what the doctor told him about the Jane Doe's condition, he repeated what the nurse told him and had a fingerprint analysis done to follow up her story.

Once Jordyn's identity and address were confirmed, the Sheriff ordered Deputy Kennedy to call the Spokane police department to find out what they knew about the woman found in the woods.

At the hospital two days later, Detective Foreman and Deputy Kennedy were led to the attending physician, Doctor Bunting. "Her name is Jordyn Hoffman. She's been missing for more than a month."

"Yes, Detective. Deputy Kennedy called and told me yesterday."

"Did she say who did this to her?"

"I just fix them, Sir. I leave those questions for law enforcement."

"Can I talk to her?"

"Yes, but keep it short. We've been keeping her sedated. Sleeping and limiting her movement eases the pain of healing broken ribs."

The doctor led the deputy and the detective into the room.

Jordyn's eyes were blackened like raccoons, her nose bandaged, and her lip split. Harry blinked back tears at the sight of her savage beating.

Detective Foreman held up his shield. "Miss Hoffman, I'm Detective Foreman with the Spokane Police Department. I'll keep this short. It's my job to track down who did this to you. Do you feel up to answering a few questions?"

Jordyn whispered something incoherent then started crying. "Can't…"

"Don't fret Miss Hoffman," he assured her in a straightforward voice, "I just need to if it was a man or a woman?" He put his badge away and walked to the bed. "Was there one person or more than one?"

Jordyn turned her face away. "I…I. Why did this happen to me?"

"Your friend said you went to see a man in Seattle. Did he do this to you?"

"Seattle? Solomon? I…." Her eyes glazed over and she seemed to be staring straight through the detective. Before her words came to her, her eyes rolled back in her head, her head lolled to the side and she passed out.

"Are you alright, Miss Hoffman? Miss Hoffman? Can you hear me?" Detective Foreman wanted to wake her, but he acquiesced when Harry placed a firm hand on his shoulder. He tried to imagine the hell Jordyn had endured, then decided that peace and quiet was the best gift he could give her.

Through a fog of haze, Jordyn lay in a stupor reliving the nightmare of her disappearance as voices floated all around her.

CHAPTER 28

JORDYN'S UBER HAD ARRIVED AT the Hotel Monaco just before midnight. Although the ride service automatically charged the fare to her credit card when she confirmed pickup, she gave the driver a twenty-dollar cash tip after he placed her suitcases on the curb. Despite her troubled mood, she left him with her best beauty pageant smile. Before walking inside, she looked up and down the sidewalk taking notice to the people gathered down the street outside a bar. What she didn't notice was the dented black sedan that had passed her Uber then turned around and parked across the street. The scratched and dented side of the car faced the curb, hidden from her field of vision. The driver cut the engine and watched her enter the hotel before exiting the vehicle.

Fifteen minutes after checking into her third floor room, Jordyn rubbed lotion into her hands as she exited the bathroom. The stress of seeing Solomon hugging that woman at The Train Station was compounded by the stress of watching him almost be run over. When she stressed, she ate, so before she went into the bathroom, she had called room service and ordered two slices of raspberry cheesecake and a Bulleit 10-year old-fashioned. That and a sleeping pill would help her sleep through the night. In the morning she'd decide whether she would go back to Spokane, or stay in Seattle and find something to do other than see Solomon.

She heard a noise at her door, assumed it was room service and thought, *Wow that was quick.* Then she heard the same beep at the door that her key made when she entered. Panic set in. The door swung open and Jordyn froze. "Glenn?" She couldn't believe he was in Seattle, and more concerning, he was in her room. "What the hell are you doing here? And how the hell did you get into my room?"

Glenn Zimmerman stood in her doorway grinning smugly as he waved a key card similar to her own. "I told the lady at the front desk that my wife checked in while I was parking the car and she just gave me a second room key."

Jordyn looked past him into the hallway and screamed, "Help!" Music from a radio in the room next door boomed louder than it should after midnight, filling both the hallway and the silence between their words.

When she screamed for help the second time, Glenn looked over his shoulder, saw nobody coming, and pushed the door closed behind him. The music from the other room lowered to a din, but was still loud enough to mute their voices.

"I missed you, Baby."

Bewilderment set into her expression. "You're out of your mind."

Glenn took three steps into the room, cutting the distance between them in half. His silver-grey eyes were cold like steel. Harsh grey eyes that looked right through her. "I came to keep you company, Baby. You weren't at your place, and when I checked with Melanie, she told me that you went to Seattle."

"I'm expecting company," she said curtly, moving toward the phone on the nightstand. "He'll be here any minute. And he won't be happy if he finds you here, so you need to get the hell out of here right now."

"Then it looks like we have a couple minutes until he gets here." Glenn rushed toward her, but instead of grabbing her, he reached for the room phone and ripped the cord out of the wall. "Especially since I watched the wrecker tow his car away."

Jordyn huffed, regarded him and tried to remain calm. She was terrified that he'd attack her if she pissed him off so she crossed her arms and stepped back, figuring that if she kept calm until room service arrived, she would be alright.

"You're not supposed to be here. I have a restraining order. You're supposed to keep five hundred feet away."

Glenn tilted his head and his eyes came to rest on the exquisitely made queen-size bed that was the centerpiece of the elegantly designed bedroom.

Flushed, Jordyn looked to where his eyes stopped. "No need to look over there, *we* are not making that trip tonight...or ever again." And she was right, but didn't know just how right she was.

Disregarding her words, he looked at the bed. "Looks mighty comfortable. But of course, I could be mistaken. It's been so long since I've had the pleasure."

"And whose fault is that?"

Glenn stepped toward her. "I'm not complaining Jordyn."

"Don't touch me" trembled Jordyn. She desperately wanted to turn and run for the door, but steeled herself to not run until room service knocked.

Glenn took two quick steps, again closing the gap between them. Before she could react, he cupped his right hand over her mouth as his left hand found her back and pulled her close. "You're all I think about, Baby." He placed his cheek next to hers and whispered, "I've missed you." His breath was hot in her ear.. He pulled her hips firmly into his and, taking a slow deep breath said, "Missed the way you smell. Missed the way you sound. Missed your heat keeping me warm."

Jordyn hated Glenn. Hated his touch. Hated what he'd done to her both at his draft party and in his apartment. She felt light-headed. His hot, smelly breath nauseating her. She closed her eyes and could feel her heartbeat. She screamed. Grabbed at his face. Reaching for his eyes, but she missed and dug her fingers into his temples when he turned his head. She jerked her hips away from him when she felt his sex harden. She closed her eyes against his desire. She had never cared for anyone the way she cared for Glenn when they were together, but remembered that no one had ever hurt her the way Glenn had either. "Damn you, Glenn Zimmerman," she screamed, twisting and turning to escape his grip before ultimately tripping over the bed's footboard and falling in an attempt to free herself.

Glenn fell with her, tightened his grip beneath her breasts. Pressed his chest against her back. Brushed his lips across her hair and planted a light kiss on the base of her neck.

"Get off of me Glenn. You hurt me. Don't you get it? I hate you! You hurt me bad and never once said I'm sorry."

"I'm saying it now, Jordyn. I'm sorry."

Jordyn squirmed to get free, but he was too strong.

"I didn't come to fight. I came to apologize. Tell you I missed you."

Jordyn moaned, her head swam, and she wondered, *Where the hell is room service?* She knew room service would rescue her; hoped someone would soon appear at her door and hear her screaming and enter the room and rescue her.

"Don't make me go, Jordyn," Glenn pleaded. "I still love you."

"If you loved me, then you wouldn't be hurting me."

"I don't want to do this, you're making me." He shifted his grip and she bit his arm. "What the hell?" Glenn grabbed her arm and spun her around. "Stay with me, Jordyn."

"No Glenn. I'm scared of you and we've proven that we don't work together. Room service will be here any minute. They'll hear us and call security. You don't want to be here when security comes."

"Let them come." He released his stronghold on her and punched her in the stomach. Jordyn folded in half with pain as he rushed to the entrance to the room, turned the deadbolt lock on the door, slid the privacy arm-bar over the hook and pushed the three-foot armoire across the door opening. "Now, if they want you that bad, they'll have to break down the door," he bolstered.

Jordyn climbed to her knees, but they buckled when she tried to stand. She had the urge to run, but her feet wouldn't move. She hoped that the security guards had room keys they could use in case of emergencies. She hoped they were strong enough to push through the barricade.

Just then, a knock came on the door giving Jordyn a ray of hope.

Glenn leaned all of his weight on top of her and covered her mouth.

A second set of three taps came to the door. When nobody answered, the voice on the other side called almost inaudibly, "I'll just leave your tray here, Ma'am."

Jordyn screamed through Glenn's hand pressed tightly over her mouth, but the sound didn't carry.

Glenn sounded like a child asking his mother to stay with him on the first day at a new school as he whined, "Don't leave me, Jordyn." He used his solid eighty-pound weight advantage to keep her pinned beneath him as he forced himself between her knees. As he unzipped his jeans and wriggled until they were down around his ankles.

"Don't!" Her words were forceful, yet barely more than a whisper.

"Can you love me again, Jordyn?" He curled his hands to the front of her body and groped her breasts.

"Stop it Glenn!" She shoved at his hands. "You can never love me the way I need to be loved."

Glenn pushed hard at her knees. Tried to force her legs open.

"Get off me Glenn. Just leave."

Glenn slumped his weight over her, pressed harder to open her legs, yanked her stockings down beneath her knees.

Jordyn yelped.

He covered her mouth with his hand.

She slapped the back of his head in rhythm to the knock on the door, thrashed her head and pulled away.

Glenn slammed her head on the Persian rug.

Her hands covered his. "Stop Glenn, you're hurting me."

Now he was fully aroused. He pressed his knees outward against her thighs and tried to kiss her, but she turned away.

She shifted her hands to around his neck and screamed, "Stop Glenn. You're hurting me." She squirmed as he kneaded his legs between hers.

He clamped his mouth clumsily on hers, their teeth clinking together painfully.

Then a rapid banging with a mush heavier hand came at the door. "This is the manager. Are you alright, Ms. Hoffman?"

"Please help me!" Jordyn shouted forcefully to ensure her words were heard above the music.

Feeling the sense of urgency, Glenn clumsily pulled his penis from his boxers. The tip glistened with pre-cum as he rocked his body sideways, forcing her knees open, his sex dangling above hers.

"Stop it," she mumbled, thrashing away her mouth as he continued to try to kiss her. She choked him again.

Glenn dropped his hips onto hers, lowered his full weight on top of her and entered her. His eyes went distant, glazed over, gone to some far-off land.

She screamed.

Glenn ignored her.

She screamed again.

Still no answer.

She pleaded for him to stop; to let her go; to get off of her and out of her room.

Glenn closed his eyes, rammed inside her, pumped in and out of her, growing stiffer with every stroke.

Jordyn swallowed a hot air balloon full of air. The narrowness of pain surprised her. Then it began spiraling outward, cramping her abdomen. She yelled, but he couldn't hear her, as the pain of his dry penis entering her stretched her roughly. She flailed her legs, punched at his shoulders; punched at his chest, slapped him in his face but Glenn's mind was gone.

The banging at the door mixed several times with the beep of the key card as the manager tried to enter the room. Glenn's barrier held and a moment later the rumblings outside the door went silent.

Glenn thrusted hard.

Her eyes leaked tears. She bit his ear and drew blood. She punched and scratched at him then desperately searched for something to hit him with; something to help her escape.

Glenn entered into a repetitively louder chorus of *Yes, yes* with every thrust until his orgasm came. Once spent, he withdrew himself and gasped, "Thank you, Jordyn."

"Rot in hell, you son of a bitch" she cried through sob-filled tears.

Glenn growled, instantly got angry, called her a bitch and punched her in the face…then punched her twice more, knocking her unconscious.

He panicked when she stopped moving. Realized that someone would soon return, then hurriedly dressed and emptied her largest suitcase so he could fold an unconscious Jordyn into the oversized travel bag. He moved the armoire and checked the peephole to see that the hallway was empty, then grabbed her purse and rolled the giant suitcase out of the room. Fearful that he'd run into hotel security at the elevator, he took the stairs down to the lobby, rolled the suitcase out the front door and was long gone when the manager returned, only to find Jordyn's room empty.

CHAPTER 29

AFTER STUFFING THE OVERSIZED SUITCASE containing Jordyn Hoffman's raped and beaten, unconscious body into the trunk of his car, Glenn Zimmerman got in and screamed like he'd been burned with a branding iron. He punched the steering wheel a dozen times before slamming his head back into the headrest, covering his face with his hands then repeatedly shouting, "fuuuuuuucccccccck... fuck... fuck... fuck... fuck... fuck... fuck... fuck... fuck... FUCK!!"

After his heartrate slowed from ultra-vibrate to tachycardic, he opened his eyes and watched for security to come rushing out of the hotel. When that pursuit didn't evolve, he started his car, pulled out into traffic and drove the speed limit to Spokane, stopping only once at a vacant rest stop to take a piss.

A half hour west of downtown Spokane, he picked up his cell phone and called his uncle. When his uncle groggily answered his phone Sunday morning, Glenn cried out, "I messed up, Darren. I need your help!"

Glenn told Uncle Darren Jordyn's address and asked him to meet him there with his hunting van. When he arrived at Jordyn's townhouse, he went inside, opened her garage door, and drove his car into her garage. Uncle Darren backed his van into Jordyn's driveway, not stopping until the rear bumper touched her garage door. He entered through the front door and followed the smell of fresh brewed coffee toward the rear of the townhouse. The two men sat in Jordyn's kitchen drinking coffee as Glenn told his Uncle Darren his version of the story, minus the part about raping her. After agreeing to take Jordyn to a drug house G-Z ran whores out of on the west end of town a couples miles past the airport, they transferred her body from G-Z's car to Uncle Darren's van.

After Uncle Darren left, Glenn proceeded to trash Jordyn's townhouse, cutting Solomon's face out of any pictures he could find of *the punk from Seattle* and putting them all in the same trashcan to make it look like Jordyn had consciously disposed of his pictures. He knocked over lamps, knick-knacks, throw pillows to make it look like a struggle had taken place. When he finished, he backed his car into her driveway, pulled his hoodie up over his head, checked that there were no people on the streets who could later identify him, went to her front door and kicked it open to break the latches and locks, then left the door cracked ajar, and drove off.

As he drove home, he called one of his goons, told him to pick up another of his goons and for the two of them to meet him at the shop. When the two goons arrived, the first one spouted off, "Boss, we got a problem," before G-Z could say a word.

"So are we going to play free psychic reader, or are you going give me the story?"

"Streets is talking about the po-po planning to run up in the place out west. Some preppie ma-fucka from the college got hemmed up and he told the cops about the spot."

"Why you ain't call me earlier?" G-Z shouted.

"Scoop just told me on the way over here after I picked him up."

G-Z turned to Scoop, "Is this information reliable?"

"Yeah, Boss," Scoop said nervously. "My man is solid with his talk."

G-Z growled, "Damn, I don't need this shit today." He took a deep breath, slapped an open palm against the side of his head six or seven times to help him think then said, "Alright, alright…I'll take care of the house."

G-Z pulled out his phone and called Uncle Darren. After he informed Uncle Darren about the conversation about the raid, he tossed his car keys to Scoop. "You two make this go away." The two goons listened as G-Z instructed them to drive his car to the opposite side of the city, smash the driver's side of the car into something to make the damage look just like the scraped up passenger side of the car, then leave it near an abandoned building and "blaze that shit."

"Yeah Boss. We got you."

"And Scoop..."

"Yeah Boss?"

"Bring me back my keys."

~

The plan was simple. Stash Jordyn in one of the rooms at the whore house. Drug her to keep her incoherent. Whore her out until she was no longer useful, then get rid of her. But after G-Z informed Uncle Darren about the pending raid on the drug house, the senior Zimmerman took the airport exit off Interstate 90 West, turned the clover leaf, got back on the interstate and drove east until he reached Lake County thirty miles later. Uncle Darren hopped out, checked to make sure nobody was around then opened the rear doors. He unzipped the suitcase and rolled Jordyn onto the van floor.

Jordyn feigned unconsciousness while she allowed her limbs to loosen up. When he looked away, she rammed her shoulder into his portly round middle, propelling them both out of the van. Uncle Darren's back landed on the ground with a bone-jarring thud. Jordyn crash landed on top of his soft girth.

"Uggggghhh!!!" Uncle Darren wailed as his ribs screamed with pain, her weight adding to the force of his impact with the forest floor. He saw that Jordyn was solidly built, but he didn't expect her to tackle like a strong safety. He felt like Troy Polamalu, Jack Tatum and Ronnie Lott had all three simultaneously leapt off the floor of the van, and run through him like he was a wide receiver cutting across the middle of a football field in a game with no referees.

Jordyn clamored to her feet. Searched her surroundings. Saw trees, bushes and forest in every direction. The sun was high in the sky, its position offering her no sense of direction. She wanted to run, but didn't know which way. Uncle Darren's moans brought her back to him. She took in his face, realized it wasn't Glenn Zimmerman—the last person she'd seen when she was conscious—but she didn't recognized this man despite the feeling that he looked familiar. She panicked when she caught sight of him pulling something metallic from his pocket. She took aim and caught his jaw with her heel. The contact was good. His head flicked around and he cried out. She kicked the metallic object from his hand, turned to face the van, and ran in the opposite direction the van was facing, deducing that it was the way back to where they had come from. When she checked behind her thirty seconds later, the man was on his feet chasing her.

The more she ran, the thicker the forest grew around her. Tree roots, fallen pinecones and thick brush tore and scraped at her bare feet. She tried not to fall. Tried to ignore the pain in her feet and ankles. Took deep breaths and evaluated her escape plan with every painful passing step. She thought that if she ran faster, she could continue in this direction and hopefully lose him in the woods; or veer right or left, find a hiding spot in the thick brush and hope that he'd run right past her.

She fell and a dust cloud exploded around her. She choked, coughed, heard him trudging through the woods as she climbed back to her bare feet. He was still following. Still catching up. The fall had broken her rhythm and she was losing the distance between them. She veered right and after running for fifty yards, she started curving right, hoping that she'd circle behind him and make it to his van. Five minutes passed and she came upon a cabin near a small pond. She stopped, hesitated, considered whether the cabin belonged to her abductor, or if it was a neighbor who could help her. A noise behind her told that her hesitation had lasted a moment too long.

Jordyn turned to see her abductor coming much closer than she thought he should have been. His face was so red it looked like he'd just won an hour-long breath holding contest. Just as Uncle Darren reached to grab her, her fight or flight instinct reinitiated and she ran toward the cabin, praying that it was a neighbor's place.

Her pursuer leapt at her as she reached the cabin porch and clapped her ankles together.

She tripped and landed hard on the single step porch of the cabin, her back crashing into the door frame. Her face skidded off the wooden floorboards and her head slammed against the wall to the right of the door. Pain shot through her body from the point of impact, traveling down her spine to her legs. Her muscles went slack. Her legs slumped as though her tendons had been snipped. There was blood in her mouth. Her eyesight blurred and her face felt hot. She heard her pursuer step up onto the porch and she scrambled against the closed cabin door looking left and right for a way to escape.

"You do exactly as I say and I won't have to hurt you none." He grabbed her arm roughly and lifted her to her feet. He expected resistance from her, but turned his face in surprise when she spit a mouthful of blood and phlegm in his eyes. He turned the knob on the door with his free hand and pushed her against the door making it swing all the way open.

Jordyn's weight carried her stumbling into the cabin. She turned around when she gained her balance. The man was much closer than she remembered. She caught sight of something metallic coming toward her. She didn't have time to work out what it was so she juked side-to-side hoping to confuse the older man and hopefully get past him and back outside. But he basically stood still like a big sloth too clumsy to move quickly in either direction. She could get around him. She didn't believe in his promised mercy. If she was going to die alone in a cabin in the woods, then she would die scratching this bastards eyes out.

She saw a small, four-pane window to her left. It was wide enough for her to fit through, but not him, so she bolted for the window, hoping to dive through it before the man could catch her. Two feet before crashing into the wall, Jordyn went airborne and lifted her forearms to cover her face. At the exact moment of impact, her abductor grabbed her around her waist, stopping her motion through the window, but not before shards of broken glass dug into her arms.

The uncle and the ex-girlfriend crashed to the floor. Her head crashed into the thick leg of Uncle Darren's handmade, wooden coffee table. The roughly-fashioned, homemade table connected with the side of her face. She thought she would pass out, lose consciousness, but she fought her grogginess, forcing herself to stay awake, focusing on his voice.

"Stop fighting me little girl. I told you I ain't go'ne hurt you none if you play nice." Just like Jordyn, he was out breath. He had lost his grip on her when they smashed into the furniture, but wrestled his way up trying to get ahold of her again.

Jordyn took advantage of his loosened grip, scrambled toward the front door and pushed the door open. He grabbed her feet and she fell outside onto her back staring at the bright afternoon sky. She tried to scream but her mouth was full of blood.

He grabbed ahold of one foot and pulled her back into the cabin kicking frantically. He stood up, towered over her and grabbed the other foot and pulled her all the way into the cabin.

Jordyn spat blood. Cried out for help, but there was nobody that deep in the woods to hear her. Desperate, she kicked free one leg, screamed, and swung her foot up into his crotch with all her might.

Uncle Darren screamed like a banshee as he tumbled to the floor atop her. She slapped at him with both hands trying to get him off of her. He grabbed her neck and squeezed tight. She scratched at his eyes. He wailed, released her neck and punched her twice, knocking Jordyn unconscious and bringing the fight to an abrupt end.

Darren Zimmerman lay next to the now motionless Jordyn Hoffman breathing hard and cursing aloud. He'd previously thought his debt to his nephew was insurmountable, but after this, they were even. Uncle Darren continued to breathe heavily as he staggered to his feet. He reached in his pants and adjusted himself despite the agonizing pain of Jordyn trying to crack his walnuts with her foot. He looked down at Jordyn, saw her chest moving and knew she wasn't dead. He grabbed two bottles of water and a couple of towels from the kitchen, wrapped her arms where they were bleeding from the window glass, stuffed the water bottles in his pocket, then picked her up and carried her off the porch and into the woods.

Uncle Darren's thirty-two acre oasis was located in the woods north of Liberty Lake. The two-building property was well-secluded. Nobody came looking for anything out there. A well-marked fence separated the twenty-five acres that were used for hunting from the seven acres around the cabin. Nobody but Uncle Darren and G-Z would ever know there was a woman hidden in the woods.

Uncle Darren shifted Jordyn into a fireman's carry and trudged the one-hundred yards from his cabin to an eight-by-eight, seven-foot tall shack he used for smoking meats during hunting season. He laid Jordyn down on some old horse blankets, wrapped duct tape around her wrists and ankles, then put the two bottles of water next to her hands. Once he was confident she'd be alright, he padlocked the single wooden door on the front of the shed and headed back to his cabin.

Jordyn would wake several hours later to find herself alone in the dark, trapped inside a shed that would be her Arkham Asylum until either someone came to rescue here, or the fat man or Glenn came to dispose of her.

CHAPTER 30

EVEN THOUGH SHE AND SAVANNAH had no idea what had happened to Jordyn since the last time she went to Seattle, Melanie was content being Glenn Zimmerman's girlfriend. She and Savannah were with Jordyn the first time she met Glenn. When he asked Jordyn for her number, Melanie offered all of their numbers—home, cell and work, chiming, "Sweetie, you can have my social security number if you want it."

Savannah called and relayed whatever information the police detective had provided during her every other day call to the police station. Solomon had claimed his innocence, but the evidence— Jordyn leaving Spokane to go see him in Seattle, and his pictures being the only ones she mutilated before she left—all pointed to him. The hotel manager had said that he heard a struggle in the room but the room was empty when he finally entered. Jordyn's father hadn't heard from his daughter, and her mother told them that she hadn't come to see her in San Francisco. Jordyn had been missing more than a month and nobody in her inner circle knew where she was.

G-Z had just finished his shower and walked into the bedroom where Melanie was watching the evening news anchor gave a thirty-second report about her friend—the missing beauty queen from Spokane—as she got dressed to go out for her birthday dinner celebration. Ten seconds after the story ended, Melanie's phone rang. "Hey Vannah," she answered, putting the phone on speaker so she could finish her makeup. G-Z turned off the TV, went into the bathroom, and left the door open so he could eavesdrop.

The news report kept G-Z thinking about Jordyn at dinner. He knew Melanie would want to spend *quality time* together after they got home, but he decided that it was time to go out to Liberty Lake and get rid of Jordyn for good. He needed to make an escape without arousing her suspicion, so when the waitress brought her grand margarita, he told her that she should go to the bathroom and check her makeup. Wanting to make sure she would sleep long enough for him to get out to Liberty Lake, take care of Jordyn and get back before she woke up, he dissolved two Rohypnol pills into her drink while she was gone—one less than the three he gave her before he drove to Seattle.

Melanie fell asleep in the car during the drive back to her place after dinner just as he had hoped. He carried her inside, took off her shoes and laid her on top of the bed, then took her house key and left.

The dusk that had prevailed when he left Melanie's house had bloomed into full-blown night as he arrived at Uncle Darren's property. He left his headlights pointed at the front of the cabin until he went inside and grabbed a camp light for the hundred yard walk out to the shed where his uncle told him that he left Jordyn. Uncle Darren had taken her food and water every other day throughout the past couple of weeks, but G-Z had not ventured out to the lake since Uncle Darren had dropped her off.

Jordyn had grown accustomed to the sounds of animals foraging outside the shed. Every week or so, the man who brought her food included a new chemlight so she wouldn't have to endure the nights in total darkness. She'd had the current chemlight for four days. A week ago she pried the head of a nail far enough loose to use it to scratch most of the way through the duct tape binding her wrists. Unfortunately, her captor noticed the frayed duct tape before she freed her wrists and applied twice as much when he came back to reinforce it later that day. She spent her days calling out whenever she heard a sound outside hoping it was a person who could free her and not an animal ready to feed on her.

The fragile shack threatened to collapse at any moment. There were no windows, one door, no soul, just a tattered wooden shell abandoned like a forlorn lover. But more than that, it bore a painful emptiness. The unmaintained out-structure exuded disgrace and shame, barenaked walls on display. She'd run full-speed—or as fast as she could generate in the confined quarters—and rammed herself into the walls of the shed hoping they'd give under the force of her weight. Unfortunately for her, the shed was more sturdily built than it looked. She did; however, manage to kick two boards loose her second week there, deducing that she could squeeze through once she'd loosened three boards. Nevertheless, her Uncle Darren noticed the loose boards and nailed all three of them tight again.

Jordyn used her daylight time to find ways to escape. She foraged through the garbage on the floor of the shed hoping to find something to help her escape. The only two useful things she found were a half-empty can of wasp and hornet spray, and a spackling chisel with a broken blade. She staged her weapons under the blanket, waiting for her captor to let his guard down so she could attack when the door was open and escape.

Jordyn thought she was dreaming when she heard what sounded like human footsteps approaching. She climbed to her feet and listened closely. Her captor always came during the day, so she hoped her late night visitor was someone who could help free her, or at least go get help.

She peeked outside through the space below the hinges where the door and the frame met. She saw a figure walking straight toward her carrying a camp light. Her first instinct was to scream, but since the person seemed to be coming straight at her and comfortable where he was going, she didn't think it was a trespasser. Jordyn continued to watch the shadow come closer until she could almost make out that it was a man. Fright set in. Her mind raced and she wondered why her captor felt the need to make a night visit. *Why was he here so late? Was he coming to let me go? Was he coming to kill me?* Her last thought seemed to make the most sense. He had come to kill her under the cover of night. With that thought in mind, Jordyn hid her chemlight under her blanket, pulled out her can of bug spray and her broken chisel, and retreated to the farthest, darkest corner of the shed and prepared to fight to save her life—to kill or be killed. She'd been this man's captive for weeks and still didn't know why. She held her breath, remained dead quiet and crouched in the corner like a cobra ready to strike, hoping that this time her instincts were dead wrong. Better her instincts dead wrong than her dead.

The door creaked open after the sound of the padlock being undone stopped. Just as the beam from the camp light exposed her hiding place, Jordyn heard the words *Where you at, Bitch?* clear as day in Glenn Zimmerman's voice. Without hesitation, she sprang from the corner and sprayed the bug spray in the direction of his voice.

"Aaaaaahhhhhhhh!!!!!!" was all that Glenn heard as the ball of infuriated humanity that was Jordyn Hoffman leapt on him like the caged animal he had made her. He shouted, "What the fu...?" as a liquid hit him in the face, stinging his eyes and a moment later coating his tongue. He stumbled and fell backwards as the wild animal in the cage plowed into his chest knocking him back away from the shed. He dropped the camp light and landed on his butt then rolled to his back as the howling apparition attacked him from every angle.

Jordyn sliced at his face with the broken chisel. She cut his ear, bit his nose, and when he overpowered her to push her off him, she rolled onto her stomach, sprang up and ran for her life.

Discarded five-gallon water bottles, overgrown weeds, pallets, and bones from decayed animal carcasses scattered in the center of the beautiful wilderness was like running through a minefield. A half-acre of human generated mess formed the foundation of the breeding ground for disease and dismay surrounding the shed. Every third step presented a new obstacle for barefooted Jordyn to overcome.

Glenn Zimmerman was behind her on the ground wiping his eyes.

Jordyn ran at top speed and was soon out of breath. Uncertain which way to go to get to people on a moonless night, she prayed she wasn't running deeper into the forest; wasn't running away from safety. Her instincts had been to run toward civilization. Run toward help. Her instincts had let her down. She heard a train's whistle to her left. She turned and ran towards the railroad tracks, ran for five minutes then stepped onto the train tracks and knelt down. She took deep breaths, trying to catch her wind, trying to remain quiet in case G-Z popped out of the woods. She touched her bare feet and felt blood, felt where thorns, sticks and other ground cover had torn her skin. Looked in every direction for a sign of where to run next.

The ground began to vibrate, Jordyn looked left and saw a freight train 500 yards away hurtling toward her. She raised her arms and waved as she walked toward the train. A moment passed and even if the driver saw her, there was no time to stop with only 500 feet between her and the front of the train. In seconds, the train would run her over, but she didn't step off the tracks. She continued toward the train, moving faster, intent on throwing herself underneath it if it meant she wouldn't have to go back to that shed. The train gave no signs of slowing. There was no whistle or screech of metal brakes. She was so close that the vibration shook her to her knees. Just as the train was about to smash into her, she flung herself to the side of the tracks into the thick brush. The engine and cars roared past the edges of the nearby trees as she watched her ride out of the wilderness race by.

Breathless, she saw a shadow down the line and figured it was Glenn. That he'd gotten up and come after her. Unlike the time the familiar looking man who she couldn't completely recognize chased her, Jordyn did not look back once as she ran. She hoped the train had crushed him, cut him in half, or at a minimum, trapped him on the other side of the tracks.

She could hear him. He was too close. She got up. Her plan was to loop around the edge of the woods and double back on the tracks toward the way the train came. Even though she knew it would be better to remain focused on running, she gave into temptation. She had to look. She had to know where he was. She turned around and couldn't see him. He was gone, but the train was still thundering past. She thought she lost him when she ran into the forest, so she changed direction and ran toward town. Toward safety.

Thirty seconds later, Glenn leapt out from behind a tree and reached for her at the waist. She managed to avoid his reach and kept running, outpacing him until a fallen tree trunk brought her to a sudden stop. He caught up and grabbed a hold of her ankle. She crashed down onto the forest floor. He was on top of her, slapping at her and shouting, but she couldn't hear him over the sound of the screaming in her mind. All he could see was her teeth and eyes.

Then she remembered that she had prepared for this moment. She realized that the broken chisel was still in her hand. She kept it from before just in case more fighting was necessary. She clutched the wooden handle hard to ensure herself that she still had it. Now that he had her pinned down, she would only get one chance. As he put his hand on her panties, she brought the metal tip to the side of his head. Glenn sat upright and clutched his ear. She sliced at him again cutting the hand that clutched his ear. Her desire to get away was strong. She struck again and again. She should have killed him, but Glenn rolled off her and, still holding the bloody chisel, she scrambled backwards on all fours like a trapped animal.

Glenn dropped onto his hands and knees, crawling after her. Part of his ear lobe hung loose, dangling from a flap of skin. His expression twisted with anger. He lunged for her ankles. She slashed at his hand, jabbing and cutting with the broken chisel. He grabbed her wrist, pulling her toward him. Face-to-face, she leaned forward and bit the hand that held her. With his free hand he clasped her neck, squeezing, keeping her mouth away from biting him again.

She gasped, tried to break free but his grip was strong. She was suffocating. She threw her weight sideways. The two of them tumbled, rolling on the ground over and over as they struggled; him trying to hold on, her trying to break free.

Jordyn was on top of him when the base of a wide evergreen stopped their motion. Without thinking, she pushed herself up then flopped down, striking him square in his privates. Glenn screamed, letting her know she had hit her target, and she raised herself up again. Glenn's second scream let her know her aim was still true.

He rolled away and cupped both hands over his aching genitals.

Jordyn shoved his leg away with all her might, stepped on his stomach as she stood, then ran, not slowing down, smashing through low hanging branches that jutted out from trees. Ran through the darkness towards what sounded like a distant rushing river. Ran until she ran out onto a paved road. Didn't stop until she was standing in front of the eighteen wheel truck driven by a red-headed woman named Brandi with Pippi Longstocking braids.

Glenn arrived at the clearing adjacent to the two-lane road just as the squealing of the truck's brakes came to an end. If he had caught Jordyn, he would have killed her. When the driver's side door of the truck opened, he slunk back into the shadow of the tree line to avoid being seen. To his surprise, a woman got out of the truck and ran to where Jordyn had fallen in the ditch. He considered taking the chance and rushing them. If he timed it right, he could surprise them. The truck driver was an innocent bystander, but as long as he ended Jordyn, killing her would just be collateral damage.

Just as he convinced himself to take the risk and step out from his hiding spot to finish what he'd started, a car's headlights appeared to his left and closed quickly on them. G-Z watched the headlights grow brighter, illuminating the two women as the lady truck driver helped Jordyn into her truck. Frustrated, Glenn Zimmerman disappeared into the woods as the truck drove off, cussing all the way back to the car he parked at Uncle Darren's cabin.

CHAPTER 31

SOLOMON HADN'T TOLD VIVIENNE ABOUT his discovery, so she was surprised when he offered to drive her to church that morning with no explanation. When he detoured away from what she knew as her regular route to church, Vivienne asked nicely where they were going instead of her normal initial response to berate the driver for missing their turn. Without hesitation, he told her they were going to the church in South Seattle where Lawrence was preaching. A huge fan of Lawrence's demonstrative pulpit performances, Vivienne left it at that, turned up the volume on the radio and sang over the gospel channel music.

Solomon and Vivienne arrived early and sat in the front pew. They didn't normally sit together at Mount Sinai, but since they were both visitors, they did at South Seattle First Baptist Church of God in Christ. Lawrence was pleased to see his friend's face when he entered the sanctuary, and even more pleased to see Mom Viv. Amari entered with the choir, sat, and raised her eyebrows in surprise when she noticed Solomon in the front row.

Once Lawrence, the church elder and the senior deacon were seated, a super soprano with heavenly pipes led the choir in a soul stirring number that raised the roof at South Seattle First Baptist. Joy and the Holy Spirit were both present as the congregation filled the sanctuary with a tidal wave of *amens*, *hallelujahs* and similar praises. After two songs, the reading of cards and prayers for the sick and shut-in, and two offerings were collected—one for the building fund and one for normal tithes and offerings, Lawrence approached the altar.

"Good morning First Baptist family. I love to see so many of you packed in here today. God truly is good!" Lawrence paused while several church members shouted their concurrence. "This morning I want to talk about faith. Faith in our fellow humans and faith in God.

"Faith is the substance of things hoped for—the evidence of things not seen! Like when I say, I have faith that someone out there will hear me, my faith is reassured by your cosigning my faith in My God."

Another round of cosigns echoed from the congregation.

Lawrence preached for forty-five minutes before the choir stood to perform their final selection. This time Amari sang the lead. Vivienne, who had been watching her son's eyes, followed his gaze until she saw Amari's face. Up until this point, Vivienne hadn't noticed the woman who bore such a striking resemblance to her deceased daughter-in-law, but once Amari stood in front of the choir to sing her solo, surprise filled her spirit more than any part of Lawrence's sermon. Vivienne stretched her face in awe when the woman appeared to be looking at Solomon. She turned to him and saw that he was returning her stare, then she pinched Solomon on the arm and asked him, "Is she the real reason we came all the way out here?"

"Yes Viv." Solomon turned to meet his mother's inquisitively judgmental face and stoically replied, "Yes she is."

"Does she know who you are?"

Facial expression still stoic, he replied, "We've met."

You've met?" Vivienne guffawed, "Oh this is going to be good."

Solomon hushed her. He sat and watched Amari throughout the duration of the song, not once looking at his mother. Once the choir finished, Lawrence made his way to the altar to conclude the day's service.

Once most of the congregation had passed Lawrence, Solo and Viv joined the greeting line. Viv said, "I love how intense Lawrence gets when he's preaching. His sermons are so passionate."

Solomon replied, "I get a kick out of how you can see the sweat beading on top of his bald head. And how he sweats so much that his glasses keep sliding off."

Right before they reached Lawrence, Viv said, "And you know he is serious when he elongates…Jeeee-zus!"

Noticing the older and younger Alexandrés laughing heartily, Lawrence asked, "What I miss?" before giving Mom Viv a hug.

As Viv teased her other son, Solomon, just like his first visit, turned his attention to the door which hid the nether reaches of the church where the choir removed their robes. When Amari returned, Solomon waited patiently for her to greet the pastor and make time for him. Unlike before, she was aware of his presence, so there was no doubt in his mind that she would have to talk to him. As Amari talked with Lawrence about the sermon, she noticed his eyes drift toward Solomon. Amari allowed her glance to follow his, all three acknowledging that there was no way she was leaving the church without having a conversation. Just when Amari concluded that she would control the narrative on today's conversation, Lawrence asked Amari for a private audience to talk to her about a friend. Amari conceded to Lawrence's plea for *leniency and listening with an open mind* before releasing a huge a sigh of uncertainty about what awaited her. She followed as Lawrence accompanied her to greet Solomon and Vivienne.

"Well hello Sister Favors," Solomon said eagerly.

"Well hello to you too, Brother?" started Amari. "What did you say your name was again?"

"Solomon!" Vivienne said, inserting herself into the conversation. "Wow child, if I hadn't been at her funeral myself, I would swear you were my dead and buried daughter-in-law standing right here in front of me now."

Lawrence's prelude softened the reality of Viv's coarse words.

Amari's first glance at the largish woman conjured images of Della Reese. When Viv called her son's name in her raspy voice, her *Della Reese* was cemented. "So I take it that this lovely lady is your mother?" She admired Vivienne's brightly adorned dress and before either the momma's boy or his momma responded, she said, "Your dress is fabulous. My mother has one very similar." Amari thought, *I cannot believe this man had to bring his mother for backup. I hope he doesn't think that I won't tell him to get lost just because she is here.*

"Yes," Solomon replied. "Vivienne Alexandré, I'd like you to meet Amari Favors."

He searched her face carefully for withdrawal, for returning anger, for something, but there was nothing. The tension, and the weight of memory and regret that he'd expected would come with seeing her again, were absent.

Amari and Vivienne shared an amiable handshake.

"So how can I help you this time Brother Alexandré? Reverend Didier says you have some news for me."

Solomon could feel the tension in her voice. In some way he could imagine that he was deserving of her curt tone, but he was too interested in telling her what he had found out since their first meeting to let her resistance dissuade his effort.

"Actually, I came here because I would like to talk about you and my wife Mareschelle." Solomon confirmed Vivienne's statement about Mareschelle and proceeded to tell her of their remarkable resemblance. He told her of Schelle's passing and how he saw Amari about town several times over the past year and how she coincidentally happened to be at the church the first time his best friend was there as the guest pastor.

"So what does all of that have to do with me?" Amari asked. She had raised her voice a little and realized that she had attracted some unwanted attention from those in the church who continued to stay after the service.

Solomon replied, "Miss Favors I loved my wife very much and when I saw you the first time I thought I was going crazy. After we spoke last, I couldn't get you out of my mind so I did a little digging into my wife's past and found out some things from her mother that I would like to talk with you about if you will allow it."

"Why don't you say what you have to say Mister Alexandré?" Amari's shift from calling Solomon 'Brother Alexandré' to 'Mister Alexandré' meant that she was trending toward angry black woman. Solomon knew that he was treading on thin ice now and would have to be careful.

Lawrence said, "I don't think here is the place. The pastor's rectory would provide this conversation the privacy it deserves."

"If it is all the same to Miss Favors," Solomon said following Amari's reference to him as mister vice brother, "If she would do us the honor of joining us for dinner, I think I can paint you a clearer picture of how what I found out about my wife might affect her."

Amari's eyes shifted from his face to his wedding ring, then back to his face. "I have a fiancé Mister Alexandré, so I don't think going on a date with you would be appropriate."

"Bring him with you. This is news that he needs to hear," Solomon exclaimed. "I would love to meet him and it would give me and Lawrence a chance to meet him, if pastor hasn't yet."

Lawrence declined, citing his and Annette's prior commitment.

"Thank you for asking me first." Vivienne huffed before taking a seat in an empty pew.

"You're welcome, mother," Solomon placed his hand on Viv's shoulder. "Dinner for you and your boyfriend are on me."

"And I guess I have to pay for my own food?" Vivienne interjected. "I know I raised you better than that!"

Amari laughed, convinced that Viv talked sweet when it served her, but her overwhelming impression was that this tough old gal was more gruff than fluff.

"No Ma, you don't have to pay for your own food. I'm paying for your dinner too. You know that!"

Solomon returned his attention to Amari and said, "Please just come and hear me out. If you decide that you don't want to stay and eat after you hear what I have to say, it's all good."

Amari searched the church anxiously. Solomon couldn't tell who or what she was looking for, but twenty seconds passed before she turned to him and said, "Alright, Brother Alexandré I give. I will join you for dinner, but this better be good. And I will have my fiancé with me just in case you creep me out like you did last time."

"I apologize for that."

Vivienne frowned and asked, "What did you do to her boy?"

"Ma, Please!" Solomon said.

Amari smiled again. She liked Vivienne, or at least she liked the way she handled her son. Solomon didn't really appear to be a momma's boy, but with some guys you never can tell.

"Great," Solomon said, returning his attention to Amari. "Let's meet at Texas de Brazil at six and see how things go from there?"

"Alright," Amari said. "Nice meeting you Missus Alexandré, I'll see you later tonight."

"Nice meeting you too," Vivienne said.

~

Solomon called the restaurant on the drive back to Seattle and made reservations for four. During his time with Vivienne that afternoon, he shared what he'd been doing since he first met Amari. She seemed excited for him, but cautioned him that bringing this woman into his life may cause him more harm than good. She questioned his motives for wanting to find out about her but ultimately let him know that he had her support no matter what happened at dinner.

When they arrived at Texas de Brazil just before six o'clock, Amari and her fiancé were waiting in the lobby. Solomon offered the man his hand. "Doctor Solomon Alexandré, nice to meet you."

Amari's fiancé accepted his handshake and replied, "Philip Wirthmore. Nice to meet you too." Philip Wirthmore—a slim, six-foot, pretty boy with a polished demeanor was every bit the distinguished gentleman he appeared to be. He had finished law school, passed the bar on his first try and trampled competitors on his way to becoming the youngest partner in the history of one Seattle's most prestigious law firms. He'd been elected Deputy Mayor before the age of thirty six and subsequently elected the Emerald City's Mayor before he turned forty. Handsome, self-confident and flawlessly dressed in a light-blue suit, yellow tie and wing-tip shoes, his demeanor wreaked of the term boorish.

Solomon introduced Philip to his mother then sought out the Maître d to announce their arrival.

"Are you really Philip Wirthmore, the Mayor?" Vivienne asked. "You look a lot older and meaner on the television."

Philip and Amari laughed.

"Yes I am Ma'am," Philip said. "I'll have to get the camera fixed."

"Hunh, and he has jokes and manners too," Vivienne said, "Young lady, this one here is a keeper."

This time Vivienne joined Philip and Amari in quieted laughter.

Their table was ready so they were seated immediately. Solomon ordered water and tea for everyone.

"I didn't want tea," Vivienne scowled. "I want a glass of wine, since you're driving."

Solomon felt like a pre-teen who'd just been found out in a lie. He told her, "I'll order an appropriate wine once you order, mother."

Viv huffed and picked up her menu.

While the waiter was off to get their drinks, Solomon started to tell them why he asked them there. "My wife was adopted shortly after birth. Over the past couple weeks, I discovered that twin girls were born at St. Bonaventure on September 17, 1980. And between my research and my conversation with the agent who handled the adoptions, my deceased wife Mareschelle is Amari's older twin sister."

Amari regarded Philip searching for his reaction. The catfishing idea entered her mind and she wondered why he picked her. She glanced at Vivienne and for some reason, Viv's expression convinced her there may be some truth to his story. She whispered, "Go on."

Solomon revealed an envelope containing his research. He handed the envelope to Amari who slid it in front of her fiancé attorney, Philip without opening it. As Philip perused the documents, Solomon informed her of the adoption agent's confession that she was forbidden by her employers to tell the adopting parents that there was another baby, even if it meant that the babies could be kept together. How her mother, a college student who'd been raped, had died from complications during childbirth and never learned her rapist's identity. He concluded his story be telling her that Mareschelle's mother still lived in Tacoma.

"Mean old bat," Vivienne interjected in between bites of her salad.

"Ma please," Solomon growled.

Vivienne stuffed salad in her mouth and then pointed as if saying, 'It wasn't me, I wouldn't dare talk with food in my mouth'.

Despite the enormity of the revelation, Amari giggled. She didn't feel like laughing, but Vivienne amused her. For the third time that day Vivienne made Amari smile. A feat Solomon had yet to accomplish.

Solomon said, "Excuse me if you consider this rude," then asked, "Do you mind if I ask about your parents?"

Amari answered, "My parents both died two years ago. My father died first and I think my mother died of loneliness three months later. I spent as much time with her as I could, but I couldn't make up for the loss in her heart."

"That's sad," Vivienne said.

"Thank you for that." Amari placed her hand on top of Vivienne's. "But it's alright. They were married for over fifty years and they loved each other until the day they died. They loved me too and I am just happy that they are together and resting.

"That's sweet," said Vivienne.

"I'm sorry to hear that," said Solomon. "I don't know what I would do without my mother around to badger me all the time." He chuckled then said, "I mean love me all the time."

Vivienne said something under her breath but kept eating.

Philip's nod confirmed the legitimacy of the paperwork for Amari.

Amari blew air. "So I had a twin sister that I never knew about?"

"Yes," Viv chimed in quickly. "And ever since the first day he saw you running around Seattle, this one thought you were a ghost. Boy thought he was losing his mind."

Amari stared off into space intently, contemplating life, love, loss and what it would have been like to grow up with a sister. After a long beat, she cleared her throat, wiped away a tear from her left eye and asked," And now that we're here, what do you want from me?"

"Well..." Solomon started, "I would like the chance to be your brother-in-law. I would like the chance to be your friend." He had pondered the answer to this question a thousand times since his first visit to First Tacoma Baptist. "I lost the love of my life way too early," he paused, took two deep breaths and comported himself. "Once I saw you, I had to meet you just so that I knew my mind wasn't playing tricks on me. I knew that if I had a piece of my Mareschelle back in my life, I would be a better person for it. I know that is a lot to throw on you out of the blue but it is the truth." He saw Philip shift in his chair when he said, *back in my life* so he regarded him and said, "Forgive me brother. I have no intention of causing any more angst than I already have. I have no idea what Amari is thinking, but all I know is that I can rest easy now knowing that I really wasn't crazy running around thinking I was seeing a ghost."

Viv stared at her son, vividly remembering how throughout her lifetime, Solo's passion toward things he honestly believed in.

Amari reached out and clutched Philip's hand. Choking back tears, she asked Solomon, "Can you tell me about my sister?"

Solomon exhaled a joyful sigh of relief. After his performance at the café during their first meeting, he wasn't certain that Amari wouldn't get up and walk out after he spoke his peace.

Solomon started telling stories as far back as he could remember about him and Mareschelle, and when he got to the part about their wedding he broke down in tears and stopped talking. He excused himself from the table and went to the men's room.

Not missing a beat, Vivienne continued the story of their wedding and told her opinion of her daughter-in-law, most of it favorable. More favorable than what she told of Mareschelle's mother.

When Solomon returned from the men's room, Amari enlightened the table about her past. Like long lost friends exchanging stories, they were surprised when the waiter approached them four hours later and let them know that it was after ten o'clock and the restaurant was closed. Solomon exchanged business cards with both Amari and Philip, jokingly recommending they see Lawrence for marriage counseling before they walked down the aisle. The couple found the honest humor in his recommendation and promised to talk with Lawrence after his next sermon.

Vivienne gave Amari hugs, kissed her goodbye and said, "It's a shame you missed having your sister in your life. We had our differences, but she was a beautiful person inside and out. If you are as good for that young man as she was for my son, then Philip is one lucky man. You stay sweet." Gentility was not a trait Solo often associated with his mother, but Vivienne surprised him that night.

"Thank you Vivienne," Amari replied.

Outside the restaurant, the mayor's town car awaited Amari and Philip. Vivienne flirted curbside with the fifty-something valet while Solomon retrieved his own car. He folded the soft cover roof of his 1938 Saliot into the trunk before returning to pick her up.

In the car, Solo wanted to scold his mother for her behavior, but he knew that he had no real reason to because she said nothing out of her normal character. If nothing else, Solo knew that Vivienne always kept it real when it came to speaking her mind about her son.

Vivienne said, "They make a cute couple. Much better than you and Schelle. She was never right for you."

"Don't start Mom." Solo knew that Vivienne never cared for Schelle and moreover, she never held her tongue about her feelings toward her deceased daughter-in-law. Every time she got onto one of her tirades, Solo wanted to rip his mother's tongue out.

Vivienne cut her eyes at him.

Solo could tell from the sinister look on her face that something devious was stirring in that brain of hers. He asked, "Is it so wrong for me to want the kind of love that Amari and Philip seem to have?"

Vivienne snorted, clicked her tongue, but remained silent. She looked out the window at passing traffic and thought, *Am I so wrong for wanting my only son to stay single. What about me? He's all I got.* Vivienne turned to face Solo and stroked the side of his head. *I never did like that Mareschelle. Her, or her stuck up Mama.*

"You know what, Ma?" Solo asked. "I need to get back to dating."

Vivienne smirked. "Boy, you're just horny. You don't need another simple woman tying you down again."

Solomon jumped in his seat, flabbergasted by his mother's words.

"Look," she continued, "just take yourself to one of them strip clubs or massage parlors, or wherever it is you men go these days and get some *me so horny* girl to take care of that for you."

"Take care of wha…?" Solo started. "Know what; never mind!"

Vivienne didn't bat an eye. She said, "Just looking out for my baby," but was really thinking, *This boy needs to get him a whore for his man needs and let me keep them heifers away from his money.*

As Solo left downtown headed for North Seattle, he told Vivienne that he had some business to handle Monday and asked her to clear his afternoon schedule. He didn't see patients on Monday morning, so the morning required no cancellations.

Vivienne, never completely renouncing the bad feelings for her deceased daughter-in-law, was not totally convinced that Solomon involving himself in this Amari woman's life was the right thing to do, but nevertheless, she agreed prior to exiting the car.

When they arrived at her house, Fred, the widowed, 65-year-old, most recent addition to the neighborhood, Viv labeled *an eight* when he moved into the house directly across the street from her six weeks prior, stopped talking to her next door neighbor and walked toward the car. Viv declined Solomon's offer to walk her inside. Instead, she kissed Solomon on the cheek and exited his car while Fred held her door open, then shut the passenger door and walked her to her door sporting a huge grin.

Solomon drove away calling, "Alright you two, don't be up in there making no babies!

CHAPTER 32

IN THE WEEK FOLLOWING DINNER with Amari, Philip and Viv, Solomon met Amari, collected her DNA swab then submitted it and a clump of hair from Mareschelle's brush for comparison. Amari was open to meeting her sister's mother. To getting a glimpse into the life of the sister she always dreamed of having, but never knew existed. When the test results confirmed a 100% DNA match for the twin girls born on September 17, 1980, Solomon called Rachel Mae Betancourt and asked her it was alright for him to come over and have dinner with her on her birthday the way he and Schelle used to. After Rachel Mae agreed, Solo told her he'd be there around three on Sunday.

At bible study Wednesday night, Solo told Viv that he was going to church in South Seattle again on Sunday then having dinner with Amari and Mrs. Be.

Viv called Rachel Mae after work Friday and told her that Solomon shared the news about her birthday dinner. She explained how she understood how hard it might be celebrating her birthday alone for the first time without her husband and asked if it was okay for to come over and cook dinner for Rachel Mae and Solo. Viv didn't care for Mareschelle as Solomon's wife, and was more or less indifferent toward Rachel Mae following her daughter's passing, but she was not going to allow another woman to share an enjoyable experience with her son without somehow being involved.

Viv didn't mention that she knew Amari was coming. Unaware of Viv's ulterior motive, Rachel Mae agreed to dinner, then conceded to Viv's coercion not to tell Solo about their duet becoming a threesome.

~

"Hello Mrs. Be." Solomon, Amari and Philip were in the church parking lot when his mother-in-law answered her phone Sunday afternoon. "I know it's late notice, and I apologize, Ma'am, but since we're celebrating, do you mind if I bring two friends to dinner?"

"Boy, you couldn't be more inconsiderate," Rachel Mae gruffed. "I already set my table and now you want me to dig out more china."

The Betancourt's dinner table seated eight, so Solomon knew there was enough room. "If you want, Ma'am..." Solomon put his phone on speaker so Amari and Philip could hear. "...I can pick up a dessert on my way."

"Ain't no need for all that." Rachel Mae always overcooked for company and Solomon knew it. When he and Mareschelle ate at her parents', they always took enough leftovers home to make lunches all week. Without asking who, Rachel Mae said, "Just bring them on."

Rachel Mae almost fainted when she saw Amari standing on her porch next to Solomon the same way she'd seen her Mareschelle stand next to him a thousand times in the past. Her knees buckled and she grabbed the door handle to steady herself. Solomon stepped to catch her, but she brushed him away with a, "Stop, Boy!" She covered her heart and looked upward. "Lord Jesus, Saints Alive. If this child ain't my Rennie, I don't know why I'm living."

Once she started calling the Lord's name, Solomon was certain she was fine, so he stepped back, allowing Amari and Rachel Mae an unobstructed line of sight.

As if God had sent her a brown angel in high heels, Rachel Mae switched gears like a race car, stepped forward, opened her arms and embraced the stranger who so strongly resembled her deceased daughter.

Solomon noticed Amari's bottom lip quiver as Rachel Mae wrapped the woman who shared her daughter's face in her husky arms, then cried as she hugged the woman long and tight. He watched the old woman rock the hunched over stranger from side-to-side, holding Amari at her much shorter height while they hugged cheek-to-cheek. Watched the delicate movement of Rachel Mae's frail hand as she dabbed at her eyes with a satin handkerchief after she finally let Amari go.

Then Rachel Mae faced Philip, eyed the man in the three-button black suit and pink Italian shirt with no tie. His chiseled chin, full lips and bright, clear eyes set in luscious caramel skin, devoid of blemish or scar, made Denzel pale in comparison. She asked, "And who is this fine looking gentleman?"

Amari took a moment to recover from the shaking and bone rattling that was Rachel Mae's joy in meeting her, then said, "Mrs. Betancourt, this gentleman is my fiancé, Mister Philip Wirthmore.

"Wirthmore?" Rachel Mae muttered. "What kind of sedity name is that? Where your people from boy?"

"Sacramento, Ma'am," Philip answered quickly. His eyes were set in perpetual awe, the rest of his face held the luster of polished bronze. "But my parents moved to Seattle when I was ten." Philip guessed Rachel Mae to be sixty, if she was a day. Her silver hair and puffy eyes were all that appeared aged above her smooth brown cheeks. Her neck was thick, but not fat. No jowls hanging low like he'd seen on some heavier women her age.

"Wirthmore?" Rachel Mae repeated. "Ain't Wirthmore the name of that there Mayor in Seattle?"

"Yes, Ma'am," Philip responded. "I…"

"You any kin to him?" she interrupted.

"Yes, Ma'am," Amari answered this time. "One in the same."

"Hmmph." Rachel Mae was a short—five-foot-four or so—

matronly woman with large, wide-set brown eyes. Her pug nose and thick, pouty lips sat on a round face that over that years had intimidated many a man, and woman. She eyed Philip and grunted, "Then why didn't he just say so? Peoples is always putting on airs about who they are. Can't just be who they be; always wanna sound important." The fire that spilled from her pouty lips brought to mind scenes of the wicked witch from *The Wiz*.

What a mouth! Amari thought as she eyed Rachel Mae, deciding whether to be insulted or tell her off. She did neither, but instead opted to bide her time and see how the visit evolved.

As she headed inside, Rachel Mae spoke to no one in particular, "Well don't just stand there with the door hanging open, come on in."

Solomon followed Amari and Philip into the foyer. The soft aroma of roasted meat wafting in from the kitchen caught Amari's nose and reminded her of childhood Thanksgivings at her parent's house. The smell swirled around her head and pulled her into the inviting comfort of Rachel Mae's quaint home. "Dinner smells wonderful," Amari said, anxious to shove a thick slice of the delicious smelling meat into her mouth. She looked in the direction Rachel Mae headed and asked, "Can I help you with anything in the kitchen?"

Rachel Mae laughed. "No Honey, dinner's all but ready." She gestured to the immaculate room full of antique furniture to her right and said, "You take my son-in-law and that gorgeous fiancé of yours into the living room and get them a drink."

Ten minutes later, Rachel Mae entered the dining room from the kitchen and called, "You kids come in here so we can eat."

Solo's jaw almost hit the floor when he saw Viv holding a casserole in the dining room next to Rachel Mae. He said, "What the…?" when his tongue regained consciousness.

"What?" Viv chided. "Don't I always cook on special

occasions?"

"Yeah," Solo conceded, averting his gaze to Rachel Mae. "But...but you two."

"And what could be more special than a birthday, a homecoming, and meeting new family?" Viv said, over her son, as she moved to find a spot to place the piping hot dish in her hand.

Amari eyed the feast set out for Rachel Mae's birthday: a standing rib roast, garlic chicken, green beans with mushrooms, sliced beets, carrots with cranberries, white and yellow corn, yeast rolls, fried cabbage and collard greens seasoned with sweet Italian turkey sausage. When everyone sat to eat, she said, "You have a wonderful home, Mrs. Betancourt. Thank you for opening it to us."

Solomon blessed the table then sliced the crown roast as Viv and Rachel Mae passed the sides. For the next half hour, silence blanketed the room as the quintet feasted on the meal Viv and Rachel Mae prepared. Solomon opened two bottles of wine—one white, and one red. Rachel Mae had baked a decadent fresh apple cake—it was her favorite and she only made it on her birthday. Viv made a rum-soaked pound cake because her son couldn't stop raving about the one he'd had during his Caribbean vacation last summer.

While *The Kids*, as Rachel Mae referred to them, sampled the desserts, Viv and Rachel Mae commenced *The Inquisition of Amari Favors* that Solomon had expected—or more like regretted.

Amari looked at Solomon, her eyes begging him for guidance.

"Go easy on her ladies," he said, we don't want to scare her off."

Amari held Philip's hand for reassurance as Viv and Rachel Mae continued their inquiries.

Did you know you were adopted before you met Solomon?
What city did you grow up in?
Where did your parents work?

Vivienne interjected, offered Amari her condolences for a second time then told Rachel Mae that Amari's parents were deceased.

Rachel Mae offered her condolences, then continued with:

Do you have any other brothers and sisters?
Do either of you have children?
Did you go to college?
Are you in a sorority?
Where do you work?
My Rennie was allergic to mushrooms; Do you have allergies?
Do you vote? Republican or democrat?
How did you meet Philip?
Have you set a date for the wedding?

As the women interrogated Amari, Solo looked upon the walls at family pictures of Darnell, Rachel Mae and his Schelle, and reflected on all of the wonderful times he had shared in the Betancourt home. He saw a picture of Mareschelle poolside in the backyard wearing a bikini and daydreamed of her on the beach during their honeymoon.

"Solomon?" a cracked female voice called in a tone meant to make it seem like she had called him more than once. The cracked voice belonged to Rachel Mae. Her call shifted the group's focus from the inquisition to Solomon.

He woke from his stupor and turned to face the direction of the cracked voice. All eight eyes at the dinner table stared at him. Just when he was about to accept the oddity of the Betancourt's presence as a daydream, he heard the calling of another familiar voice. He blinked hard as his mother's voice dispersed the bedroom scene.

"You alright, Baby?" Viv's voice pulled him back to the present.

He closed his eyes tightly again, either in the ecstasy of relief or in the rigors of concentration. When he opened them, he met Amari's eyes first. He struggled to look away, but it was impossible. His impure memories of her sister were written all over his face, transferred to her sister and were now tinkering somewhere on the border of that heated sensation that rushes between madness and pleasantry. A few beats of awkward silence passed in which he experienced the unfamiliar sensation of embarrassment. He stole a glance of the picture hanging on the wall above Rachel Mae's head of Mareschelle in her wedding dress. "Just thinking about my Schelle."

He looked to Philip, hoping he didn't see the lust in his eyes, and saw in his gaze what looked to be understanding in a clipped, jerky gesture that eased the tension tightening the muscles in his face.

Philip told Solomon, "Losing a loved one is hard. But you have to know that they want you to keep living and loving after they're gone."

Amari placed her hand on Solomon's, told him, "If you ever get lucky enough to find love again, grab it and don't let go. Fight for it like a junkyard dog and take the risk of getting hurt because if you don't take that risk you may miss the next best thing to ever happen to you. The only one you'll be cheating in the end is you. If you've ever wanted a woman to be happier than you, then be smart enough to look past her eyes into her heart and soul.

Having both lost their husbands—one to divorce, one to a stroke—Viv and Rachel Mae cosigned Amari's and Philip's thoughts; that carrying Mareschelle's memory was good, but he had to move on.

Years of pseudo strength had proven ineffectual. Allowing himself the experience of finally mourning his wife's death, Solomon repeated *why* several times, then *why did you leave me, Schelle?* Prior to that moment, he had never allowed himself to weep or crumble in public. At her funeral he barely cried, but now as tears streamed down his face, he didn't care who witnessed his cleansing.

Once Solomon was solidly back in their present space and time, Rachel Mae asked Amari, "Have you ever met your grandmother?"

Amari sat stock still for a moment. Of all the questions she imagined Rachel Mae asking, THAT was not one of them. She gripped Philips hand tighter as tears welled in her eyes. After a beat, she managed to squeak, "No, Ma'am."

"Well then we need to fix that right away." Rachel Mae's smile brightened the room. She knew Amari's grandmother still lived in a nursing home on the other side of Tacoma and moreover, knew how ecstatic Bonnie's mother would be to meet her other granddaughter.

During his reverie, Amari answered every question to Viv and Rachel Mae's satisfaction. They talked about family. Rachel Mae recapped Mareschelle's childhood. Vivienne thought about Mareschelle's inability to bear children, but decided Rachel Mae's birthday party was the wrong setting to address that issue. However, when Amari asked about Mareschelle's passing, Rachel Mae said, "You and I can have a private conversation about Mareschelle's health issues at a later date. I can't talk about that today." When the inquisition ended, Rachel Mae announced she was going to get a cup of chamomile tea with honey and asked if anyone would like some.

Amari said yes.

Two cups of tea in hand, Rachel Mae joined Amari in front of the picture of Mareschelle in her wedding gown. She said, "Seems like yesterday. It was a noon wedding. Rennie wafted down the aisle holding on to her father's arm like her daddy was a superhero. Oooh honey, the church was packed with all of Rennie's high school and college friends, cousins from her daddy's side of the family here in Washington, and some of mine from Oklahoma. I wore a pale green dress that Rennie picked out for me. Told me it was her favorite color, that it reminded her of her favorite orchid, and that if I wore it, she would be the happiest girl on the planet. It wasn't the glitziest wedding you've ever seen, but it was elegant and it was the wedding that my baby wanted. My Rennie was so happy that day."

Amari wrapped her free arm around Rachel Mae's shoulder and hugged her tight. "Mrs. Betancourt, I would be honored if you would sit in for my mother at my wedding."

Rachel Mae's answer was an onset of blubbering tears.

Amari smiled, hugged her twin sister's mother as tight as she could and sipped the delicious tea while she stared at her sister in her wedding dress.

It was almost nine when Rachel Mae walked her guests into her foyer. Phone numbers, promises to visit or to meet for lunch, and invitations to stop by anytime they wanted were shared between Amari and the two elder women. Solomon and Philip exchanged numbers—Philip inquiring about Solomon's sports' allegiances, and Solomon inviting him to Woody's for poker night with the Horsemen. Both agreed and gave dap on the porch while the ladies exchanged hugs and kisses.

When Solomon didn't see Viv's car outside, he asked, "Hey Viv, explain to me again how you got here?"

"I didn't explain the first time," Viv laughed devilishly. "And if I must tell, it was my friend Fred. And I told him you'd bring me home."

Solomon, Amari and Philip laughed all the way to their cars.

Viv stayed back on the porch with Rachel Mae until *the kids* were out of earshot. She held her hand and stood a step below Rachel Mae so they'd be at eye-level while they talked. "Girl, I know things haven't always been the greatest between us, but I think it's about time that changed. We are blessed to have great children, and even though your baby girl isn't with us anymore, that shouldn't stop us from being family. So if it's alright with you, I'd like us to try and spend some time together."

"Hell Viv, you're right. We old gals got to stick together."

Viv and Rachel Mae hugged for a long moment. As Viv walked to Solomon's car, Rachel Mae asked, "Hey Girl, you play Bid Whist?"

"Hells yes!" Viv exclaimed. "And Tonk too!"

"Good," Rachel Mae replied. "We play every third Thursday. I'll call you."

"Sounds good, Girl."

As Solomon held his car door open for Viv, Amari called. "Hey

Brother-in-law?" As Solomon contemplated a sarcastic retort, she continued with, "If you own one, would you consider dusting off your tux for me?" then she slipped into Philip's car and rode off with the Mayor of Seattle the same way Solomon saw her do when he imagined Mareschelle getting into a car at an art auction once upon a time ago.

CHAPTER 33

TREY THOMAS ACCOMPANIED DETECTIVE CHRYSTOPHER into Solo's office on Monday afternoon, eight days after dinner at Rachel Mae's. "Good news or bad?" Solo asked after shutting the door behind them.

Trey nodded to the detective indicating that he had the floor.

"Detective Foreman called from Spokane. He said they have a woman they've identified as Jordyn Hoffman in a hospital under police protection."

Solomon's knees buckled. He grabbed his desk to steady himself, then waved Trey off when the attorney stepped to help him.

"Spokane police want you up there for a lineup," Trey told him.

"What are we waiting for?" Solomon belted out. "Let's go!"

"Slow your roll, Son," Trey continued. "There's a couple things we need to discuss first."

"Jordyn is alive. What else do we need to talk about? Let's go."

"They are still kidnapping charges pending," Trey continued. "And you are still the prime suspect."

"That doesn't make any sense. How can that be?"

Detective Chrystopher flipped open his notebook "When I talked with Spokane police, he said that the woman truck driver who brought her into the hospital put in her statement that the only three words Miss Hoffman spoke before she passed out were Seattle, Solomon Alexandré."

A woman truck driver? Solomon immediately thought of Brandi, the burly woman truck driver who'd accosted him at the rest stop. He chuckled for a moment then thought, *Figure the odds,* knowing she couldn't be the only woman truck driver in Washington State.

"She's alive," Detective Chrystopher continued, "and that's the good news; but the bad news is that your name is the only name she gave them. And that makes you their prime suspect. They told me that they placed Miss Hoffman in a medically induced coma two days ago after she came out of surgery to help her injuries heal, but they expect to wake her up tonight or tomorrow. Spokane Detectives want you there to discuss anything she tells them when she wakes up."

"Why would I kidnap her? That just doesn't make any sense."

"Don't worry, Son," Trey said. "I will be with you the entire time."

Detective Foreman's call to Detective Chrystopher requested Seattle PD detain and transfer Solo to Spokane. Trey Thomas cleared his calendar to make the trip to Spokane with Solomon.

"Finish up whatever business you have going on today. Go home tonight and grab what you need," Detective Chrystopher instructed.

"I don't need nothing," Solomon barked. "We can go now."

"No need for all that," Trey told Solomon. "Take tonight and get yourself situated. My company jet will take us to Spokane in the morning."

~

When Darren Zimmerman listened to the news report that an unidentified woman had been found near Lake County, he panicked. The reporter didn't mention if she was conscious, or if she had spoken to the police, or where she'd been found, but he knew that if she wasn't dead, it would only be a matter of time before the police came knocking down his door. He had done what G-Z had asked because G-Z had come to his rescue three years earlier when he got carried away choking a prostitute while having sex and killed her. G-

299

Z helped him get her out of his house and helped him bury her in the woods on the hunting grounds near his cabin. To make certain her body wouldn't be found, they cut down a tree and laid the tree over the fallen leaves they used to cover the dirt over her grave.

At sixty-five and recently diagnosed with advanced liver cancer, Darren decided that spending the remainder of his days in prison was not an option. The next morning after showering, eating his favorite pancake breakfast, cleaning his kitchen and making his bed, he dressed in his fanciest three-piece suit, took out his cell phone and made a video confession of his part in Jordyn's disappearance. Having some fleeting sense of culpability, he added the story of the prostitute buried in the woods, giving markers so she could eventually be found, but leaving his nephew's name out of the part about the prostitute.

He called the police station and asked for the name of the detective leading the investigation of the Jordyn Hoffman case. Once he had Detective Foreman's name, he wrote it on the outside of a manila envelope, turned off his phone, and put his cell phone on the charger to refresh the battery. He had called his utility companies early that morning to put an immediate stop to all of his services, Darren put his cell phone in the manila envelope and put the envelope in the glove box of his car. He arrived at his job dressed in his suit, told his boss about his liver cancer and told him that he was retiring, effective immediately. He cleaned out his locker then sat and waited for the Human Resources rep to see him.

After twenty-four years in an abusive marriage, his wife took their only child and left him. His daughter called him from New Mexico just before Halloween two years prior and told him that her mother had passed away. He hadn't seen his wife or now twenty-six year old daughter in twelve years, but he still loved her despite her telling him in their one and only phone conversation that he was a piece of crap father, and husband. After he had verified with his HR rep that all of his insurance and beneficiary paperwork correctly identified that his daughter would receive all of his benefits, he drove to the liquor store and bought two bottles of their most expensive tequila.

Darren arrived at his cabin just before dusk that night. He parked his car fifty yards down the dirt driveway and walked to the cabin in his three-piece suit, leaving the manila envelope with the words Detective Foreman written on the outside as the only item in the trunk of his unlocked car. He made a big fire in the fireplace then drank ninety percent of a fifth of tequila over the next couple of hours as he reminisced over the pictures of his wife and daughter he'd brought from his house. When the tequila and his tears made the pictures too blurry to focus on, he stumbled over to the gas stove and turned the left burner knob until he could hear gas escaping the burner. Darren stumbled back to his recliner and washed down a dozen sleeping pills with the last of the high-priced Mexican liquor. He threw the bottle into the fireplace, reclined his chair and closed his eyes.

The gas explosion would burn Darren's cabin to the ground before they discovered him and after a thorough search of his car, the manila envelope would be delivered to Detective Foreman three days later.

~

Detective Foreman camped out in Jordan's hospital room for two days before she was coherent enough to tell him her story. Solomon and Trey Thomas had arrived in Spokane and were sequestered at a hotel for two days waiting for her to be coherent enough to observe a lineup. Fortunately for them, their waiting wasn't in vain.

From her hospital bed, Jordyn recalled for Detective Foreman her trip to Seattle. She summarized her brief entanglement with Solomon including their disagreement at the club and her leaving Solomon's place after someone tried to run them down in the street. Through tears, she recounted Glenn Zimmerman breaking into her hotel room at the Hotel Monaco then assaulting, raping and choking her unconscious. She described waking up in the back of a van with a stranger who imprisoned her in a shed out in the woods. Told how she fought Glenn Zimmerman weeks later when he came to that shed to kill her. How she stabbed him with the broken chisel, bit through his ear and escaped after she kneed him hard in the genitals and left him lying in the woods. How she ran to the road and blacked out when she saw the truck's headlights screaming toward her.

The blood on the broken chisel recovered with Jordyn's clothes was identified as belonging to Glenn Zimmerman. Before that night ended, with a warrant for his arrest in hand, Detective Foreman lead a SWAT team to Glenn Zimmerman's storefront office to arrest G-Z. He and twelve of his workers were in the store when police arrived. The police surprised the unsuspecting group of petty thugs and it appeared the arrest would go down without any shots being fired.

When the SWAT Team came through the door and yelled for everyone to *Freeze* and *Get down*, Glenn was in the back room. The young wannabe thugs did as ordered. G-Z heard the commotion and came out flapping his arms and telling everybody to be cool. The situation seemed benign until one of G-Z's goons ran out from the back room pointing a machine gun. SWAT cut him down with two bullets. At the sound of gunfire, a couple of G-Z's other thugs went for their guns. When the shooting finally stopped, Glenn 'G-Z' Zimmerman and six of his goons were dead.

Serving the arrest warrant for G-Z's Uncle Darren proved futile when a week later the coroner's report identified Darren's body as the body found in the fire at the Liberty Lake cabin. The cabin that sat on the same piece of land determined to be the property Jordyn where was held captive.

CHAPTER 34

THE GLENN ZIMMERMAN NIGHTMARE CONVINCED Jordyn to leave Spokane. She moving San Francisco for a fresh start with her mother and a job as a physical therapist with the Golden State Warriors. She'd sold her townhouse, quit her job and was pleasantly surprised when she saw Solomon walk into her farewell party.

Savannah invited Solomon to the party once she'd finalized the arrangements. She told him Jordyn was riding the train to San Fran by way of Seattle and Portland but insisted that he come see her in Spokane because her layover in Seattle was only for two hours in the middle of a workday. Solomon left his car at the Seattle railway terminal and bought a round trip ticket to Spokane, the return leg of his trip matching Jordyn's. He didn't want to think of her as damaged or emotionally needy. He told himself that he should honor her. That he should recognize her survival.

After the charges against him were dropped, Trey Thomas flew back to Seattle, but Solomon stayed for a week, helping Savannah clean up Jordyn's townhouse. When she came home from the hospital he stayed with Jordyn for a being the Good Doctor.

Melanie confessed that she'd had a crush on Glenn since college, and that she figured she could finally have him with Jordyn interested in Solomon. When she learned that Glenn Zimmerman had been charged with kidnapping, she told the detective that she ran into Glenn as she was leaving the train depot after dropping Jordyn off. That she and Glenn ate lunch and then had sex that afternoon, and when she woke up later that evening, Glenn was gone. Melanie was charged as an *accessory after the fact* for not coming forward and telling the police that he told her that he "took care of Jordyn and her punk boyfriend when he was in Seattle." As a punishment, her three-year probation sentence paled in comparison to the wicked ass-kicking Savannah gave her in her basement.

After hugging her, Solo escorted Jordyn to the bar to order drinks; a brown ale for him, a three-olive dirty martini for her. He said, "Savannah invited me. I hope you don't mind me crashing."

"I'm glad you came. Saves me the trouble of hunting you down in Seattle."

His face drooped before he said, "I'm sorry that this happened to you. That something like this would uproot you from your home."

"I believe that everything happens for a reason," Jordyn smiled.

"Savannah told me that you're moving to San Francisco."

"Yes, kind sir, I am," Jordyn said, pulling him to her and wrapping him in her arms. "My train leaves day after tomorrow."

"I know. I bought the same ticket for the Spokane to Seattle portion." Solomon returned her embrace. "I figured it would give us a chance to talk."

"I'd like that." Jordyn smiled her pleasure in travelling with him again. "I miss you, Mister Doctor Solomon Alexandré from Seattle."

"I miss you too, Miss former Washington State beauty queen Jordyn Hoffman from Spokane."

He whispered, "I love your perfume," before letting her go.

"It's new," she grinned. "It's called *Totally Interesting*."

"And that you are, Jordyn Hoffman. Totally. Interesting." As the server returned with their drinks, he said, "I want to apologize for…"

"It's cool," she interrupted, nervously poking her fingers in her hair. All around them, strangers were sipping drinks, smiling and having light and flirty conversations. Jordyn had a million things she wanted to say to him, but it didn't quite seem like the right time or place. So instead of standing there looking like a teenager awkwardly fiddling with her prom dress, she said "Dance with me, Solomon?"

Solomon led her to the dance floor where they'd remain for the next hour.

In every breakup, there is that period when you wonder if you made the right decision. People go back and forth, get back together again just to break up. Sometimes two and three times before they know for sure. He slipped his arm around her shoulder and pulled her close. He was warm and she felt safe and new in his arms. For a few moments, she remembered being with him and the world was all right.

The band was still jamming when they left the party at the upscale tapas bar. Both hot and sweaty from dancing, they carried their coats as they walked out into the cool night air. Halfway down the block, she let her hair down and shook it around her shoulders. They walked hand in hand past the square where he'd first seen her dancing, past the restaurant where she'd stolen his SD card, past several bars and shops in the downtown area as they journeyed the three blocks toward the Light Rail. When a stiff wind blew two blocks from the club, she shivered and put her coat on.

Two women exited a lingerie and lace shop. The powerful aroma of loud perfume lingered in the air behind them. One of them eyed Solomon then smiled knowingly at Jordyn as she passed. Four young men drinking beer and talking loudly in front of a crowded bar saw the attractive couple that didn't look like them enjoying each other's company and started casting dispersions. One of the men spouted, *Look at the whore walking her black dog,* at their backs as they passed. A second one added, *Whore Bitch,* loud enough for them to clearly hear.

Jordyn leaned forward, trying to encourage Solo to walk a little faster.

Traitor, added the third man reluctantly. They sounded like they wanted to test Solomon's manhood; like they wanted to start a fight.

Jordyn bristled. Pulled closer to Solomon. She knew they were drunk and thought they might have had guns.

Solomon chose to ignore them—at first. Chose to stay calm and pray they let them pass without incident so that he wouldn't end up back in jail.

Black bastard wanting to stick his dirty dick in her fine white lineage, the fourth guy yelled, needing to say something just so he wasn't left out.

That comment brought Solomon to his breaking point. He'd been punked by assholes in Spokane before and was not going to let it happen again. He turned to oblige their desire, to give them a piece of the angry black man they so desperately seemed to be wanting a piece of; to stomp them until it would take three or four policemen to pull him off of them.

"No Solomon." Jordyn stepped in front of him, wrapped her arms tightly around his waist, pressed against his front and leaned into him. "Please don't. For me. Please, let's just go."

Solomon clinched his jaw and fists tight and prepared for battle, didn't seem to notice her first plea, but eased his forward motion a beat later when Jordyn dug her heels in and stiffened her body against his. Without looking back, Jordyn begged Solomon to walk away—after a huge sigh and a frightening growl, he did. A beer bottle flew like a missile past the side of her face. Jordyn felt his muscles tense again, she pulled him forward and began running. Another one crashed against the sidewalk a few feet in front of them just before they ran up the stairs onto the elevated train platform. Jordyn impressed Solomon with how effortlessly she jumped the turnstile. They stopped at the far end of the deserted train platform and listened for the stampede of footsteps that never came. When the train arrived, they quickly entered the most forward car where she sat in silence, scared and shaken, her heart beating like a hummingbirds wings.

Solomon calmed quickly once the train started moving and pulled Jordyn into him. She smelled so good. Her skin so soft. Her sculptured features so beautiful. He breathed as she breathed. His only thought was of kissing her. He wanted to mold his flesh into her flesh, sink beneath the surface of her skin and dive into her.

Her sweet high from the club was gone. Her libido was gone. She was frightened, wanted to erase the past few minutes, but she couldn't. Having sex was the last thing on her mind.

"Are you okay?"

She nodded, but she wasn't.

Once they reached their station, she removed her shoes and padded barefoot over the block-and-a-half from the Light Rail to Savannah's condo. Savannah had arranged to stay at her boyfriend's house to give them some privacy after Solomon confirmed on the phone that he would come to the party. They'd forgotten to leave a light on, so it was dark inside when they arrived. Jordyn cursed when she stubbed her toe on the way to the light switch. She offered Solomon a seat, but he followed her into the kitchen. Still shaken by the drunk stranger's foul words, she busied herself and put water on for tea, avoiding his touch as he silently followed her around the kitchen.

"And who is that," Solomon asked when he heard the whimpering puppy in the corner poking at the gate to his crate.

"This little love bug is my new puppy, Bulleit." Jordyn pulled the puppy from his crate, rubbed his belly making his leg quiver, then kissed him on the head. "He's a rescue, just like me," she said proudly as she presented Bulleit to Solomon. "And he's starting his new life in California—just like me."

Solomon played with Bulleit as Jordyn poured them both a cup of chamomile tea with honey then sat across the table so she was out of his reach. She avoided his eyes, concealing the secret feelings she didn't feel comfortable sharing.

Those bastards, she thought. *Why do people have to be such assholes? Men like them don't care that he's educated, has his Doctorate and owns his own business. Don't care that he's a religious, God-fearing man who rarely misses church. All they see is the color of his skin.* She questioned what made her think she could comfortably be with him in this world. He wasn't a white man, and as far as men like them freely roamed the world, Solomon couldn't protect himself if they collectively decided to harm him. How could she want a future full of uncertainty that the man she loved could be taken from her at any time just because his skin tone didn't match hers? As she quietly sipped her tea, she imagined having a gun, slipping out after Solomon fell asleep, shooting those four stupid bastards and killing everybody else she came across who thought the way they did.

"Sorry if I'm not being good company, but those guys on the street back there pissed me off. What gives them the right?"

Solomon held both her hands, weaved his fingers in between hers. Massaged the muscle between her thumb and forefinger with his thumb. Rubbed her with one hand and held Bulleit with the other as he asked, "So really, other than pissed off at those cowards, how are you?"

"Me?" Jordyn let out a sigh long enough to fill a balloon. "I'm fine for the most part. I have a job waiting for me. You know how I am—straight workaholic. Won't be happy unless I find a way to work 10-12 hours a day and a few dozen more on the weekend; but, I'm counting on my new pup to help me become the new me." Jordyn reached over with her free hand and rubbed her new puppy's head. "I'm good for now, Solomon. After I put Spokane and the last five years behind me. I'll be able to figure out what my next chapter looks like."

"As long as you're in it, that chapter will look great." Solomon told her he knew her last day in Spokane would be busy. Told her that he didn't want to keep her up late and that he'd be going after he finished his tea.

She said, "I really want to apologize for the way I acted last time I visited you in Seattle. I shouldn't have acted like that at the Train Station."

"We were all emotional that night. I'd much rather forget it."

"I was a mess. We've never really talked about it."

"And we don't have to."

"But I..." she started.

"Ancient history." Solomon squeezed her hand tighter. "I'm just happy that you are okay now. None of that matters anymore."

Jordyn gripped Solomon's hand and walked him into the living room. She sat down on the small loveseat with her arms crossed. Made room for Solomon, still holding her puppy in one hand, to sit and lounge next to her.

"Sure you're okay?" he asked.

"Yeah, I'm okay. Just tired of trying to be strong all the time." Jordyn leaned her head onto his shoulder, said, "I think I have a couple unresolved issues when it comes to you."

"Okay."

"You were special to me, Solomon." Jordyn chuckled for a minute then said, "Like Viola Davis told the little girl in the movie *The Help,* 'You is Sweet, You is Kind, You is Important', that's how I think about you."

"Like I'm a helpless three-year old little girl?" Solomon struggled to hide his smile despite knowing that Jordyn couldn't see his face.

"No silly boy." Jordyn tapped him on his leg with her free hand. "Like the kindest, gentlest, most gentile man I have ever met. You make me feel important, Solomon Alexandré. You make me feel special in a way that no other man ever has. And the fact that you are a decade older than me and will make some woman other than me happy once she finds you and figures out how to make you happy, saddens me when I think about losing you."

"What do you mean?"

"I didn't want to be just another one of the girls on your list. Didn't want to be someone you kicked out before your newspaper hit the front porch. That's why I got so mad when I saw you hugging that woman backstage. Your explanation made perfect sense, but all I could see and hear was red. All I could see was another woman keeping you from being with me, and I wanted nothing to do with that so I overreacted, and ran—and we know where that got me."

Solomon saw a tear drop into Jordyn's tea.

"Well to be honest, you telling me about you being a finalist for Miss America was intimidating. Even though you are younger than me, that shit was a big deal. I assumed that beauty queens only dated celebrities, or handsome, rich and famous guys. And even if we did cross that line into familiarity, I would somehow become the old guy who quickly bored you."

"I guess I told you too much about me on that first date, hunh?"

"I'm not saying that," he chuckled. "But loose lips sink ships."

"I did say too much, but I was feeling you Solomon. Feeling you like I've never felt any other man. Something about you that night made it easy…no, comfortable for me to be open-kimono honest and tell you whatever was on my mind. Always have and always will feel that way."

"You didn't tell me any more than I told you about my past."

Jordyn ran her fingers through her hair. "I know, but men and women are judged by different standards."

"Hell, you made it seem like men are no big deal. The dime for a Baker's dozen."

"Solomon, a woman tells the truth because she is feeling him. Not because she wants him to think of her as a ho. She wants him to accept her as she is, with no secrets and no bullshit."

"That's not the way I see you, Jordyn."

"It wasn't just that though."

Solomon sipped his tea.

Jordyn said, "One question."

"Okay?"

"And be honest. If you can remember."

"Sure."

"How was it with me?"

"How was what?"

"Don't make me say it."

"Say what?"

"You're going to make me beg aren't you?"

"I don't know what you're talking about, Jordyn."

"I'm talking about the sex, Solomon. How was sex with me?"

Solomon guffawed, giggled and then laughed for almost a solid minute. "Hnh, hnh, hnh, Jordyn Hoffman, you haven't changed a bit!"

"Well?"

Solo blushed, then answered. "You were uhh…something else."

"Oh really? Something else, good? Or something else, bad?"

"Yes really! Trust me, I haven't forgotten. It was good. No, it was great. I just…at the time, there was nowhere it could go. I had too much clutter. Like you just said, too many unresolved issues."

"Leona?"

"Not just that." Solomon kissed her on the top of her head. "I was married when we first met; that time you stole my SD card." He shoved his hip into hers to let her know he was joking. She giggled and shoved back. "And despite how much I loved my wife, I found something about you very attractive. Then when we officially met, I was an emotional wreck because my wife had passed; and Leona had gotten shot and I ended up losing her as a girlfriend."

"You're not over her, are you?"

"To be honest," he paused and pushed his lips up into a soft smile. The kind that held old memories. In a soft tone he offered, "Some relationships you never fully get over."

She didn't say anything, just rubbed his leg and pressed her head deeper into his shoulder.

"And then I met you, and you listened to me. That was all I needed."

Jordyn nodded because she understood how he felt. How complicated life could be. He was a great guy. She thought, *maybe that's why I tripped so hard*. She patted his hand, gave him her empathy. "My timing has always been bad when it comes to personal relationships, but I'm trying."

"Good. And stay that way. Keep getting better." The conversation, despite the content, felt uncomfortable. Maybe because it was the kind of dialogue you had when you needed closure to move on with your life when it ended. "You're a talented, stunningly beautiful, young woman. San Francisco seems like exactly the place for you to find the unexpected life-changing opportunity that you deserve."

"And don't forget headstrong," she interjected with a laugh.

Solomon repeated her suggestion. "And I fully expect a headstrong women like you to discover that you truly are the diamond ready to be slipped on some lucky man's finger."

Jordyn set her teacup down then wrapped her arms tightly around Solomon's middle. She closed her eyes and squeezed back tears as she held him like she'd stop breathing if she let go. After bear hugging him for more than a minute, she loosed him, made eye contact, then pretended to check her watch without actually looking at the time. That good old body language that said that it was time for the fat lady to break out in song. Her heart wanted him to stay, but if he did, he would see her cry like a baby and she didn't want that. "I'm really going to miss you, Solomon."

"I'm really going to miss you too, Jordyn."

She looked at her watch again, actually seeing the time this time, and told him that the bed in Savannah's guest room was very comfortable if he wanted to stay.

He feigned not being upset when he realized that she meant he would be sleeping alone. He tried to kiss her once more at the guest bedroom door but she moved her head so his lips landed on her cheek. He her retreat to Savannah's bedroom then closed the door, stripped down to his boxers, and slid into the comfortable queen-size bed, closed his eyes and fell asleep.

Jordyn turned on the TV in Savannah's bedroom then buried her face in a pillow so he couldn't hear her and cried herself to sleep. She knew Solomon wasn't the one who hurt her, but the thought of losing him made her cry.

When Solomon awoke the next morning, Jordyn was curled up inside of him on the guest room bed. Her back was to him as he inhaled her, pushed her hair back and saw the streaks on her cheek where tears had dried. He exhaled, wished he knew the words to comfort her, held her a little too tightly and disturbed her sleep. Saw that her eyes were red and puffy from crying when she opened them.

Jordyn rolled over to face him, wrapped her arms tightly around him and in a whisper purred, "I'm sorry."

Solomon kissed both of her eyelids.

Jordyn buried her face in his neck. Didn't even flinch when her forehead rubbed against his scratchy, unshaven chin. She fluttered long lashes across his Adam's apple, kissed him along his collar bone a dozen times then closed her eyes and cried herself back to sleep.

CHAPTER 35

THREE CARS WERE PARKED OUTSIDE Solomon's house when he and Jordyn pulled onto his block. Neither would admit it, but they were both dead tired. Solomon recognized a song they had danced to during his first visit to Spokane and turned the radio volume up as he pulled into his garage.

Jordyn grabbed his arm as he went to open his door. "Wait a minute."

"What's wrong?"

She had been texting when they first pulled out of the train depot parking lot but fell asleep during the ride to his house and dropped her phone. She fumbled around, looked ready to cry when she said, "I can't find my cell phone."

Solomon shut his door. "It has to be here somewhere." He leaned back and rummaged on the floor behind the passenger seat while she checked around her feet. "Is this what we're looking for?" he said, handing her a leather square with a hand strap that looked like a checkbook cover.

Jordyn kissed him then grabbed the puppy carrier from the back seat.

Solomon paused at the back porch,. "Dammit. I left my wallet in the glovebox. Give me a minute, Jordyn, I'll be right back."

"May I borrow your door key?" Jordyn asked squirming uncomfortably. "I need to use the bathroom."

Solomon dug his key from his pocket. Told her, "If I'm not there when you finish, pick out a bottle of wine for us to sip on." When he entered the house, his mother and the Four Horsemen greeted him. Viv was in the kitchen putting the finishing touches on one of Solomon's favorite meals; Tarragon roasted spatchcock chicken, maple-glazed Brussel sprouts with bacon and almonds, and smashed new potatoes. She'd also picked up a couple loaves of black bread, and for dessert, caramel apple cobbler with whipped cream. Now in her late sixties, she didn't spend a lot of time in the kitchen, but she loved cooking for her son and his friends. He kissed his mother then tried to introduce her to Jordyn.

"You're late boy," Viv interrupted. "I've already met this pretty girl. Now I see why you couldn't stay out of Spokane." Jordyn smiled. Solomon chuckled, then raised a questioning eyebrow when the Viv he knew surfaced. "She's a little skinny and her melanin is a little lacking, but she seems nice."

Vivienne's words washed over the room like a giant North Shore wave, silencing everyone except Jordyn. Solomon's smile evaporated as he searched for the words to shield Jordyn from the impact. The words that came would've ruined everyone's night, so he stayed mum. Desmond and Lawrence looked away, embarrassed. Kenny laughed out loud at Viv's words, then said, "And on that note, I'm going downstairs to get some more wine. I think we're going to need it."

When she saw their reactions and his mother's words finally sank in, Jordyn's smile faded too.

Vivienne Alexandré never had a problem doting on her son; no matter the place or the company, she would tell people how she felt about Solomon and what she thought of their relationship with her son. And this dinner conversation would be no different. As everyone savored their dessert, Vivienne left half of her small piece of cobbler on her plate, emptied her wine glass and sat back. She observed Jordyn for a beat then folded her arms across her chest and said, "You don't look stupid, so I assume you already know that you are with a good man. But I want you to know that my son is a very special man. I don't know why he's kept you a secret, but something must be wrong if he ain't never introduced me to you before."

"Yes, Ma'am. That's probably my fault. I know…"

"My Solomon has never done wrong a day in his life," Vivienne cut Jordyn short. "When they made my son, they broke the mold."

Kenny guffawed loudly and Desmond started coughing.

"Excuse me?" Viv warned, averting her eyes between them. "You two have something to say?"

"No Miss Viv," they sang in tandem, having previously sampled doses of Vivienne's wrath and not wanting to go down that road again.

"My son worked two jobs when he was in high school to help us out. Kept his grades high and earned an academic scholarship to college. Never once complained; even after his daddy left me to raise him by myself."

"Now is not the time, Viv," Solomon interrupted her monologue.

"Sounds like you had a lot on your plate, Missus Alexandré," Jordyn said, reaching across the table and placing her hand on top of Solomon's.

"And I did a good job if I say so myself." Viv never had a problem patting herself on her own back.

"Well if nobody else thinks so, I do," Jordyn said, laying it on thick.

"You didn't finish your dessert, Viv," Solomon interjected.

"Like I was saying," Viv disregarded her son's attempt to silence her. "He's never been one to brag on himself; that's always been my job. Brag on him and protect him. He's the only son I have, and I'll be damned if I'm going to lose him to you or any other heifer."

"Alright, that's enough Mom!" Solomon's tone and the use of the M word silenced Vivienne. "Jordyn's been through a lot. What happened to me and to her was not her fault. She's starting a new life and leaving all of that behind her. She's my guest. She's here as my friend and our complicated history is off limits. I mean it Viv, it will not be tonight's topic of conversation." Solomon glared at his mother.

A long beat later, she conceded.

"Now," Solo continued, "Can we enjoy the rest of this wonderful dinner and end the night on a high note?" He held Viv's gaze as she grabbed the bottle of wine.

"Your son is truly an amazing man." Jordyn said loudly, her volume bringing all eyes to her. "This guy told me about a lot of his accomplishments, and some of the things he had to endure along the way, but I had no idea about the depth of his struggle. I understand why you are so proud of him. You have every right to boast, brag and be proud of him. You raised a remarkable man."

Kenny coughed, "Bullshit," into his napkin, making everyone laugh.

"So you're going to be staying with your mother?" Lawrence asked when the laughter quieted down.

"At least until I find a place near work," Jordyn replied. "In fact, she flew into Portland yesterday for some business. She's staying there until my train arrives so we can ride to San Francisco together."

"Oh, that's nice." Vivienne added to let everyone know she would not be silenced. She averted her gaze back to her son before saying, "Spending time with your mother is what good children do."

Solomon shoved pie in his mouth, drank wine—and ignored Viv.

CHAPTER 36

SEATTLE PAPARAZZI BILLED AMARI'S WEDDING as the social event of the season. Viv and the Horsemen were there with dates. Amari and Mareschelle's biological grandmother, Daisy Chatman, sat in the front row next to Rachel Mae and the two empty seats covered for Amari's deceased parents. Every flavor of co-worker, girlfriend, politician and Seattle A-Lister filled every seat in the cathedral to watch Mayor Philip Wirthmore marry his beautiful bride.

When Solomon and Jordyn knocked on Amari's dressing room ten minutes before the start of the wedding, they found Amari's bridesmaids inside trying to comfort her because just two minutes prior, the wedding coordinator had come up and announced that Philip and his best man hadn't arrived.

"Please go find him," Amari begged Solomon through her tears.

Jordyn stayed with the bride and her maids as Solomon rushed to his car. As he waited for traffic to ebb so he could escape his parking spot, the mayor's USV pulled up next to him, blocking him in. Solomon got out when he recognized the SUV. He yanked the rear door open and the stench of tequila hit him head on. When he saw Philip and his best man half-dressed and still drunk, he got in instead letting them get out. He ordered the driver to, "Just circle the block until I tell you to stop," then pulled out his cell to call Kenny.

"Yo?" Kenny answered on the first ring.

"Yo, is your bag in your trunk?" Solomon asked.

"Always."

"Good. Meet me at your car. I got an emergency."

Kenny kept an overnight bag in his car complete with bottled water, energy drinks, a toiletry kit filled with mouthwash, cologne, deodorant, body wipes, headache powders and caffeine pills. Everything a man needed to start his day when his night never ended.

Twenty minutes later, Philip approached the altar from the side door. Solomon stood in the foyer preparing to give Amari away. He marveled how ten years after his wedding day, Amari looked exactly like her sister. Same makeup, same lipstick, same gorgeous face under the veil. As he looked at his wife's twin in her wedding gown, he wasn't thinking of presenting her to Philip, but instead, thought of his Schelle and their wedding day during their twenty-seventh summer.

Just before high noon, Darnell Betancourt and his daughter joined ushers behind closed doors at the Eternity in the Light church in Tacoma. Solomon waited at the altar with his fellow Horsemen and Pastor Carroll. A horde of a thousand butterflies swarmed his insides and as he waited, he had picked at his fingernails and fidgeted with every loose string on his tux. He wasn't nervous about getting married—because marrying his Schelle made him the luckiest man on the planet. He was nervous about forgetting his vows. Public speaking—or better yet, talking in front of large crowds—was not yet his forte, which made him nervous about embarrassing Mareschelle.

The organist began the *Wedding March* when the ushers opened the sanctuary doors. Mareschelle was beautiful. Her face angelic. Her hair exquisite. Her stunning, white, elegantly luxurious wedding gown had an haute couture sophistication. She smoothed the sides of her dress, cupped her bouquet to her chest and smiled at Solomon for approval before entering the sanctuary.

Unable to take his eyes off his bride-to-be, Solomon couldn't stop smiling. He had always thought her beautiful, but he had never seen her look more beautiful than right then.

The anxiously awaiting church congregation stood and, as if God had placed a brown angel in peep-toe high heels by his side, Darnell escorted his daughter down the aisle. When they reached the altar, he raised the lace covering her face, unveiling her beauty for all to behold. He kissed her cheek, said *I love you, Pumpkin*, then turned to face his future son-in-law. In the most intimidating whisper Solomon had ever heard, he told him, "You take care of my Baby, you hear." It was apparent how much he loved his daughter, and from the repercussions inferred in his tone, Solomon knew he could never let anything happen to *his Pumpkin*.

"Yes Sir," he said calmly, battling the urge to vomit.

Darnell turned and joined his wife walked in the front row. He kissed her on the cheek with the same tenderness he kissed Mareschelle. Solomon smiled at his future in-laws, then turned his attention to Schelle. If he was lucky, that would be him and Schelle sitting there in thirty years. The wedding march ended when the pastor began to speak.

"Dearly beloved, we are gathered here today to observe the union of Mareschelle Betancourt to Solomon Alexandré." His husky voice was so strong that he didn't need the microphone to be heard in the back row. "The union of matrimony is a lifelong commitment never to be entered into lightly. It is to be entered into in the face of God so that the union shall be blessed in the name of the Lord forever and ever. We are also gathered here today to get to this thing called love. Love is a powerful word; so powerful that Solomon and Mareschelle have chosen to express that love through their own vows."

Pastor Carroll faced Mareschelle and nodded his approval for her to start her vows.

Mareschelle beamed when she regarded Solomon. "I have dreamed about my wedding day ever since I was a little girl, and I've been told that on her wedding day every girl is a princess. Fairy tales always end with the handsome prince marrying the beautiful princess, and today I finally get to be that princess. Solomon Alexandré, I have loved you from the day we met and, despite all the convincing it took me to convince you that I was the woman you were meant to be with, I know I am your Mrs. Right.

"My heart smiles when I see you. You are a loving soul and a gentle man, who today I willingly give myself until the end of time. Thank you for being my Dark Knight, my partner, my protector and my lover..." Her quartet of bridesmaids giggled in series. They'd shared a bottle of wine in the dressing room and were tipsy. Mareschelle waited for them to stop before continuing. "...And most importantly, thank you for being my friend. Today we promise for better and for worse. I can honestly say I have no idea what that means, but as long as I'm doing it with you, I can't wait to find out.

"Thank you for loving me unconditionally. You complete me and because of that, I promise to love you as my forever husband as long as there is breath in my body." Tears streamed down her face. "As I enter your kingdom and become your forever faithful queen, I pledge to always stand lovingly by your side. With this I vow you my forever, and a love so true that it will burn in me until my life's fire is extinguished."

By the time she was finished, every woman in the church was wiping away their own tears. Some of the men had pulled out handkerchiefs. Following a chorus of amens and hallelujahs, Reverend Carroll turned to Solomon and said, "Whenever you're ready, son."

Solomon sniffed twice, blew air then said, "Mareschelle Renáe Betancourt, you are the rarest flower that I have ever known. Your smile radiates like a thousand moonbeams dancing on a golden river of sunlight, and I will eagerly awaken every day to catch a glimpse of the magnificent beauty that you shine into my world. In my hands I will hold you, keep you, and with all the strength in my body," he averted his eyes toward her father before he said, "give my last breath to protect you from any and all harm.

"This sacred pledge will forever join us at the heart and I will forever cherish you like the precious gem you are. I too have loved *you* since the day we met and as true as your love for me may be, the depth and breadth of my love for you will carry us through all time and eternity. I revel in the thought of being your forever husband, and I promise to be all the man you will ever need until the day I am no more. That is my promise to you."

His 'all the man' comment made a couple of the bridesmaids giggle even louder this time. Their two bottles of Moscato while they helped Mareschelle dress, getting the better of them.

When Solomon stopped talking, every lady in the church was crying tears of joy. He had won each and every one of their hearts. Mareschelle led the sobbing, and even though the tears running down her face had streaked her makeup, she would not wipe them away.

Pastor Carroll said, "Let there be anyone who contest this beautiful union speak now or forever hold their peace."

Darnell gripped Rachel Mae's hand tightly when he noticed her neck starting to crane. Kenny stole a peek at Mom Vivienne. Her lips were pursed so tight she could have snapped a toothpick. The rest of the church was silent. Nobody uttered a sound. "Being that there is no contestation to this union; Solomon and Mareschelle, I now pronounce you, husband and wife."

Solomon exhaled a long sigh. He couldn't wait to hear the words that came next when Reverend Carroll proudly announced, "Sir, you may salute your bride."

Solo drew Schelle into his arms. Pressed his lips to hers, and instead of the lingering, passionate kiss he so desired, he reluctantly settled for a chaste kiss as the deep, stereophonic sound of throat clearing simultaneously emanated from the vicinities of both Viv and Mrs. Be. The organist played a joyous tune as they exited the church. Solomon couldn't stop smiling as he escorted his bride down the aisle and through the doors at the back of the sanctuary.

Mareschelle broke into a big smile when she stopped at the open limousine door to throw the bouquet. A small pushing match ensued on the church stairs before a short, plump, brown-skinned girl with a cropped haircut came away with the bouquet.

"We did it," Mareschelle said. "We're married!" She held up her hand to take a good look at the two-and-a-half carat, emerald-cut platinum wedding band. "This is the happiest day of my life." Then they disappeared into the limo and the crowd waved as it whisked them away to meet a cruise ship on their way to a ten day cruise to Tahiti.

CHAPTER 37

THAT NIGHT AFTER AMARI'S RECEPTION, Solomon grabbed a bottle of sparkling wine from the cooler in his man cave and two champagne flutes from the butler's pantry. when Jordyn exited the powder room, he was in the hallway, his arms splayed, holding the glasses and wine. He told her, "I'm going to shower and change. After you get comfortable, let's meet down here so we can enjoy this the right way." After he escorted her upstairs to his guest bedroom, he showered, moisturized, spritzed cologne then put on microfiber lounge pants and a sleeveless Tee that read MISTER MIDNIGHT. Downstairs he ordered Alexa to play *smooth grooves*, filled the champagne flutes, then sat on a recently purchased oversized loveseat where he waited for his guest.

Jordyn showered, washed her hair then twisted it in a towel while she dried herself. She turned sideways in front of the mirror, raised herself slightly on her toes and marveled at the flatness of her stomach, the firmness of her breasts, and the smoothness of her sun-browned, almost golden skin. She slid on her panties and fuzzy slippers then rubbed moisturizer on her face. She put on a satin robe, went out into the hallway and called *Marco* to locate Solomon.

Everything about her physical being; her eyes, her lips, her hair, even her soft feet that she slowly rubbed along the inside of his thighs, made him long for sex with her; every move she made intensely focused his unquenchable sexual appetite.

After they both finished their first glass of wine, he leaned in, but not too much, and Jordyn did the same. He was aroused. Her nostrils flared with each breath exhaled. They were both turned on. Both maintained eye contact as she bit the corner of her pillow-soft lips. He licked his. Her breath quickened; her cheeks flushed; she shuddered and a moan escaped her lips. He wanted to taste her more than anything in the world, and apparently she recognized his desire.

Jordyn loosened her robe and straddled him. Then she pulled his t-shirt over his head and tossed it fall to the floor. He was topless but that wasn't enough for her. She wanted to see—and feel—all of him. They showered each other with passionate, consuming kisses; behind ears, on nipples, on necks and bellies, over each other's heart.

When he reached for her panties, she stopped him. The desire rippling through him warmed his blood, flushed his cheeks. He asked. "What's wrong?"

"I umm...can't." She wanted to have sex, but menstrual cramps meant her cycle was close. "I think my aunt's about to make her visit."

"What aunt?" Solomon frowned. Her mother was meeting her in Portland, so why was she playing games with him?

"My metaphorical aunt, Silly," she said. "You know, Bloody Mary." Jordyn covered her mouth with one hand and pointed downward. "But, if you don't mind..." She wanted him badly, didn't want to rush one second of one minute of their last night together. Feeling an imperious sexual urge, she slid off his lap and gently pressed his knees apart. "Before I venture off and never see you again, I'd like to know a little bit more about what goes on inside that magnificent mind of yours." She freed his excited manhood from his boxers, licked her lips, sipped her wine then took him in her mouth.

Solomon gasped, slammed his head against the back of the sofa.

Her mouth was cold on his penis. After a long minute, she released him, removed a strand of hair from her eye, bit down sensuously on her lower lip, and regarded him. She wrapped him in her left fist, stroked him slowly and flashed a devilish grin. "How about I ask you some questions and umm…check your temperature while you answer them?"

Unable to form the words to disagree, Solomon nodded.

Jordyn asked him the first of several questions, dipped her head and swallowed him whole. For the next twenty minutes, this cycle of asking him a question while she stroked him with her hand, alternated with him trying to answer while she stroked him with her mouth.

Jordyn watched Solomon writhed through a joyful agony. Words eluded him. Her erotic power was far greater than she realized. After pleasing him for almost an hour, she succumbed to her overwhelming urge. Bloody Mary may have been coming, but that train was still on the tracks far off in the distance, over the river and through the woods.

She led him to his bedroom and flopped down onto the great haven of his massive bed. His underwear came off under her power, then hers under his. When he caressed her body, his hands felt as if they were designed for her breasts; his lips and tongue for her sex. She wrapped him in a condom and climbed naked onto his lap. She buried her face in his neck and whisper groaned, "I want you to do everything a man does with a woman. Everything you want to do to me."

He did everything he knew how; and when he was unsure, she told him with her words and guided him with her hands and hips, and called out to ancient gods long forgotten. "Talk dirty to me, Baby," she moaned as her fever continued to rise. "Oh God that feels good." She yanked the plastic clip from her hair and it shattered when she threw it against the wall.

Solomon lay beneath her on the chaise as Maxwell, D'Angelo, Chante Moore, and Prince encouraged him to make love like a movie star. He was in a zone. Sex poured from him like blood from a wound. The champagne stoked his fires while Jordyn Hoffman stroked his heart. He looked deep into her eyes and could feel her energy all around him. Touches that invoked moans. Moans that grew into shouts. Shouts of *Don't stop, Baby,* that reverberated off his bedroom walls.

Jordyn felt a rush of heat that started in her toes and moved through her like a beam of light. Her heartbeat sped up, her breaths went shallow and she felt dizzy. She'd never let a man affect her like that before, not even the first time she and Solomon made love. She hummed her torment, nibbled on his ear, then turned and rode him reverse cowgirl in a full gallop. She pleaded in a staccato for him to "Don't...ever...stop... Baby."

For almost two hours, they repeatedly built up a head of steam and let that love machine run out of gas as they tried to scrub away the awful memories of the Train Station, the Alumni Gala, the firebomb, their individual assaults, her rape and kidnapping, his arrest, and everything else negative and hurtful brought about at the hands of Glenn Zimmerman. Desperate sex included the exchange of several orgasms; on the chaise, in the shower and on the balcony, then finally subsiding into sleep on the bed, folded into each other after sharing one last long, slow, intense orgasm.

When Solomon woke the next morning, Jordyn was not in his bed. They had fallen asleep in each other's arms, and slept good and hard. Their slow lovemaking reminding him of those Calgon commercials—*she took all of his stress away.* He looked up to see his bathroom door open and the light off, then he turned to the hallway door, and there, on the doorknob, hung her panties—purple, silk, expensive—her way of letting him know that it had not been a dream. That she really had been there. *Damn,* he thought, *what I wouldn't give for a little more of her this morning.*

He discounted her absence as her way of not wanting to endure the feelings that accompany saying a final goodbye, so he showered before going downstairs to forage through the meager provisions in his refrigerator. It wasn't until he noticed the key fob to his Audi missing from the wooden bowl in his kitchen that he questioned Jordyn's whereabouts.

He checked the time, recapped the night before then vigorously searched his kitchen and dining room for his keys. He decided to go check the spares he kept in a lockbox in the guest room, but stopped when the back door opened and Jordyn came in with two bags containing their breakfast. Solomon exhaled, relieved that his paranoia was misplaced, that his thought of something else happening to Jordyn was unwarranted. He went to Jordyn, placed the bags on the counter and hugged her like he'd lost her; like he wanted to when he first found out she was alive.

~

Jordyn's three hour train ride from Seattle to Portland departed at 4pm. For an hour before boarding, they sat in the station and shared a turkey club wrap in a basil-tomato tortilla, whole grain sun chips and two bottles of flavored water. A brooding fog of silence hung about the table, clearly articulating their romantic discontent. Jordyn Hoffman—who was trusting by nature, but cautious by experience—knew that he would lie if she asked him *What's wrong?,* so instead she asked him, "How was your sandwich?"

Solomon rubbed her puppy's mane and stared into the rim of his glass. "I'm eating it," he said stonily without raising his head. "It'll hold me until dinner."

"I know what you're feeling, and it's not easy for me either."

"What else do you want me to do?" he asked.

She peeled herself from her chair, swallowed hard and said breathlessly, "Just hug me. Just hold me," she sobbed. "That's all I need right now." Her eyes were closed, but she felt the change in air pressure as he moved around the table and leaned into her. She opened her eyes as he took her in his arms. She felt his biceps twitching as she allowed her arms to dangle until they lost the ability to resist grabbing him. Then she buried her face in his chest, inhaled him and hugged him for dear life.

She had been with him completely, knew their time had officially come to an end, but she wanted to indefinitely suspend that ending. Wanted to freeze time and steal Solomon Alexandré from the real world. Make that moment last for the rest of her life. Would make room for nothing outside of their relationship. "Solomon, I..." she looked up at him, urging him with her eyes to ask her to stay, although she knew in her heart that he could not. Had he asked, she was ready to be with him forever. Had he asked, she was ready to marry him and make a family.

But he didn't ask.

It was as if she had inside her a glass ampoule that held her soul separate from her body. When his words didn't come, she clenched and the glass shattered like her window shattered by that brick.

Instead he asked, "Will you call me when you arrive?"

"Unless every phone in the universe stops working," she chortled through her tears.

He asked her to stick out her hand and close her eyes, and she did. "How do you like it," Solomon said, placing an object in her hand. "It's a World War II challenge coin. My grandfather gave it to me when I was a boy. He got it from a soldier he met from France."

When she opened her eyes, Jordyn curiously examined the front and then the back of the two-inch wide, silver circle.

"It's not worth much. I just thought..." he said, reaching over to take it back. "But, if you don't like it..."

"I love it," Jordyn blurted out uncontrollably. "I love it."

"Great!" Solomon smiled bright and wide. "Then it's yours."

"And I will cherish it forever." Jordyn stretched up onto her toes, placed both arms around Solomon's neck, kissed him on his cheek then pressed her body against his like there was no tomorrow. She said, "I want to thank you, Solomon Alexandré, for being a wonderful presence in my life. Every girl deserves an amazing man like you in her life; even if it is only for a season."

"And every man deserves a woman as exciting, cool, and sexy as you," he said, wiping a tear from her eye when she released him.

She wiped the lipstick off his cheek then said, "Call me if you ever cross the Golden Gate Bridge."

They gave each other one last hug with their faces turned in opposite directions before she picked up her bag and her new puppy.

He stood next to her, absorbed her apprehension about her new life, cupped her chin and motioned toward the trains and repeated her sentiment. "You are an amazing woman, Jordyn Hoffman. Any man who doesn't treat you like the queen you are is a fool."

They hugged one last time. Jordyn held his chin and kissed his cheek. That inevitable goodbye was hard to get to, but she was finally ready to move on and it was easy to walk away after that. She had promised herself that she wouldn't, but she looked back. Hard not to look back at a man who had you creating a new language in bed and wearing ice packs between your legs to soothe the throbbing. She said, "I guess with me out of the picture, you'll soon be flying solo again?"

Solomon didn't stare at her directly, but at the whole of her. Her colorful, but well-coordinated ensemble consisted of sandals, frayed jeans, a loose blouse and a floppy pink and yellow hat that concealed eyelids that fluttered like the wings of a butterfly behind expensive designer frames. He admired the former beauty queen from Spokane from the soul outward. The dreamy expression, the sheepish grin, told her that his mind was on a journey, contemplating *what if*; he and she both alternating between the outcomes of that mental speculation. "Probably won't be real soon, you are kind of a hard act to follow."

She nodded, chuckled, shook her head and smiled back with the same, *Yeah what if?* wishing he'd been single when they first met.

He walked away smiling. Sinless speculations. Faultless dreams.

She took that smile as a win. Took that win and hummed her

small victory as she headed toward her train to ride off into the sunset. Ride away to her new life in her new town with her furry, new, best friend.

As he reached the ride share waiting for him, he heard Jordyn yell at the top of her lungs, "Look out Seattle, the Love Doctor is back and better than ever!"

Without looking back at the future that wasn't meant to be, Solomon considered life with her as his queen then climbed into the taxi and rode the smile Jordyn had caused all the way to Viv's house.

Hair bouncing in the gentle breeze, her face one big smile, Jordyn was free from the nightmares of the terrible person in Spokane who had never loved her the way she deserved. Letting go felt good. Feeling good made her happy. Happy with simply being Jordyn.

CHAPTER 38

JORDYN HOFFMAN WAS ALIVE AND WELL and flying solo toward her new life in California with her new puppy, Bulleit. Solomon found relief in the resolution of the mystery of her disappearance, but now with her out of his life, he also found himself flying solo once again. Six hours after her departure, Desmond slid into his booth at Woody's Bar and Grill where Solomon sat nursing a long pour of 14-year scotch. He pointed at Solomon as he called to a waitress, "Monique, please bring *Doctor Down in the Dumps* a Wagon Wheel." Then he snatched away the almost empty scotch glass.

Solomon barked, "Yo, Bruh, why you take my drink?"

"Because you know I ain't going to let you sit up here and drown your sorrows in this glass. We didn't let each other do it when we lost our wives and we damn sure ain't doing it now because some woman left town."

"Well, I ain't drowning my sorrows, I'm just toasting to her safe trip."

Desmond let that marinate then asked earnestly, "So she's gone, huh?"

"Yeah, Bruh. She's gone for good."

"You don't know that. You two may cross paths again someday."

"If we were meant to be together, she'd still be here." Solomon leaned back and asked himself why he didn't get on that train with her. He rationalized starting a practice in San Fran. That Desirée could take on a new partner and since she only had a handful of hours left to complete her marriage counseling certificate, she could reschedule them or he could see his current clients virtually until she finished her certification.

But was moving to San Fran to start a relationship with Jordyn realistic? First there was the age difference. He was good with a four- or five-year difference, but a decade was beyond reasonable to him. Maybe not right now in their late 20's and 30's while they're still humping like rabbits, but as they matured and the sex slowed down, it would be challenging, if not downright awkward and unbearable. No, they were just too different.

"Well, if you're hungry," Desmond continued, "you are gonna love the Wagon Wheel. It's our new house sampler platter. It's got sizzlin' shrimp, bangin' beef tips, jalapeno hotties, poppin' potatoes, crazy cluckers and veggie sticks."

"Sounds good, but I can't eat all of that."

"Kenny just called. He and LD will be here soon."

After a waiter landed a pitcher of beer on the table, Solo said, "Alright then, give me my drink back until they get here."

Fifteen minutes later, Woody's was closed, and the Four Horsemen were discussing money, drinking beer and demolishing the sample platter.

Desmond asked, "You guys ever watch *The Chi* on Showtime?"

Solomon, KD, and LD grunted, shrugged and nodded their answers.

"Well, the lead actor on the show is this young chef who buys a food truck after quitting his job at an upscale restaurant because his boss never gave him any credit when the customers complimented his food. He is just getting his name known around town when he's shot and killed."

"Damn!" Solomon said through a mouthful of beef tips.

"And why did we need to talk about this while we're eating?" Kenny asked before shoving another jalapeno hottie in his face.

"Because I'm thinking about starting a food truck," Desmond said.

"Sounds like a good idea." That was Lawrence. "I see them around town a lot on the weekends and at lunchtime downtown."

"Cut me in for a quarter and I'll front you the truck," Kenny said.

"And I'll pitch in five G's for the initial food load out," Solo added.

"And if you bring it to the church for lunch on Thursdays when we feed homeless, the Outreach ministry will cover the tab on those days," Lawrence said.

Desmond said, "Sharet's nephew just graduated top of his class from culinary school so we hired as our new sous chef. I figure I'd provide the truck, he'd do the cooking and it would be a great way to expand the restaurant's name around town."

"Sounds like a plan partner," Solomon chimed in. "Let's do it."

"And it might put a little more change in our pockets," Desmond grinned.

"That right there," LD huffed. "Only the simple things in life matter."

"Right, the simple things," Kenny started. "A glass of single malt to give me a buzz when I want it, enough food to fill my belly when I'm hungry, and enough money to treat a woman to dinner so she can treat me to some ass later. That's what'll keep me happy...the simple things in life."

Right on cue with being happy with the simple things conversation, Desmond's favorite song started playing on the jukebox. And to make it even better, his favorite sedative was still behind the bar. Desmond excused himself from the table and Solomon followed him to the bar to refill his scotch from one of the private bottles they kept underneath the bar.

Sharet Thompson wouldn't be what you called a pretty woman,

but she was part owner and manager of a very prosperous Woody's Bar and Grill. With her MBA from the University of Portland, she helped Desmond with business decisions that helped improve Woody's financial profile which convinced Desmond to give her a ten-percent ownership share in Woody's.

"You okay, Baby," she asked Solomon in a buttery smooth lilt.

"Yeah Sharet, I'm good."

Sharet never drank with customers when she was working, and she bared no bones about cutting a customer off when she thought they'd had too much. She was a true business professional, and Desmond's patrons love her as a bartender. After she caught Solomon's gaze long enough to discern if he was drunk, she asked, "Is LD driving you home tonight?"

"No, Baby. I got an Uber on standby," Solomon chided then kissed her on the cheek after she refilled his glass with a single shot of scotch.

Sharet cooed when Desmond walked up behind her, wrapped his arms around her middle and whispered something in her ear too quiet for Solomon to hear. She leaned her head back and giggled, then kissed her beau on the cheek.

Like an intelligent third wheel, Solomon felt the crowded space of their unspoken words and knew they needed their alone time. He said, "Don't make no babies up here in our place of business," then he yielded and smoothly glided back to the booth to join Lawrence and Kenny.

Desmond took the towel out of Sharet's hand as she was drying a glass and led her to the dance floor. He was five when his parents moved to the United States from the West Indies. He had a temper, but was a great dancer; both qualities his friends attributed to him being an Antigua island native. The blue light that Desmond had installed over the dance floor set the mood as he slow grinded with Sharet like the two of them were the only two people in the room at a basement house party.

The buzz from that music and his three glasses of ginger tea with nutmeg took Desmond to a place where his mind was at peace. He held Sharet close while they danced; invaded her space as only a woman's lover should. Holding a good woman like Sharet in his arms as he slow dragged tamed the beast in Desmond that his temper brought to the surface.

Sharet was good for Desmond. She was a sensual, free-spirited woman whose spirituality matched her passion for life. A devout believer, she hadn't missed a Sunday church service in over sixteen years.

Sharet was way too much woman for him, but Desmond deserved points for trying. Anyone could see how easy it was for Desmond to fall for such a lovely, well-rounded woman, but their happily ever after was not written in the stars. After a year of dating, being lovers and sharing a beautiful personal and professional relationship, they exchanged house keys, but agreed they didn't want to live together. Desmond and Sharet had talked about marriage, but agreed that they weren't ready to jump the broom again. Sharet's husband physically abused her. Desmond's wife died during childbirth.

"I don't know who Wood thinks he's fooling," Lawrence said as they watched the pseudo-couple dance. "But he really loves that girl."

"Good for them," Kenny said, startling both Lawrence and Solo.

"You have to have your own family," were Lawrence's words to his younger brother at the table fifteen minutes later as Desmond and Sharet danced to their fifth song. "You have to have your own kids. Without that you end up living your life vicariously through a neighbor, or best friend and everything they do with their family. Nieces and nephews are great, but you want your own to keep you from being a lonely, bitter person. Eventually, you become disparaged because you never have anyone to call your own. You never have anyone of your own to cherish. You never have anything of your own to partake in. You always find yourself participating in someone else's life to the extent that you get upset when that person forgets to call and invite you. Then you feel left out, or even worse, excluded, when that once-in-a-lifetime, greatest-thing-in-the-world happened and you weren't there to partake in it because it happened with someone else's family. So it may take you a little while longer to find Missus Right, that perfect somebody for you, but you have to do it. You gotta have a wife. You gotta have your own family. God didn't intend for us to be single and alone all of our life."

"Aaahhhh," Kenny sighed after emptying his beer glass. "I'll start my family and consider kids once I stop fantasizing about Tyra Banks coming to visit me in a Hooters outfit. Until then it looks like I'll be cruising Seattle in search of the next Missus Right Now."

"More like, in search of a new heartbreak," Lawrence replied.

Sharet joined Desmond at the table after they finished dancing. Solo had called for his ride share and was giving dap to the Horsemen when her phone rang. After a couple of back-and-forths with Leona, Sharet named everyone still there with her at Woody's, mentioning Solomon's name last, just as she hugged him and he mouthed *goodnight*.

Solomon shook his head when Sharet offered him the phone, but she handed it to him anyway. He stepped away from the group and asked, "Hey Red, What's crackin'?"

"Nothing much," Leona answered. "At the house vibin' to my Girl Magic playlist and sampling some wine called *Snoop Dogg Cali Red*. It's got *red* in the name, so you know I had to try it." They laughed. "Anyway, I heard that mess about your girl toy is all cleared up?"

Solomon detected the hint of jealousy in her words and smiled. "Yeah, your competition has finished with me and moved on to the next round."

"Competition? Oh no Honey, never that? Leona Pearson has no

competition." They laughed like old friends. Like Forever Best Friends. Then her cell phone chimed and Solomon waited while she checked a new text message notification. She returned and asked him, "Hey, are you still down to do that radio interview I told you about?"

He thought for a moment then said, *I can rock with that,* then paused again before saying, "As long as you do it with me."

"Hang on a second since I got you on the phone." Before he could dissent, Leona put him on hold, made a call, and told the man who had texted her that she had 'The Love Doctor' on the phone. Then she clicked back over to connect the three-way call. "Anthony Walters, I have Doctor Solomon Alexandré on the line and we want to know if you were for real about having him on your radio show, or if you were just talking smack?"

They listened as Anthony introduced himself to Solomon, told him about his show and that after talking with Leona, what he thought his listeners would get out of him interviewing Solomon.

When Anthony finished, Solomon cosigned the concept, agreed to meet with him and thanked him for the opportunity before Leona interjected, "Monday works for us. Thanks, Walt. Love you Boo."

They laughed again after Leona disconnected the radio man.

Solomon's cell phone vibrated and he checked to see a notification that his ride share was five minutes away. He jokingly asked Leona, "You don't play around, do you?"

"Doctor Alexandré, have you ever known me to play games."

Solomon smiled ear-to-ear, then said, "How could I forget?"

A beat passed before Leona said. "I didn't mean to keep you."

"Keeping me is not the issue, Red. Never was. But, it is late and my ride is here, so I should let you holler at your girl."

"Love you, Cuz!" Leona sang.

"Love you more, Red." The smile on Solomon's face was frozen in place as he rejoined his friend's table and handed Sharet her phone.

Desmond asked Solomon, "You two good?"

"Yeah. I'll see her on Monday."

"Did she trip about Jordyn?"

"Nahh Wood, she ain't that type."

"You're right, she's better than that." Desmond cosigned.

"I appreciate you, Bruh." They exchanged a handshake and another hug before Solo turned to leave.

"Well since you can't push up on her no more—you two being first cousins and all," this was Kenny, "You good with a brother shooting his shot?" Kenny flashed a Cheshire cat smile at Solo and smoothed down his goatee before pouring another glass of beer.

"More getting shot down than shooting your shot," Solo retorted.

"Come on KD," Sharet chimed in. "Everybody in here knows my girl is not feeling you like that."

"Maybe not right now, but she's fair game now that's she's kinfolk to my man and no longer subject to the Bro Code.

"Wait a minute," Solo said. "Wood; LD; does the Bro Code rule for not dating exes apply in this situation?"

Lawrence looked away then said, "My name is Bennett…"

When Solo looked to Desmond, he said, "…And I ain't in it."

"Man," Kenny started, "Y'all ain't shit." Everyone at the table laughed but Kenny. He said, "Well you know that old saying, when one door closes, three more open. And since that one is closed for you. I might try and see what's behind door number three."

After a beat, Sharet said, "Bro Code may not apply Kenneth Didier, but as Leona's best friend, I know for certain that when it comes to my girl, all three of those doors are closed for you."

This time even Lewis—the tall, reedy janitor with a vicious overbite and bulging eyes—laughed as he swept the floor around them.

Solomon hugged Sharet then gave each of the Horsemen dap before heading out. As he crossed the sidewalk he thought about how memories were funny in the way that they retained what they wanted, and discarded what they didn't. The mere articulation of Leona's name when they were on the phone stimulated the memory of kissing her. A guilty pleasure, like so many others, that he'd never again have the pleasure of experiencing.

EPILOGUE

BASICK MEDIA CORPORATE OFFICES OCCUPIED the entire third floor of an office building on Rosemont Boulevard, just off Middleton Street. A dermatologist's office on the second floor advertised weight loss by freezing away stomach fat. The first floor of the building housed Queen Sam's Used Books, and more importantly, Kim's Kitchen, a Seattle culinary landmark where Solomon dined regularly. After work, he went to Kim's to meet with a producer from Basick Media about the details of him appearing on the talk radio show Leona had called her friend about. With that meeting concluded, he sat alone finishing off the last of his waffles and four chicken tenders. A hush rolled across the restaurant when a caramel complected woman entered looking as pure and sweet as the syrup on his plate. For a moment, he believed he was looking at his dead wife, Mareschelle. Frozen like a statue, he stared at the rare beauty— a fork full of chicken and waffles dangling midair.

Had he conjured her? Was he daydreaming? Could this be the woman he thought he saw buying white lilies from the street florist? Maybe it had to do with the fresh, salty air, or being far enough away from the confines of a jail cell, or perhaps it was the prospect of meeting someone new. Or, maybe he missed his wife so much after flirting with Leona the other night that he willed this woman to appear?

He wanted to go to her, but he couldn't. He was mute, paralyzed, barely breathing and as useless as a three-dollar-bill. Statuesque and lovely were the only words to describe the woman standing at the register with her back to him. His eyes worked, and if they had a voice they would be screaming *Mareschelle, please turn around and talk to me, Baby*! If they had hands, they'd tug at her back, desperately urging her to turn around and face him. Talk to him and prove he wasn't going crazy.

Finally, as if his eyes had the power of telepathy, she turned and faced him. He anticipated a nod; hoped for a smile; prayed for an embrace; instead, their eyes met and he received a stare as blank as new printer paper. It wasn't Mareschelle. It was just a woman. A cute woman, but not the one he'd talked himself into wanting her to be.

"Have we met?" the woman asked, now noticing his stare intently boring into her.

"I don't think so," he answered politely. "But, you remind me of a girl, that I, once knew," he instinctively replied in a sing song voice.

"You can do better than that," she said, recognizing the popular tune.

"No need. I wasn't trying to pick you up, Pretty Lady. But if you'd like to join me for a bite, I'm certain I'd enjoy the company."

"Maybe next time," she smiled. "I'm late for an engagement."

The sway in her hips suggested he should follow and try again to convince her to stay. Now that he'd seen her face and knew it really wasn't her, Solo watched the woman shaped like Mareschelle walk out the door with her bag of chicken wings. And just like that gorgeous doppelganger, his appetite was gone too. He left his food on the table, paid his bill, gave Kim a hug and a kiss, and then exited to make his way home.

~

Halfway down his driveway, Solomon slammed on his brakes when a rabbit scurried across his path. At first he wanted to curse, but then he laughed as he remembered Schelle slamming the brakes on his car the first time he let her drive because she refused to run over a bunny rabbit.

It was their first official date, and she had agreed to go out with him, but only if he let her drive. Mareschelle loved race cars. Her father had gotten into dirt car racing right after high school and had introduced her to racing. Solomon's college car was the 1976 silver and black Pontiac Trans Am his father left behind when he joined the service. When he told her it was the same car from the *Smokey and The Bandit* movie, she just had to drive it. She told him if he really wanted to go out with her, he would have to let her drive his hot rod. He did, and he did. He picked her up at the Huskie book store and, after playfully asking her to show him a driver's license—which she did—he surrendered the keys to his prized possession.

"Took you long enough," she purred as she slipped into the driver's seat. "Don't worry, I can handle this too," she teased, leaving the rest unsaid.

He got in beside her and let himself be the happy passenger, going wherever she wanted to take him.

Mareschelle spun the tires and burned rubber as she sped off of campus. Eager to feel the power of a muscle car, she stayed off of the highway to avoid police and took the back roads toward Everett. Twenty minutes later, after spinning and drifting through winding curves and streaking down deserted backroads at speeds approaching one hundred miles an hour, Mareschelle found herself about a mile from civilization, heading toward the vintage movie theatre on the eastern outskirts of Everett.

She was making good time, enough for them to buy popcorn and soda before the movie started. She had slowed into the forties and had just reached over and placed her hand on top of Solomon's when a rabbit hopped out of the bushes and stopped dead-center in the middle of the road. Mareschelle was peeking at Solomon, but when she caught sight of the rabbit, she squealed and slammed on the brakes. They both lurched forward as the Trans Am quickly slid to a stop leaving a plume of dust behind them like the wake on a speed boat.

"What the hell are you doing?" Solomon shouted.

"Bunny rabbit," was all she managed to say, shocked at how quickly the car stopped. Twenty feet ahead of them the fat bunny rabbit sat stock still in the middle of the road.

"What?" he challenged again.

"Look."

Solomon turned from Schelle to see the brown ball of fur sitting on the road without a care in the world. "You almost killed us for a stupid freaking rabbit?"

"But he's so cute."

"Cute?" Solomon was incensed, but when he saw the genuine look of concern for the rodent on Mareschelle's face, all of his anger quickly faded. "Yeah," he exhaled hard and said without taking a second glance, "I guess it is cute."

Mareschelle smiled and revved the engine, hoping to scare the rabbit off the road. It didn't move. She released the brake and as the car started rolling forward, the bunny rabbit leisurely hopped along the side of the road. "See, Silly Rabbit," Mareschelle chided, "he just needed a little nudge."

Solomon looked off into the tall brush as they passed the spot where the rabbit disappeared. He mumbled, "Next time, his ass just needs to be roadkill."

A beat later, they were talking and laughing again. Ten

minutes later they had their tickets and were walking into the vintage, newly-restored, single-screen theatre to watch the Dorothy Dandridge birthday celebration film fest.

With the rabbit gone from his driveway, Solomon parked, pulled his rucksack from the passenger seat then headed toward the back porch where he saw his neighbor sipping a beer.

"What's up, Majac? Why you sitting out here all alone?"

"All good, Partna, just enjoying the cool night air. I missed not being able to enjoy nights like this when I was underway on my submarine."

"I can't imagine. But, how are Tessa and the baby?"

"They're good." Majac took a swig from his bottle. "I know it's late, and I don't want to hold you up, but I need to holler at you about something serious when you have a free moment."

Solomon dropped his bag. "I thought you said you and Tessa were good?"

"Yeah, we're good, but my homeboy, Jaz, and his wife, Crystal, are going through it right now."

"I heard he was doing a movie. What's up with that?"

"Yeah, that sore subject is the source of their drama."

"I got you," Solomon said and pulled out one of his business cards. "Have them call my office and setup a consult. Will that work?"

"Sounds like a plan," Majac said then tipped his bottle at Solomon before he left.

Two hours later, with his laundry done and two bourbon cocktails in his wake, Solomon popped some popcorn and locked all of his doors before retreating upstairs. Once again, he was alone with his thoughts; the chronic thoughts of losing Mareschelle, the taunting thoughts of being related to Leona, and most important, the nightmarish thought of being accused of killing a beauty queen from

Spokane. Thoughts of the guilty pleasures he had experienced with them consumed him:

Making love in the rain.

Road trips.

A mutually shared love for music.

Holding hands and walking barefoot through the grass in the park.

The intimate pieces of a woman—

the hollow of her neck,

the small of her back,

the intensity of her stare,

and the intimidation of her sigh.

Makeup sex after a knockdown, drag-out argument, and the incomparable experience of sharing her orgasm.

The taste of first kisses, and most importantly...experiencing True Love!

With the memories of the last two years clearly in his rearview, Solomon could loose the thoughts of those women and finally get on with his life; focus on flying solo. Once in bed, he swallowed two sleeping pills containing a mix of ashwagandha, valerian root and lavender, drank a cup of chamomile tea and turned on the television.

Beginning with that drive to Everett and that silly bunny rabbit, movies had played a significant role in his relationship with Mareschelle. He switched the TV to a movie streaming network, pressed *Play Now*, then, barely thirty minutes into his wife's favorite movie, *Carmen,* he found his favorite guilty pleasure aside from the company of a woman—the pleasure of a good night's sleep.

Acknowledgments

THIS WRITING THING CHALLENGES ME. Conforming to the rules over and again while trying to convey a thought in a manner that a reader will enjoy brings me to the brink of a migraine. And let's not get into the harrowing abyss of the prolonged tête-à-tête. All that being said, venturing down this rabbit hole brings me peace in my happy place.

Shout out to my Beta-Readers: Stephanie Smith and Maureen Jackson from the Mocha Authors Book Club in Chesapeake, Virginia; the BESTEST book club in all of Virginia. Thanks to Brooke from Golden Life Publishing for hyping my characters after reviewing each version. Thank you to my poetry writing daughter India 'CJ' Sexton for enduring my persistent 'Tell me what you think about this idea?' banter. I can't wait for your poetry book to drop so I can recommend it to my readers.

Rumor has it that laughing adds years to your life. If asked, my children will claim that I will live forever because I am always 'laughing at them', and for the most part it's true, but only because they say the funniest Shiznit!. But, their faces, their smiles and their laughter is my greatest joy. That, and Twizzlers!!

My wife of more than 30 years continues to support, encourage, critique, understand and love like nobody else on this planet! Saying I Love You may be redundant, but our THREE decades of redundancy truly is a beautiful thing! Now we gotta figure out how to raise the bar for our next thirty!

If you are reading this, Thank You for taking this journey with me. Without awesome people like you, this two-year obsession of my life would be no more than a digital file lost in the ether or a 6x9 paperweight hiding in a library near you. If you've enjoyed this vacay from reality, please share with a friend if the spirit moves you.

Love You ALL for all your support.

Let's talk real soon about Chemistry Matters: Book 4.

As Always, Enjoy the Read!!!

H. Adrian

CPSIA information can be obtained
at www.ICGtesting.com
Printed in the USA
LVHW030840010223
738313LV00003B/184